Brandishing Betrayals

Devil's Psychos MC Book 2

M.E. Thornwood

Midnight Dreaming Publishing

M.E. Thornwood

Midnight Dreaming Publishing

P.O. Box 312 Elburn, IL 60119

Interior design by Atticus

Edited by: Cantina Book Club

Cover by: RJ Creatives

ISBN: 978-1-962688-09-3

ISBN: 978-1-962688-08-6 (e-book)

CONTENTS

IF YOU ARE MY family member, thank you for your support, I love you dearly, but DO NOT READ THIS BOOK. This is not for you. We will not be having an awkward conversation about the contents of this book.

Brandishing Betrayals is book 2 of a trilogy and must be read after Brandishing Beginnings to make sense. It is a dark Reverse Harem/Why Choose romance, meaning the main female character will not choose between her loves interests. There will be group scenes and dark themes including Motorcycle Club Culture, primal play, Shibari, and dubcon scenes. This is a BDSM romance with on screen negotiations and themes that are not suitable for every reader.

For the full list of trigger warnings, please check the author's website. Brandishing Beginnings is book one of a three book series and will end on cliffhanger.

M.E. THORNWOOD

Author Note: If you find any errors in this book, please contact the author at m.e@methornwood.com

To those who have to hide the truth from those you love,

because it's safer for them.

Prologue

Maya Henderson

I SLAMMED MY EYES shut as I crashed into a brick wall. Not an actual brick wall, if the muttered, "Shit," was anything to go by. Heavy hands landed on my upper arms, steadying me.

I snapped my eyes open and gasped when I saw the leather Motorcycle Cut, with the patch on the front that read Devil's Psychos. *Fuck.*

My heart pounded in my chest and blood rushed through my ears. My eyes widened in disbelief. How was this possible? I looked up into the darkest brown eyes I'd know anywhere.

"Maya," Marcos Candela breathed, his grip on my upper arms tightening. Astonishment and disbelief filled his face as he stared down at me.

"Marc," I whispered, unable to gather words. I looked up at the love of my life, with wide eyes. I trailed my gaze over him, taking in every detail. His hair was still buzzed short against his skull, his eyes were such a dark brown they were almost black, and a dark goatee framed his plump lips, looking every bit as kissable as I remembered.

My gaze raked over him, before I glanced over his shoulder and saw another sight that sent my heart racing. "Jase," I gasped softly, my eyes raking over the second love of my life.

"Hey, Darlin'," Jason Langford drawled smoothly as ever. Whether he had been affected by my sudden appearance or not, he didn't let on.

His steely gray eyes bore right through my soul. He was tall, a good foot taller than my five-three frame. He was lanky too, with a slim muscular build. Athletic build. His blond hair was cut short and styled into a messy, bed-head fashion that suited him. He wore a silver chain around his neck, and a plain, gray fitted t-shirt under his Devil's Psycho Cut. A barbell was pierced through his left eyebrow. There were gauges in his ears, along with several other piercings.

He was still as fucking hot as he was ten years ago, even if he did seem to have more hardware. He had aged well and his face was clean shaven. His smooth voice made me shiver, like it always used to. It was like honey, a smooth drawl that set my core on fire. Always had.

"What are you guys doing here?" I asked, looking between the two of them. My heart racing.

"Dagger's in surgery," Marcos answered softly. He finally let go of my upper arms and I felt cold and unbalanced, immediately missing his touch.

I shivered slightly and tucked a stray hair behind my ear. "Is he okay?" I asked, fear plaguing my heart. The third and final love of my life was hurt and in surgery.

"He'll be fine," Stone answered, giving nothing away.

My eyelids fluttered; his voice always got to me. For a man that didn't talk much, he used to have me eating out of the palm of his hand whenever he spoke softly to me. Some ten years later, and his voice was still napalm to my soul.

"Mom!" a young boy's voice called out from behind me, breaking me out of my stupor.

I froze, my heart pounded in my chest. Blood rushed my ears, as my whole world was caving in around me. I didn't want them to find out this way. I had planned on telling them, telling Marcos, but I wasn't ready yet.

"What the *fuck*?" Jason's voice was a booming crack in the silence.

I jumped, not used to hearing that tone from Jason, *ever*, even Marcos startled at his tone. Marcos stared over my shoulder, in disbelief and awe.

"How?" Marcos asked, his voice soft. His eyes locked on my son, Lucas.

I squeezed my eyes shut in panic. How the hell would I ever explain this? I needed time. *This wasn't supposed to happen this way!*

"Mom," Luke called again.

I quickly glanced over my shoulder to see my little boy, staring at me with wide eyes. He had dark black hair and deep brown eyes, just like his father. His left arm was in a sling, and he was sitting back on the hospital gurney he'd been brought in on from school.

I gave him a pained smile. "Just a minute, honey," I said.

"Maya?" Marc's voice was sharp, her name a question.

"Mom, I want to meet him," Lucus said. His voice was steady and sure. He may be just a nine-year-old boy, but he knew what he wanted.

I closed my eyes and took a deep breath. *Fuck.* I needed more time. I couldn't do this. They were going to hate my When I opened my eyes, I couldn't meet Marc's gaze. "Would you like you meet your son?" I asked him softly, staring at the Devil's Psycho patch on his cut.

"I would love to meet my son," Marcos said softly. He brushed by me without saying another word, and walked into the exam room beyond.

I watched him extend his hand to Lucas and introduce himself. "I'm Marcos, what's your name?" he asked gently.

"Hi," Lucas said. He put his hand in Marc's and maintained eye contact while he shook his father's hand. "I'm Lucas, my friends call me Luke," my son answered.

I gasped softly, and quickly covered my mouth, as tears welled in my eyes. I'd always known Marcos would be a great father, I felt horrible denying him all these years. I would never be able to explain why.

"What the fuck is this, Maya?" Jason growled quietly. His hand wrapped around my bicep and pulled me toward him.

I faltered as I was jerked forward. Jason Langford was not one to fuck around, *ever*. My heart raced; I couldn't do this.

"Did you know you were pregnant when you left us?" Jason demanded, cutting right to the heart of the matter, his slate gray eyes bore into mine.

I gasped at the intense anger I saw in those eyes; anger, hurt, betrayal, all of it clear as day on his beautiful, handsome face. At least it was to me. I'd always been able to read him when no one else could. The club had given him the road-name of Stone, because he was usually a stone-cold mask.

I'd always been able to read him, though. And he always saw through my bullshit.

Until now.

I nodded slowly. "Yes," I murmured and lifted my eyes to meet his gaze. I needed him to believe the worst in me. I needed him to want nothing to do with me. It was safer that way, safer for all of us.

His glare intensified, the vein in his jaw throbbed as he clenched his teeth. Even after all these years, he was sexy as hell when he got worked up. "Why?" he snapped.

"Do I need a reason?" I shot back and raised an eyebrow at him. I put my hands on my hips, brushing off his grip on my bicep, and glared up at him. I knew I was being unfair. It had been ten years since I last saw him. I didn't know anything about the man before me, not really, not anymore.

Jason growled deeply again. He never was one for game playing. He had patience for a lot of things, but lies and bullshit were not one of them. "You've changed," he snapped, his gray eyes rolled over my face.

I rolled my eyes and shrugged a shoulder. "Sure have," I said, nonchalantly.

"Not for the better," Jason added, his eyes narrowing in contempt.

I glared back him. I forced myself to appear angry and disgruntled, rather than the hurt and anguish I really felt. All I wanted to do was lean into him and let him wrap those strong arms around me. I wanted to hear him tell me everything was going to be okay, and that he would take care of me, protect me from here on out.

Instead, I met his glare and crossed my arms over my chest. I squared off with the big bad wolf and steeled my spine. I had to keep the distance between us. My safety and my son's depended on that distance. "Don't worry, *Stone*," I drawled. "I'm not here for you."

He stepped closer to me, like he was trying to intimidate me. "Don't worry about that, doll face. You proved your worth in the end. Less than nothing."

It took everything inside me to not break under those words and his distance. The pure venom in his tone rattled me to the core. This was not my Jason. My Jase, would never look at me with such contempt in his gaze.

Tears welled in my eyes at his words. Pain stabbed my chest, like a physical blow, as my heart shattered into pieces over his words. Thankfully I was saved from answering as the doctor walked up, clipboard in hand.

I turned from Jason as the doctor glanced my way and nodded once, before he walked into the exam room.

"Alright little dude," the doctor spoke loudly. "Are we ready to get a cast on and get out of here?"

Luke looked at the doctor nervously.

I walked over and grabbed my son's hand. "We sure are, aren't we Luke?" I said and forced myself to push through the pain and tears and smile at my son. I could be strong for him. I would be, strong for him. I had to be. I had no other choice.

Luke eyed me, seeing my pain. He squeezed my hand before he turned to the Doctor. "Let's do this," he nodded.

"That's what I like to hear. Why don't we get out of here? I'll wheel you out, your parents can follow me and we'll head up to orthopedics on the second floor," the doctor said.

No one bothered to correct him.

I held my son's hand as the doctor wheeled the gurney out of the exam room and they headed for the elevator.

Halfway down the hall, when it was clear that Marcos wasn't following, Luke told the doctor to wait.

I glanced back to see Marcos and Jason in a discussion, before both men did a manly hug with a back slap, before Marcos was striding toward us.

Jason didn't follow.

Maya

IT WAS A MISTAKE to come back here.

I looked around the massive backyard, taking in all the smiling and laughing faces at the family barbeque. There were rough and tumble bikers wearing leather cuts covered in patches labeling them either a Devil's Psycho or Ravager Knight drinking and smoking. Kids ran through a sprinkler in the yard while others jumped into the in-ground heated pool. Wives and girlfriends chatted around the pool or with their men in yard and garage.

Alcohol flowed and laughter rang out. The smell of a pig roasting in the driveway made my mouth water. A group of leather clad men stood around the spit on the driveway—the trailer the spit was attached to, was a state-of-the-art mobile kitchen on wheels.

It was a gorgeous early spring day in northern Illinois. The unseasonably warm weather had everyone was smiling and laughing, happy and carefree—everyone but me.

Scenes like this used to be as familiar to me as breathing. I had grown up in Creekton before I moved to Chicago. After almost a decade in Chicago with my son, I moved back to Creekton, or rather Mourningside, to take care of my aging parents after the car accident they had endured.

Now, I felt like an outsider. A simple backyard party, like the one around me, broke my heart. It reminded me of what had happened back then, and what could have been had I stayed all those years ago; had I not uprooted my life and moved to Chicago.

My son, Luke, ran through the sprinkler and did a running jump into the deep end of the heated swimming pool. He was a spitting image of his father, from the dark brown eyes to the dark brown hair, even the tanned skin of his Mexican heritage.

My heart squeezed when he came up laughing and yelled, "Dad! Dad! Did you see?"

"Heck yeah, I saw! Great jump buddy! Big splash!" Marcos "Killer" Candella yelled across the backyard, a huge smile on his goateed face. He leaned his arms over the top of the four-foot fence that surrounded the pool area, and watched Lucas from behind a pair of silver, wrap-around sunglasses.

It hurt to look at him, broke my heart. It was my own doing, though, nothing to be done about it at this point.

At thirty-four years old, I was no stranger to heart break, but what I'd once had with Marcos was something different. Not just Marcos, his two best friends as well, Jason "Stone" Langford and Nico "Dagger" Gage. The four of us had been inseparable back in the day.

Until I left.

The day I packed up my room in our old farm house rental had been the hardest day of my life.

Until I came back here.

Now it seemed like every day was one of the hardest of my life. Anytime I was around Marcos, Jason, and Nico, was too hard. It hurt too much being around them. I'd all but avoided them in the last six months I'd been back home.

Marcos would come over to the house to get to know Luke, but I gave them space, and mostly left them to their own devices. Eventually they started going out, meeting up with Jason and Nico, and having their own adventures.

They weren't at the 'spending the night' stage yet, but I knew it would be soon. Marcos hadn't wanted Luke around the biker life yet. It was one of the few things we agreed on.

So much for that, I thought as I looked around at all the bikers and their families scattered around the backyard.

Maya

I sat around pool, wondering what I was still doing at the party. My reason for being here had been whisked away in a flurry of excitement as Kara's water broke and her three boyfriends had rushed her to the hospital.

Kara had begged me to come to the party and I found that I couldn't tell my friend no, not anymore, not after rekindling our friendship after almost a decade. We had met in college and grown close after learning we both hailed from the same shitty little town of Creekton.

I had been a junior when Kara was a freshman. As freshman's weren't allowed cars on campus, I had offered to take Kara home on weekends and holidays. From there, our friendship had grown, until I eventually met Kara's older brother Marcos... and his friends.

When I graduated and moved back to Creekton/Mourningside, I had run into Marcos, Jason, and Nico at a bar on graduation night. I had learned the truth that night about them being members of an MC. And after our history of hooking up during my college years, seeing them again had only cemented us all being together.

The rest was history.

We had started hot and heavy and burned hot and heavy through our two-year relationship. If things hadn't gone down like they had at the end, I probably would have stayed with them—probably would have raised Lucas with them.

It hurt too much to think about the what ifs. Just like it hurt too much to sit in this backyard and stare around at all the happy families, knowing I had fucked up my chance at a happy family a long time ago.

I was just about to get up and tell Luke it was time to go home, when a body fell heavily onto the chaise lounge beside me.

I looked over at the tall blond-haired Adonis, Nico Gage sat tall in all his Italian glory. Deeply tanned and tatted skin, bright blond hair that hung down around his broad-shoulders and the brightest blue eyes I'd ever seen. Thick muscles strained beneath a gray t-shirt and his black leather biker cut. The horned devil on the patch on his shoulder stared me in the face.

I groaned internally, knowing my chance of escape was likely thwarted. Nico would want to sit and talk. It was what he liked to do. Talk.

I'd purposely been avoiding him for the last six months, knowing there nothing I could say. I couldn't tell him the truth. I had to keep him and Marcos and Jason at a distance. It was the only way.

"Well hello there, Pretty Dreamer," Nico said as I met his gaze. "I think you've been avoiding me."

I swallowed thickly. I looked down at my hands before I forced myself not to fidget under his intense scrutiny. I turned to face the pool, hoping to appear calm and cool, bored even.

I needed to push him away, and keep him away.

"Not everything is about you, Nico." I shrugged and turned back to him.

His bright blue eyes narrowed slightly, though an amused smirk tugged at the corner of his lips. He didn't buy my act for one minute.

Fuck.

Jason once might have been good at reading me, but Nico was better. Nico knew my soul on a whole other level. He would be the one I'd need to be careful around. He wouldn't give up as easily as Marcos and Jason.

Nico knew me so deeply, I often wondered if we hadn't been made of the same soul at one point, and had split apart some eons ago. He was my heart and I was his.

Or we had been, at one point.

He chuckled gruffly. "Oh, Little Dreamer," he shook his head. "Let's not lie."

I glared at him. "Let's not act like you know me, Nico. It's been ten years. You don't know me." I rolled my eyes and looked away from him.

He chuckled again and leaned toward me. "That's where you're wrong, Little Dreamer." His voice was low and close to my ear.

I turned my head to find him only inches away from my face. I gasped softly.

He smirked at my reaction. "I can see how uncomfortable you are here. This isn't your scene anymore." He tilted his head toward the yard full of people.

I huffed a laugh. "It was never my scene."

He smiled widely, showing off bright white teeth. "Another lie," he shook his head. "You used to own these parties."

He was right, I had owned these parties. People and parties and socializing had been my thing back in the day. I grew up with half of them in Creekton and the other half weren't any different than those I'd grown up with. They'd all come from the same rough and tumble small town.

"I may have owned those parties," I said. "But I didn't like them and I'm done doing things I don't like to do. I'm not that same girl anymore," I admitted, looking away from him.

I saw him frown out of the corner of my eye.

"No," he agreed softly. "I don't think you are."

I turned back to him and gave him a tight smile. "Do you think you could take me home? I'll leave my car for Marcos to drive Luke home later."

Nico was slow to agree. He looked me over slowly, like he was memorizing my face, or trying to see into my soul. It was unsettling and sent a shiver down my spine. I didn't want him looking at me too closely. He was likely to find something I didn't want him to see.

"Sure, Little Dreamer," he agreed. He nodded once at me, before he slowly got to his feet. "Let me tell Marcos the plan and we'll head out."

I nodded and dug out my keys. I handed them to Nico and stood up. "I'm going to say goodbye to Lucas."

I walked away before he could say anything more.

Luke was climbing out of the pool when I walked over. "Hey mom! Did you see that?" He grinned brightly at me, all the happiness in the world shinning on his face.

I smiled easily. "Sure did! It was awesome!" I high-fived him. "I'm gonna take off, alright? Your dad will drive you home later."

Luke nodded, smile still stretching across his face. At this point in his relationship with his father, he had no problem going home with Marcos. "Alright! I love you! See you later!" he shouted. He bounced up and pressed a quick kiss to my cheek, before he turned and jumped back into the pool again.

Sadness welled up inside me at his quick dismissal. There had been a time when he was a young child, that he couldn't leave my side without a huge production of waterworks and hysterics. Now, I barely got a kiss if I was lucky, and he was on his way again.

Nine and going on Nineteen.

As I turned away from the pool, my eyes caught on Nico and Marcos talking along the fence surrounding the pool. Marcos's face turned toward me, and though he had on mirrored sunglasses, I knew his eyes were on me.

I ignored him and headed for the front of the house. There was no reason for me to hang around here anymore. Not with my son occupied and his father wanting nothing to do with me.

Instead of walking past all the men congregated on the driveway, I chose the opposite side of the house. Walking through the grass, I rounded the side of the house and stopped in my tracks as I came across a scene that stopped my heart cold: Jason was pressing a leggy blond against the side of the house. Her long legs were wrapped around his waist and her head was thrown back in ecstasy as his thrusting hips bounced her fake tits in her skin tight crop top.

His face was buried in her neck, so he didn't see me frozen there.

I debated on turning around, when a heavy arm dropped around my shoulders and Nico's deep voice said, "Ready to go, Dreamer?"

I jumped and Jason lifted his head from the woman's neck as her eyes popped open. With both sets of eyes on me, I felt a blush heat my cheeks.

Nico nudged me forward, keeping his arm around my shoulders.

I squared my shoulders and owned it.

Stone's steely gaze locked on mine as I walked by. His gaze raked over me, before a smirked tugged at his lips. My stomach clenched; it was the most emotion I'd witnessed on his face in the last six months. "Always did love to watch," Jason goaded, his voice low.

I tripped over my own feet. I hated that he could get under my skin so quickly. "Wasn't much of a show." I shrugged as I passed them. "I've seen better."

Nico chuckled softly as we headed for his motorcycle. "Little Dreamer, you're playing with fire."

I didn't have a response...'cause he was right.

Three months later

Maya

S EEING JASON WITH THAT woman had haunted me for days, even months later, the hurt and anger warred within me. I knew I didn't have a claim to him; knew he'd probably been with hundreds of women in the last ten years. I had no right to feel this pain, not after I walked away from him—from all three of them. Still, it tore through me and kept me up at night.

I had done what I had to ten years ago. Now I would have to live with those consequences. I couldn't let them near me to find out the real reason I left.

"Mom," Lucas pulled me out of my thoughts. "I'm thinking of joining the football team."

"What football team?" I asked, looking up from the book I was reading.

"There's one through the park district, I think? Or it's a travel team? I don't know, but a lot of the guys at camp were talking about it," Luke explained.

"What's the name of it?" I picked up my phone, prepared to google.

"Panthers."

I typed in Panther football Mourningside, IL into google and quickly found the website. I spent the next ten minutes looking into the registration details and scheduling. "Practice is three nights a week in the evening with games every Saturday. Practice is from four to six—oh."

"Oh," Luke frowned, realizing the same thing.

I worked till four-thirty every day. I wouldn't be able to get him there.

"Would Grandma be able to drive me?" Luke asked, his voice dejected, because he already knew the answer.

I shook my head sadly. "I'm sorry baby. You know she can't drive right now."

Luke huffed out a heavy sigh and turned back to the TV.

My heart broke as the disappointment settled on Luke's beautiful face. "Let me ask your dad, alright?"

Luke perked up at and grinned.

I slowly typed out a text message to Marcos.

I sent the message and exited the messaging app. I sighed internally, knowing that Marcos had been working his ass off the last several months, trying to save up to buy a house, so he could have a place for Luke to stay with him on the weekends.

My phone pinged a moment later. I opened the message app and saw Marcos's reply.

Straight to the point, as usual with Marcos. I forced down my disappointment from his one-word answer. I was grateful he was willing to do anything for Luke, but the distance Marcos put between the two of us hurt.

I shoved down the pain and disappointment and forced a smile on my face. "Your dad said he could take you."

"Yes!" Luke shouted and jumped off the couch, pumping a fist into the air in excitement. "Heck yeah!"

His enthusiasm was infectious. I laughed and jumped off recliner to hug him. "Thanks mom!" He wrapped his arms around me in a tight hug.

I hugged him back, savoring his happiness. "No problem honey." I held him a moment longer before he pulled away, bouncing over to the couch.

"I can't wait to tell the guys tomorrow!"

I grinned and picked up my phone. "I'm gonna jump on the computer to register you, OK?"

Luke just nodded, already enthralled in the TV program.

I walked down the hall to my old childhood bedroom. Not much had changed in the room since I'd gone off to college. I hadn't spent much time at my parents' house after college. I had moved in with Marcos, Jason, and Nico almost right away.

I settled on the full-sized mattress and pulled my secondhand laptop off the nightstand. I pulled up the website info again and opened the registration page and paused—registration was six-hundred and fifty dollars.

My heart sank, clenching in my chest. It was too expensive. How was I going to pull this off, plus pay for my student loans, and help my parents with their bills? Things were tight enough as it was before I moved back to Mourningside. I thought of how happy and excited Luke had just been—the happiest I'd seen him since learning we were leaving our home in Chicago.

I couldn't take that away from him, even if it meant I went without something else. I sighed and reached for my purse on the floor. I pulled out my wallet, taking out my credit card, and prayed there would be enough on the balance to pay for this—already calculating how much gas was in my car and how much food was in the house.

My parents' car accident had eaten away at their savings and mine. Medicare didn't cover a home nurse and state-run care facilities were horrible. I would do everything I could to keep my father home for as long as possible.

My father's injuries had been extensive. He had already been slowly losing his mind to dementia before the accident, but since the accident, he mostly lived in his own world. He was bedridden and required a full-time nurse.

Thankfully my mother's injuries weren't as extensive. I counted my blessings that my mother was still able to move around, mostly on her own, and that she still had her mind. Though she was homebound now, no longer able to drive since the accident, she was able to help put dinner on the table most evenings, if she was up to it. Her energy levels were not what they used to be though; the accident had just taken too much from her body—she was frail.

I paid the fee for football and let out a deep breath when I received the payment confirmation. *Thank God,* I thought. I wouldn't be crushing my son's dreams and wouldn't have to have an embarrassing conversation with Marcos where I begged him for money.

Marcos "Killer" Candela

I SET MY PHONE down with a frown. Maya had texted about Luke wanting to join the football team. I had expected it, Luke talked nonstop about it when we hung out together, but any conversation with Maya anymore was rough.

Dagger fell into the La-Z-Boy besides me in the clubhouse lounge. It was pretty quiet around the clubhouse these days, since the death of our former president Larry "The Butcher" Buckley and patched brother Henry "Ace" Harding. With Buckley's death and the club vote, I was now president. I had immediately implemented some changes, including a ban on cocaine and any hard drug usage in the clubhouse.

My club didn't seem to mind, most of the heavy users had been Ace and Buckley anyway. It might have been six months since

Buckley had killed not only Ace, but a Prospect and Janey, one of the Devil Chaser's—the women that hung around the Devil's Psychos, looking for sex—but many of the women were still leery as fuck about the Psychos.

"What's going on, Marc?" Dagger asked, cracking a beer can as he leaned back in the recliner.

I shook my head, feeling the weight of the world settling on my shoulders. "Maya texted. Luke wants to play football, but practice starts before she gets off work. She wanted to know if I could swing takin' him to practice Tuesdays, Wednesdays, and Thursdays. He's got to be there at four."

Dagger raised an eyebrow. "You started that security gig with the Irish..." he trailed off.

I nodded, I was well aware of what I had signed up for with the Irish: protection detail, four nights a week, while the IRA was in town. "I'm going to need you and Stone's help with this one."

"You've got it," Stone's deep voice came from over my shoulder.

I turned to see my friend and brother, and nodded.

"Yeah man," Dagger also said. "You know you've always got us."

I sighed, grateful. "I know."

Stone moved around the recliners and slowly took a seat on the couch in front of me and Dagger. "Have you talked to her at all?" he asked.

I shook my head. "Any time I tried, she shuts down. I stopped asking."

Maya had refused to tell me why she kept Lucus a secret. She also refused to tell me why she left. She pretty much refused to tell me much of anything that wasn't directly pertaining to Luke.

I didn't know what to think about it—about her. She was an enigma now. Stony silences usually met my questioning—when I'd still tried—so I stopped asking.

"You?" Stone asked Dagger.

Nico shook his head. "She seemed sad when I drove her home after the party at Kara's. She didn't say much of anything, tried to push me away, like usual. But I'm tellin' ya man, she seemed sad."

Stone rolled his eyes, but didn't comment.

I sighed.

"There's something more going on here—with her," Dagger continued. "This isn't Maya."

Stone chuckled sardonically. "It's been ten years, bro. You don't know her anymore."

"Did we ever?" I asked, frowning.

"We did," Dagger said vehemently. "We knew her, inside and out—"

"We thought we did," Stone cut him off. "We thought we knew her, owned her—then she left. Just packed up one day and was gone..."

For a man that didn't speak often, Jason got really talkative when he got passionate about something, I thought.

"She was scared!" Dagger defended her. "She had been in a fight with that chick, what was her name? Letty? Letica?"

"Leticia," I supplied, frowning. "Tish," I added.

"Tish," Dagger nodded. "She had that bloody cat fight with Tish the night before. She was covered in the bitch's blood when we dragged her off Tish, yelling at her."

"She never did say why they fought," Stone shot back. "All we know it what Bear and my dad said. About Dax and Tish. You don't think they threatened her, do you?"

"I don't know... maybe? She took off the next day, and refused to answer our calls after that," I said. I rubbed a hand over my beard covered jaw, staring off at the wall, lost in the thought.

"Talking was always hard for her," Dagger said.

"And we had ways to make her talk," Stone grumbled.

"So what are you saying? We tie her up? Make her talk?" I said, half joking, but half serious—we needed answers.

Stone huffed, "No. She doesn't deserve it. Ignore her, Marc. She's not keeping Luke from you. She wouldn't dare, not now. Hang out with your son and ignore the baby mama drama."

Once again, the silent one, knew just what to say to cut through the bullshit. "Not sure I can do that, brother," I sighed. "I'm not sure you can either." I finally looked away from the wall, to turn to Stone.

The man in question, sat on the couch before him, utterly fucking still, like his namesake. His face an expressionless mask that grated on my nerves. I loved the dude, but sometimes he was little too unfeeling.

"Funny, not what you were doing when we walked up on you and that Devil chaser the other day," Dagger smirked, taunting Stone.

Stone shrugged a shoulder. "Just called her out for watching me fuck the chaser. She always did like to watch."

I frowned. "When was this?"

"When I was taking her home from the party. We ran into him on the side of the house, balls deep in Vivian," Dagger explained.

"What'd Maya say?" I asked.

"Said it wasn't much of a show and that she'd seen better," Dagger replied.

I chuckled softly and ran a hand over my buzzed head. A headache was starting to form between my eyes, the pressure a dull ache at the moment. I knew if we continued with this conversation, I'd be down with a full-blown migraine. "Then what?" I questioned, regardless.

"Then we left," Dagger shrugged. "I dropped her at home. She walked inside before I could ask her anything."

"Of course, she did," Stone deadpanned.

I rolled my eyes and stood up. I couldn't listen to them bicker anymore. "I'm heading out," I said, and walked away.

It was early evening still, if I played my cards right, Luke would still be up. I checked the time on my phone, nodded to myself, and headed for the door.

Chapter Four

Maya

I HEARD THE HARLEY from a block away. Luke was laying on the couch, head in my lap, and completely zonked out. The TV played softly, some Marvel movie or something. I had been reading on my Kindle since he turned the movie on.

The Harley engine grew louder, until it cut off down the driveway. Marcos knew my parents went to bed early, so he parked his bike at the end. It was a few a minutes before he walked up to the door. He paused in the picture window, looking into the living room.

I waved him in, unable to get up and answer the door for him. He was quiet as he entered, pulling the screen door shut softly, not letting it slam. He was equally quiet as he closed the heavy wooden door and turned to face me.

I watched him carefully. There was something different about him tonight—something softer. "When did he pass out?" he asked softly, his voice deep.

"About an hour ago."

Marcos nodded and bent over to untie his boots.

I watched him warily; I didn't want him to stay. I needed him to leave in fact and soon. "What are you doing?" I asked, when I couldn't take it any longer.

"I'll put him to bed for you, so you don't have to wake him," Marcos said, not looking up from his laces.

I went to say something, but stopped, and closed my mouth. It would be nice for him to move Luke to bed without waking him up. God knew it had been years since I had been able to carry him to bed.

I set down my Kindle as Marcos walked toward me. When he slid his hands under Luke's body and carefully lifted Luke into his arms. My heart fluttered as I watched the careful concentration on Marcos's handsome face. He was thinner than I remembered, his cheeks no longer as full as they had been ten years ago.

At forty-one, Marcos was only getting more attractive with age: the hard edge of his jaw and sharp lines of his goatee, his dark chocolate eyes that were dark as night. He was broad-shouldered and corded with muscle, his leather cut hung to his frame, and the muscles in his back rolled as he lifted Lucas effortlessly from the couch.

I stood up and walked in front of him, leading the way down the hall. I pulled the blankets down on Luke's bed and stepped out of the way, giving Marcos room to lay Luke into bed.

Once Marcos pulled the covers up around his son, he pressed a soft kiss to his forehead before he stood up. He didn't leave turn to leave though. He hovered over Luke a moment, just watching him, before he slowly stepped back.

I waited in the doorway, leaning against the frame, watching him. It broke my heart seeing how tender and careful Marcos was with Lucas. He was a great father already, in such a short period of time. I hated that he missed out on the first nine years, hated that he wasn't able to be with Luke full-time.

Before Marcos turned for the door, I turned around first and headed back to the living room. I took a seat on the couch again and picked up my Kindle. Marcos didn't stay once Luke was down, so I opened my book and started reading while Marcos took his time in the bedroom.

I glanced up when he stopped in front of me. He was looking down at me... for the first time in months, he met my gaze. I couldn't decipher the emotion on his face. Gone was the blank mask or his blatant annoyance when I was around, instead there was a questioning look and a slight frown on his face...like he was trying to figure me out.

I kept my features neutral and waited for him to speak up. He opened his mouth to say something, but then there was a buzz from his pocket—his cellphone vibrating.

Whatever peaceful calm that had settled over him while in my home had vanished the moment the phone buzzed. He turned away from me and shook his head. He reached into his pocket as he headed for his boots by the front door. "Yeah," he answered his phone with a grunt.

I watched him slid his feet into his unlaced boots, not bothering to lace them.

"I'll be right there." He didn't even bother to turn back or acknowledge me, he just turned for the front door and walked out, quietly shutting it behind him.

I glared at the door. Somedays I really hated him. He treated me like I wasn't there. It drove me crazy. I didn't know what to do...if there was anything I *could* do.

I shook my head and stood up and walked to the front door. I flipped the deadbolt, letting the snick and click of the bolt sliding home echo through my soul. A finality.

I left *him*. I needed to remind myself of that fact. I left him for a damn good reason, and that reason was sleeping down the hallway. I would have to harden my heart and get over my feelings when he was around. He would be around a lot moving forward.

It was the only way I would survive, the only way I had been surviving the last ten years. I pushed back my shoulders and steeled my spine. I could do this, I had already come so far, I could keep my walls up and keep moving.

Maya

The yellow carnation was tucked under the wiper blade of my beat up Honda Civic. One simple, beautiful flower in a happy shade of yellow. It looked friendly and nonthreatening...but I knew better.

The sight alone, chilled the blood in my veins. Ice trailed down my spine as I froze in my tracks. My heart pounded in my chest as my breaths came out in short pants.

This wasn't happening...This cannot be happening.

"Mom?" Luke asked from beside me, his voice cutting through my alarmed distress.

Startled, I shrieked and flinched away from his voice.

"Mom, what's wrong?" Luke asked, turning to face me. The nine-year-old boy was immediately on alert.

My hand flew to my chest and I gasped for breath as I turned toward my son. He looked worried, scared even. Lucas reached for my hand and I pulled him toward me. "Come on, let's go," I ordered, my voice sharp.

I looked around the main street frantically, searching for any sign of anyone watching—any sign of *him* watching. I pushed Luke toward the car all while pulling my keys out of my pocket and scanning the street.

"Mom, what's going on?" Luke questioned, clearly frightened and picking up on my distress.

"Get in the car, Luke. Now," I ordered, pushing him toward the vehicle.

He moved quickly and climbed in the backseat without another word. I tossed my bags in the passenger seat and quickly climb in the beat-up old car. I glanced around the busy main street again, before I pulled out of the parallel space and onto the street.

"Mom, you're scaring me," Luke said softly from the back seat. "Why is there a flower on the windshield?"

I hadn't removed it. I had left it there and drove off as quickly as I could. Now, driving down the street with a stupid yellow carnation under my wiper blade, I knew I couldn't stop. I had to get out of there, get far away from Mourningside as I could...only I couldn't.

I had my parents to take care of—the whole reason I moved back to Mourningside in the first place. I had hoped after ten years he wouldn't care about me any longer, not since I kept my mouth shut all this time. I had done what he asked.

I'd proven at this point that I wouldn't talk... why was he harassing me again?

I didn't stop driving until I pulled into the long driveway of my parents' house. My knuckles were white on the steering wheel and I was barely breathing when I shut the engine off.

"Mom?" Luke asked softly from the backseat.

"Yeah, baby?" I asked, hanging my head. I finally released the steering while and took a deep breath.

"What's going on?"

I took another deep breath and let it out slowly. I leaned back in my seat and forced myself to relax. No one had followed us, I hadn't seen anyone in the street, I was relatively safe at the moment. "I'm sorry I startled you honey. The flower was just a surprise...from an old friend. I didn't mean to frighten you." I put a brave smile on my face before I turned to face him.

Luke eyed me skeptically. He wasn't stupid. He was nine years old and wise beyond his years—an old soul as I often referred to him—he would see right through my bullshit if I wasn't careful. "You were terrified, mom," Luke said softly.

"It's nothing for you to worry about, baby. Let's just get your equipment in the house. We can order a pizza for dinner and watch that new action hero movie you were talking about."

"Alright! But no peperoni!" Luke shouted, before he threw open his car door and climbed out.

I pushed the button to release the trunk before I too climbed out of the car. I grabbed my purse and groceries bags. I doubled checked for my phone before I closed my door, just as Luke finished in the trunk and shut the lid closed.

We made our way into the house, trying to be as quiet as possible when we walked in. My parents usually took afternoon naps together, as much as they could with my father in a hospital bed. My mother had pushed her twin bed up next to my father's, after we'd removed the king-sized bed, to make room for the hospital bed.

My mother made it work though.

I quickly unloaded the groceries while Luke put all his new football pads and gear away. It was supposed to be a fun summer day. We had hit the football pre-camp equipment pick up, met the coaching staff, and Luke had seen a couple of his friends from the day-camp he went to while I worked.

I had been able to meet the moms of his friends and exchange numbers; we even set up a playdate for the boys the following weekend at the local pool. Then Luke and I, had hit the grocery store for some odds and ends things we wanted, plus the ice cream that Luke had requested. We had talked about going rollerblading or bike riding that afternoon, depending on how my parents were, but now I wasn't sure that was a good idea.

Fucking hell man... I'd been back in Mourningside nine months now. Nine months and I'd had no sign that HE even knew I was back. HE lived in Creekton anyways, not Mourningside.

After ten years, it shouldn't matter anymore. What happened back then—what I had witnessed—he should know by now that I wouldn't say anything. I even left town because of him, because he had told me to— well, threatened me.

I had just finished putting away the groceries when my mother hobbled into the kitchen. At sixty-five, Elaine Henderson was hunched over and acted more like she was going on eighty-five. The accident had really taken its toll on her.

"Hey honey," my mom greeted me with a smile.

I forced a smile on my face. "Hey Mom, how are you feeling today?"

"Alright, dear. You guys were up and out early this morning," she commented as she shuffled toward the coffee pot.

"Yeah, equipment pick up was at eight, then we ran some errands. I returned those books to the library for you and picked up a couple more. I also got everything you wanted for dinner tomorrow." I turned to face my mother, watching as she grabbed her mug out of the drying rack next to the sink and slid it toward the coffee maker.

"Oh that's great honey," my mother said absentmindedly.

I frowned, watching my mother. She seemed lost in her own head, not really paying attention to me at all, but only engaging because I was standing in the kitchen. My mother was like that with me a lot, absent. We weren't that close. We'd had a rocky relationship when I was growing up and we had fought a lot. My mother would always compare me to my older sister Jenna, it was always *Jenna's doing cheerleading, or Jenna's got straight A's. Jenna's going to be a doctor.* It drove me nuts growing up and only served to shove a wedge between me and my sister.

It wasn't until college that my relationship with my sister grew. Jenna understood our mother had idealistic notions on what children should be, instead of loving and accepting the children she had. Jenna and I had spent two years partying together at college, healing our relationship, before she graduated and moved to Chicago for her residency.

We had grown close, so when shit went down ten years ago with *him*, Jenna had invited me to Chicago to live with her while I got on my feet. Jenna had also helped me get a job at her hospital. It was the fresh start and support I had needed, during the most heartbreaking time in my life.

Now, I was close with my sister. Jenna had been my rock all these years and had helped me with Luke. We had lived together in Chicago, until Jenna had met her husband, Brad Daulson. When the two of them had decided to move in together, Jenna had left the apartment for Luke and I. Jenna had given me everything over the years.

When our parents had their accident, we had discussed options for their care. It had made more sense for me to move back home. Jenna had a husband and two young kids, and had a career to think about. She was hoping to become Head of Surgery one day.

I had been struggling month to month to pay rent in an expensive city on my own. My son had been left at sitters and day camps when I worked and the neighborhood around us had slowly descended into crime. It made sense for me to move in with my parents, even if the last time I had lived in this house, I had been kicked out.

In the almost ten years that I had lived in Chicago, I had reconciled things with my mother as best as we could. With both of us living two hours away and neither one on talking terms with her, Mom had broken down and admitted how wrong she had been. She had come to Chicago and had a big reconciling weekend with both of us, and Jenna had only agreed to moving forward if Elaine would really try and treat me better.

Our mother had agreed, but it had been slow going. There were too many years of hurt for me, and I didn't really trust her after being kicked out last time. I tried though, for Jenna, and I really had missed dad, despite how he had broken my heart as well. After the accident, I had realized how little time I had left with my father, so I decided to suck up whatever hurt and anger I still felt for my mother and moved home to help take care of them.

My parents' home in Mourningside was two hours south-west of Chicago. It was in an unincorporated neighborhood with large lots and plenty of room to run around and play outside. It boasted a great school district and Lucas had classmates down the street.

Luke had bloomed since moving to Mourningside, especially his relationship with his father.

While it had been the best thing for Luke—or so I thought until that stupid fucking carnation had shown up on my windshield—I just wasn't sure if it had been the best thing for myself. Looking at my mother as she splashed half and half in her coffee, I wondered again why my mother didn't seem to care about me as much as Jenna.

"What do you have planned for this weekend?" my mother asked.

I glanced at the clock; it was just after one in the afternoon. After my scare with the flower on her windshield, I honestly didn't feel like doing too much. "Laundry probably," I answered, off handedly.

My mother hummed and shuffled away from the kitchen; her cup of coffee cradled between her hands and her quota for small talk reached for the day. I wondered why my mother even bothered asking, as she clearly didn't care.

Marcos

THE BABY'S CRY WAS the first thing I heard when I walked into my sister's house. My niece had a set of lungs on her to rival her mother's. I would know, being ten years older than Kara, I had practically raised her as a baby.

The next thing I noticed was the pile of laundry stacked on the couch in the living room and mess of papers strewn across the dining room table. It wasn't like the four of them to have a messy house.

I glanced around the house—there was no one to be found.

Lilah was still crying upstairs and she didn't sound like she was getting any softer. I took the stairs two at a time, and headed down the hall toward her bedroom, wondering where the hell her parents were.

I got my answer when I walked into the infant's bedroom and found all four parents sitting on the floor or in her rocking chair, heads leaned back and eyes closed—like they fell asleep sitting up and hadn't heard the baby.

I ignored them and reached into the crib and picked up the fussing six-month-old. "Shh," I murmured, smiling at my niece. "It's okay, mamacita, shh," I cooed softly.

Lilah soothed her tears once she was lifted from the crib. I settled her into the crook of my arm and started rocking her gently. God, I loved these moments with her. I rocked her a moment longer before I walked over to her changing table and got to work changing her diaper. I felt like it wasn't that long ago that I was changing Kara's diapers.

"What's happening?" Kara mumbled, jerking awake.

I glanced over my shoulder at my sister. Her blond hair was in disarray, her makeup was smudged on her face, her clothes wrinkled. She was a hot mess. I glanced at her men and saw they weren't much better. Johnny was leaning against the wall, next to the crib, missing a shirt, and had dried spit up on his sweatpants. Derrick's long brown hair was stringy and greasy; there were dark circles under his eyes even as he slept in the rocking chair. And Kevin's usually spikey hair was flat on his head, his shirt was inside out and he was in his boxer briefs.

Clearly the four of them were exhausted beyond belief.

"Marcos?" Kara asked, her voice groggy.

"Si, Lil Manita," I murmured softly, not wanting to wake her guys.

"What are you doing here?"

I chuckled softly. "Just wanted to see my girl. Go to bed sister, I've got her tonight."

"Whaa?" Kara asked, clearly not awake yet.

I finished up with Lilah's diaper and zipped up her sleeper before I picked her up and turned to face my sister. She was still sitting on the floor half asleep, a dazed and confused expression on her face. I frowned slightly. "Necesitas dormir," *You need sleep.*

"Si," Kara responded. "Ella no ha dejado de llorar. NO sabemos que hacer." *She won't stop crying. We don't know what to do.*

I nodded slowly; I had a feeling it was something along those lines. The four of them had been great parents and been especially great about switching off and taking turns. It was highly unusual for the four of them to be this fucking exhausted. "Go to bed, sister. I'll take her tonight."

Wood creaked to Marcos's left as Derrick slowly got to his feet. "Shit man," he grumbled.

I chuckled, seeing the big burly man so disorientated was a little bit funny. "Go, all of you," I ordered them, as Johnny and Kevin slowly regained consciousness. "Get some sleep tonight. I've got her."

"Seriously man?" Johnny grumbled, running a hand through his short blond hair.

"Yeah guys, go. Sleep all night, we'll just be hanging out. Get a full night's rest without interruption."

"Thank you," Kevin said, not even glancing back as he headed out the door.

I laughed and cooed at Lilah, ignoring them all as they filed out of her room. Kara padded over and pressed a kiss to my cheek, while rubbing Lilah's head. "Thanks, big brother, I love you," she murmured, before she left the room.

"Love you too, Lil Manita," I replied softly to her retreating form. "Alright Lil Mamacita," I cooed down at Lilah. "What do you say we head downstairs and make you a bottle. We'll get you some of Tito Marc's teething meds and get you some sleep too. It sounds like you've been a tiny terrorist."

Lilah gave me a big smile like she knew exactly how much she'd been terrorizing her parents.

"Alright, good plan." I nodded my head and walked out the door.

Marcos

Several hours and three diaper changes later, I finally got Lilah down for bed. She was passed out on my chest and I was not about to move her. Not at all. I had kicked off my boots hours ago and shrugged out of my cut as soon as I needed to burp the little girl. In my blue jeans and plain white T-shirt, I was as comfy as I was going to get for the night.

I snuggled down into the corner of the fluffy sectional couch and closed my eyes. I'd already shut off most of the lights, only leaving on the dimmed accents lights that were aimed at the fireplace. Just enough light to walk around, but not enough to bother me while I dozed off.

Only I couldn't sleep. The moment I closed my eyes and tried, my thoughts raced in my head. I immediately thought of my son Lucas and how much I had missed out on the first nine and half years of his life. All the teething sessions and diaper changes, all the first roll overs and steps, and all the damn cuddles. I had missed out on so much, and it hurt my heart to see my son and know I'd never have those moments with him.

Luke was a great kid and the two of us had hit it off immediately. Luke had asked about me regularly growing up and Maya had told him everything she knew. When Luke started asking about meeting me, Maya had moved them home.

While some of that hadn't exactly played out quite that way, Maya had never denied me my time with Luke since knowing he existed. She may not be open about *why* she left in the first place, but she was open with sharing her son with me now.

I needed to get a house, as soon as possible. The one-bedroom apartment I lived in was not enough space for the two of us, and if I was honest, I missed living with Stone and Dagger. After Maya had up and left, we'd tried staying in the same house, but things hadn't been the same. Things hadn't been the same for quite a while, if I was honest.

I needed to bring up the subject with his brothers, see what they thought about moving in together again. Maybe we could pool our money and buy something faster than what I'd be able to.

Our previous club president Larry "The Butcher" Buckley had run the club's finances and businesses into the ground. The income we earned from the club had most of us barely making ends meet. In the six months since I took over as president of the MC, I had made some great changes in the way we ran our businesses.

I also had mended business relationships that Buckley had let go by the wayside, or had shat on all together, like the protection detail with the Irish. The IRA didn't come through often, but when they did, they appreciated the extra protection. They were not friendly with the Russian Bratva and moving guns was a tricky business.

I knew Johnny and the Knights worked with the Bratva, and had dealings with the Seratelli crime family as well. Nico had his own ties to the Seratelli's through his mother. The whole web of crime syndicates that wove through Mourningside and Creekton was intricate. Add in the Las Serpientes... and we were all fucked.

Lilah let out a little coo on my chest that stopped my grim thoughts and brought me back to present. I needed to set her down in her basinet and get some sleep, I had a feeling she would be up again in a couple hours.

With a reluctant sigh, I set my niece in the pack n play bassinet that my sister had set up in the living room, and grinned when Lilah didn't fuss. I grabbed the thick fleece blanket off the back off the couch and wrapped it around myself as I laid down and closed my eyes.

Chapter Six

Maya

"MOM, CAN I RIDE down to the creek with the guys?" Luke asked, pulling me out of my thoughts.

I turned away from the back picture window I'd been gazing out of and looked at my beautiful nine-year-old son. He was the spitting image of his father: tanned skin, dark hair and eyes, and the same chiseled features as Marcos.

I frowned slightly, wondering if it was safe. The carnation on my car the day before had rattled me of all sense of security I thought I'd had. Maybe I had been naïve to think that after ten years, HE would have forgotten about me.

I really didn't want to have to explain it all to Lucas though. He was used to going down to the creek with his friends in the neighborhood. "Yeah, alright. You got your watch on you?" I asked, referring to the smart watch he wore, that allowed him to call me in case of an emergency.

"Yep!" he smiled brightly and took off toward the door.

"Be home by five, for dinner!" I called after him.

"Ok!" he shouted back as he tore out the door.

I chuckled to myself, spirits lifting at the sheer joy Lucas exuberated. Feeling better, I glanced at the time and saw it was early afternoon, still plenty of time to cut the grass before dinner. I headed to my room and changed into a strapless bikini top and a pair of cut offs. It was the middle of July in central Illinois, and it was hotter than hell outside, so I was going to take advantage of it and work on my tan while I cut the massive yard.

I'd been mowing for about thirty minutes, cutting in and around all the planting beds by hand with the push mower. When I saw a shiny black Silverado pull into the driveway I frowned. I wasn't aware of any plans that Marcos had with Lucas. While he was getting used to dropping by unannounced lately, he still usually texted to make sure we didn't have plans.

I pulled my cell out of back pocket as I cut off the mower. A quick glance at the screen showed no missed notifications of a text or call, so I pocked my phone again and wiped away the sweat from my brow with a bandana I'd tucked in my back pocket.

I didn't go to the truck though; I waited for him to climb out. I couldn't see through the tinted windshield, so I was surprised when the passenger door opened as well. I waited with my hands on my hips, panting slightly and dripping in sweat, as Marcos and Jason climbed out of the truck and Marcos stalked over.

I watched as both men slowly survey my body, their gaze raking over me hungrily. I knew I looked damn good; I'd worked hard to keep my body in shape over the years. My tits filled out my bikini top, the tanned smooth skin of my upper body was on display, showing off several of the tattoos I'd gotten over the years and the piercings I'd added, like nipple piercings I knew were visible through the fabric of my red bikini.

My eyes landed on Jason, watching as he closed the truck door, but didn't move toward me. His gray eyes showed a storm-cloud of feelings, but his face was otherwise his usual stony mask of indifference. He was dressed in his usual summer attire, a white T-shirt with his Devil's Psychos leather cut over it, and despite the heat, he wore blue jeans with white shoes. His blond hair was cut short and styled in a spikey bedhead look.

Marcos was dressed the same as usual for him too, a black T-shirt under his cut, blue jeans, and black boots. A pair of sunglasses covered his eyes, hiding them from me, but even then, I knew he was watching me was he stalked toward me. "Hey, is Luke around?" Marcos asked.

I wanted to roll my eyes when he didn't even ask me how I was doing. I knew he didn't care. All he wanted was his son, and I was being patient with him regarding his unscheduled drop-ins, but he was starting to get on my nerves.

I shook my head. "He's down by the creek with friends."

Marcos nodded slowly, running a hand over his buzzed hair. "Right," he said.

There was an unbelievably awkward pause as I waited for Marcos to figure out what he was doing. I looked past him, to Jason who was standing with legs spread and his hands in his jean pockets, eyes on me.

I stared back until Marcos said, "When will he be back?"

"I told him to be home by five," I answered. I steeled my spine, waiting for him to say something...anything.

"Right," he finally said, nodding.

I frowned, watching him. I'd never seen him look so defeated before, so... lost.

"I guess I should have called him," Marcos said softly.

Again, I just waited, while I had thought it as well, I wasn't going to tell him that. He would say I was being uncooperative, then we would argue about me keeping him from Luke again. I was sick of the arguing, sick of the accusations. I needed them to stay away from *me*, not Luke. So I kept my distance.

"Alright," Marcos nodded again and turned away, not saying another word.

I watched him climb in the truck before I looked over at Jason. He was still standing next to the truck, staring at me. It was a little unnerving. His stormy gray eyes locked on mine, but I didn't move, and didn't back down. I wasn't afraid of Jason "Stone" Langford—he may be an asshole, but he'd been mine at one point.

Finally, he turned away without a word and climbed back into Marcos's Silverado.

I waited until they pulled out of the driveway before I turned back to the mower and started things up. I had shit to do and waiting around on men who couldn't get their heads out of their asses wasn't one of them.

Marcos

I shifted in my seat, as I drove away from Maya. "Fucking shit," I groaned, and tried to adjust my very hard dick, without being too obvious about it.

"Yeah," Jason grunted, also shifting in his seat. "She's gotten more defiant."

I frowned. Was that it? "She still as stubborn as ever," I said.

"To think, we had trained that out of her at one point," Jason sighed.

I didn't want to think about the past. It only made me angry and upset most of the time. We'd had a great life together back then, the four of us. We had been extremely happy back then. The guys and

I had talked about inking Maya with our mark and even marriage as a possibility...until she left.

Now there was this impenetrable wall between us and her, and we were finding it impossible to break through it. She stood firm on the other side, not budging.

I shook my head, trying to clear my thoughts. I couldn't afford to think about the past, all I could do was think about the future. Or present. Right now, I was going to drive down the street to where the creek was and look for the spot that Luke had shown me, where he hung out with his friends.

I pulled over on the side of the road when I saw Luke down the ravine next to the creek. He was throwing rocks into the water with a group of kids. I recognized a couple of the boys, but the girls I didn't know. One girl in particular was standing closer to Lucas than the others. She had blond hair down to her waist that looked smooth and shiny.

I got out of the truck and slowly walked down the ravine, not wanting to startle any of the young kids. "Hey Luke, your dad's here," one of the boys called out—Jaxon maybe?

Luke turned to look over his shoulder and smiled when he saw me. He turned around and slowly made his way toward me. I was a little surprised he wasn't running and jumping into my arms like every other time he saw me, but I shrugged it off. "Hey, Dad," he greeted with a smile, as he neared.

"Hey buddy, I was just in the neighborhood and thought I'd drop by and see if you wanted to hang out?" I held my fist out for Luke to pound knuckles; pretty positive the kid didn't want to hug his father in front of his friends.

Luke frowned and he hit his fist against mine, and briefly glanced back to the girl by the creek. I had to fight my smirk at the fact that my son appeared to have a little crush, until Luke said, "Sorry, Dad. I'm hanging out with my friends today. Maybe we could do dinner tonight? Mom said to be home at five."

I felt my heart breaking. The kid was nine and he was already brushing me aside to hang out with his friends. I nodded easily, though, not wanting Luke to see my disappointment. "Alright buddy, I'll talk to your mom. If not, I'll give you a call tomorrow and we'll set something up for this week."

"Sure, sounds good," Luke nodded, looking for all the world to see, a cool kid, just making plans.

I plastered on a grin and let the little dude impress his friends. "Alright bud, I'll see you later." I held out my knuckles again and Luke pounded them once, before he turned back to his friends and walked back to the girl near the water.

I headed up the ravine, not looking back before I lost my nerve. Goddamn, things were not going my way lately. Depressed, I climbed back in the truck and started driving away, before Stone could comment.

"What was that about?" Stone asked a moment later, when we turned the corner.

"He has plans," I sighed. "I should have called him."

There was a long pause in the truck before Stone spoke up. "Stupid how shit turned out. She never should have left."

I shook my head not wanting to get into it with him. We'd argued about it a lot in the last six months since Maya had returned and as many times as I had questioned Maya, she refused to answer me. "We need to find out why she did," I finally said, driving slowly through the neighborhood. I was lost in his thought, wondering what I should do now that my plans with Luke were canceled.

"Were her nipples pierced?" Stone asked out of the blue, shifting in his seat.

Immediately I felt my cock stir in my jeans. "Yeah, man," I murmured. "A couple new tats on her arms too."

Stone grunted. "You think Dagger's right? Something more going on with her? That shit with Tish was pretty brutal. Maya had never reacted like that before...and the beat down she delivered on Tish? Maybe it rattled her?"

I frowned. "She claims she knew she was pregnant when she left, but she was drinking that night, wasn't she? That part doesn't make sense. Even if she was rattled about the fight, that's no excuse not to tell us, anyone of us could have been the father."

Stone grunted again. "Just cause he's your mini, don't mean me and Dagger aren't his father too."

A smile finally pulled at my lips. I nodded slowly, "Yeah man."

"What's the plan? You're just driving aimlessly here," Stone said.

"I dunno. Go home I guess?" I shrugged.

"We could go back to Maya's like you told Luke. Have dinner with them," Stone suggested.

"Dinner's hours away yet, and should we impose like that with her parents?"

"Yes. Let's go impose, put a little pressure on her," Stone said.

"And what, stand around watching her cut the grass why we wait? My dick won't be able to handle that, bro."

Stone chuckled sardonically. "She was already pretty sweaty. It's hot as balls outside."

"Fucking hell, bro," I groaned, but turned the truck around the block again and headed for Maya's parents' house. "I guess we're doing yard work then."

Another minute later we were pulling into the driveway. "Holy fucking hell," Marcos groaned, taking in Maya as she continued to cut sections of the yard with the push mower. She wasn't facing them, so she probably hadn't seen them, but they had full view of her bare back, and massive fucking tattoo the spanned the entire thing.

"Holy shit," Stone breathed.

Massive angel wings spread across the smooth expanse of olive skin, with intricate shading and detailed feathers. It was a masterpiece of a design, true artwork. And it was hot as hell.

"Fuck meee," I groaned.

"You sure she didn't know we were coming over today? Purposely dressed like that?"

"No," I denied. "I didn't know I was coming here until I said it to you...that's just how she always dressed in the summer, bikini and cut offs."

"I remember," Stone grumbled.

Maya turned toward us, mowing the next row of grass, and we watched as her tits bounced as she moved. Her hips swayed seductively, and my eyes immediately zoomed in on her narrowed waist and the tattoos inked on her ribs and down her side. She had a gorgeous hourglass figure, with big tits and thick thighs that I just wanted to smother my face in between. "Fuck," I breathed.

Maya didn't stop mowing until she reached the driveway. She shut off the mower and waited.

"I guess we're doing yard work, bro," I told my buddy before I got out of the truck.

"Fuck my life," Stone grumbled, but opened his door.

Maya didn't say anything as I rounded the front of the truck. She stood where she was and watched both of us warily. I was getting really tired of her silence, of her careful watchful eyes. She saw too much and showed too little, despite being half naked in the blazing sun.

"Luke was hanging with his friends, said he had plans," I explained as I walked toward her. "He said to ask you if we could stay for dinner."

Maya stilled, her limbs locking tight. I wouldn't have noticed had I not been watching her so carefully for any kind of reaction. She was so good at masking her feelings, I found I had to watch her extra closely. Her eyelids fluttered slightly, and her nostrils flared, her limbs locked, all for just a moment before she nodded slowly. "He with a girl? Blond hair down to her ass?"

"Yeah," I nodded.

"Melanie, she lives next door." Maya pointed behind her, where the nearest house was a good hundred yards away.

I nodded absently, "It cool if we stay for dinner?"

Again, Maya froze ever so slightly. I smirked internally; I loved getting under her skin. She clearly wasn't used to it anymore. She shrugged a shoulder. "Sure, dinners at five thirty, I'll be mowing." She bent over slightly to pull the rope on the mower to start it and I got a nice view down her bikini, almost seeing nipple, before she straightened and turned away from us, creating another row as she walked away.

"Awfully big yard to be doing by hand," Stone commented.

"Yeah, I've seen her using a tractor before," I said. "There's a shed out back."

Stone grunted, but turned toward the backyard. We walked around the side of the house and headed for the shed tucked back behind the detached garage. We found the tractor We were looking for in the open shed, along with a weed-whacker and blower.

I jumped up on the tractor and tried to fire it up. When it sputtered and refused to turn over, I quickly realized why Maya was cutting the front yard by hand. "Well shit," I grumbled and climbed off the tractor.

Stone popped up the front hood and looked underneath. The tractor was an older model John Deer that had clearly been taken care of well, but with how Maya's dad was meticulous about his shit, it made sense. Since the accident, I hadn't seen him. Maya said he was bed-bound, which was why she moved home in the first place.

Stone messed with the spark plugs, pulling them out and putting them back again. He put his hand on the seat and leaned, putting weight there for the sensors to register it, then tried cranking the engine again. When it fired right up, he motioned to me.

"Alright, I'll drive, you trim." I pointed toward the weed-whacker hanging on the wall.

We spent the next two hours mowing the lawn and weed whacking around trees and bushes. After Stone finished, he pulled out a sidewalk edger and cleaned up the overgrowth around the driveway and sidewalk. Then he went around blowing the grass off all the surfaces and blowing any grass in the street back into the yard.

There was no reason for grass to be in the street, it killed bikers daily. Blow the damn grass back into the yard and save a life.

At some point, Maya had gone inside, leaving us to finish without her. I was annoyed and grateful at the same time when she disappeared. She had been an utter distraction and my dick was still hard as nails in my pants from her barely there clothing. I was getting sick of her stonewalling though, the absolute nonchalance from her was rage inducing.

I was already planning everything I would bring up during dinner. I was tired of her brushing me off, I wanted answers—and if I had to put her on the spot in front of her mother, I would.

Maya

I WAS LOSING MY mind. Jason and Marcos had both stripped off their shirts in the late afternoon heat and humidity. Why the fuck where they staying? Marcos really needed to get over the fact that Luke had plans. He didn't call the kid, he didn't make plans with him for today, he couldn't be upset when Luke already had plans with his friends.

I went inside when I had finished mowing the front yard and it was clear that the guys had fixed the tractor that wouldn't start. With one of them riding the tractor and the other one weed-whacking and edging, there really wasn't anything else for me to do. Not outside at least. I went inside and took a quick shower before I went into the kitchen to set the table and check in with my mother.

My mother had a pot of homemade spaghetti sauce simmering on the stove and a fresh loaf of bread cooking in the oven. The house smelled divine.

A quick glance at the clock showed I still had an hour until Luke would be home. With dinner taken care of and the table set, I found myself with an hour of down time. Feeling out of sorts, I looked out the back picture window at the two men taking care of the yard and sighed. It had been a very long time since I had seen them doing physical labor.

Both men were in amazing shape. Marcos was shorter and stockier than Jason, who was built lankier like a runner, where Marcos was more compact like a football player. It made sense as he had played in high school. They both had, but only Marcos had a passion for it until he dropped out of school.

Clearly both men still kept up with their workouts, if the near zero percent body fat was anything to go by. Watching the rippling muscles from the window had my heart pounding in my chest. I wasn't sure how the fuck I was supposed to sit through an entire dinner with the two of them, Luke, and my fucking mother.

Feeling on edge, I turned toward the liquor cabinet and pulled out a bottle of Vodka. I was going to make myself a cocktail, sit in the front room, and read a book. I wasn't going to look out the back window and watch the stupid, sexy, sweaty men do lawn work. No. I wasn't. No.

Once I was sitting in the front room, far away from the back window, I opened my kindle and pulled up the last dark romance novel I had been reading. I took a sip of my cocktail and tried to jump back into the scene where the Dom had his Sub tied to a St. Andrews Cross. He had strapped a magic wand to her high and had it pressed against her clit.

Even the sexy punishment scene was enough to pull me out of my thoughts. That was better said than done though, not when my own Doms were in the backyard, sweaty and shirtless, looking for all the world a hot steamy piece of man pie, all but imploring me to drop to my knees and beg for forgiveness.

Goddamn, how many times had I had that very thought? If I just explained it all, dropped to my knees for my Doms and explained why I had to leave back then, why I disappeared in the first place—and begged for their damn forgiveness—they would have to understand, right? They would see and understand why I did what I did, wouldn't they?

Annoyed with my thoughts, I set down my kindle and took a long pull from my cocktail. The reusable plastic straw was bright pink and helped the alcohol go down so smooth. I didn't know how I was going to get through this damn fucking dinner. Why the hell would Luke invite them to dinner?

I groaned and stood up. I stalked toward the back window and peered outside. Marcos was still riding the tractor around in straight rows, but Stone was standing on the back patio, not ten feet from the window.

He had his back to me, so he didn't see me, and was hunched over the weed-whacker he had propped up on the wooden patio table. He had a fresh roll of weed-eater string and was undoing the current line around the head of the machine.

I watched his deft fingers easily unwrap and pull apart the line. Those thick, long fingers that were so talented at doing any millions of things—most of which I was intimately familiar with.

In the six months since I'd returned, I'd barely spoken to Jason—not since our very first argument. The one where I'd blatantly lied to him at the hospital. He had been pissed, beyond pissed really. I couldn't remember a time that his steely eyes had ever glared at me that way. It had hurt me—still hurt.

Sweat dripped down his back, his jeans hung low on his hips. I warred with myself before I finally grabbed two bottles of water out of the fridge and headed for the door. It was the least I could do, right? He was helping me out, after all.

I braced myself for his stony silence and gruff attitude. "Here," I murmured, and set the bottles on the table out of his way, but still close enough for him to reach.

He grunted, but didn't turn to me.

I ran my eyes over his torso before I turned back for the backdoor. "Thank you for the yard," I said.

God, that was awkward, I thought as I walked back in the house. I wasn't going to stay around and wait for his judgment. I knew I would get that tenfold from him at dinner, unless I got lucky and he outright ignored me, like had been doing the last six months.

Back inside, I berated myself for even going outside. It had been a dumb idea, and I was only opening myself up for heartache. I needed to stay away from them. The damn yellow carnation left on my windshield the day before was all the proof I needed that HE still remembered and was still watching.

My heart sank. HE was still watching, and my boys had been here for hours, being domestic and fixing my tractor and mowing the lawn. If HE *was* watching, I could only imagine what he was thinking.

Fuck, I'd been stupid. I should have told them to fuck off and schedule plans with Luke later.

There was nothing I could about it now. I went into the kitchen and started prepping a salad for dinner to keep myself busy. I forced myself not to look out the back window, until the front door flew open and Luke came running in the house, right on time at five p.m. on the dot. "Woah! Where's the fire buddy?" I asked, looking up from the book I'd finally been able to read.

"Dad's staying for dinner?" he asked, looking around.

"Yeah, he's out back with Jason," I said, feeling a tinge of pain in twist as Luke referred to Marcos as Dad. He'd only recently started doing it, finally feeling comfortable with their relationship.

"Yes!" Lucas cheered and headed straight for the back door.

I looked around the window, to see both Marcos and Jason were standing around the picnic table when the door flew open. "Dad!" Luke shouted and went running toward his father.

Marcos was shirtless and sweaty and caught Luke with ease, holding him tighter when Luke realized he was sweaty and tried squirming to get away. Marcos laughed as he tickled Luke while holding him tight against him. The smile that lit up Marcos handsome face was breathtaking. He really was aging like fine wine with his chiseled jaw and cheekbones, his dark eyes and goatee. He embodied tall, dark, and handsome.

I turned away from him and Lucas when I couldn't take it anymore. It was then, that I noticed Jason was staring at me, watching me as I watched Marcos and Luke. He had his arms crossed over his bare chest and he stared me down in that silent, dominate way of his. It was the same stare that used to have me lowering my eyes and sliding to my knees.

I dropped my eyes, but I fought the urge to drop to my knees. He wasn't my Dom. I wasn't his Sub. We had too much baggage and history between us to ever go back to that dynamic anyways. Those dynamics were built on trust. Trust and communication. Neither of which I was accountable for at the moment.

I sighed and turned away from the window. I headed back to the living room and picked up my book, just as my mother came out of her bedroom and entered the kitchen. She would start the noodles and finish up dinner. I had a few minutes to get myself ready for the epic shitshow that was about to be family dinner. I only hoped I came out the other side in one piece.

Jason

I WATCHED MAYA RETREAT from the picture window, her eyes down. I could see the emotions warring over her face as she watched Marcos with their son. She was both happy and sad as she looked at the boy with his father. Tears pooled in her eyes, as a sad smile tugged at her lips.

For the first time since she had returned, she was showing emotions other than annoyance or anger. For the first time since she left us ten years ago, I could see the regret in her caramel-colored eyes.

Was Dagger right? Was there more to the story of her leaving? Was it possible she was hiding something from us? Was it possible that she *lied* to us about leaving?

I didn't know what to believe. Up until this moment, I had believed her at her word when she told me that she knew she was pregnant and wanted to leave us. Life back then had been a mess. We had been at war with Las Serpientes, Marcos and I had been shot, and Nico had done time in County.

Then there had been the brawl that Maya had gotten into with Tish. But knowing that Tish had been Hillcrest's girlfriend, that Hillcrest had her infiltrate our clubhouse and had come onto Marcos that night, it made sense as to why Maya had delivered an epic beat down. Maya had never been shy about fighting. Not back then.

She was an angry and possessive thing back then. I used to call her Hellcat. I hadn't even seen a spark of that old Maya since she'd returned. She had kept her emotions under lock and key, and kept up her damn façade whenever we were around.

Even when I tried to get a rise out of her while I was fucking Vivian, she didn't get angry. Annoyed, maybe, but nowhere near as passionate or worked up as she would have gotten years ago if I'd gotten under her skin. Not that I would have fucked someone else back then. I wouldn't cheat, but she was known for her fiery temper, and I liked to rile her up.

"I can't wait for football to start!" Luke's excited voice pulled me from my musings of Maya and the past. I glanced over to see Luke beaming up at his father. "Thank you for agreeing to bring me. Mom won't be home from work yet, when practice starts."

Marcos grinned down at Luke. "No problemo, little dude. I'm glad I get to spend time with you. I used to play football when I was your age. I played all the way through high school."

Until he had to drop out, I thought. Life had a funny way reminding you of the past.

"That's so cool!" Luke exclaimed. "Brody's big brother is a quarterback for the Jr. High, and he gets all the chicks!"

I laughed heartily at the young man's excitement. "That what you were doing today? Hangin' with that girl?"

Luke, for all his exuberance, only blushed slightly. "Sure. Maybe. Melanie lives next door. We're just hanging out."

I smiled and shook my head in awe. The kid was nine. What did he know about girls and 'hanging out'?

There was a knock at the window, and we looked over. Maya was motioning us to come in and eat.

"Food!" Luke cheered, pumping his fist in the air.

"Let's eat," Marcos agreed, picking up his shirt off the table and pulling it over his head.

I also pulled on my shirt, feeling the clean cotton stick to my sweaty skin. I'd kill for a shower right now, but I was not about to ask Maya for that.

We followed Luke inside and slowed to a stop when we saw Elaine Henderson dishing up spaghetti. She gave us a look of contempt before she said, "Hello boys," like we weren't forty-year-old men.

"Hello, Mrs. Henderson," Marcos and I said almost in unison.

"I'll eat with your father, dear," Elaine said, picking up a bowl and plate and setting them on a tray.

Maya looked up from the salad bowl she was prepping and frowned. "Ok," she said, looking a little confused.

I watched the two women with interest. Maya never used to get along with her mother. They would butt heads constantly. She also never would have let her mother just walk away when she clearly had questions. This new Maya, the post-move and non-confrontational Maya, didn't say anything to disagree. Instead, she pulled out another tray and quickly made up another place setting, before she poured two glasses of milk and added them to the tray. She walked away, following after her mother, with the tray of food and drinks.

Luke sighed and watched her go. "I don't think Grandma likes you much."

"Why do you think that?" I asked.

Luke shrugged and played with the food on his plate.

Maya walked back in a moment later, cutting off the conversation as she breezed past us and began making another plate, before she moved on to the large salad bowl and dished herself a portion.

She moved to the table a moment later and set down her dishes, then she turned back to the fridge. "You guys want a beer?" she asked, over her shoulder as she opened the fridge.

"Sure," Marcos grunted.

I just nodded when Maya met my gaze. She looked away quickly, opening the fridge and pulled out three beers. She left them on the counter for us to grab and walked over to the table.

It was a six-person table. Maya took a seat next to Luke on the far side of the table. Marcos walked over and took the seat across from Luke, leaving both ends of the table open. Deciding to ruffle Maya's feathers a bit, I took the seat next to her, at the head of the table.

Her movements froze only slightly as I sat down my plate and beer. Had I not been watching; I wouldn't have noticed. She hadn't expected me to sit down next to her.

When we were all seated at the table, I grinned internally. Maya was utterly uncomfortable as the awkward silence descended on the table.

"Mom, when does football start?" Luke asked, starting up the conversation.

"Next week," Maya and Marcos responded.

Maya looked up from her plate to Marc who sat across the table from her. He nodded once at her, and she nodded in agreement.

"So what are we doing next weekend?" Luke asked.

"You're meeting up with your friends Saturday at the pool," Maya said, pulling out her cell phone and opening her calendar app. I looked down at all the dates filled in and narrowed my eyes. Her schedule was full, every single day of the week had several colors of things going on, even the weekends. "Sunday, you have Tyler's birthday party."

"Oh yeah," Luke grinned.

"You're going to Chicago?" I asked, not bothering to pretend like I wasn't looking at her calendar, taking note of every damn appointment listed. There were several doctor's appointments listed each week. I could only assume it had to do with taking care of her parents.

"Uh yeah," Maya said, not looking at me, as she set down her phone and locked the screen. "It's Jenna's birthday. We're going to spend the weekend at her place. Luke's going to hang out with his cousins and some old school friends."

Marcos frowned, glancing at Luke as the boy cheered happily.

"You're pretty busy," I commented, staring at Maya.

She shrugged a shoulder and didn't give me much to go off. "Almost seems like you're purposely keeping Luke too busy to see Marc," I accused, leaning back in my chair.

Marcos shot me a look and shook his head.

I just shrugged a shoulder and waited. Once again, I was surprised when Maya didn't rise to the bait. It was Luke that spoke up. "Uh no," he shook his head. "I have friends, I have a life too. I'm trying to do both and see everyone," he said so matter-of-factly, I turned from Maya and focused on Luke. "I've been spending every minute with Dad lately," he said and glance at his father. "And I love that, I do. But like... I'm missing out on my friends too."

Marcos smiled easily, though I could see the hurt in his gaze. "I get it man. You've got a lot going on. We'll figure it out."

Maya watched Marcos, and I swore I saw actual concern on her face. "Football starts next week. You guys will see each other then, and Sunday dinners are open. We could plan on those?" She suggested, tossing Marc an olive branch.

"Yeah, that sounds good," Marc nodded.

Maya picked up her phone and slid to August. I saw two free weekends in the middle of the month. She set the phone down again and locked the screen. I noted she had it set to thumbprint scan. "We've got a couple of free weekends before school starts, maybe you and your dad can plan something fun for then?" she asked, looking at Marcos for confirmation.

Marc smiled and nodded, and Luke cheered. "Yeah. I'll set it up with your mom. We'll figure it out."

Luke was so excited as he quickly finished his dinner. Once he bounced away from the table and headed out to the living room, Maya turned to me with a glare. "Don't fucking do that."

I smirked. "Do what?"

"Pit him against us," she growled, finally showing a bit of emotion and anger, finally showing a hint of her old passionate self. "Luke is not a baby. He knows I would never keep him from his father. It was his idea at to move back here in the first place. He wanted to meet his father. He made that choice. I won't keep Luke from Marcos, if that's what Luke wants. He will also make the choice to see his friends if he so chooses."

"Funny how you *say* won't keep him from his father, yet you did… for nine years," I said, leveling her with a glare.

Out of the corner of my eye, I saw Marcos's shift in his chair as he watched the two of us get into it. "Yeah, I did," Maya glared at me. "I fucking left you and didn't look back. I'm here because my parents need help and Luke wanted to meet his father. That's it."

I ground my molars and I clenched my jaw in anger. I wanted to strangle the life out of her for being such a selfish bitch.

"Enough," Marcos grunted. He picked up his plate and beer bottle and walked over to the sink. He set his dishes in the sink and left the room. "Hey man, you wanna play video games?" he asked Lucas in the living room.

Maya stood from the table and started clearing her half-eaten plate.

I lashed out, standing and grabbing her by the throat. I wrapped my fingers around her neck and glared down at her, pulling her toward me. She gasped and clawed at my hands, immediately dropping her dishes to the table with a clash. I didn't care. I pulled her toward me. When her face was inches from mine, I growled low, "I know you're a lying cunt, but I will find out the truth, even if I have to kill you for it. I won't allow you to hurt my brother, or take his kid from him."

I squeezed her neck tighter. Her face turned red, tears welling in her eyes, and when she started struggling, I squeezed even tighter.

Her eyelids started to flutter. Her hands wrapped around my wrists first, as if she could pull me off her, before she reached down and grabbed the fork from her plate. Her movements were sluggish as she stabbed the fork down into my arm.

I hissed in pain as the tines of the fork broke through flesh. I dropped her immediately.

She began coughing uncontrollably after I let her go, as if she couldn't get enough air in her lungs fast enough. She would have crumpled to the floor, if she hadn't caught herself on the table first. Deep coughs left her chest heaving, as tears rolled down her face.

I shook my head in disgust and turned away from her. I walked out the backdoor, not looking back.

Maya

I GASPED AND PANTED for breath as the backdoor closed behind Jason. That stone-cold mask he always wore, falling back into place after he choked me. My knees wobbled as I got to my feet. My neck hurt. I hoped it wouldn't bruise. I worked in a women's clinic. I couldn't be showing up to work with bruises on my neck.

I couldn't do this. I needed a minute to myself. The pain, not just physical, but the emotional pain was too much to bear. The utter look of hatred on Jason's beautiful face, would haunt my dreams for the rest of my life.

Once again, my heart broke, as I thought of all the things I'd fucked up by running away to Chicago.

"Mom," Luke asked from behind me.

I pushed myself up, forcing my wobbly legs to straighten. I quickly wiped the tears from my eyes while my back was to Luke.

"Mom, are you okay?" Luke asked.

"Yeah, honey," I croaked, my voice hoarse. It hurt to speak. I mentally swore, Jason had squeezed my neck so roughly, he actually hurt me.

I heard Marcos's heavy boots before I saw him. "Luke, go finish that level for me, alright? I'll be right there," Marcos said.

He walked over, turning so he was in front of me and looked me over. His eyes widened when he took in the tears. "Fuck," he gasped, reaching out for her neck.

I flinched away, bringing my arm up to block his touch.

He immediately backed off, raising his arms in surrender. "Shit Maya. I'm not gonna hurt you," he said softly. "Just let me see."

My body shook as more tears leaked out of my eyes. I didn't move when he lifted his hand again. I squeezed my eyes shut as he curled his finger under my chin and gently lifted my chin up so he could look at my neck.

"Motherfucker," Marcos growled, his voice low.

I flinched away again, jerking out of his hold and backed away.

"Maya," Marcos breathed.

I shook my head and turned away from him, b-lining for my bedroom. I prayed on everything I was, that Luke would stay in his room for a while.

Once I was in my room, I shut the door behind me and leaned back against it taking a shaky breath. It took me several long minutes before I felt steady enough to walk into my attached bathroom.

I turned on the light and flinched when I saw the damage Stone had inflicted. Tears fell freely down my face, as I leaned in closer to peer into the mirror. My neck was bright red and already bruising in spots.

I gasped at the damage. How was I going to explain this to my mother? Luke? How the fuck was I going to go to work? I couldn't, not looking like this. Fuck. It was Sunday. I didn't have many sick days. I was still new on the job, and between my parents' appointments and Luke's schedule, I wouldn't have many days left.

I had to worry about the fall flu season once Luke was back in school. I needed to save a couple days in case he got sick. Tears poured down my face as a sob broke out of me. My throat was on fire, my neck ached. I turned away from the bathroom and went back into my bedroom. I curled up in bed, pulling a pillow over my face to stifle my sobs. I couldn't let Luke hear me, or my mother.

Thankfully my parents' bedroom was on the other side of the house, off the kitchen, while the other three bedrooms in the house were in a hallway off the living room.

I heard the front door close and the house fall silent. I wondered what it meant. Did Marcos leave? Would Luke come looking for me? I needed to get up and pull myself together. I couldn't let Luke see me like this; it would freak him out.

I was stronger than this. *Time to put on your big girl panties and pull yourself together,* I thought.

I slowly pulled myself out of bed and into the bathroom again. I turned on the shower, and slowly undressed. I would take a hot shower, cry some more, then *bitch the fuck up and get my shit together.*

I was in full on pity session, tears mixing with water, while I sat on the shower floor, hugging my knees to my chest, when my bathroom door opened slowly.

"Little Dreamer?" Nico asked softly, knocking as he walked in the steaming bathroom.

I watched Nico's beautiful face as he walked in the bathroom. With his chiseled cheekbones and shining blond hair around his shoulders and bright blue eyes, he looked every bit of the avenging angel he often aimed to be.

A sob tore through me at the sight of him.

"Hey pretty girl," he murmured as he squatted down outside the shower, pressing his hand to the clear shower door.

"Where's—" I broke off when I started coughing again.

"Easy now," Nico said. "Marcos took Luke with him. They're out seeing a movie. We've got a couple hours."

Another sob tore through my chest, racking my body. I squeezed my legs tighter and buried my face into my knees. Thank fuck

Marcos had the decency to take care of Luke and call Nico to take care of me. He knew I wouldn't turn Nico away.

A moment later I heard the shower door slide open, before the water shut off. "Come here, Dreamer," Nico murmured.

I looked up to see him holding out a towel, spreading it wide for me to step into once I climbed out of the shower. I stared longingly at it a moment before I finally reached a hand out to him.

He let go of the towel with one hand and reached in the shower to help me to my feet. I didn't even care that I was naked before him—he'd seen it all already, anyways. I stepped over the bath edge and into the cool bathroom. Nic was quick to wrap me up in the white fluffy towel. He wrapped it tight around my body before he pulled me tight against him.

He rubbed my back as held me snuggly.

I sniffed as I breathed in his spicey scent. The cologne he wore, the same he wore back then, was a welcome hit of Novocain straight to my battered soul. I rested my head against his chest and let the sobs consume me.

I didn't know how long he held me tight. He rubbed my back and whispered in my ear the whole time, soothing me as much as he could.

When I finally pulled away from him and wiped my face, I couldn't look at him. We were barely even friends anymore and here I was covering his shirt in my snot as I bawled my eyes out.

"Come on, Dreamer, let's get you dressed," he murmured softly. He wrapped an arm around my back and guided me into my room.

Once I was settled into comfy sweats and baggy T-shirt, I avoided Nico's eye as I climbed into bed. I rolled on my side and put my back to him. I heard him sigh, before there was a click of a switch and the bedroom plummeted into darkness. I heard the rustling of clothes before the blankets on the bed were pulled back and he climbed in behind me.

He slid his arm under my head, while his other arm wrapped around my waist and pulled me backwards against his hard body. He spooned me tightly, leaving zero space between us. "Is this okay, Pretty Dreamer?" he asked, his breath hot against my ear.

I nodded and hugged a pillow to my chest.

"Just rest, babe." Nico pressed a kiss to my temple and I could almost pretend that nothing had changed between the two of us, that I hadn't broken his heart when I'd left him ten years ago. I drifted off to sleep, wishing I'd wake up ten years in the past and made different decisions.

Marcos

I T WAS LATE BY the time I got back to the clubhouse. After Stone had fucking choked Maya, I had to get Luke out of the house. I didn't want my son to see her hurt. Luke should never have to see his mother hurt like that.

Motherfucking Stone and his goddamn temper. I couldn't believe Stone had hurt her like that. The bruising around her neck...Jesus fuck man.

I had called Nico to take care of Maya, while I'd taken Luke to the movie theater. We ended up watching the latest Marvel action movie, and it was after eleven when I took Luke back home. I had managed to convince Luke that Maya was already sleeping, so I tucked him into bed myself, making sure he brushed his teeth and washed his face.

After Luke was in bed, I cleaned up the kitchen, knowing how Elaine would throw a fit if she saw it a mess in the morning. Maya and her mom butted heads a lot, mostly because Elaine was a critical bitch. I didn't want Maya to have to deal with her on top of the pain she was most likely experiencing.

It was almost one a.m. when I stepped into the clubhouse. While it was quiet by our standards, people were still awake and moving around. I found Stone drinking alone at the bar that ran along the back wall.

I saw red the moment my gaze narrowed in on my brother. Stone's back was to me, but my growl of rage gave me away. Stone barely turned toward me as my fist connected with his jaw. The hit knocked Stone back, but I was faster, and I grabbed Stone by the front of his shirt and punched him again across the face.

"Oh shit," someone grumbled behind me.

I didn't know who, and didn't give a fuck. All that mattered was breaking Stone's fucking face. "You're fucking coward," I spat at my brother as I hit him again.

Stone didn't even fight back, he sprawled back against the bar, blood coating his face as I pummeled him again.

"Pres," Axel spoke up from behind me.

I stopped, my fist still in the air, as I took in Jason: bloodied and beaten, swollen and blinking lethargically as he stared up at me. I was breathing hard, my chest heaving, as I stared down at my brother. "You'll stay the fuck away from her," I ordered, lowering my fist.

Jason gave a small nod of understanding.

I took a deep breath and glanced around the room. Axel was standing in the opposite corner, his boys Phoenix and Blaze with him. Axel eyed me warily, but I did what I came to do, so I turned and left the way I came, heading back out of the clubhouse for my bike.

I rode around for hours before I headed home to my apartment and showered. I was still too keyed up to sleep, even though it was going on seven a.m. After I showered, I sat down and ate a bagel for breakfast, my thoughts drifting once again to what Stone had done to Maya.

What the fuck had my brother been thinking? Yeah, Maya had left us, and yeah, she didn't tell us that I had a kid, but none of that was an excuse for Stone to put his hands on her like that.

Not Maya. Not then, or now, or ever.

The bruising that had immediately bloomed across her pale skin would haunt me for the rest of my life, as would the way she flinched away from me like she thought I would hurt her as well. I hoped to God that Stone didn't cause any permanent damage.

Whatever I might've been feeling for my ex-girlfriend, I definitely did not want her harmed. I needed to see her. I needed some kind of reassurance that she was alright. I couldn't shake the fear that clung to me still.

When I finished eating, I hit the road again, this time heading back to her house. It was going on eight in the morning though, so I hoped she was home and hadn't gone to work.

By the time I got to her parents' house and parked at the end of the long driveway, I knew she wasn't home. Her car was gone and Dagger's bike was still parked near the street. I pulled out my cellphone and quickly called Dagger.

When I was immediately sent to voicemail, I cursed and growled into the phone, leaving a message, "Dagger, what the fuck? Where the fuck are you?"

A text message pinged on my phone before I'd even hung up the call.

Dagger

We're at my place.

I didn't even think about it, I slid my phone back in my pocket and started up the bike again. It wasn't until I was halfway to Dagger's that I thought about what I'd even say to her, if she'd even want to see me.

After keeping her at arms-length for the last six months since she'd returned, and practically ignoring her unless it pertained to

Luke, I knew she wouldn't be receptive to anything from me. I didn't care, though. I needed to see her.

Chapter Eleven

Maya

I woke the next morning to the alarm on my phone blaring from the nightstand. I tried to roll over, only to roll into a hard body. I froze, startled.

"Easy, Little Dreamer," Nico's deep voice muttered in my ear.

I relaxed slightly, only for the memory of Jason's hand wrapped tightly around my neck, to crash over me. I shimmied out of Nico's hold and leaned over him to grab my annoying phone off the nightstand on Nico's side of the bed. It was five a.m. I snoozed the alarm and clutched my phone to my chest as I rolled back over.

Nico curled around my back again and held me tight. "When do you have to leave?"

"I start at seven," I responded, my voice hoarse. My throat hurt, it was dry and scratchy and sore. "We have to leave by six-fifteen so I can drop Luke by the day camp at six-thirty, and still make it to work by seven." I whispered the words, not wanting to break the moment, but also because it helped my throat. I loved every minute wrapped up in Nico's arms, even knowing I didn't deserve it. It hurt to speak though, everything felt raw.

Nico hummed softly and held me tighter, like he knew exactly what I was thinking. "Call into work today, take Luke to camp and we'll hang out at my place."

I sighed. "I don't have many sick days. I can't."

"Baby, your voice sounds like you ate glass," he muttered.

I grunted. He was right, and my throat fucking hurt, but I did not have the time off to spare. "I have five sick days left for the year. I can't afford to use them, not with my dad being how he is and school starting next month. Luke gets sick every fall with the back-to-school ick."

Nico hummed again, and my phone alarm started going off again.

I sighed and extracted myself from his arms and got out of bed and headed for the bathroom. I had to shower still, since I didn't wash my hair last night. I had to make Luke lunch for camp, and I had to— "Shit," I swore, when I looked in the bathroom mirror. The bruising around my neck was already dark red and purple.

"Fuck, Dreamer," Nico cursed as he walked into the bathroom, blinking at the light. "That's not good."

Tears welled in my eyes as I took in the red and purple finger-prints around my neck. Blood welled under the skin. I looked rough. "Fuck," I whimpered. I couldn't go to work like looking like this. I worked in a women's health clinic; my boss and coworkers would know immediately that there were handprint bruises around my neck. I wouldn't be able to explain them away.

Nico immediately turned me away from the mirror and pulled me into his arms. "Take the day, baby," he said softly in my ear. "Take the day. You have us now. If Luke gets sick in the fall, we can be with him."

I frowned and leaned into his chest. Would they really be there if Luke was sick? Yes, yeah, they would. I knew in my heart that Marcos would drop everything if he knew his son was sick, and if he couldn't, Nico would.

I thought I would have been able to include Jason on the list of people that would drop everything for my son, but after last night, I wasn't so sure. Jason had never physically hurt me like that before, even when he used to punish me in the past, he had never left lasting marks anywhere other than my ass.

Would he drop everything for Luke? I didn't know, and I wasn't sure I wanted him around my son.

"Call in, baby. We'll go to my place for the day. I'll take the day off, too." Nico rubbed up and down my back soothingly as he spoke softly.

"Do you live with them?" I shifted in his arms, pulling away slightly to look up at him.

Nico frowned and a shadow passed over his blue eyes. "No," he shook his head. "We have our own places now."

I saw it in his eyes, what he wasn't saying. I saw the pain and heartbreak there. The pain and heartbreak that I put there. "Nic," I spoke softly.

"Don't." He shook his head.

I didn't listen, though. "How long has it been since you've lived with them?" I pressed him. I needed to know, even though I had a feeling I already knew the answer.

He gave me a tight look. "Since the rental house...since you left." Nico ran a hand through his shoulder-length blond hair, musing the messy locks.

I gasped, my mouth dropping open in shock, even though I had known it in my gut. "Nic," I murmured.

He shook his head sadly, "We fell apart after you left, Maya."

Tears welled in my eyes and I had to look away from his beautiful face.

"Maybe if we knew why you left in the first place," he said softly, running a knuckle over her cheekbone.

I could see what he was doing, how he was hoping to lead into *that* conversation, but I couldn't do it. Not yet... not today. I needed more time. I shook my head sadly and stepped away from him, letting his hand drop from my face. "I can't, Nic. I can't."

"One day, Little Dreamer, you're going to have to tell me. Even if it rips out my heart, you're going to have to tell us why." He spoke gently, but firmly. His voice was deep and melodic as it rolled over me.

I knew he was right, but I couldn't tell him. One day maybe, but not today.

"Alright babe, take your shower. Get ready for the day, I'll get Luke up." Nico left the bathroom after that, closing the door behind him.

I sighed and turned to the shower. I didn't have any more time for self-pity. I needed to get in the shower and get moving. I needed the morning routine to appear as normal as possible to my mother. The last thing I needed was my mother screeching on about 'those boys are bad news'.

Maya

"Bye Mom!" Luke yelled as he jumped out of my car at day camp.

"Bye, love you!" I called after him, before the back door slammed. I wondered if he even heard me, as he ran toward his friends near the elementary school the day camp was held.

A horn honked behind me and I cursed and drove forward. "Alright, alright," I grumbled.

"This is intense." Nic commented with a laugh as he glanced around the coned-off area that was the drop off lane.

"You should see it during the school year. It's a cut-throat business, drop-off line," I smirked.

"I bet," Nic laughed. "Is this his school too?"

"Yep."

"He looks like he made friends pretty easily."

"Yeah," I sighed. "Moving here in January might have helped. It was the middle of the school year, so he was able to meet people. We got lucky that he was in the same class as a couple of the kids from the neighborhood. It was the mom of one of his friends that told me about the day camp, which was godsend, because my mom really isn't able to do much more than take care of my dad...Luke would have been so bored at home."

"I'm glad you're back," Nic said, as I slowly pulled out of the parking lot and onto the street.

I gave him a tight smile and nodded once. "Me too."

Nic reached over the center console of my Civic and rested his hand on my thigh. He gave it a gentle squeeze and left it there. It was a warm weight on my leg that made concentrating on anything, let alone traffic, more difficult.

"Make a stop at Buttin's, will ya?" Nic asked, referring to the local grocery store.

I nodded and pulled into the parking lot.

"Great. I won't be long," Nic said as I found a parking spot. "Stay here."

I nodded absently and waited, my mind playing over the events of the night before for the hundredth time. How Jason's gray eyes had glared at me with such hatred and contempt. How he hadn't batted an eye when I had tears running down my face, and how it took me stabbing him with a goddamned fork, for him to not kill me.

For the thousandth time, I wondered if I made the right choice a decade ago, if I had stayed, what would have happened? There was a flash out of the corner of my eye, and glanced to my left. When I didn't see anything, I looked away, messing with the radio.

It was another ten minutes in the car, before Nico finally walked out of the grocery store, his arms laden down with plastic grocery bags. I popped the trunk for him to load everything into, listening to the bags rustle as he set everything down.

A moment later he was climbing back in the passenger seat again and had a bright ass smile on his face. I raised an eyebrow at his jovial expression, not really feeling it myself. "Ready?" I asked.

"Absolutely, Little Dreamer. Let's go!" He slid his hand onto my thigh again, as I started up the Civic.

I rolled my eyes and backed out. "Where am I going?" I asked, as I drove through the parking lot toward an exit.

Ten minutes later, I pulled into the parking of an upscale town-house complex. The kind where the garage was on the main level, and everything was built above it. It looked new and modern from the outside. "Park in front of the garage," Nic directed me.

As I put the car in park, Nic got out and walked up to the garage door. On the side of the frame, I eyed a keypad. He punched in the code and a moment later the door started to open.

I popped the trunk and shut off the car, before I gathered my phone, keys, and purse. Once I had my stuff, I climbed out. Nico was already grabbing the bags from the trunk. "Come on," he called, shutting the trunk before I could help.

I locked the car and followed him inside the empty garage. His motorcycle was back at my place, and knowing Nico, his truck was probably at the clubhouse until winter.

He led me up a set of carpeted stairs to the main level. It was an open concept living, dining and kitchen area. In the back corner, tucked behind the kitchen was a door that was opened to the bathroom. The stairs turned and continued up to a third floor, where I assumed the bedrooms were.

Everything was new and modern, masculine in shades of gray and black. Not much in the way of art or décor, but there was massive plush sectional that dominated the living room, centered around a massive TV that took up half the wall.

For the first time that morning, I smiled. "Very nice," I told Nico, glancing at him as I headed for the couch.

He beamed brightly at me and I had to fight back the surge of butterflies in my belly at seeing that sexy ass grin aimed my way. Instead, I settled onto the fluffy couch and got comfortable. I had a solid eight hours of free time and I was going to use every minute it.

I grabbed the remote off the coffee table and flipped on the TV. I had shows to catch up on.

Marcos

W HEN I ARRIVED AT Dagger's townhouse, I pulled my bike alongside Maya's beat up Civic—the same Honda Civic I'd helped her buy brand new eleven years ago. Her first brand new car. She'd been so excited and damn proud of herself and I'd been so happy for her and proud of her too.

She had worked so hard through college, and then after when she got her first *career* job, using her degree. It had been shortly after her parents had thrown her out of their house. My heart hurt every time I thought of the past and what we had back then. There wasn't a day that went by in the last decade that I hadn't thought about her, hadn't missed her.

She was the one that got away...and now she was back. I only wondered if I could set aside my own feelings of hurt and resentment to move on.

I let myself into Dagger's garage using the keypad on the garage door and headed into his house. Upstairs, I walked into the living room to find Dagger sitting on the couch, his back to the stairs, as he watched TV quietly...alone?

Dagger turned to me immediately and pressed a finger to his lips, motioning for me to be quiet. I frowned and walked quietly into the living room. Maya had her head on a pillow in Dagger's lap and a throw blanket draped over her—she was sound asleep.

I walked around the couch and eyed her warily. Her golden blond hair was pulled back in a messy bun, her curls in disarray. The blanket was pulled up to her chin, so I couldn't see the bruising on her neck.

"How is she?" I asked, voice soft, as I walked closer.

Dagger shrugged a shoulder and gave me a so-so wave of his hand.

I sighed and moved even closer. I wished I could touch her, hold her. I wished things weren't so fucked up between us. I kicked off my boots and took a seat on the couch at Maya's feet. She was curled up, so there was plenty of room unless she stretched out.

I made myself comfortable on Dagger's stupidly plush sofa.

It wasn't long before I was nodding off to sleep myself.

Marcos

I woke to the shifting of the couch and feet sliding over my lap, dangerously close to my dick. I grabbed the feet before they could hurt me and cracked open an eye. Maya had rolled over onto her back and stretched out, but looked like she was still sound asleep.

I glanced at Dagger; my brother was sliding his fingers through the curls on Maya's head. He must have pulled her hair out of the bun and was toying with it.

I smirked, knowing how damn pissed Maya got about people fucking with her hair. "Stop," she grumbled, sleepily slapping his hand away.

So maybe she wasn't asleep after all.

Dagger stopped, a wide grin on his face as he stared down at her. I could see his feelings written all over his face. Dagger wasn't like Stone or I. He didn't bottle his emotions up as badly as we did. He was more open with his feelings, and he forgave too easily.

Seeing him, utterly in love with Maya still, I had to look away. It didn't sit right. We couldn't just go back to how things were, too much had changed between us all. I only wanted to make sure she was okay, and that Stone hadn't permanently harmed the mother of my child.

Now that she had rolled onto her back and the blanket had fallen away, I could clearly see the bruising around her neck. Deep red bruises, purpling in color, mixed with tinges of blue, wrapped around her neck. Some spots you could make out where Stone's fingertips had been.

My heart stopped as I cleaned closer and studied her neck. I didn't notice her watching me, until she said, "Why are you here?"

I looked up from her neck to see a sliver of amber eyes watching me from beneath thick eyelashes. Her voice was thick and raspy; she sounded like she had smoked two packs of cigarettes a day for life. It was rough.

"Wanted to see how you were," I said, shrugging a shoulder nonchalantly.

Her eyebrows furrowed as she frowned, her eyes darting between mine, watching me warily. The uneasiness on her face killed me, watching her walls go up before my eyes, tore through my soul.

As her mask slipped into place onto her face, a cool composure that hadn't just been there, she slowly pulled her feet off my lap and sat up. She looked away from me and grabbed her hair tie off the coffee table where Dagger had tossed it and gathered up her thick curls.

She stood from the couch while she finished tying up her hair, and walked toward the kitchen. I watched her go, knowing I was making her uncomfortable. In the kitchen, she grabbed her extra-large travel mug, the stainless-steel one with the handle on the side and a straw that all the online girlies went crazy over.

She took a sip of whatever she had in there, before she turned and met my stare. Her eyes narrowed in a glare as she stared back at me. "I beat the shit out of Jason," I said, not really sure why I was telling her.

"Good." She didn't seem to care at all.

"Dude," Dagger sighed and shook his head. "You should probably go."

I turned to my brother and frowned, but I knew he was right. Maya was clearly uncomfortable with me here; she'd been resting peacefully before I showed up. Now she looked like she was crawling in her skin.

"Alright," I agreed and nodded.

Maya watched me warily as I stood from the couch and walked toward her. "I'm sorry about Jason," I said.

She didn't respond, just stared at me.

I nodded again and turned toward the stairs. "Dagger, I'll see you tonight."

"Yep," Dagger replied.

I left them and went downstairs and out the garage door. I would give her space for now, but I wasn't going to leave her alone. Now that I saw how guarded she was around me, I had a feeling she was hiding something, and I would find out what it is, no matter what it took.

Maya

After Marcos left, I settled back on the couch with Nico and wrapped several ice packs around my neck. We watched another movie while I did twenty minutes on and twenty off with the ice. Nico made me hot coffee to sip and we chilled on the couch for the rest of the afternoon.

I couldn't remember the last time I had such a peaceful day. Nico didn't talk much, other than to ask me if I wanted food or something else to drink. When it was time to go home, I had to fight back the tears.

"Hey Nic," I said, my voice thick.

"Yeah, babe." He looked up from his phone to look over at me.

"I'm sorry I left you," I said softly. I watched as pain flashed in his blue eyes before I continued. "I'm sorry I hurt you."

Tears welled in my eyes as his eyes shuttered closed. He turned away from me and ran a hand over his face, rubbing at the scruff covering his jaw. "It would help, if you could tell me why?" His voice was hoarse, like he was choking back his own emotions. When he turned to me again, his blue eyes were red rimmed, the tears slid down his cheeks. "Can you tell me why?"

A sob choked me and curled in on myself, as I shook my head vehemently. "I can't, I'm so sorry," I sobbed.

I kept shaking my head as sobs wracked my body.

Nico moved quickly, pulling me against him and onto his lap. I buried my face into the crook of his neck as I cried uncontrollably. "Fuck, baby," Nico groaned, and held me tight.

I gripped the back of his shirt, as I held onto him for dear life—like he might disappear from me forever. "I'm so sorry, I'm so sorry." I just kept chanting it over and over.

He rocked me body slowly, back and forth. He didn't say much as he held me, occasionally murmuring that I was okay, even though we both knew I wasn't. I had fucked up so many times in the last ten years and it all had started when I walked away from them.

Only time would tell if I could redeem myself, to ever have a semblance of a friendship with them again.

Maya

Wednesday had been a relatively slow day in the office. It was our late day, so we wouldn't get busy until most people got off work. I was sitting in the small lounge of our Clinic, eating my homemade lunch, when there was commotion up front at the desk.

Lots of cooing women saying, "Oooo", and "Ohhh", and 'Aww'.

I had just looked up from my phone when the lounge door opened and a massive bouquet of yellow carnations and orange lilies was carried in, covering the face of my coworker.

I froze, my sandwich still halfway to my mouth as fear pooled in my belly. My heart pounded and my breath caught in my throat. "Oh my God, Maya!" Jayla, the front desk girl, gushed as she walked in with the bouquet.

I quickly schooled my face, forcing myself to smile and put down my sandwich as Rori and Aeyla walked in the lounge, with huge smiles on their faces. "Someone must really love you," Rori said.

"Uh, yeah," I forced a laugh. Thank God these women didn't know Flower Language and had no idea the true meaning behind the yellow Carnation and orange Lily.

They were not friendly flowers. In fact, they were quite the opposite. Orange lilies symbolized hatred, pride, disdain, and contempt; while yellow Carnations symbolized disdain and disappointment.

It was not a friendly or romantic bouquet of flowers by any means, and the true meaning rattled me to my core.

HE had found me.

HE knew where I worked.

HE was watching me.

I had hoped the first yellow carnation on my car last Saturday had been a fluke, or a reminder. This was an all-out assault. The line had been drawn in the sand, and I was standing behind enemy lines.

Jason

M Y WHOLE BODY ACHED, even almost a week after my beating. Marcos had done a number on me and I had deserved every punch.

I fucked up.

I fucked up bad.

Shit with Maya might not have been great before, but fuck. I never wanted to hurt her. That wasn't me. The fear in her eyes would haunt me forever. Even now, the thought of it drove me out of bed.

Unable to sleep, I tossed the blankets off me and reached for my jeans on the floor next to the bed. I pulled them over my naked cock and carefully zipped up, before I headed for the door of my dorm style room at the clubhouse. Ever since Maya had left us ten years ago, we had gone our separate ways, no longer living together.

It was too painful a reminder of what we had lost.

And we never shared another woman.

Our lives had been utterly destroyed when Maya left us, and seeing her now, hearing her say it, it still fucking tore my heart out. I felt like shit for choking her, but hearing her say those words in my mind on repeat, only made me want to choke her again. *I left you on purpose.*

It was bullshit.

Dagger wasn't talking to me, and Marcos, man. I hadn't even seen Marcos in the last week. As president of our club, he had to be present, and he must've been, because no one else said anything. But I hadn't seen him.

I stumbled down the hallway barefoot, heading for the fridge behind the bar in the main room. The room was mostly empty at four a.m., the party having died down around two.

I grabbed a beer and turned to survey room. The lights were dimmed low, but I could still make out the sprawled and passed out bodies that littered the floor—brothers who hadn't made it to their own dorms, or hanger-on's that crashed on the floor or couches instead of driving home. There were a couple half naked women on or under the men as well.

It was the typical scene of early Saturday morning at the clubhouse.

What wasn't typical, was the bright light emanating from president's office down the hall from the barroom. I scratched my brow with my middle finger before I took a sip of the Coors. I grabbed another beer from the fridge and headed toward the light.

I rolled my eyes at the stupid pun in my head.

The light on in the office could only mean one thing: Marcos was in the building and didn't want to be seen.

Well fuck that. I had shit on my mind I needed to say, and Marcos was just the one I needed to hear it.

My bare feet slapped on the polished concrete floor as I walked down the hall. The office door was half closed, so I pushed it open as I stepped inside.

Seated behind the desk, Marcos had his head down as he poured over the stacks of papers in front of him. In the six months since Buckley's death, Marcos had pulled the club from the brink of death and bankruptcy, saving us, but we were still scraping by.

I saw how it weighed on my brother. The stress he carried as president was hard. But add in the stress of trying to form a relationship with a son he hadn't known about, and the tense relationship with our ex... it was a lot for any man to handle.

Marcos never complained about it, though. He never bitched and moaned, he just shouldered it all, so others didn't have to, and pulled us out of the bullshit Buckley had sunk us into with Las Serpientes.

The fucking snakes were circling, demanding payment for Buckley's death. Buckley apparently still owed them money for the death of the Ravager Knights MC President Mac 'King' Taylor—money the club didn't have.

I knocked on the doorframe of the office, waiting for Marcos to acknowledge me before I walked into the lion's den.

"Yeah," Marcos grunted before he glanced at the door. His face was unreadable, so I couldn't tell if he was surprised to see me or not.

"Hey," I said, stepping into the office and closing the door behind me.

Marcos looked over my bruised face before he turned back to the papers in front of him. "What do you want?"

I ground my teeth as to not lash out at my brother's gruff attitude. "To apologize."

"I'm not the one you owe an apology to," Marcos shot back immediately.

Again, I gritted my teeth. I may owe Maya an apology, but I doubted she'd let me anywhere near her any time soon to deliver it. And I wasn't ready to face her yet. I moved further into the office and set both beers down the desk between us. I took a seat in chair in front of the desk. "She's the mother of your child, I'm sorry I hurt her, man," I apologized, despite the fact that Marcos didn't want to hear it.

Marcos shook his head and let out a low sardonic chuckle. "You know what I don't get?" he finally said, looking up to meet my gaze. "How you—the man who used to be so fucking obsessed with her back then that you would borderline stalk her—could *hate* her so much now, that you almost fucking killed her?" The anger radiated off Marcos in waves.

I gritted my teeth again and forced myself to relax. I couldn't explain my irrational rage when it came to her. "She fucking left us," I ground out.

Marcos nodded. "Yeah bro, she did. I'm not saying you have to be in a fucking relationship with her, or even be *nice* to her. But don't fucking try to kill her!"

I looked away, gritting my teeth. I fucked up, I knew that already.

"Dude, Maya is not your mother," Marcos said.

I snapped my gaze back to my brother and glared. "Don't."

"No, you fucking don't. This bullshit you have with Maya is the same. You think she fucking abandoned you. She might have left us, but she came back, and she would never abandon her child. She's not your mother."

"And you're okay with her walking out on you? Not telling you, you had a kid?" I snapped, getting pissed off.

"Of course not," Marcos shook his head. "I won't deny that she broke my fucking heart, and that some days I can't even fucking look at her. But she's a damn good mother, and will do anything for him. And she's done a damn good job of raising him so far on her own."

I sighed and looked down at my bare feet, before I reached for my beer on the desk. I pushed the unopened one toward Marcos. "I'm sorry. I'll apologize to her and figure out how to curb my anger."

Marcos reached for the beer and popped the can open. He took a long sip as he leaned back in the chair. He ran a hand over his chin thoughtfully, "I think Dagger's right about her. Something's not adding up."

"Come on, man," I said shaking my head, not wanting to hear it for the hundredth time. Dagger was bad enough, but now Marcos?

"You didn't see her," Marcos snapped. "Monday, I went over to Dagger's. He had convinced her to call into work, to heal," Marcos glared at me. "She was sleeping when I got there. So I hung out for a while. Seeing her go from unguarded to instantly on the defense when she saw me..." he shook head and looked away. "I think she's hiding something."

I rolled my eyes. *Of course, she was hiding something, she was a fucking liar,* I thought. "Like what?" I humored my brother.

Marcos shook his head again. "I don't know, man. I talked to Nic yesterday. He said before she left his place, she apologized for leaving us, for hurting us. When Nic asked her if she could just explain *why* she had done it, she started sobbing. She said she couldn't tell him, and became inconsolable the harder he pressed."

I narrowed my gaze on my buddy. Marcos clearly believed whatever happened was a breakthrough into the inner workings of her mind, but I didn't see things like that. In fact, I thought it was a convenient way for her to get Dagger to stop asking questions. She knew how easy it was to manipulate Dagger's feelings; she knew Dagger would stop at the first sight of a tear in her caramel eyes. It was a little too *easy* for my liking. I kept it to myself though. I knew my buddies were looking for any hint or sign or reasoning for her ghosting us back then.

I was pretty sure we weren't going to get the truth out of her, though. Maybe it was time to do our own investigation into her.

"I met with Johnny and his boys this week. I've got a couple jobs I'm gonna bring to the table tomorrow, drug running, security, things like that."

I nodded, accepting the change of subject.

"Nic is meeting with his cousin tomorrow," Marcos said, dropping an anvil like it weighed nothing.

"What the fuck, dude?" I growled, leaning forward as if that would help me hear better.

Marcos nodded solemnly, taking a sip of beer before he responded. "Las Serpientes are pressing in hard, even the Knights are feeling the squeeze. Shit's about to pop off, and we are not in any kind of position to defend ourselves, even with the help of the Knights. We need help."

"And the fucking Mafia is who were asking for help from?" I growled, getting to my feet. "How the fuck could you make him call them?"

"I didn't," Marcos shook his head, not even rising to the bait. "Nico offered. Leo and him are working through shit."

"And what the fuck will Nic owe the Seratelli's after this? What's the fucking cost?" I snapped, pacing behind the two chairs set before the president's desk.

"We'll find that tomorrow I assume. Or is it today? Fuck," Marcos groaned and rubbed his temples.

"He's going today? Fuck. Are we going with him?" I asked.

Marcos shook his head. "No. He's on his own. I'm picking up Luke from the pool this afternoon and he's spending the night at my place tonight."

I stopped pacing, "Your first overnight?"

"Yeah." Marcos sighed, rubbing his hand over his buzzed hair.

"Damn bro, congrats," I said, truly happy for my brother.

Marcos shook his head. "I haven't seen Luke all week. I've given Maya space since last weekend. The sleep over was her idea."

Rage roiled in my gut. "You should be able to see Luke whenever you want to."

"Bro, you need to lay off. I have been seeing Luke whenever I want. You heard him at dinner; he's missing his friends. And I wasn't the one that fucking choked the shit out of Maya. Yeah, I gave her some fucking space this week and Dagger's been checking in with her daily. You really fucking hurt her bro. She had to take time off work, time she doesn't fucking have, because she's new on the job. She's stressing about when school starts and Luke gets his usual back to school cold, who's going to take care of him. She's got a million appointments to take her parents to, she can't afford to take time off."

Guilt stabbed at me again. I shoved my fingers through my messy blond hair and pulled. My fucked up was pretty epic this time.

"You don't seem to get it, brother," Marcos said as he stood up. "My name isn't on the birth certificate. I can't sue for custody. No judge in their right mind would grant me any kind of rights based on my felony record, let alone my current title of president of a criminal organization."

I scoffed, I hated that affiliation when anyone thought of the MC, regardless if it was true or not. I opened my mouth to argue my point, but quickly shut it when I saw the look on Marcos's face. "You shouldn't have to live in fear of her taking him from you."

"I wasn't afraid of that, until you fucking hurt her!" Marcos exploded rounding the desk and stomping toward me. He got right in my face as he spoke. "She's made it pretty fucking clear, that she'll do whatever is in Luke's best interest, and if she thinks in its Luke best interest to stay the fuck away from us? From me? You better believe I'm gonna beat your fucking ass again. I'm fucking serious, brother. Stay the fuck away from her. And if you do run into her, you keep your damn mouth shut."

"Alright," I agreed immediately. "Fuck."

Marcos shook his head and turned away; he grabbed his beer off the desk chugged it back.

"For what it's worth man, I am sorry. I've been making myself sick over hurting her," I admitted, my voice low.

"Yeah. Me too," Marcos mumbled.

Chapter Fifteen

Nico

I RAN MY HAND down the zipper of my leather cut, wondering—not for the first time that day—if I should take it off and meet my cousin in plain clothes. I haven't seen my cousin Leonardo in ten years, but I knew for a fact that Leonardo would be dressed in a suit, the made-men always wore suits.

I looked around the outside of the fancy as fuck restaurant where I was told to wait and narrowed my eyes. This wasn't my scene. I steeled my spine and walked into the building, holding the door open for an older Italian couple, as they walked out with their boxed-up leftovers in hand. Murmuring a brief greeting, I headed into the restaurant after they passed.

The restaurant was busy inside. The hostess looked up with a cheery smile that immediately froze in place as she took in my attire. "Can I help you?"

"Nicolai Gage, I have an appointment."

The woman immediately looked down at her podium and frowned. She pulled a yellow sticky note off the reservation book and looked up. "Yes. I see. Right this way." She nodded once, then turned toward the dining room, not bothering to grab a menu.

It didn't matter, I didn't think I'd be eating anyways. I followed her as she wound her way through the busy restaurant, ignoring the eyes of the diners as they passed by. She led me through the main dining room to a hallway in the back. We walked down the hall, past the bathrooms and the kitchen and two private dining rooms, to an office tucked around a corner.

The woman knocked on the closed door and waited. It was a moment before a gruff male voice said, "Come in."

"I've got it from here, darling," I murmured to the girl.

She jumped, startled and nodded, before she walked away quickly.

I took a deep breath and pushed open the office door, finding the room exactly as I expected. Dark wood covering the walls, a deep red carpet on the floor, and in the center of room, seated behind a massive mahogany desk, sat my cousin Leonardo Seratelli.

Dressed in a sharp three-piece suit that probably cost more than what I paid monthly on my condo; Leonardo Seratelli looked every bit the mafia Don he was. Tall and broad shouldered, with tanned olive skin and black hair that was fucking coiffed back away from his handsome as fuck face, but he had the same fucking blue eyes that I had.

All and all, Leonardo was a formidable man, even if he looked like a damn pretty boy. Not that I had much room to talk, I just covered myself in leather and blood, and didn't front with a suit.

"Cousin," I greeted as I walked in the office and shut the door behind me.

Leo looked up from the cell phone in his hand and narrowed his gaze on me. "Not sure you still hold that title, Nico." Leo's deep voice was as commanding and every bit authoritative as the rest of him, cutting me to the bone, with one simple sentence.

"Alright, I deserved that," I admitted.

It might have been ten years since we saw each other, but clearly the animosity was still there. "What do you want, Nicolai?"

"Full name, damn," I joked, cracking a smile.

Leo stared at me with a hard gaze, his bright blue eyes icy. He rose slowly to his feet and buttoned his suit jacket closed. "I haven't seen you since you turned your back on the family ten years ago and you want to waste my time with jokes?"

I swallowed thickly. "No, of course not."

"Then hurry up and speak, Nicolai." Leo's slightly accented voice grew thicker with the pronunciation of my full name, rolling off the tongue and sounding almost musical. The bastard always sounded so damn sophisticated.

God, it grated on my nerves. But I was here for the club, so I needed to get over whatever insecurities my cousin made me feel by just standing there. "Look, I'm sorry, alright? I walked out ten years ago and I'm sorry."

Leo narrowed his eyes. "You're fucking '*sorry*'?" He leaned forward, placing both hands on the desk in front of him. "I *needed* you, and you fucking turned your back on me." His voice was a low menacing growl that I was sure put the fear of God into Leo's adversaries, but it had the opposite effect on me.

No.

Instead, it ripped out my soul to hear my cousin's utter contempt. I had done that, put that divide between us. We had once been the best of friends growing up, but life had dragged us separate ways, and in the end we fell apart.

"You're right," I admitted.

Leo's eyes narrowed again, like he couldn't believe what he was hearing. "Why are you here, Nicolai?"

"Can I not just want to see family?" I asked sagely, knowing I was toeing the line.

"Then why haven't you seen your mother in six months?" Leo shot back. He straightened and shook his head. "I don't have time for your bullshit, Nicolai. Get out of my sight." He dismissed me with a wave of his hand.

"Leo—shit—I'm sorry, ok? I'm sorry I walked out. I'm sorry I left when you needed me. I've recently discovered just how badly I fucked up back then."

Leo hit me with a hard stare and for a moment I thought I was staring at my Uncle Augustino—Leo's father—a man I hadn't seen I'd been arrested and framed by Hillcrest. Augustino had come to visit me in county after someone had tipped him off that I had been picked up.

Augustino had basically said that I was on my own—not that I had expected the family to get involved anyways. There wasn't any love lost between me and my uncle. We had said our words several times over the years, but my arrest had been a deciding point for Augustino.

I was no longer welcome within the family, the family would honor the coke deal with the Psychos, but contact would remain between leadership, and I was not welcomed.

I had agreed.

While I had been in jail, though, Maya had left us and my Uncle Augustino had been murdered. It had been a tumultuous time. While I had only been locked up for less than twenty-four hours, it had been the most monumental twenty-four hours of my life.

"I'm sorry I wasn't there for you when Augustino died," I said. I ran a hand through my blond hair and sighed, looking down at my scuffed boots. I wondered how the fuck I was going to right this wrong with my family.

"What do you want, Nico?" Leo sounded tired.

I looked up to find my cousin sitting back down in his desk chair. Leaning back, Leo rested his elbows on the arms of the chairs and steepled his fingers in front him, his hard blue eyes watching me warily. There was a quiet resolution set on his face. "The coke trade with—"

"Jesus fucking Christ!" Leo snapped.

I immediately stopped talking, knowing I had already lost any ground to stand on with my cousin.

"The coke trade was given to the Knights. End of story. I brokered the deal with Mac Taylor. It's done."

"And if Johnny Taylor doesn't want to move coke anymore?" I hedged carefully.

Leo shook his head, reaching out for his phone off the desk. He sent a quick text and stood up. "I'm not having this conversation with you, Nicolai. The Knights have the coke. It's done. Get out of my sight. Go see your mother."

The office door opened behind me and I glanced over my shoulder to see two muscled goons in tailored suits walk in the office. Sighing, I knew when I was beat. "I'm sorry about Uncle Augustino. When I found out about him, my girl had just left and my head wasn't in the right place. Not that it's an excuse to not be there for family, but I thought you should know. I'm sorry." I turned to the door, without waiting for the men to escort me out.

"Your girl," Leo said when I reached the door. "What happened to her?"

I paused in the door, wondering just how to answer that question. "I did," I answered grimly.

Leo gave me a nod, and I left the office, a heavy feeling sinking in my gut.

Nico

I took my cousin's advice after I left the restaurant and headed west, to my mom's house. The neighborhood my mother lived in was nothing but McMansions set back on massive lots. It was a gated golf course community and boasted its riches and manicured lawns. The house my mother lived in—and I had grown up in—was no different.

It was a world away from the nitty gritty life that I had carved out for myself with the Devil's Psychos.

I may have grown up here, but I found myself—and Marcos and Jason—when I was in high school running the streets of Creekton. It had been an act of rebellion after my father was killed, to go against the family and get myself into trouble in Creekton, but instead I had found my own family in Marcos and Jason and had never looked back.

This time, I removed my cut and draped it over my handlebars before I headed up to the front door of my mother's house. It was a point of contention between us, and as I was already going to be in deep enough shit with my mother for not showing up for six months, I would try not to add any fuel to the fire if I could help it.

The front door opened before I could knock on it. The older woman that answered it had been with the family since I was a child. "Nicolai!" Guilia greeted me with a bright smile. "It's so good to see you," she said, before switching to rapid fire Italian as she pulled me into a tight hug.

I answered her back, slipping into Italian, a genuine smile lighting up my face.

Guilia was just pulling away from me when I heard my mother's heels clicking on the marble floors. I had to steel my spine before I saw her.

Teresa Seratelli-Gage was still as beautiful as ever. In her early sixties, with blond hair pinned back into an elegant chignon, her bright blue eyes sparkled, even as they narrowed into a glare as she took me in. Her bright red lipstick accented her lips as they pursed while she slowly surveyed me from head to toe. "Nicolai." She finally greeted and moved closer, opening her arms to me.

I flew into her embrace, trying to remind myself that she was a frail woman now, and I was no longer a little kid, but the urge to hide in her arms was strong. She may be disappointed in me, but she still loved me and still would hold me. It was because of that disappointment that I had stayed away to begin with. I hated to let her down, so I stayed away thinking it was better for her.

"Momma," I murmured, hugging her tightly.

"My boy," she whispered, her voice thick with emotion.

"I'm sorry, momma."

Thersea pulled away and shook her head. "I'm glad you're finally here, son. Guilia, will you prepare lunch, please? We'll take it in the sunroom." My mother looped her arm through mine, and I got the hint to bend my elbow and guide her toward the back sunroom that overlooked the back patio and pool.

The mansion was enormous, way too big for my mother to live here all alone—except for Guilia. I had tried many times to get my mother to sell the place and downsize, but she had refused time and time again, stating it was the last piece of my father she had left, and she wouldn't give it up.

"Talk to me, Nicolai. What's been going on with you in the last six months?"

I took a deep breath. "Maya came back, in January."

My mother gasped and turned to look up at me, stopping abruptly. "You're serious?" she asked.

I nodded. "Yes. She came back to take care of her parents. They were in a car accident in November, I think. And when they were released from the hospital and the rehabilitation center, they still needed a lot of help, so Maya moved back to help them."

"Oh that's wonderful! Not about her parents I mean, that's horrible news. But I'm so glad she's returned."

"She came back with her nine-year-old son." I let that hang out there a moment, watching as my mother's eyes light up.

"Nine-year-old?" she gasped.

I nodded slowly. "Marcos is the father. I mean they haven't done a test, but he looks exactly like Marcos."

Tears welled in my mother's blue eyes as a bright smile lit up her face. "Oh, that's wonderful news. And how is she? Single?"

I barked out a laugh, shaking my head. I continued walking toward the sunroom, tugging my mother along. "She is single, and we see Luke often—that's his name, Lucas."

"What a beautiful name. You have pictures, don't you? You must show me immediately."

As we sat down at the table in the sunroom overlooking the back gardens and pool, I pulled out my phone and dove into everything going on lately with Maya, Luke, and the guys. "Oh, Nico, they're both beautiful."

Nico

After a nice lunch of catching up and showing my mom a million pictures of Luke and Maya, I guided the conversation to my recent visit with my cousin Leonardo. My mother sighed and looked out at the backyard. "I wish you would have called me before visiting him."

"Why?"

"Because the family isn't happy with you, Nicolai, not that they weren't before, but they tolerated you because your business dealings benefitted them. This mess with the MC's is not good for the family."

"How do you know of all of that?" I narrowed my eyes on her in shock.

"Because I still see Leonardo every week dear. Family dinner at his mother's house."

"Fuck." I sighed. I had forgotten about the family dinners. They were every single Sunday, at Leonardo's home parents' home. His mother still hosted the large gathering, employing the help of several servants.

My mother pursed her lips at my use of crude language, but didn't say anything this time around. "What did Leonardo have to say when you saw him?"

"He told me things were a done deal with the Knights. And to go see my mother."

My mom smiled and shook her head, affection clear in her eyes.

"While he was right about that last part, he's wrong about the Knights. It's imperative that I speak to Leo. The Knights want out of the deal and the Psychos need help. I need help, mom," I implored. "Maya is being threatened, and I'm pretty sure by Dax Hillcrest, the leader of Las Serpientes—"

Teresa hissed as she heard the name of the gang. They were notorious—but Teresa knew they had kidnapped Kara.

I pressed on. "The serpents are threatening Maya, it's why she left us in the first place. She's scared and won't tell us everything. And I can't kill him, because Kara is worried that it will somehow impede her father's hearing. I could really use Leo's help."

Teresa was silent as she chewed on her bottom lip, lost in thought.

I waited, needing my mother to agree to help me.

"I suppose you want me to speak to Leonardo?"

"Please, mom. It would mean—"

Teresa shook her head, cutting me off immediately.

I waited, watching her warily.

"You've screwed up a lot with the family over the years, Nicolai," she started, speaking softly, meeting my gaze with her own hard stare. "The family will require retribution." She looked worried.

I swallowed thickly and nodded. "I understand. I'm willing to make amends."

"Nicolai." My mother sighed.

"Mom." I reached for her hand, "I get that, I know you're worried about me, but I'm begging you. Please, talk to Leo. I need this. Maya and Luke are in grave danger and we can't help her."

Teresa sighed heavily, jerking her head once. "Ok. I will talk to Leonardo this weekend."

"Thank you." I got up and hugged my mother fiercely. "Thank you."

"Nicolai, I cannot guarantee anything. You offended your uncle and the family years ago. You will have to issue a formal apology to the family and accept whatever penance they deal out." Her breathing grew shaky. She knew how cruel and hard the family could be. While I wasn't a traitor, they might treat me like one. My punishment could mean my life.

"I understand, momma." I pressed a kiss to her cheek as I got to my knees before her. Resting my forehead against hers, I spoke softly. "I need to protect Maya though. Luke may not be my blood, but he's my son nonetheless."

A sob shook my mother's tiny frame and I hugged her tightly.

"It'll be ok, momma. I promise."

BRANDISHING BETRAYALS

Chapter Sixteen

Maya

THE WEEK WAS LONG and slow, but uneventful. My nerves were shot and I had perfected my make-up skills by the end of the week, even when I opted to wear a thin turtleneck under my scrubs in the office. Thankfully the women's clinic was always kept cold and I usually wore a sweater over my scrubs, so the switch to turtleneck underneath wasn't a stretch and barely a blip to my coworkers.

By Saturday, the coloring on my neck was looking a little better, but I knew it would be a while before I would be able to stop with the make-up.

Since Monday's encounter with Marcos, he'd made himself scarce throughout the week. It wasn't until Friday that he had finally texted and asked if he could see Luke over the weekend. I had agreed and told him he could pick up Luke from the local pool on Saturday after he was done hanging out with his friends.

They were going to attempt their first sleep over at Marco's apartment.

My nerves were shot at the idea of Luke spending the night away from me, so I opted to distract myself with some retail therapy on Saturday afternoon. Not that I had much money to spend, but Friday had been payday, and I could walk around the outdoor mall and window shop a bit. It was beautiful, if not a scorchingly hot summer day.

I was browsing a window display of a black lacy dress, wondering if I'd ever live the kind of life that would allow me wear something so spectacular, when I was broken out of my thoughts by someone speaking to me.

"Well, well, well, what do we have here?" a nasally male voice crooned from behind me.

I halted in my tracks. Ice slid down my spine. I knew that voice—that fucking voice—it was the voice of my nightmares. Dillion "Dax" Hillcrest.

I turned my head slowly and met the mismatched gaze over my shoulder, the pale light blue eye and the deep dark one a night and day opposite. The thick jagged scar that ripped his face in half, was as raised and puffy as it was ten years ago.

Dax towered over me, still as intimidating as he was back then. Fear coiled in my belly, as my heart raced rapidly. This wasn't happening, I couldn't handle this again. It nearly killed me last time.

"Hillcrest," I responded coolly, forcing myself to appear as aloof as possible, as I slowly turned to face him. I might be terrified, but I was no longer the scared little girl he ran off ten years ago. I would not show him fear.

A sneer pulled at his scared face. "You think you're tough now? Now that you're back with your motorcycle club, being their whore? I've seen them sniffing around you again." His voice was as nasally as it was before, and its rasp sent shivers down my spine.

I couldn't afford to piss him off, I knew that. He wasn't above hurting me, or my loved ones. He had demonstrated that before, but I couldn't roll over either. I was not the same naïve little girl anymore. I rolled my eyes, "I'm not with them."

"No? Just share blood with them?"

A chill broke out across my skin, pebbling my flesh despite the summer heat. He knew Lucas was theirs. Fuck. I hadn't even known if he was still alive until he dropped that flower on my car last Saturday.

I knew it was only a matter of time before he found out. He had been watching me for weeks, or longer, even if he'd only been dropping flowers for the last week.

Dax chuckled darkly. "Yeah, puta, I know all about your baby daddy problems...And Candela sure has been coming over to your parents' place a lot lately. How does he feel that you left because of me? Wonder if that son of yours knows he could have had his daddy if you had told them all those years ago."

My breath caught in my throat. I'd wondered that very same thing, every damn day of my life, for the last ten years. Every time I looked at Luke, I wondered if I should call Marcos and tell him the truth.

"Maybe I should tell Candella the child is mine," Dax drawled, crossing his arms and cupping his chin with his thumb and forefinger in a thoughtful expression.

"You're an asshole," I snapped, done with his shit.

He lashed out before I could react. His hand wrapped around my throat and he shoved me back against the window of the store hard and fast, before I could stop him. My hands came up and gripped around his wrist, trying to pull him off me. He crowded into my space, using his body to keep me against the glass.

He smelled of stale cigarettes and cheap cologne. The leather jacket he wore was torn and shredded in places. His teeth were yellowed and his breath stank as he breathed hot air in my face. "I think you're forgetting your place, whore."

I struggled against him. I dug my fingernails into the hand around my throat as I gasped for breath.

"I told you never to come back here," he growled in my face, his multi-colored eyes glaring down at me.

I focused on the gnarly scar bisecting the left side of his face as I struggled to breathe. "You don't control me," I ground out, between clenched teeth.

He squeezed my neck tighter.

"Everything alright here?" a man's voice asked, somewhere behind Dax.

He let go of me instantly.

It took everything I had to stay on my feet and not cause a scene in the semi-busy outdoor mall. I looked over his shoulder to see a security guard in a black T-shirt that had a company logo on the front left. "Yeah," I muttered, "fine."

Dax walked away, shooting me a look over his shoulder as he pushed past the guard.

I didn't wait around either. I took off in the opposite direction, ignoring the security guard and hightailing it for the parking lot.

Things were quickly getting out of hand with Dax Hillcrest, and once again I wondered if I should go to Marcos or Nico and confess everything.

Chapter Seventeen

Marcos

"Hey man," I greeted Nico as I walked into the club-house Sunday evening.

"Hey bro." Nic smiled and stood from the couch he was sitting on. I leaned in and slapped his hand with Nico's in a brotherly handshake-hug, that involved a lot of back patting.

"How was your weekend?" Nic asked.

I grinned widely. "It was great. Amazing. I picked up Luke from the pool. Then we got dinner at McGrady's and hit the arcade. It was awesome."

"Why do you look so exhausted?" Nic chuckled.

"I gave him my bed. I slept on the couch, or tried to. I didn't sleep much." I groaned and took a seat on the loveseat across from where Nico had been sitting.

Nico frowned. "Time to buy a house?"

"It's past time." I sighed. "Shit's tight, you know? I've been saving, but we aren't earning what we used to, and nothing legit that'll convince a bank to give me a loan."

Nico was completive for a moment as he rubbed a hand over his jaw.

"We could do it together," Stone said from behind me.

I looked over my shoulder at my buddy, frowning slightly. "We haven't lived together since Maya left."

Jason rounded the couch slowly, running a hand over his spikey hair. "Yeah...and we haven't been doing well on our own either."

"So what are you saying?" I asked, leaning back to look at my brother.

"We pool our resources. I've got cash. I haven't spent much in the last couple years," Jason clarified.

"Same. I've been squirrelling money away from the jobs," Nico said. "We know you were paying for Kara's undergrad, but you should talk to her about that. I bet she doesn't know."

I sighed. My sister definitely didn't know and I hadn't planned on telling her either.

"Dude, Kara is rolling in cash, she would be so pissed if she knew you were paying her loans for her. She probably thinks they were paid off by her father," Nico said, shifting on the couch. "There's no way she'd allow you to continue to pay them if she knew."

"Talk to her," Jason said. "Then we can pull our funds together and put down a hefty down payment on a house. I know you've been looking in the neighborhood where Maya's at. And Kara lives in that neighborhood too. It makes sense for us to move there."

My heart fluttered in my chest. "You guys would do that?" I didn't know why I asked it; my brothers would do anything for me.

"Hell yeah!" Nico exclaimed.

Jason smirked. "You know we would."

"I guess I'll go talk to Kara tomorrow," I said. "Tonight, we need to talk business with the club."

Marcos

An hour later we were sitting around the large wooden table in church, waiting for the last of our guys to file in for our weekly meeting. Usually, I held it on Saturday nights, but I had Luke last night, and I still wasn't ready to bring my son around the clubhouse yet, and definitely not on a party night. The kid was still too young for that shit.

"Next order of business," I said, looking around the table. "With things calm now between us and the Ravager Knights, we need to have a sit down with the Italians."

Nico sighed from his spot to my left.

"Probably should have done that a while ago," Jerry Langford spoke up.

I nodded slowly. "I agree. The Knights have agreed to end the Coke trade with the Seratelli's. I think it's only right we approach the Italians as the replacement. It would give us a way to earn a steady income again and we can push it through the same trade routes we're using for the Heroin."

"Why did the damn Mafia go to the Knights in the first place? We've always run their Heroin. Why the fuck did the Knights get the Coke?'"

"Not sure," I shook my head. "Whatever deal Mac Taylor struck with the Seratelli's; Johnny didn't know about it. It was toward the end of Mac's life, maybe he was getting greedy. It's anyone's guess, because he went against the Bratva too."

A rumble of murmuring went around the table.

"Nico, I need you to speak to your cousin," I said, turning to my buddy. "Set up a meeting." I had to say this formally in front of my club, even though I knew Nico already went to Leonardo once. We had to do things above board.

Nico eyed me warily, this was a dangerous game to play in front of the club, but we needed the brothers to agree to Nico meeting with his family on behalf of the club, otherwise he would be considered a traitor. He nodded at me. Things may be rocky between Nico and his family, and they had enough unresolved family drama to write a book about, but Nico would reach out—again—simply because his club president had asked it of him.

"We looking to smooth things over with the Seratelli's or are we vying for the coke trade?" Bear asked, crossing his large arms over his chest.

"How do we feel about both?" I asked, looking around the room once again. "I was hoping to smooth things over, clear the air. The shits that happened with the Knights and Seratelli's and the Bratva, it would be nice lay everything out on the table."

"You'll never get the Russians to agree to a sit down with the Italians," Jerry Langford said. "And what about the Irish? How are they going to handle things if we start working with the Italians?"

I rubbed a hand over my scruffy jaw. My brothers were asking legit questions that I myself had thought about over the last several weeks. I nodded solemnly. "I have those same questions. This is why we need a sit with the Italians. They're in our backyard. We have to deal with them every time we head into Mourningside, and they're Nico's blood. We need a better understanding of what we're dealing with here. And the Irish know we've got ties to the Italians. It's only a recent development bent that we haven't."

"And you think Leonardo Seratelli will agree to meet?" Jerry asked.

"He will," Nico said gruffly.

"You can't know for su—"

"I can." Nico said, cutting off Jerry. "My mother is his God-mother and aunt. Her brother was Leonardo's father."

Murmurs rumbled around the table. While it was common enough knowledge, they didn't talk about it often—Nico didn't talk about it all.

"And you see your cousin often?" Jerry raised an eyebrow, already knowing the truth. He knew Nico well enough over the years, being Jason's best friend and all.

"Not in ten years," Nico admitted. "He's been asking my mother about me." Nico shrugged, running a hand through his wavy blond hair.

"I think it's a solid plan," I said, jumping in the conversation. "We let Dagger set up the meeting with his cousin, and if Seratelli doesn't want to meet with him, I'll make a formal call through Giovanni."

A rumble of murmuring went around the room.

"So you sit down with Seratelli, discuss the coke trade and the backhanded dealing with the Knights? Then what?" Phoenix asked, drawing my gaze across the table to the brown eyed man.

"What do you mean?" I asked.

"What are we doing about Las Serpientes? Vince Carmichael? I feel like we still got unfinished business there."

"Carmichael is in County without bail, awaiting his trial. The District Attorney is working with the Knights attorney Freddy Danvers and my sister, to make sure Carmichael stays behind bars for a very long time. As for the snakes…" I trailed off, glancing between Phoenix, Blaze, and Axel. "What do you suggest?"

The three men exchanged a look. "We're not gonna lie here," Blaze said. His dark black hair was covered by a backward ballcap and his green eyes shone bright in florescent light. "We have a personal interest in what happens with the snakes."

"My little brother was killed by Dax Hillcrest twelve years ago," Axel said. His gray eyes cutting to mine.

I cursed under my breath. I had known something had happened with Las Serpientes and Axel's crew, back in the day. It was what made the three of them join up to begin with, but I had never known the full story.

"I'm sorry man," I said.

Axel nodded curtly. "Yeah… I have a bit of a vested interest in Hillcrest and the snakes."

I rubbed a hand over my buzzed head, thinking. "I get that, I do. They kidnapped my sister." I shook my head. "My hands are tied on that for right now. You know we made a deal with the Knights to let the D.A. handle Carmichael right now. My sister thinks that if we go after Las Serpientes on the outside, they'll retaliate on the inside and do something to fuck up the case against Carmichael. As of right now, my sister needs him alive."

Axel narrowed his gaze at me. I could feel the anger behind that glare. "If things change—"

"If things change," I interrupted him. "We will vote as a club as how to handle Hillcrest and Las Serpientes."

Axel blew out a breath and looked away.

Chapter Eighteen

Marcos

I WALKED INTO MY sister's house late Monday night, after texting her to see if she was still awake. I was dreading the conversation I was about to have with her and prayed to God her men would give us space.

I let myself in through the backdoor, walking into the kitchen. I left my boots on, as I walked through the large kitchen in search of my sister. I found her curled up on the couch, nursing a glass of wine. There was a book propped up on a pillow in her lap, she looked comfy and cozy, and utterly relaxed.

I hated that I was about to piss her off, especially now that we had finally got into a good place in our relationship. "Hey lil Manita," I greeted.

She looked up from her book and gave me a soft smile. "Hey Marquitos." She unfurled herself from the couch and walked over to greet me with a hug. "Want something to drink?"

"I'll take a Whisky," I said, squeezing her tightly.

She hummed as she pulled away. "Important meeting, requiring whisky, late at night? What's going on big brother?"

I sighed as I stepped away from her. I ran a hand over my buzzed head and paced away from her.

Kara was quiet as she poured me a glass of whisky. She slid it over on the counter toward me, before she walked back into the living room and grabbed her glass of wine. Once she was back in the kitchen, she took a seat at the large island and waited, watching me expectantly.

I sighed as I walked over to the island. I took a sip of my whisky and rubbed a hand over my scruffy jaw. "Look, I'm sorry okay."

She frowned, "Marquitos—"

"Just let me get this out, OK?" I shot her a pleading look.

She pursed her lips together, her blue eyes narrowing on me, but she nodded once and let me continue.

"I hate to admit this, but I'm struggling a little bit financially, and well..." I rubbed a hand over my jaw again, hating that I wasn't able to just spit out what I needed to say. *This fucking vulnerability shit sucks.*

"Marcos," Kara said, pulling me out of my train of thought. "Whatever you need. You can have. How much money do you need?"

"It's not like that." I shook my head vehemently. "I just need to stop paying your student loans. If I don't have those payments, I'd be OK."

Kara gasped.

I couldn't look at her. I could only imagine the pain in those blue eyes. I knew I was hurting her. *This is such bullshit.*

"What do you mean you're paying my student loans?" She snapped. "Marcos! What the hell!"

I finally looked over at her. The anger was evident, but so was the pain.

"I thought my dad took care of my loans! I never would have expected you pay for them! Marcos! We said when I applied for those loans, that they would be my responsibly when I graduated! It only made sense! Why in the hell would you be paying them? My dad told me he took care of them for me! I thought he rolled my undergrad into the Harvard payments!"

"He and I might have gotten into an argument about them. I told him I could take care of you just fine, and would pay it."

"Jesus fucking CHRIST," she swore. She shook her head in disbelief. "That has to be close to eighty thousand dollars! What the fuck, Marcos!"

I took a long pull from my whisky, letting her rant. Some-times it was better if she just got everything out in the open. "I'm just asking you to take over the monthly payment, *Manita*. I'm sorry you didn't know; I didn't want you to. But now with Luke and shit with the club, money is tight, and I'm trying to buy a house."

Kara sighed and tossed back her wine, emptying it in one gulp. "Did you bring the papers?"

I pulled out a stack of opened envelopes from my inner pocket on my cut. The clear film on the envelope window crinkled as I handed them over.

Kara took the stack from me. She set the stack on the counter in front of her and pulled open the first envelope. Her face was a range of emotions as she read over the billing. Her mouth dropped open when she took in the monthly payment due. "Marcos this is a damn mortgage payment!"

"Look, if you can't do the whole thing, just pay half, and I'll take care of the other—"

"No." She snapped, cutting him off with a glare. "I'll take care of this. What the fuck, Marcos! You should have told me about this sooner! I would have paid this years ago!"

"I didn't want you to be upset. I still don't want you to be upset. OK, sister?" I sighed.

Kara shook her head. "It's not OK, brother. I'm sorry you had to deal with this. I'll take care of it."

I smiled faintly and opened my arms. She flew into me, hugging me hard, making me rock back a step. "I love you, lil Manita."

"Love you too, Marquitos."

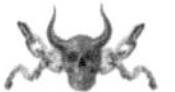

Marcos

"I talked to Kara last night about the student loans," I told Stone and Dagger as we sat down to lunch the following day. The restaurant around us was bustling, so I wasn't worried about anyone overhearing our conversation.

"That's good," Dagger grinned. "I bet she was pissed!"

I chucked sardonically. "Sure was. But she's going to take care of the payments now. It frees up fifteen hundred a month."

"That's a damn mortgage payment," Stone grunted.

"That's what Kara said," I sighed.

Stone pulled out a piece of paper from the inner pocket of his cut and set it on the table, in front of the three of them. "This is what I can chip in for a down payment."

Dagger pulled out his own folded piece of paper. "This is what I've got."

I frowned and reached for both pieces of folded paper. "Shit," I muttered when I took in the large sums written down. "Seriously?"

Stone just shrugged.

Dagger grinned broadly. "Yeah dude! Let's do it!"

I shook my head. "After all these years... are we really talking about living together again?"

"We always lived together before—until Maya left," Dagger said, smiling sadly. "Besides... maybe things with her will come full circle."

Stone snorted and shook his head.

I glared slightly at my buddy across the table from me, before I turned to Dagger and frowned. "I don't know about all that, but it would be nice to not live alone anymore."

"Bear has a friend that's a realtor, I'll reach out tomorrow," Jason said.

Chapter Nineteen

Maya

"Girl, I don't know what the fuck to do," I sighed into the phone. I had just gotten done telling my older sister the latest news of Hillcrest stalking me and how I was trying to keep everything afloat with my son and our ailing parents. I was feeling hysterical and getting myself worked up. "It's too much. I can't take it anymore."

"It's okay," Jenna said. "It's going to be okay."

I wished I could believe that, I really did. "Dad's bills are piling up and Luke just had a damn growth spurt. He's going to need all new clothes before school starts." I sniffled as tears welled in my eyes.

I'm such a shitty mom. I can't even afford new clothes for my son.

"Hey, you don't need to worry about Dad's bills. Just let them go," Jenna advised.

I shook my head. "They'll stop treating him if we stop paying. You know that, Jenna. You're a damn doctor."

"Yeah, and I also know they can't refuse to care for a patient!" Jenna shot back. She sighed and I heard her take another deep breath. "Look sis, I know you moved there wanting to help mom and dad as much as you can, but Dad's not going to get better from this. He's barely hanging on as it is. You should bring in hospice care and relieve some of the burdens and stress from you and mom."

"But he's not dying...hospice won't come until he's close to the end. Besides being completely bed bound and nonverbal... he's not dying." I was tired of the same argument I'd had countless times with my sister. For being a doctor, Jenna could be completely uncaring sometimes.

"He needs more care than either of you can provide. He should be in a facility," Jenna said.

"Which we can't afford and insurance won't cover." I rolled my eyes. "Look Jen, I can't do this right now."

"I'm sorry Maya. I wish I could help more."

"Don't worry about it, sister. I'll take care of it." I didn't know how, but as usual, I'd figure it out.

"You should really talk to the police or your guys about what's happening with Hillcrest. I might not agree with what they do, but they'd be the ones to help."

I shook my head again. She *could not* go to my guys about Dax Hillcrest. It would only cause more problems across the board for all of us—which was the last thing we needed. "Maybe," I conceded, placating my sister.

"Are you still coming up here next weekend?"

"Yep." I didn't know how I'd afford the gas and whatever else we'd need up north, but I would make it happen. I knew Luke was looking forward to seeing his old friends.

"Alright. I'll see you then. I love you," Jenna said. As usual, she just brushed things under the rug, acting like they weren't as big a deal to her as they were to me.

"I love you too," I told my sister before I hung up the phone. I felt more dejected than I had before I'd spoken with Jenna. My sister just didn't get it.

I left my room and headed out into the living room to find my mother sitting in the recliner. It was rare that my mother left my father's side—he often got agitated if he was left alone for too long.

"Was that Jenna?" my mother asked, cutting right to the chase.

"Yeah," I said, taking a seat on the couch across from her.

My mother hummed noncommittedly, not looking away from the TV. "Are you still going up there next weekend?"

"Yes, that's the plan."

"And what of Luke and his father?"

I ran my hands through my messy curls, pulling my hair from the roots. I was so sick of these damn conversations. "Marcos knows we're going up there."

My mother tsked under her breath.

I rolled my eyes. "What?"

"I just think he should be with his father. He's been without him for too long."

I gritted my teeth. "And I'm not keeping him from Marcos. We're going to see Jenna for three days: Friday through Sunday." I spelled it out for my mother, trying to reign in my temper.

Again, my mother hummed.

"I gotta go, Mom. I'll be back later." I stood from the couch, not caring that it was almost eight o'clock at night. I couldn't stay in the house a moment longer.

I went back to my bedroom, threw on some jeans and put a bra on under my T-shirt, then grabbed my keys. I didn't know where I was going, but I couldn't stay home a moment longer. Thankfully Luke was out with Marcos, doing who knew what, but I was glad for the alone time.

I needed a fucking drink and drove down the road to a local hole in the wall place on the boarder of Mourningside and Creekton. It probably wasn't the smartest place to go, considering the location, but it was close to home, and the drinks were cheap.

I walked in the mostly empty bar and looked around, remembering it was a Monday night, and most people didn't go to bars on Monday nights—other than regulars. I took a seat at the bar and quickly ordered a whisky neat from the rough and tumble older man that was bartending that evening. Prison tattoos covered his hands and neck, and a gray scruffy beard covered his jawline. He had a screwed gaze that screamed, *fuck around and find out.*

I had no interest in finding out. *Thank you very much.*

The bartender had just set down my glass of whisky when the door chimed behind me. I didn't even look over my shoulder, just pulled open my phone and opened the Kindle app. I'd nurse my whisky, read some smut, and go home when I felt calmer.

"Well holy shit!" a female voice called out from behind me. "If it ain't Maya Henderson in the flesh."

I looked up from my phone and turned to see over my shoulder. "Jesus fuck," I laughed. "Slade fucking Cooper."

"Hot damn, girl," Slade said and walked right toward me. She had a wide grin on her beautiful face. The woman was utterly gorgeous with long silky black hair that fell to her waist in a smooth sheet and the most piercing green eyes.

I slid off my stool and greeted my old friend with a hug. "You look amazing," I said, as I hugged the woman tightly.

"So do you! It's been too long!" Slade gushed. "What are you doing here?" She asked as she pulled away.

"I moved back, in January," I admitted, instantly feeling bad that I never informed my friend. We had been close at one point. Slade had done all my tattoos over the years, but in the last eight months since I'd been back, I hadn't had time to reach out.

"No shit?" Slade said, eyebrows raised in shock, as she slid onto the barstool next to where I had been sitting.

"Yeah." I sighed, and took a seat. "My parent's got into a bad car accident last fall. I had to move in with them to help out."

"Ah shit. I'm so sorry, girl." Slade's green eyes crinkled in the corners; sympathy evident on her face.

I nodded and sipped my whisky.

"The usual, Slade?" A gruff voice asked.

I looked up to see the bartender standing before us.

"Yes please, Bobby. Thank you." Slade grinned at the bartender before she turned back to me. "Drinking alone on a Monday night, that's gotta sum up how things are going lately, though?"

I chuckled sardonically. "Pretty much." I took a sip of my whisky and shook my head. "What brings you to a bar on a Monday night?"

Slade chuckled and shrugged. "Nothing as depressing as you, probably." She smirked and bumped my shoulder with mine.

I laughed and shook my head.

"Monday's I usually meet my dad here after we close up the shop. We're just down the road. He was finishing up with a client and I finished up early. Figured I come down here, read a book and have a drink before the old man met me."

"Funny, I thought I'd have a drink and read a book, while I cooled off and tried not to feel so damn pathetic."

"Ouch. Let me guess, living at home as an adult, sucks?"

"So fucking much," I groaned. "I've never been close with my parents; you fucking know that. But my mom is just like oblivious to everything, and trying to balance her judgement and Marcos's anger, not to mention fucking Stone's... it's rough."

Slade sighed. "Maybe you should just fucking tell them the truth then." She shot me a pointed look that cut right through me.

"And what will that accomplish? You were there back then; you know what was happening! And he knows I'm back. He's already fucking starting again." I choked on a sob, before I quickly swallowed it and took another sip of my drink, throwing back what was left in the glass.

"Jesus fuck," Slade groaned. "Dude...you gotta tell the guys. Killer and Stone are gonna flip the fuck out, and Dagger man... he's gonna go ballistic."

"I know." I rubbed a hand over my face, thinking how weird it felt to hear Slade use Marcos's road-name, before I held up my empty glass for the bartender. Bobby made quick work of setting down another whisky neat before me, while I contemplated my life choices.

"What's he doing?" Slade asked.

"Leaving flowers on my car, sending them to my work. He confronted me at the mall the other day." I sighed and sipped my drink.

"Dude." Slade turned abruptly to face me. She wrapped her hand around my shoulder and squeezed it until I turned to look at her. "You're in over your head. Please, please, talk to Marcos about this. Talk to your guys, explain it to them. Hillcrest is not to be fucked with. You haven't been here in the last ten years; the man's grown more unhinged since you've left. He is dangerous."

I frowned as I took in the utter fear that came over Slade's beautiful face. It wasn't like my friend to be scared of anything or anyone. She tattooed outlaw bikers on the regular, her shop was set up between the two territories and when the Ravager Knights and Devil's Psychos had beef last year, she had taken sides and told the Psychos she wouldn't be tatting anyone while they were at war with the Knights. It had been a bold move, but Slade didn't give a damn.

To see her so pale and on edge, it sent a shiver down my spine.

I didn't get a chance to respond, though. The door chimed, singling someone entering the bar, and both of us looked over to see a tall man with a small potbelly walk in. He was bald with piercing green eyes that matched Slade's. "Yeah girl," I said absently as I watched Art Cooper walk over. "Hey, Mr. Cooper." I smiled up at the man.

"Well, hey-hey!" Art grinned broadly. "Maya Henderson! How you doing, girlie?"

"Doing great!" I put on a bright smile, though I didn't feel it in my soul. "I was just heading out though! I'll have to come by the shop soon."

"Yeah you do that girlie!" Art smiled.

I threw down some cash to cover my drinks and a tip for Bobby. I wrapped my arm around Slade's shoulders in a sideways hug and pressed a kiss to her cheek. "Always good to see you. I love you. I'll see you soon." I walked away before Slade could reply, throwing open the bar door and heading out into the night.

Chapter Twenty

Marcos

IT WAS GOING ON eleven p.m. when I finally pulled my truck into Maya's driveway. Luke had dozed off in the backseat, his head propped against the window. I never meant to keep him out so late, but after the movie, we got ice cream and we sat talking in the truck while we ate it.

Thankfully Maya hadn't started texting me, asking where we were—not that she did that ever. No, Maya left me alone when I was with Luke. Shit, she left me alone, period. She only ever reached out to me when it was regarding Lucas.

And I never reached out unless it was regarding Luke either. I sighed softly as I shut off the truck. I'd have to carry Luke in the house and put him to bed. Maya was probably already in bed as it was late on a Monday night and she had work in the morning.

Thankfully the living room lights were still on, so I might have a chance that the house was still unlocked. Otherwise I'd have to wake Luke to get the key out of his pocket.

It took me a couple minutes to get Luke into my arms and out of the truck. I carried him up the driveway and to the front door. I could see through the picture window that Maya was sleeping on the couch. I managed to get the unlocked front door open without waking either Luke or Maya.

I spent the next ten minutes pulling off Luke's shoes and pants, and tucking him into bed. I picked up Luke's bedroom a bit and when I was sure my son was sound asleep, I shut off the light and closed the door.

In the living room, Maya hadn't moved from her spot on the couch. She was practically naked, dressed in the smallest booty shorts I'd ever seen, skintight and barely there. She had on a tiny crop top as well, that was loose on her curvy frame, exposing the bottom half of both creamy tits.

"Fuck," I groaned as let my eyes roam over her curvy body. Her light brown hair up in a messy bun, the white crop top doing little to hide the piercings on her nipples through the shirt, along with her belly button piercing, making me wonder if she had any other piercings on her body. She definitely didn't have them back when we had been together.

I ran my hand over her bare thigh, marveling at the smooth tanned skin. It had been so long since I touched her, so long since I felt the heat of her body against mine. I slid my calloused hand over her thigh, around her hip, and under her ass. I gripped her plump ass cheek and roughly squeezed.

She let out a soft sigh and shifted on the couch.

I froze. *What the fuck are you doing, dumbass?* I couldn't be caught feeling her up. I shouldn't be doing this at all. We might have been into somnophilia when we were dating, but we were no longer dating and I was being a perv.

I slid my hand down the back of her thighs and under her knees while sliding my other hand under her upper back. I slowly pulled her into my arms and lifted her from the couch. I would be good and put her in bed and leave—that's it.

I lifted her from the couch and stifled a groan as she snuggled into my neck—just like she used to. I carried her down the hall to her bedroom and pushed open the door. I was surprised to see her room still looked like it belonged to a teenager, down to the old rock band posters that were still hanging on the walls.

I never realized how little she had lived here after college. I knew when she moved in with me and guys back then, that it had been quickly after graduation. She hadn't been in a good place with her parents, but I would have thought over the last decade apart, they would have talked things out. Seeing her mom last week only cemented the fact that I really didn't know Maya anymore.

I gently laid her down on her bed, before I pulled the sheets and blankets out from under her. Once she was tucked in securely, I sighed and stepped back, watching her intently. My cock was hard as a rock in my jeans and I briefly had a thought of jacking off right there, but refrained, and thank God for that because there was shuffling in the hall before Luke peaked his head in the bedroom.

"What are you doing?" Luke asked, his voice thick with sleep.

I jumped, clutching my heart. "She was asleep on the couch. I carried her to bed, just like I carried you to bed."

Luke nodded, frowning slightly. "She doesn't usually fall asleep on the couch."

"She was probably waiting up for us. We got home late." I kept my voice low, trying not to wake Maya. I walked toward Luke and nudged him out of the way. "Come on, back to bed with you," I murmured.

I spent another ten minutes settling Luke back into bed after the kid brushed his teeth and put on PJs. I was exhausted by the time I finally closed and locked the front door behind me and headed back to my truck. It was times like this, where I desperately wished we all still lived together, so I wouldn't be going home alone to a cold and empty apartment.

Chapter Twenty-One

Maya

I STRETCHED IN BED as my alarm blared obnoxiously on my phone from the nightstand. I reached out blindly, grabbing the cell and snoozing the alarm. I needed a few more minutes. It wasn't like me to go out on a Monday night, let alone drink.

I remembered passing out on the couch while waiting for Luke, then nothing else. "Luke!" I called out in a panic, remembering.

Luke stumbled into my room. "What, mom?"

"What time did you get home?"

"Late. Dad tucked me in. He carried you to bed and was tucking you in when I woke up. I brushed my teeth and he tucked me back in." Luke climbed under the covers next to me and curled up.

I smiled and pulled him into my arms, cuddling my baby. "He carried me to bed?"

164

"Yep."

I didn't know what to think of it. Marcos was acting different since Jason's assault. I hadn't seen Jason either in the weeks since that fateful dinner. It was all confusing and made my head hurt to think about.

I tried not to think about them. I tried not to think about a lot these days: Marcos and the guys, Dax and his threats, and the money I would need to come up with for my father's continued treatment. It was all too much and I was beginning to feel like I was sinking.

I just needed to get through the rest of this week, then come Friday I would be headed north to Chicago for a weekend with my sister. I needed that very much right now.

"Start getting ready for camp, alright? Today's the first day of football, so make sure your bag is ready to go: water bottle, snack, all of that." I hugged him tighter to me, before I let him go and climbed out of bed.

"Yeah, mom."

My head swam as I stood up, alluding the hangover I was clearly sporting.

It was going to be a long day.

I was exhausted by the time I pulled into the parking lot later that day. I'd gone home after work and changed my clothes. I helped my mother cook dinner and ate a small salad before I left to go pick up Luke from practice at six. I would wait to eat dinner with him.

The football field that the Panthers organization used was owned by Mourningside Park District. It was located about ten minutes from the house in one of those outdoor multi-sport complexes with multiple baseball, soccer, and football fields. There was also a skate park, playground, tennis courts, and badminton courts on site. It made finding the right field to be at confusing.

I had given Marcos a detailed site plan of the park that I'd found online, and labeled the football field by number, I even highlighted the closest parking to the fields—anything to make it easier for him to drop off Luke to practice on time.

By the time I parked in the lot closest to the field Luke was currently playing on, I had five minutes to spare. I got out of the car and walked over the field, searching for not only Luke, but also to see if Marcos was still there.

Dread curled in my stomached when I found Stone leaning against the side of the bleachers, one booted foot crossed over the other. His arms were crossed as he took in the kids practicing, the gray T-shirt he wore under his black leather cut stretched across his muscular biceps. A black baseball cap adorned his head, and mirrored aviators covered his eyes from the blazing summer sun.

He looked fucking hot as hell, and butterflies fluttered in my belly as I slowly walked toward the field.

Exhausted and nursing a hangover still, the last thing I wanted was to deal with Jason and his bullshit. I looked around, frowning when I didn't find Marcos anywhere. Ignoring Jason, I walked right on past him without sparing him a glance, on my way to the front of the bleachers.

"Maya." Stone's low voice sent a shiver down my spine as it always did.

I didn't stop, though. I scanned the bleachers of the all the waiting parents and found a large empty space halfway up. I took a seat looking out at the field, as the boys ran around.

Heavy footsteps sounded from behind me, as someone walked down the bleachers from the top. My bench sagged as someone took a seat next to me. I looked up, just as Dagger's heavy, ring covered hand landed on my thigh.

I arched an eyebrow at him, ignoring his hand, and waited.

He leaned over and pressed a kiss to my cheek. "Hi, Little Dreamer. It's been a while."

I rolled my eyes and turned back to the field, brushing him off. I didn't know what kind of games him and Stone had planned, or what he had roped Nico into, but I wasn't interested.

Thankfully the coach seemed to be wrapping things up on field. All the boys were huddled up around him, each down on a knee, listening.

"I get you not talking to him, but why me?" Nico asked.

I sighed and shrugged a shoulder. "I'm tired, Nic. What are you doing here?"

"We came to see Luke practice. Marcos was having dinner with Kara tonight, so we offered to stay and watch his first practice."

I frowned. "You don't have to, though. Coach said parents can drop off and pick up."

Nico squeezed my thigh. "We wanted to. We don't get much time with him."

Guilt tore through me at his words. It was always fucking guilt when I thought about leaving them ten years ago, about keeping Luke a secret from them. I had once thought they'd be my *happily ever after*. Funny how life turned out sometimes.

The coach ended practice right then and all the boys on the field turned for their bags lined up near the bench. I stood up and walked away, letting Nico's hand slide from my thigh. I walked down the bleachers and toward Luke, who was talking to the coach a minute longer than the other kids had.

I walked closer, hanging back a few feet to give Luke some space. The coach, a bald-headed man with a beard and a start of a pot belly glanced at me and smiled. "You must be mom." He held out his hand and I smiled and stepped closer, shaking his hand.

"Yes, I'm Maya."

"Coach Tim Boone. Nice to meet you." We briefly shook hands. "I was just telling Luke here, for never playing before he's got talent!"

I beamed. "He gets that from his father." I ran a hand over Luke's sweaty hair.

"That's great! It was Dad who dropped off?"

"Yeah. Do parents need to stay during practice? We work opposite schedules most days," I said, covering for our situation.

"Oh no, not at all," Coach Boone said with a smile. "Most parents drop off and come back. First practice we tend to see them stick around, but once the weather turns, they'll be in their cars."

I laughed, feeling relieved.

"Good work today, Luke." Coach Boone patted Luke on the shoulder before he turned to another parent.

"How do you feel?" I asked Luke with a smile.

Luke groaned and started walking toward his bag. "I'm OK, I think."

I laughed and followed after him. It only took him a minute to strip off his shoulder pads and practice jersey. Chucking everything into his bag along with his helmet and water bottle, Luke was ready to go a moment later.

"Can we get burgers? I'm starving," Luke commented as we started walking toward the parking lot.

"Not tonight babe. Grandma made food at home."

"What'd she ma—"

"Hey guys, good practice, Luke!" Nico smiled broadly as he walked over. Jason trailed several feet behind him.

"Thanks! Thanks for coming!" Luke beamed.

"We wouldn't miss it, dude," Jason said, moving closer. He held out a hand for a high-five. Luke jumped and slapped his hand against Jason's.

I sighed internally. Even after what Jason did to me, I still enjoyed seeing Luke close with him, was still happy they had formed a bond in the last eight months.

"Dad said he had to work today?"

"Yeah, a job came up." Nic nodded. I eyed him, because that's not what he told me, but I didn't mention it, because they didn't owe me anything. For all I knew, Marcos had plans with his sister, then got called away.

"Can we get burgers?" Luke asked again.

"No, Luke. I told you already. Grandma made dinner." I shook my head.

Luke groaned.

I narrowed my eyes at him, giving him one of those 'mom looks' that was meant to put the fear of God into him.

He met my gaze and quickly looked down.

"Say *good-bye*."

"Bye guys. You coming to dinner Sunday?" Luke asked.

I froze slightly, realizing how Luke had just played me. *Fuck my life.*

"Uh, if it's okay with your mom?" Nico asked, tactful as ever.

I forced a smile on my face. "I did say Sunday family dinners. It's fine. We're coming back from Chicago that day. So we'll probably just do take out."

"Mom, we should bring home Gino's East from the city!" Luke exclaimed.

"It'd be cold by the time we got it here," I sighed, trying to keep him off that. I really didn't have the cash to buy dinner for everyone. I was barely going to be able to afford the gas to get there and back.

"It's okay, Luke. We'll pick up something and bring it. That way it'll be hot when you get home and your mom doesn't have to worry about it after a long drive." Nico smiled and my heart warmed as the relief of not having to pay for another a meal, after what was sure to be an expensive weekend.

While the guys were saying their good-byes, I climbed into the front seat of my car. I was just closing the door when someone stopped it. Looking up, I found Jason standing there with his large hand on the top of door, pulling it back toward him. "Can we talk?" His voice was low, as not to draw attention to us, but I knew Nico was probably helping by distracting Luke, so Jason could confront me.

Fear spiked in my gut. "No."

"Well then you can listen, while I speak," Jason said.

Anger twisted through me. "No," I said again. I turned toward the door, reaching out for the handle without looking up at him.

He stepped between the door and car before I could grab the handle, cause my hand to graze over his dick. Recoiling back, I snapped at him. "What the fuck, Jason?"

Crouching down, Jason got in my face. Fire blazed in his eyes as he braced one hand on the steering wheel and the other on the back of my seat. His slate gray eyes were a storm of emotions as he glared at me.

Feeling caged in, I leaned back as far as I could with the center console behind me, digging into my back. He had successfully cornered me and there was nothing I could do without making a scene—and I did not want to draw Luke's attention to them.

"Can I just fucking apologize, already?" His voice was low and deep, that sensual fucking tone that always drove me fucking wild.

I was too incensed to listen to him. "No. You can't." *Period*, I thought in my head, reminding myself to keep him away and to keep him upset with me. It was safer that way.

"Well, I'm going to."

I rolled my eyes and looked away, turning my body toward the steering wheel, as to not have to look at him further.

He grabbed my jaw and forcefully turned my face to his. Stifling a gasp at the raw pain storming in his gray eyes, I gritted my teeth and waited.

"Look, I'm sorry I hurt you. I'm sorry I let my anger and rage get the better of me." The low melodic tone of his voice sent shivers down my spine. With just two sentences, I could feel my resolve cracking. *His god damned voice!*

Words escaped me, keeping my teeth clenched shut, I didn't respond.

He watched me carefully, his gaze roaming slowly over my face, taking in every detail as he absently stroked my cheek with his thumb. "I never should have put my hands on you."

I swallowed thickly, blinking back tears. God, I wanted nothing more than to lean into his touch and have him wrap his arms around me. But I couldn't. I wouldn't put herself, or Luke in danger like that. I didn't know who was watching and it seemed like Dax was watching at all times now.

Steeling my resolve, I blinked away tears and took a breath before I responded emotionlessly. "Ok. You apologized. Let me go."

Jason blinked, his mouth slowly opening. He looked almost dumbfounded by my response and it fucking *killed* me.

I had to stay strong, though. I HAD to keep them at arm's length. My family depended on me.

He slowly dropped his hand from my face, his eyes searching mine as I glared at him. *Walk away Jason.* "Why did you leave, Maya?"

"I already told you—"

"I want the truth," he demanded. His brow furrowed as stared contemplatively at me.

"I don't owe you anything. I'm still wearing the bruises you gave me from the last time we had this conversation. Leave me alone. *Please*." I emphasized the word almost imploringly.

Jason ground his molars, a vein in his temple popping. His stone-cold stare cut right through me. I couldn't give in; I stared right back. His eyes roamed over my face, as if trying to see through my lie, or look for any hint that something else must be truth.

I had to stay strong. I couldn't let them in.

"Mom!" Luke called out. "You ready? I'm starving!"

"Yeah, honey. I'm ready," I called back to Luke, my eyes still on Jason.

The vein in his jaw popped again as he ground his molars. Ignoring him, I put my key into the ignition and cranked on the car. "This isn't over," he ground out, before walking away.

I took a deep breath, then turned to close my door again. Luke climbed into the back seat and was buckling up as Nico squeezed into the doorway before I could close the door. "Jesus," I gasped.

"Nah, not Jesus. Still Nico." Nico laughed at his own joke.

I rolled my eyes, despite the small smile pulling at my lips. I've never been able to stay angry with Nico for long. Our relationship had always been different than with Marcos or Jason—lighter, more carefree. I had missed him more than anything in the last couple days.

"Have a good night, beautiful," Nico said, and then pressed a kiss to my cheek before I could stop him.

He stepped away and closed my car door before I could say anything.

I sat there slightly dazed for moment, before Luke spoke up in the backseat. "Ready mom?"

"Yeah, honey," I said, jerking myself out of my thoughts and put the car in drive. I glanced around to make sure no one was around me before I pulled out of the parking spot, thoroughly ignoring the two bikers that were about twenty feet away, watching me intently.

Chapter Twenty-Two

Maya

"Girl, you look so much better today, than you did when you got here Friday night," Jenna exclaimed Sunday morning as we sat down to breakfast in Jenna's dining room, while Jenna's husband Brad entertained the kids in the eat in kitchen.

I let out a self-depreciating laugh, "Oh you mean, when I was exhausted and stressed to holy hell after a week of too much shit happening? Then rolled in here at eight p.m.? Of course, I look better than I did then."

Jenna shook her head, a sad smile gracing her lips. "Not what I meant, and you know it."

The week dragged on for me, by the time I was loading up the car Friday evening after work, I was exhausted and more than ready to hit the road. Between work, seeing Marcos and the guys at football—all three of them had shown up for Wednesday and Thursday's practice. Then add in the fucking flowers that Dax Hillcrest had left me everywhere I fucking went, plus the stress of taking care of my sick father, it had been a godsend to get some time to unwind with my sister.

The stress that had melted off of me as she drove down Lake Shore Drive through downtown, following the lakefront as I headed to my sister's home in Lakeview. Even though I had shown up looking haggard Friday night, I had still felt the weight of the world lift away the moment my sister wrapped her arms around me. It had taken everything in me not to break down and cry.

"I've been under a lot of stress," I sighed. "The guys are always around now. They stay through Luke's football practice. I get there and they're hanging around. He's loving every moment of it, of course. And I can't fucking blame him, but it's so hard."

"Don't you think it's time that you told those guys the real reason you left? You didn't have a fucking choice, that dirt bag practically chased you out of town." Jenna practically growled the words.

I swallowed thickly, dropping my head and staring into the cup of coffee I cradled in my hands. "I don't know." I sighed heavily. "In the days before I left them, Dax had shot both Marcos and Jason, had his girlfriend infiltrate their clubhouse, and had Nico framed for something he didn't do. The man is utterly dangerous and holds sway with the police. He's already threatened Luke and our parents. Do you really think it's smart to tell Marcos, Jason, or Nico? They would fly off the deep-end and start a fucking war with Las Serpientes, and then we'd really be in danger." I sighed again, setting down my mug and running my fingers through my messy hair.

"I think you're not being fair," Jenna said slowly.

My eyes shot to my sisters, not believing what I was hearing.

"Hear me out," she hedged, raising her hands up in surrender, "just a minute."

I kept my mouth shut and waited.

"What if you still don't tell them, and Dax doesn't care that you've been keeping your distance and he STILL decides to lash out? What then? Now your boys have no idea what happened to you, or Luke, and they're left in the dark forever."

"But he—"

"OR!" Jenna spoke over me. "Or, you confess to your men. Come clean about why you left back then, how utterly fucking terrified you were, and tell them how it's all starting again. Tell them Dax Hillcrest has been harassing you for fucking YEARS—because I know he's sent people out here to check up on you—don't fucking deny it."

Tears welled in my eyes as my sister called me out. Dax had been checking up on me for years. Once a year, I had received a flower in my mailbox, like a fucking reminder that he was still out there, and could get to me anywhere I went.

"What if the club could help? What if starting a war with Las Serpientes is exactly what needs to happen?" Jenna pressed on. "Aren't you tired of living your life in fear?"

A broken sob choked out of me, as I tried to stifle it. I *was* tired of living in fear, so fucking tired. Every day I it got harder to get up and go to work, harder to make it through the day. I was constantly looking over my shoulder, expecting to see him creeping in around a corner. Then the added stress of being around my men every night this week and unable to touch them, knowing that if I broke down and sank into their arms, I'd feel better for a moment, only to fear that Dax had seen me and would try to kill someone I loved.

"Oh honey," Jenna cooed, and immediately wrapped her arms around me.

I fell apart in my sister's arms, letting out all of the stress and pressure I had been carrying around for months. "They hate me." I choked the words out between gasping breaths.

"Maybe they do," Jenna said, not one to sugarcoat things, "but you haven't given them a reason to trust you either."

I knew that of course; I'd purposely been pushing them away. I've needed to push them away.

"You need to think about telling them the truth. At this point, it's the only way. You're only going to make yourself sick with worry, when they could be protecting you and Luke. You owe it to your son to make sure he's taken care of."

I swallowed thickly and nodded minutely. There wasn't anything I could say. I *was* making myself sick with worry.

Maya

The drive home from Chicago was quiet. Luke played on his tablet with headphones in while I set my music low and zoned out while driving. I pulled into my parents' driveway right at five p.m. Marcos's black truck was already parked on the street in front of the house, three doors opened immediately as I pulled in.

Luke jumped out of the Civic as soon as the car was in park. He tossed his tablet and headphones to the seat next to him, and greeted his dad loudly, running toward the truck.

I sighed and took my time undoing my seat belt. I was sure I looked like crap, my hair a mess and my eyes were likely bloodshot. I had spent the drive lost in thought with tears swimming in my vision every now and then. Between the chat with my sister that morning and my appointment with my therapist the morning before, my nerves were fried.

I really didn't want to sit through a family dinner with my ex-boyfriends when my walls were crumbled around me. I was too raw, too fucking emotional. I ignored the rowdy boys at the end of the driveway and popped the trunk on the Civic.

Climbing out of the car, I steeled my spine, but kept my head down. I really didn't want to draw attention to myself, at least not until I managed to grab a shower and clean up. "Mom!" Luke called out as we walked up the driveway.

Forcing a smile on my face, I glanced over my shoulder at the four guys walking my way. "Yeah, babe," I called back.

"Dad brought pizzas!" Luke's enthusiasm always warmed my heart.

"That's great!" I said, grabbing my duffle bag out of the trunk and slinging it over my shoulder. "Why don't you help me unload the car really quick, then you can find plates and silverware for your dad. I'm gonna take a quick shower."

"Sure mom!"

I breathed a sigh of relief as I grabbed my pillow and headed for the front door. It wasn't until I was behind my closed bedroom door, did I finally let my shoulders fall. This was going to be an epic nightmare. I was going to have to get my walls up and cemented quick, or I was going to have a break-down during dinner.

Marcos

The guys and I followed Luke and Maya into the house. Maya immediately headed for her bedroom to shower, leaving Luke to help the guys set up pizza and gather plates and silverware. "How was your weekend, bud?" I asked my son.

Luke grinned broadly. "It was great. I hung out with my cousins and got to see all my old friends. Mom invited them to come down here to visit down here for my birthday."

I paused, "And when's your birthday again?"

"November 11th. It's on a Saturday this year. Mom was going to talk to you about plans, but she was thinking my friends might be able to come down too." Luke's excitement warmed my heart, even if I was annoyed to not have been included in the initial planning stages. It would be my first birthday with his son. Was it asking too much to want to spend the day alone with my kid, without a bunch of strangers hanging around?

I plastered a smile on my face for my son's sake, though. "Yeah, I'll talk to your mom and we'll figure it out."

"Thanks dad! I really want you to meet all my friends! And my Chicago friends to meet my friends here!"

Sensing my mood, Nico spoke up. "What else did you guys do when you were in Chicago? Did your mom go meet any old friends?"

"No," Luke shook his head. "She hung around Aunt Jenna most of the time, but she did go see her therapist on Saturday morning."

"Therapist?" Nico asked, raising an eyebrow.

"Yeah, Mom's been seeing one for a while now. She says she gets sad sometimes or overwhelmed and that it helps to talk to someone."

I narrowed my eyes, wondering what that was all about. I shared a look with Jason while Nico kept the conversation going with Luke. "Yeah, that sounds helpful. Does your mom get sad a lot?"

Luke's shoulders dropped and he looked away from Nico to stare out the window. "Yeah," he nodded slowly. "She gets really scared sometimes. Usually after she finds flowers on her car. I think someone leaves them for her. She gets really freaked out and then I usually hear her crying her room later. She doesn't want me to know she's upset, but then she's sad for days after."

My whole body tensed. "When was the last time this happened?" I tried to keep my voice even and not spook my son, but my blood pressure was rising quickly.

"I dunno, a couple weeks ago maybe? The day we picked up my football equipment, there was a bouquet of yellow flowers on the car when we got back to it. Mom seemed really scared. She doesn't seem happy that we moved here..." Luke's voice trailed off. He dropped his gaze to his hands and sighed. "I think she was happier in Chicago."

"Did the flowers ever happen in Chicago?" Nico asked, setting a hand on Luke's shoulder.

"No, I don't think so. Not that I know of anyways. Like I said, Mom seemed happier there."

I swallowed thickly, my warning bells ringing in my head—something wasn't right with this picture. I shared a look with Nico then turned to Jason.

Jason was staring at Luke with narrowed eyes, his head tilted slightly, like he was trying figure out a puzzle.

"It's possible your mom was happier in Chicago," Nico hedged. "There's a lot going on here. Your grandparents' accident was hard on your mom, and she's still dealing with that."

"Grandma isn't very nice to her either." Luke spoke softly glancing around to make sure that Elaine wasn't around. "And I know mom worries about money. I was honestly surprised she was able to pay for my football. I know it was really expensive."

I had to grind my molars not to react to that. Maya hadn't said a word to me about money trouble. She hadn't said a word to me about a lot it seemed.

"What's child support?" Luke asked, turning to look at me.

I had to take a moment to gather my thoughts, but Nico beat him to it. "It's when one parent pays money to help the other parent take care of their child."

"Oh." Luke doesn't look at me, but I can see the wheels turning in his head.

"Usually, child support is set up through the courts, meaning a judge tells which parent is allowed to raise the child and the other pays to support that. Your mom and I never set that up, because she's done such an amazing job raising you."

"And you didn't know about me," Luke deadpanned.

I nodded immediately. "And I didn't know about you. I also didn't know your mom was struggling. But that won't happen anymore, ok? You don't worry about it; those are grown up problems. I'll talk to your mom and we'll figure it out."

Luke nodded solemnly.

"What else did you guys do this weekend? Anything fun?" Jason asked, changing the subject.

"Aunt Jenna took us to play laser tag while mom was at therapy! It was awesome! I totally killed my cousin Chase."

Nico, Jason, and I all laughed at his enthusiasm. I faintly heard the click of a door opening down the hall, signaling that Maya was done with her shower. "Come on, let's get food."

Chapter Twenty-Three

Nico

I SAT DOWN HEAVILY in the chair at Skin of a Different Breed. Slade's booth with covered in artwork, all done by her, showing off her magnificent skill. "Hey Nic," Slade greeted as she walked out of the backroom.

"Hey Slade," I replied, but didn't glance at her, as a multi-colored massive flower piece was in the middle of display, a piece I was very familiar with. "This Maya?" I asked.

Slade slid across the floor on a rolling stool and looked where I was pointing. "Yep," she answered.

My eyes were drawn to the right, where there was another picture—this one was of Maya's back—I could still see the large floral piece down her side, but this one was showing her back, and the massive angel wings tatted there in extraordinary detail. "Holy shit," I murmured, sticking my face closer to the picture. There were words tatted into the wings: redemption, remorse, resilience, strength, breathe.

"You haven't seen that?" Slade asked, startling my gaze away from the picture.

"No." I shook my head. "When did you do this?"

Slade looked up from the instruments she was unpackaging from their sterile packs and squinted at the picture. "About five years ago, maybe? The date should be in the corner."

I leaned back in and sure enough, written small in the upper right corner was the date. Five years ago. "How long did this take?"

Slade looked over again. "We did that in 3 twelve-hour sessions. Then one final touch up session a year later after everything was healed up."

"She came here for those?"

"Yeah," Slade replied, her voice a little softer this time.

"And these?" I asked, pointing to the pictures the right, showing Maya's thighs and arms, where there were skulls and more flowers wrapped around them. I saw the date said three years ago.

"No, those I did in Chicago at an expo. Maya always came to the convention center when I was in the city."

I hummed under my breath as I took in all the new ink my girl had gotten in the last ten years. And yeah, she was still my girl. No matter how long we'd been apart, no matter what Marcos and Jason said, I would always consider Maya my girl.

"We had dinner with them last night," I said, turning away from the cubical wall of photos to look at Slade.

Slade Cooper was a beautiful dark angel, utterly gorgeous and unbelievably sweet. She had long black hair to her waist, piercing green eyes, and was tatted and pierced *everywhere*. For as sweet as she was, she was no pushover, though. She was used to tatting rough and tumble bikers, made men, and even the Don of the Seratelli Crime Family. She didn't let anyone walk over her or use her for information—including me.

She leveled me with her steady gaze and raised an eyebrow. "Yeah? How was that?"

I sighed. "I dunno. Maya seemed sad, kinda out of it through dinner. She didn't eat much, and kind of just pushed her food around her plate."

Slade sighed and picked up the transfer paper. She motioned to the chair and I followed her direction. I pulled off my cut and shirt, folding them together and leaving them on the spare chair in the corner. "Did something happen?"

I frowned, thinking about the night before. "They came home from Chicago. They spent the weekend with her sister."

Slade's poker face was intact as she applied the transfer paper to the skin on my chest. "You think something happened?"

"I don't know what to think. Maya came home looking kinda sad and out of it, from the weekend away. Luke said she saw her therapist on Saturday. When Marcos asked him about it while

Maya was in the shower, he said that sometimes she got sad or scared."

"That's valid," Slade said, pressing down on the paper on my chest, before she slowly peeled it away. "Everyone has their moments."

"Slade, I know there's more going on here. I know you're still close—"

"Maya is one of my best friends, Nico. I won't tell her secrets." She snapped at me, her eyes narrowing.

I frowned, watching Slade's face carefully. "I know. And you're loyal to a fault, but if something serious is going on with her…"

"That's Maya's business. If she wants to divulge that with you, then she will." Slade picked up her tattoo gun and got to work. It wasn't like her to be so short or abrupt, it also wasn't like her not to ask me about tattoo placement, usually she had me check things out for any adjustments I might want before she got to work.

Clearly, I had struck a nerve.

"I get that it's Maya's business," I said a half hour later, breaking the silence of the steady buzzing coming from the tattoo gun. "I do, Slade. But this is Maya, if there's something seriously going on with her, I would want to know."

Slade paused, pulling the needles back. She sighed heavily. "I can't tell you what's been going on with Maya, but I can tell you this: look deeper. Think about it harder, Nico. Maya is tough as nails and will always shut out the world. Something must have happened that made her seek therapy. For a girl that never opens up and can't talk about her feelings, why would she volunteer her feelings to a stranger?"

My mouth popped open. "You know something."

Slade looked down, refusing to meet my gaze.

"You definitely know something. Slade, what the hell happened?"

She took a deep, shuddering breath, and when she lifted her head, I could see tears lining the eyes of the bad ass tattoo artist. She blinked them away quickly, taking another deep breath. "All I'm saying is, maybe there's more than meets the eye when it comes to Maya. Please, be gentle with her, Nic. She needs you now more than ever."

My heart clenched in my chest. "What do you mean?"

Slade shook her head and pressed the gun to my skin again.

When it was clear that Slade wouldn't tell me anymore, I dropped my head back to the chair and sighed. *What the hell was going on?*

Nico

I was lost in thought later that night while I sat in the living room of Marcos's small apartment, still thinking about my conversation with Slade. *How much did we not know? What really happened that drove Maya away ten years ago?*

"Earth to Nic," Marcos said, snapping his fingers in front of my face.

I blinked out of my thoughts and looked up at my buddy who standing in front of me. "What?"

"Dude, where's your head? We've been talking about the realtor finding us a bunch of places to look at this week," Marcos said, stepping back and sitting down on the couch.

I ran a hand through my hair and sighed. Jason walked over with a plate of food and handed it to me. I nodded in appreciation. "You guys wonder if there was more to Maya leaving?" We've had this conversation before, but I couldn't help but bring it up again.

Jason huffed, but Marcos sighed. "We've talked about this before." Marcos ran a hand over his buzzed head.

I shook my head. "I saw Slade today. Something wasn't sitting right with me after what Luke said last night."

"About what?" Marcos asked slowly.

"About Maya seeing a therapist." I looked at my brother, really looked at Marcos. The man was sitting across the living from me, sprawled out in the only recliner in the small living room that consisted of a couch and one recliner situated before the TV.

Jason and I were sitting at the small two-person dining table, set up behind the couch, in the very small one-bedroom apartment.

Marcos didn't look comfortable with us in his place. He'd been bouncing his leg all evening, antsy, agitated. His leg stopped bouncing long enough for him to digest the words that I spoke, then he picked up his rhythm with abandon, bouncing his leg faster if possible.

"Slade alluded to more going on with Maya. Her entire cubical is decked out in photos of all the ink she's done on Maya's body. She's still one of her best friends, even after all these years. Slade wouldn't say what was going on, she just told me to dig deeper, because it's not like Maya to seek out a total stranger to spill her guts to, when its already so hard for her to let anyone in."

"She say why Maya left back then?" Marcos asked.

I shook my head and picked at the plate of food before me.

"We know why she left," Jason said. "She said she was done with us."

"I don't believe that at all," I said.

"What do you believe?" Marcos asked, cutting off any snark from Jason.

I ran my hand through my long blond hair. "I think something more is going on. Something spooked her back then. That fight with Tish—what was it that Bear said—Hillcrest sent Tish into the clubhouse that night to instigate that fight?"

"Yeah," Marcos murmured the word slowly. His hand rubbed over his scalp, while his eyes stared off into the distance, like he was lost in thought.

"What if she was threatened? What if Tish got in her head? Think about it—" I started.

"Then she would have come to us. She knew we would have protected her," Jason cut him off.

I shook my head. "Just hear me out. What if she was threatened and she was spooked? What else happened that week? You two were both shot, I was arrested—framed by Hillcrest—and Tish started that cat fight. Is it really too far of a stretch to think maybe they got to her, too? Maybe that's why she left, she was scared?"

"And Luke?" Marcos asked.

"Maybe she thought she was saving her child by running? Keeping him away from the dangerous lives that we live," I reasoned.

"That's a bullshit excuse," Jason shot off.

I rolled my eyes; my brother's hard black and white thinking was getting old. Jason refused to give Maya any leeway. "You need to see things from her point of view, *brother*." I stressed the endearment.

"That whole day doesn't add up," Marcos said softly. "She wasn't right after our scene together. Why was there a saline bag on the counter? Do you remember that? She was dehydrated after everything we did."

"I think about that night all the time." I sighed. "I should have used my safe word that night. We took things too far."

Marcos nodded slowly. "I think we did—I did. I took things too far that night."

Jason eyed us both contemplatively, not speaking.

"What if she dropped that day?" I asked.

"Sub-drop?" Jason asked, raising and eyebrow.

"Yeah," I nodded. "We did next to no aftercare, after an extremely intense scene. I told you, Marcos, the next morning. We shouldn't have left her alone. She should have woken with one of us there."

Marcos nodded slowly, his eyes far away as if he was reliving the scene in his head. "We had to be at the clubhouse though. The out-of-town clubs were comin' in."

"Yeah, but you and Stone could have gone. I could have stayed back," I argued for the hundredth time.

"Yeah." Marco huffed, finally agreeing with me after all these years.

"I don't buy it," Jason grumbled.

I snapped my gaze to narrow my eyes on my buddy. "Why not?"

"It doesn't make any sense. Even she had dropped, she would have come to us."

"She did fucking come to us!" I snapped, raising my voice. "She showed up at the fucking clubhouse to find that bitch Tish hanging all over Marc!"

"Some Devil Chaser is not an exc—"

"Stop fucking making her into some one-off devil chaser! She was a God damn plant by the leader of a rival fucking gang! Fucking treat the situation with the seriousness it deserves!"

"I have been!" Jason sniped back. "She fucking left us! You don't think that hasn't torn me up all these fucking years?" He leaned forward slamming his hand on the table. "She was the God damn love of my life and instead of talking to us, she fucking walked out the door!"

I sat back, watching my stone-cold killer of a friend, lose the emotionless shield he held tightly in place and succumb to the feelings that were ragging inside him—finally. "I think we need to find out *why*," I stressed the word.

"It doesn't fucking matter!" Jason shouted, getting to his feet. "It's not going to change damn thing! If she was in trouble, she didn't fucking come to us! She fucking ran! She didn't trust us enough to take care of her." He acted like it was so cut and dry, it was fucking infuriating to me.

"We literally had just spent the night before punishing her! We strung her up and whipped her!" I shouted, getting to my feet to face off with Stone. "We had NEVER done a scene so intense before that night, and we gave her next to ZERO after care afterwards. You saw the fucking saline bag on the counter the next morning! She was fucking dehydrated! We did that! Why the fuck would she come to us? She had no reason to trust us! She was fucking hypothermic the night before and we fucking left her alone! We're fucking *lucky* all she did was run away. What if she was seriously injured? What if she fucking died?"

The silence that rang out in the room was deafening. Besides our labored breathing, none one of us moved. I could see the dawning horror in Jason's eyes as it finally sank in his thick skull after all this time—how seriously we had fucked up that night.

"Nico's right," Marcos spoke up from across the room, his voice soft.

I sat back down and took a deep breath before I looked over at Marc. Marcos was still sitting in the recliner, his eyes slightly out of focus, but they narrowed on Jason who had turned to look at him.

"We could have lost her that night, and it was all my fault," Marcos said.

"It was my punish—"

"It was my idea to take her outside," Marcos cut off Jason. "My idea to string her up in the woods. It was my fucking fault she got hypothermia to begin with. And my fucking fault we left her alone the next morning."

"We need to talk to her." I ran my hand through my hair, needing something to calm me down. I finally felt like I had gotten through to my brothers—made progress—but we still had a long way to go. I knew neither Marcos or Jason would forgive Maya for leaving and not telling them about Luke sooner, I knew this wasn't them declaring their love for our girl again, but it was a breakthrough nonetheless. At least they could finally see Maya's side to the things. Who knew if it would help anything in the long run.

"We've tried talking to her, she won't talk." Marcos sighed. "You try—try to get her alone."

I nodded solemnly. I didn't like that idea. I wanted us to corner her as a group, force her to speak, but I also didn't want her to shut them out completely too. "Yeah," I muttered. "We should all get tested too," I added, rubbing his jaw.

"For fucks sake," Jason muttered.

I glared him. "Don't act like you haven't quit the pussy in the last several weeks."

Jason crossed his arms over his chest defensively, but didn't say anything.

"I'll set it up, this week, we all get tested." I turned to Marcos.

"Yeah," Marcos agreed, rubbing a hand over his buzzed head.

"Fine," Jason grunted.

I nodded, already reaching for my phone to call the local clinic we used.

"We need to talk about the house," Marcos said, changing the subject. "The realtor said our old rental house was for sale if we want it. Kara fucking gave me a lump sum of back pay for her student loans—said she'd skin me alive if I didn't buy the house of my dreams for my son."

I chuckled softly, shaking my head. "I bet you fucking fought her on that."

"She said she would refuse to name me padrino and ask someone else." Marcos chuckled darkly, shaking his head. "I fucking taught her well."

I laughed, feeling lighter for the first time all night. "Fucking, Kara."

"Fucking, Kara," Marcos agreed.

"So we have more than enough to put down on the house. Is that the one we want?" Jason asked.

"Yeah. That's home," Nico agreed.

"Yeah," Marcos nodded.

"I'll have the realtor move things along then," Jason said. "Looks like were buying a house."

"Our house," I added, feeling content.

"Home," Marcos said.

Nico

I GAVE MAYA THE week to calm down after her weekend up north. I stayed away from Luke's football practice Tuesday, Wednesday, and Thursday, despite helping Marcos by dropping him off at practice while Marc delt with the Irish.

By Friday though, I was done waiting. Marcos had Luke this weekend, and Jason and Marcos were going to take him out on Lake White Buffalo in Mourningside to get some water time. They talked about going fishing, camping, and swimming. I was a little jealous of missing out, but I wanted that alone time with Maya.

The plan was to wine and dine her Friday night after work, then get her to spend the night at my place and treat her to a massage at the Spa on Saturday. I would convince her to stay the whole weekend if I could, but knowing she had spent last weekend away from her ailing parents, I knew I was pushing my luck if she agreed to stay at all.

I followed Marcos over to Maya's Friday night. When we walked up to the front door, Luke was playing a video game in the living room and Maya was curled up on the couch reading a book. Her curly golden-brown hair was pulled back from her face in one of those claw clips, and she had already changed out of her scrubs into a pair of leggings and an oversized shirt. She looked fucking delectable.

Marcos knocked on the door, for propriety's sake, before he opened the door and walked in the house. Luke looked over with a grin and a quick, "Hey dad!" before he turned back to his game. He pushed some buttons on his controller but quickly saved the game and signed out of whatever he was playing.

"Hey Little Dreamer," I grinned wickedly when I walked into the living room.

"Nico," Maya smiled, though her eyebrows pulled together, furrowing in confusion. "What are you doing here?"

"I was thinking that me and you could go out to dinner."

"Just the two of us?" Her eyes darted between Marcos and I. "Aren't you going with for the guy's weekend to the lake?"

"Nah, I've got plans tomorrow. I couldn't commit to the whole weekend. Thought me and you could get dinner though." I spoke smoothly, gliding past Marcos to stand in front of Maya.

She swallowed thickly as she stared up at me, slowly sliding her bookmark between the pages. "I uh."

"You should go, mom! Dinner with Nic will be fun!" Luke encouraged her.

I would have to remember to give that kid some money next time I saw him.

Maya looked dumbfounded.

I smirked internally, knowing she wasn't one for surprises. "Go put on a dress. You have ten minutes." I threw down the order, wondering if her submissive side would come out to play, or if her fiery spirit would.

She narrowed her eyes at me, before those beautiful amber eyes of hers slowly slid down my body, taking in my dress pants and green dress shirt. Her lips parted as her eyes widened as her eyes slowly slid back up my body. I'd even washed and brushed out my shoulder length blond hair for her tonight. I smirked and cocked an eyebrow at her, waiting for her to make up her mind.

Maya shot a glance at Marcos and Luke, both of whom were watching her. Luke smiled at his mom, while Marcos remained emotionless, but I knew he was hoping she would take the bait. "And where are we going?" Maya asked, setting her book aside.

"You'll have to come with me to find out," I shot back.

An amused smirk tugged at Maya's lips as her gaze returned to me. "Ok."

Excitement roared within me as I smirked down at her. "Ten minutes," I reminded her.

Maya stood up quickly from the couch and moved over to Luke. "Alright buddy, have a good weekend with your dad. I love you."

"Bye, mom!" Luke wrapped Maya in a huge hug. "I'll see you Sunday!"

Marcos gathered up Luke's bag and pillow and headed for the door, he glanced back at me and gave me a subtle nod, before he walked out of the house with Luke in tow.

Maya zipped off to her bedroom and while she was gone, I headed down the opposite hallway in search of her mother. I found Mrs. Henderson walking toward me though, so I didn't have to search. "Mrs. Henderson," I greeted with a smile.

Mrs. Henderson raised an eyebrow at me. "Nico?"

"How are you? How's Mr. Henderson?" I played things sweetly.

Elaine pursed her lips and headed for the kitchen. "He's doing alright, for what it is," she answered pragmatically. "The nurse that comes in during the day is wonderful."

"Oh, that's nice that you have help." I nodded.

"Yes, well we wouldn't be able to keep my husband home without her, or Maya really. She's the one that helps move him and that's when the nurse isn't here."

I swallowed hard. "So it's the nurse or Maya?" I asked. "How'd you manage while she was in Chicago last weekend?"

Elaine shrugged a shoulder as she headed over to the fridge. "I can manage a little bit here and there. We have Clarice bathe him twice a week and help get him situated. Besides feeding and helping him use the bathroom, there's not much that needs to be done."

"You can help him up and get him to the bathroom?" I questioned, wondering just how strong Mrs. Henderson was.

"No, dear. He's bed bound."

"Ahh." Nico could read between the lines on that one. *Wiping his ass.* "Did you have any plans this weekend?" I asked, trying to politely speed her along.

"No, I'll be staying home with my Harry. Why, dear?" she asked, cutting straight to the chase while she peeked into the mostly bare fridge. She pulled out a glass container, containing left-overs most likely and set it on the counter and closed the fridge, before she turned to me.

I smiled sweetly at the hunched over woman. "I was going to take Maya out to dinner tonight, and was hoping to spend the day with her tomorrow. If she agrees, of course. I just don't want her to feel pressure if you needed her here."

Elaine pursed her lips again, her eyes narrowing on me. "And what exactly are you planning with her?"

"You know dinner tonight, maybe a movie. Tomorrow, I booked her in at the spa downtown. Thought maybe she could spend the day de-stressing."

Elaine didn't seem happy about what I had planned for Maya. Was she going to tell me no? Or would she give Maya flack about it later? I really didn't want Maya to get into it with her mother. They fought enough as it was... or at least they used to ten years ago.

"Nico?" Maya asked, as she walked into the living room.

I left Mrs. Henderson in the kitchen without an answer and headed into the living room, finding Maya walking toward me, looking utterly breathtaking. A short-sleeved black wrap dress hugged her curves and fell to mid-thigh. It was classic and tasteful and stunning. "Gorgeous," I grinned and immediately walked over to her. I reached for her hip and pulled her against me, and pressed a hard kiss to her lips before she could say anything else.

She was breathless when I pulled away from her a moment later.

"Come on, let's go. I already told your mom I was taking you out for dinner."

Maya frowned slightly and glanced at the kitchen, but she didn't comment. She gathered up her purse, phone and keys and followed me to the door. "Bye mom, I'll see you later!" she shouted over her shoulder.

Once outside, I let out a deep breath. Elaine had never liked any of us, and we had mostly kept our distance, but she was even more grouchy—if possible—in the six months since we'd started coming to see Luke. It was a good thing Marcos mostly just picked up Luke to hang out and they didn't have to hang around the house.

"So where are we going?"

I smirked, though she was behind me, and led the way to my sleek sports car. I opened the passenger door for her and turned to face her with an easy smile. "Your chariot awaits, Little Dreamer."

A blush colored her face immediately and I had to bite back a smirk. She was falling right into my hands. Once Maya was safely tucked into my car, I closed the door and walked around the hood. Sliding behind the wheel, I started the vehicle and pulled away from the curb before Maya could say a word. I was moving fast tonight. No time for questions, so she couldn't back out.

Maya

I glanced around the fancy restaurant in disbelief, even though we'd been here a while. On my second glass of wine and feeling *good*, I had a permanent smile on my face as I dug into my food. Everything was tasting magnificent. Nico had been a complete gentleman since he picked me up, and he kept me laughing all throughout dinner.

I was on cloud nine. It was almost enough for me to drop the guard around him and just have fun—well, mostly enough. I had dropped my guard just a bit and I was having a great time, but

I couldn't lose site the big picture here. I wasn't supposed to be overly friendly, but Nico was always so easy to get along with, so easy to talk to.

It was just another thing I had missed dearly in the last ten years.

After the waiter cleared our plates and refilled my wine glass—my third of the night—I smiled coyly at Nico. "Was this your plan?" I asked, leaning an elbow on the table and resting my hand on my chin. I didn't care if it wasn't appropriate—my mother's damn etiquette lessons be damned—I needed to know if this had been his plan all along. "Wine and dine me? Get me drunk?"

"Sure was, Little Dreamer," Nico smirked.

I rolled my eyes at him. "What's next, you suggest we head back to your place?"

Nico's smirk widened. "That was going to be my suggestion. It's like you read my mind."

Taking another sip from of wine to think over my answer, I frowned slightly. If all of this was his plan—and knowing it Nico, it was—then I'd walked right into his hands. Why? Why go through this whole elaborate sham of a date, if he was just going to get me drunk? And I'd only drank so much because I was nervous of being alone with him. He also knew that—knew how I had to keep my guard up around them.

Maybe I should go with him back to his house. I could call him out for his elaborate plan. I shook my head. "I don't think that's a good idea," I hedged.

Nico grinned devilishly. Putting both elbows on the table, clearly having zero qualms about table manners and etiquette, he leaned toward me. "Come on, Little Dreamer, me and you still have plans tonight."

He pulled away and stood up before I could say another word. I pursed my lips and grabbed my wine glass, gulping down another massive *sip* of wine. When Nico turned away, I scrambled to my feet. "Fuck you, Nic."

Laughing, Nico reached back for my hand and wrapped his fingers around my wrist. He pulled me toward the door and I briefly wondered if he was going to pay or not. When he got to the maître d' at the door, I watched him shake his hand and the other man smiled graciously as he closed his hand around a wad of cash.

That sneaky motherfucker, I thought as I was dragged away by Nico.

Nico

I didn't drive Maya home. No, I wasn't going to give her an out, not now. Yeah, I was playing dirty, purposely getting her drunk in the hopes of loosening her tongue so she would finally fucking talk to me, but I didn't care. I wanted answers and I wanted them now.

Pulling into my two-car garage, I parked my car next to my Harley. I shut off the engine and got out, all before Maya could explode. She had been silently stewing the whole drive home. Her fingers had dug into the leather seats when she first noticed I was driving *away* from her mother's house and instead headed across town to my townhouse.

Heading upstairs, I didn't bother to stop on the main floor where the kitchen and living rooms were, instead I headed straight up to the second floor where my bedroom was. Maya was hot on my heels, dying to rip me a new one, I was sure, but she didn't even stop to realize that she had followed me right into my bedroom.

I turned to face her once she was fully in the room and grinned. "Well, go on," I smirked. "Let me have it."

She narrowed her eyes in a glare. "You tricky motherfucker," she started immediately.

My blood rushed to my cock immediately as her passion fired up. *God, she was fucking beautiful.*

"You got me fucking drunk, just so you could lure me back to your place? This the whole reason you couldn't spend the weekend with the guys? Someone had to stay back and seduce me? That your fucking plan, Nicolai?"

I fucking groaned as my full name came out of her mouth, dancing across her lips in a sensual cadence. She's *never* said my full fucking name. I almost wondered if she even knew it. But this? Holy fuck. This was fucking hot.

"Say it again," I breathed, moving toward her.

She glared at me, crossing her arms over her chest. "No."

Standing in front of her, I reached out and grabbed both of her hips and pulled her closer to me. "Little Dreamer," I murmured softly. "Please?" I was not above begging.

Maya sighed and rested her hands on my chest, rubbing them back and forth slightly, almost absentmindedly. "Nicolai."

Squeezing my eyes closed, my hands gripped her hips gently. I opened my eyes slowly and leaned my face closer to hers. "I'm sorry for my part in what happened that night."

Confusion furrows her brow. "What night?"

"The night we punished you, before you chose to leave us. The night we strung you up in the woods."

Like fucking clockwork, I watched as the walls to Maya's soul slam shut. Her eyes narrow on me as her body shuddered in my grasp.

I continued before she could shut me out completely. "We broke your trust and I should have used my own safe-word that night. For that, I'm sorry. I'm sorry that we took things too far and that you felt you couldn't trust us."

Tears begin to well her steely gaze and I knew I was getting through to her. Until she abruptly and forcefully pulled away from me, shoving me backwards. "No," she snapped. "You don't get to fucking apologize for that night. Not ten fucking years later!"

I took a deep breath and squared my shoulders, preparing for the fight I was about to instigate. I needed her caught unaware and off guard. I needed to break through her carefully crafted shields and *let me fucking in*. I needed answers. The truth!

I needed her to break, so I could put her back together, piece by piece.

"Maya. I've thought of that night every single day for the last ten years. We took things too far that night. I almost ended the scene several times because I thought Marcos was taking things too far—being too over the top with your punishment. I regret that more than anything. I should have made your safety a number one priority."

A shuddering sob rocked her body as she stepped away from me. Her hand covered her mouth and she shook her head vehemently. "Fuck you, Nico." Taking a shaking breath, she quickly wiped her face and glared at me. "Fuck you for saying that to me now."

I watched as she walked away from me, pacing my bedroom like a caged lion.

"Stop fucking trying to make me talk!" she finally yelled.

I crossed my arms over my chest and leaned back against the bedroom wall, waiting patiently. "You will. One day." I nodded at her.

Again, her eyes narrowed down to slits as she glared at me. "Like I fucking told Stone!" She spat his road name in disgust. "I fucking left you, because I didn't want you anymore! Stop making this out to be anything more that!" She stalked closer to me, her eyes ablaze. "I don't fucking love you anymore."

I laughed through the pain that engulfed my heart. "You keep telling yourself that, sweetheart."

"You know I had to go see a sex therapist after that night? You know I have issues with being restrained?"

"Hard to know if you weren't. Fucking. Here." It was a cheap shot, but I'd do anything to break through her walls. I needed her to crumble.

Pain flashed across her face for but a moment, before she quickly slammed her walls back into place. "No." Shaking her head she walked away from me again, continuing her pacing across my bedroom.

"You found out you were pregnant and you took our child away from us." I hit harder.

She faltered momentarily and I knew I had her. I would get the truth on if she knew she was pregnant before or *after*. It could change everything. "You're right," she snapped, turning back to me. She walked closer, looked me dead in the eye and *fucking lied*.

"I did know I was pregnant. I found out I was pregnant before I left. That morning, before you guys strung me up in the cold, I found out I was pregnant. Then I cleaned your house and you guys strung me up and punished me for breaking one of your inane *rules*—and I got hypothermia.

"I woke alone and so dehydrated I had to give myself IV fluids. Luckily, I had medical training, huh? Why the fuck would I stay? The three of you lost my respect that night as my Dom's. You really think I would stay? Raise a child in that environment?"

My heart broke all over again. I knew this wasn't her, though. She was lashing out. I would need to push her more. I laughed in her face and leaned down, getting closer. "You gave yourself to us, begged us to be our whore."

I registered the resounding *smack* of her slapping me, before I registered the pain radiating out across my face as my head was pushed to the side.

"Fuck you, Nico."

I laughed again—softly—a low menacing laugh that had her eyes widening in fear. I lashed out and wrapped a hand around the back of her neck and yanked her to me, her body falling against mine. Her hands splayed across my chest as she caught herself. "Don't you dare fucking lie to me, Maya." I slid my fingers through the hair at her nape and twisted it around my fist. "You consented to everything, don't fucking lie and act like those two years weren't everything you fucking wanted."

"Until they weren't," she muttered. "Reevaluate and renegotiate, right Nic?"

Stunned and confused, I abruptly let her go. She only stumbled back a foot or so, but the distance was enough. *Reevaluate and renegotiate.* Those were the words she had written on her note all those years ago—along with her safe-word. I still didn't understand what they meant. "What the fuck does that mean?"

"Ask Marcos."

I shook my head and pushed off the wall, getting into her space again. "I'm fucking asking *you.* You wrote those words in that note. You fucking left us. You fucking ripped out my damn heart that day."

A gasp startled out of her and her eyes widened as she stared up at me looming over her. I hoped that she could read the pain on my face as clearly as I could read the lies on hers. "Nico," she murmured. She raised her hand, as if to touch my chest, but thought better of it and dropped it back to her side.

"Stop fucking LYING!" I shouted.

"I CAN'T FUCKING TELL YOU!" she screamed back.

Fucking finally! Finally, we were getting somewhere, I thought.

"Why? Is someone threatening you? Was it Trish and Hillcrest? The fucking Las Serpientes?" I demanded.

Her eyes widened for a fraction of a second before she shook her head vehemently. "I don't know the fuck you're talking about. I don't know who that is."

I laughed and got in her face again, wrapping my hand around her jaw—I held her face still. "Your lies are getting old, Maya."

She swallowed thickly and licked her lips, her eyes were wide, pupils dilated. "Nico." Her breathy plea sent all the blood in my body straight to my fucking dick.

"Oh my, Little Dreamer," I crooned softly. "How I wish to watch you break all over my dick." Her eyes fluttered closed as she panted softly. "All you have to do is tell me who's threatening you."

Her eyes snapped open and her lips parted. All the fucking confirmation I needed. Now to work the fucking information out of her, only her lips slam on mine before I could press the issue further.

I groaned and wrapped my hands around each side of her face, cradling her head as I deepened the kiss. Her fingers dug into my dress shirt, nails digging into my chest beneath. One of my hands moved to the back of her head to hold her nape, while the other slid down her neck and chest to grope at her ample breasts. "Fuck, Maya." I panted against her lips.

"Nico, I need—"

"I know exactly what you need." I picked her up and tossed her down on my mattress, landing on top of her and claiming her lips again. Our mouths moved together, tongues battling for dominance. Her hands didn't even bother with my shirt, immediately they homed in on my belt and zipper.

Maya made quick work of undoing my pants and sliding them down my hips. I kicked them off and hoisted her dress up around her waist. Breaking the kiss, I looked down at our bodies, at the black lace covering her core. "Fucking beautiful," I muttered, before I tugged them off.

I dove into her pussy a moment later, not giving her time to think. That was my goal tonight, to get her out of her head. I needed answers and I wasn't afraid to play dirty to get them. If she hated me later, so be it.

I lapped at her folds, sucking and nibbling my way to her clit.

Maya arched off the bed, her hands immediately buried themselves in my hair. "Nico!" She moaned loudly.

I sucked on her clit while tugging off my boxers with one hand. Once I was naked, I slid two fingers into her soaking core and curled them forward, finding that spongy spot behind her clit. Pressing my fingers upward and sucking hard, I circled my fingers inside her, forcing her body to submit to my control.

"Ah fuck! Nico!" She screamed as she shattered.

I smirked against her skin and kissed up her body, over the curve of her belly and her ribs, leaving wet kisses trailing all the way. I sucked a nipple into my mouth, swirling my tongue around the bud as I slid my cock through her folds and lined myself up.

"Nico," she whimpered.

I moved swiftly up her body and claimed her mouth in a passionate kiss, my tongue delving deep and silencing her cries as I notched my cock at her entrance and thrusted in hard and fast, all in one move.

She arched against me, crying out into my mouth as her fingers gripped my shoulders. Her nails dug deep into my skin as she both tried to push me away and pull me closer. I ground my pelvic bone against her clit, her pussy clamping down on my cock as the aftershocks of her orgasm still ravaged her body.

"So fucking tiiight." I groaned against her lips. Trailing wet open-mouth kisses down her jaw to her neck, I found that sensitive spot in the crook of her neck and sucked down hard.

"Nico," she gasped.

I snapped my hips forward, cutting off any words she might have spoken. Setting a brutal pace, I fucked her hard and fast. Reaching down, I wrapped hands around her thighs and pulled them around my waist, changing the angle as I tilted her hips up.

"Fuck!" she called out.

With one hand, I grabbed two pillows and shoved them under her hips, keeping them elevated. "So fucking good for me," I praised her.

A whimper was all the sound she could make as I used her body roughly.

I pushed her knees up to her chest and threw her ankles over my shoulders. Her passionate cry only spurred me on as she fought to push me back and put her legs down. I was stronger than her, though. I held her tight and fucked her harder.

"Oh shit, oh shit." She panted and thrashed beneath me, the new angle allowing me to hit her g-spot head on.

I smirked as I could feel the telltale signs of her impending orgasm—the first flutters of her cunt around my dick. "That's it, Little Dreamer," I murmured, my eyes drinking in her beautifully flushed face. Sweat clung to her brow and hair stuck her forehead. Her dark makeup was smudged around her eyes. She was utterly breathtaking. "Come for me."

Maya yelled as her body seized up and her pussy clamped down on me. "Nico!" Her keening wail filled the room.

"That's it, pretty girl." I continued fucking her through her orgasm, laughing as she gushed her arousal around my cock. "So fucking good for me."

"Nico," she cried, tears running down her face.

I smirked down at her, nowhere near done with her. "You're in for a long night," I warned her, before I pulled out. Not giving her time to catch her breath or speak, I dropped her legs from my shoulders, letting them fall to bed. "Up," I commanded, before I pulled her up and forced her over onto her hands and knees.

Slipping the pillows under her hips again, I shoved her upper body down onto the mattress, so her ass was presented in the air, on glorious display for me alone. "Good girl," I murmured, running a hand over the magnificent globes of her ass. I swatted one cheek playfully and groaned as I watched it bounce. "Fucking fantastic."

"Nic," Maya mumbled, trying to turn to her face to look at me.

I slammed back inside her, keeping one hand on her hip and the other on the center of her back, holding her in place. Her moans were loud and breathy as I restarted my relentless pounding. "Such a good girl for me, Maya. This pussy is sucking me in, begging to be owned all over again. Isn't that right my Little Dreamer?"

A sob tore out of her, her body shuddering with every breath.

I didn't stop, didn't console her. She was mine to own and bend and break, and break she would, all over my motherfucking cock. "No one else can own this pussy like I can. No else but me and my brothers."

Maya's sobbing wails are my only answer.

I smirked down at her, enjoying her tears and her cries. "I'm going to wreck this pussy."

"Nico, Nico, Nico." She chanted my name.

"That's right, Little Dreamer. I own you now." Gliding my hand up her sweat soaked back, my fingers threaded through her damp hair. I twisted the locks around my fist and pulled her head up, yanking her body backwards into my chest.

My other hand skated up her body, groping a tit before I wrapped it around her throat and squeezed. Snapping my hips, I held her upright and chuckled darkly into her ear. "There you are, my Little Dreamer. Right where you belong, at my mercy."

Her eyes rolled back and she gasped.

"So good for me."

Maya whimpered.

"You didn't want to leave me—us—back then, did you baby?" I crooned the words as I fucked her hard.

Her eyes snapped open, her mouth dropping as a gasp is startled out of her.

"Answer the question."

"No!" she shouted, her body shaking as her pussy fluttered around me again, as her orgasm pooled inside her.

"That's it, Little Dreamer." I soothed her, my voice soft. Taking my hand from her hair, I slithered it down her body to her clit and rubbed circles around her nub. "Tell me what happened."

"Nico!" She cried my name and I slowed my pace. "Please," she begged.

"Why'd you leave me?" I kissed her neck sensually, nibbling at her flesh.

"I—"

My fingers dropped from her clit and toyed with her opening, slipping over her wet folds before I sunk a finger inside her, alongside my cock.

"Oh fuck!"

"Why'd you leave me?"

"I didn't—I didn't want to. I swear, I didn't want to leave." She panted hard between each word, her breath ragged and harsh.

"Why'd you leave me?" I ground my palm into her clit while slipping in a second finger.

A sob tore out of her, her body shuddering. "I didn't have a choice!"

Finally, we were getting somewhere. "You always have a choice." I curled my fingers toward her g-spot.

Crying. "I didn't. I didn't. I couldn't!" She was sobbing fully at this point and I withdrew my fingers and kissed her neck softly. I carefully pulled out of her and gathered her in my arms. I maneuvered her on the mattress until we were laying down on our sides.

"Shh," I murmured, pulling her against me. I draped her leg over my hip and angled her hips so I could slip back inside her pussy. Only when I was fully seated again, did I wrap my arms around her and pull her against my chest. "Why, Maya?"

She shook her head vehemently, sobs choking her breath. "I can't say—Nic I can't! I can't!"

"Shhh."

"I'm sorry, I'm so, so sorry." She sobbed harder, clutching me tighter.

I snapped my hips against hers, thrusting deeper, reminding her that I was still rock-hard inside her.

She cried out.

I rolled her on to her back and resumed my pace. I captured her lips in a watery kiss, as I swiveled my hips against hers.

"Please, please," she begged.

"That's it, baby. Come for me." I picked up my pace.

"Nico!" she screamed as her cunt clamped down around my cock.

I fucked her through her orgasm all while my own built within me, my balls tightening. I groaned low in my throat as I rocked my hips against hers one more time, before I shuddered as my orgasm rolled through me. "Fuck." I dropped to my elbows, hovering above her, while I caught my breath.

Maya's hands were wrapped around my waist, loosely sliding over my sweaty skin. Her eyes were closed as she lay there quietly catching her breath. She looked utterly beautiful, fully fucked out of her mind, lax and carefree.

"You love me?" I spoke the words softly, but with conviction.

Her eyes flipped open. The emotion I saw in her amber depths made my breath catch in my throat. "Yes. I never stopped loving you. I will always love you." Her voice was raw, scratchy from her sobs.

"I love you too, Maya. I always have and always will."

Tears welled in her eyes again. "I'm so sorry."

"Tell me why, baby. Who's threatening you?"

She immediately started shaking her head. My heart broke watching her become so completely distressed and succumb to her fear. "No, no. Please, Nico. Please, don't ask me. I'm sorry. I can't tell you-I can't, I can't."

"Shh. It's alright baby. Shh. I've got you."

"I can't Nic, I can't. Please."

"It's ok, it's ok. You don't have to tell me. It's alright. I've got you." I slid out of her and laid down next to her. Pulling her into my arms, I whispered reassurance as I held her close. Eventually Maya's sobs tapered off and her breathing evened out as she fell asleep in my arms.

I sighed and ran my hand through my messy blond hair. The two of us were still half-dressed, having only gotten naked from the waist down. I eased out of her arms and off the bed without waking her. Making quick work of shedding my dress shirt, I headed for my attached bathroom and took a quick shower.

My mind was reeling. Worry gnawed at me. Someone was threatening her—that I was sure of—I just wasn't sure who. And she wouldn't tell me; that much was obvious by the way she completely broke down when I pressed the issue.

This changed everything.

I would have to tell Marcos and Jason as soon as they got back from their weekend at the lake, or maybe I would join them tomorrow after I sent Maya on her way to the spa? I was hoping to pick her up after though, when she would be relaxed and languid, maybe she'd be more open to talking then?

I shook my head. I couldn't push her. Not now that I knew she was in danger. Clearly, she thought something bad would happen if she told me, otherwise she would have come to us back then. Someone had something over her, and it was keeping her away from us after all this time.

Anger clawed at me. I had to push it down, control it. Now was not the time to fly off the handle. I needed to gather as much evidence as I could. In the meantime, though, I had a beautiful woman in my bed, that had finally let her guard enough to admit that she still loved me.

I was not about to let that go to waste. Finishing up in the shower, I toweled off and walked back into my bedroom naked.

Maya was still sleeping when I returned.

I pulled on a clean pair of boxers and carefully tugged back the blankets from under her, before I hit the lights and fan on the remote and slid into bed. Tucking the sheets around us, I pulled her back into my arms.

With her head tucked safely beneath my chin, I took a shuddering breath and let myself fall asleep.

Maya

THE NEXT MORNING, I woke up with a raging hang-over. My head pounded in time with my heart and my stomach rolled. I slunk out of bed as carefully as I could, to not wake Nico and rushed to the bathroom before I spilled my guts all over his carpet. I managed to get the bathroom door shut softly and turn on the shower, before I was hovering over the toilet bowl, puking up the remnants of too much wine from the night before.

I wasn't much of a wine drinker. I usually stuck to vodka. Vodka I could handle, wine made me sick.

Thankfully once I got it out of my system, my stomach immediately felt better. I found a brand-new toothbrush still in the packaging on the counter for me and his toothpaste in the medicine cabinet.

After I brushed my teeth, I peeled off last night's dress and stuck my hand into the walk-in shower, testing the water temp. I had to adjust so it wasn't so scalding, but I slipped inside anyways, letting the hot water wash away what remained of my hang over.

My thoughts drifted to last night and a blush coated my cheeks at the thought of everything that transpired. God, he had been relentless in his search for the truth. He had played my body like a damn fiddle and shredded my emotions apart.

I couldn't even be mad about it.

Briefly I wondered if that had been his plan all along, but even if it was, I couldn't blame him. Not when I was keeping secrets from him about literally everything.

He loved me.

I had known that was true the first time I saw all three of them again—Marcos, Nico, and even Jason. They all still loved me, and I still loved them. It's why it was so hard that I couldn't tell them the truth.

And I almost broke down last night and told him the truth.

I would have to pull away again, *push them away again*. It was going to hurt. Fuck, it was going to hurt. But I had to. Luke's life was in danger, my men's lives were in danger; Hillcrest could and would kill any one of them if I opened my mouth.

No, it was safer this way. Everyone was safer this way.

By the time I got out of the shower and toweled off, a new resolve had settled over my shoulders. I could do this. I had to.

Nico

I sensed the change in her mood the moment she walked out of the bathroom. Her dress from the night before was back in place, her hair was wet, but brushed down her back, and her mask was fully in place before she walked into my bedroom. I laid there a moment longer debating on if I should even bother trying to get her back into bed or not. "Morning."

"Hey," she murmured.

"Hungry?" I asked, slowly sitting up and turning to get out of bed.

"I should go."

I clenched my teeth and took a deep breath. I knew she'd react this way, I would just have to play it cool. "Let's get breakfast, Little Dreamer. It'll help your stomach."

"Nico." She sighed. "I really need to go home."

"I spoke to your mom yesterday." I got out of bed and pulled a pair of jeans out of my dresser. "Told her I made you plans at the spa for the day. She seemed cool with it."

Maya narrowed her eyes at me. "Nic—"

"Maya, please." I walked over to her, stopping just short of getting into her space. "Please, let me do this for you. It's already booked, already paid for. Enjoy the day at the spa. Slade's going to meet you there. Have some girl time. Massages, facials, the works, it's all on me."

Her lips parted as disbelief flashed in her eyes.

I smiled easily and gathered her into my arms. "I love you, baby," I admitted easily. "I want you to relax today. Don't worry about anything. I'll take care of it all."

"Nico, I don't know what to say."

"Say yes. Just say yes."

"Yes." Her eyes twinkled as a smile broke across her face. "Thank you."

I grinned. "You can thank me later."

She smiled but shook her head. "Your thanks was last night. I need to go home tonight. I can't leave my mother two weekends in a row to completely care for my father alone."

I didn't let the grin drop from my face as I nodded easily. Pulling her into my arms, I held her against me. "Alright, baby." I nodded. "I hear you."

Maya blushed at the endearment and I vowed to myself to make it happen every single time I saw her going forward. She was so fucking beautiful. "Thank you, Nico."

"Anytime, baby." I leaned in and pressed a kiss to her lips. I was shocked when she met me halfway, pushing herself closer to me. I groaned as her tongue came out to play, deepening the kiss. "Fuck, Maya."

She giggled softly at the same time her stomach rumbled loudly.

"Breakfast it is." I laughed and slowly pulled away. "Let me find a shirt and we can go. There's a family restaurant by the spa."

Maya

I was on cloud nine as I checked into the spa. Nico had walked me in and spoke to the manager, before he kissed me soundly on the lips and walked out of the building. The desk girl greeted me with a warm smile and then walked me through the spa, highlighting key areas and showing me where the indoor pool, hot tub, and sauna were, all of which I'd have access to in between my treatments. "You have an hour to relax and enjoy the common areas before your first treatment. Here's a list of everything you're scheduled for."

"Thank you," I nodded at the woman, taking the paper, as she left me at the locker room.

"Hey girl!"

I looked over in shock, finding Slade Cooper sitting on the locker room bench, not twenty feet from me. "Slade damn! Hi!

I'm so glad you're here. How did this come to be? Like I know Nico set it up, but you agreed?" I laughed.

"Your man invited me. He came up to the shop to talk. Said it was an all-expenses paid day!" Slade grinned, tossing her long black hair over her shoulder. She stood up and walked over to give me a hug.

"That's Nico, always over the top." I shook my head as I stepped back from my friend.

"That's interesting," Slade smirked. She reached up and gripped my chin, tilting my face back to look at my neck. "Would you look at that."

I rolled my eyes and jerked my chin out of Slade's grasp. "Stop. It's nothing."

"A neck full of hickeys and paid day at the spa is not *nothing*." Slade chuckled and stepped back.

"He took me to dinner last night too. Got me drunk."

"To sleep with you?" Slade questioned, her metaphoric hackles immediately raising.

"To get me to spill my secrets." I sighed and sat on the bench in the center of the locker room.

"And did you?" Slade asked, her bright green eyes sparkling.

"No. Not really." I deflated, my shoulders dropping. "I told him I couldn't. He used sex as torture to get me to speak."

"Hot damn." Slade let out a breath. "I want that."

I laughed immediately and shook my head. "It was pretty great...it was like before."

Slade sighed. "Girl, you're being so stupid about this. Those men are still head over heels for you. They would kill for you. Why not just let them take care of the problem?"

"Because they would kill for me." My voice is soft. Looking away from Slade's probing gaze, I sighed heavily as tears welled in my amber gaze. "Last time I thought about telling them, Hillcrest shot both Marcos and Jason, then he framed Nico and had him arrested. He has the power to completely upend my life—Luke's life—and I'm not willing to risk that. It's bad enough I kept Luke away from his father all these years."

Slade let a slow breath, like she was biting her tongue and looking for strength to not snap at me. It was something she had to do a lot around me these days. We've fought over this very damn topic too many times. "So what did you end up telling Nico last night?"

"Just that I couldn't say anything. He read between the lines. Kept asking me who was threatening me. He specifically asked about Tish and Dax. I didn't say anything more than that."

"Jesus, Maya! That was your fucking out! You should have come clean right then and there! He straight up ASKED YOU if it was Hillcrest!"

I hung my head in shame. "I know. I knooooww."

"Maya, I love you, but this scares me. You need to come clean. Soon. Or I might just have to get involved."

I looked over to see the serious set to Slade's face—the hard gazed leveled on me. Swallowing, I nodded slowly. "I hear you."

"Good. Because you know I'm usually Switzerland in these things. But you're putting both you and your son at risk. I can't sit back and watch it."

Maya

After our very serious start to the morning, we moved onto easier topics as we both lounged around the pool area and through our treatments. Some treatments we had next to each other, like manicures and pedicures, and others we had apart like our facials and massages. For lunch, we ate in the attached restaurant, while sitting in fluffy bathrobes.

In the end, it had been one of the most relaxing days of my life in years. I couldn't remember the last time I felt so amazing. When it was time to go, I asked Slade for a ride home, but Slade laughed. "Nah boo, your man has that covered too." Slade pulled out a bag from one of the lockers and handed it to Maya. "I was told to give you this, threaten you into the dress, and then leave you here. Nico will pick you up for dinner in a bit."

My mouth dropped open in shock as I slowly reached for the bag. "He really went all out."

"Sure did. Maybe it's time you actually *talked* to him," Slade hedged again. Thankfully she had let the topic rest since the morning, but now that I was inevitably going to see Nico again, Slade had picked up her pestering again.

"Yeah," I said almost mindlessly as I opened the bag. I huffed out a laugh as I checked out the contents. Inside there were a pair of black leggings and an oversized t-shirt that I was pretty sure was Nico's from back in the day, along with clean under garments and a pair of flipflops.

"Alright girl, today was fun. I hope you have a good time tonight." Slade stood up, now fully dressed and walked toward me.

I hugged her tightly. "Thank you for today. I'm sorry I'm so distracted."

"I'm sorry I'm pushing. I just want you safe. I love you," Slade said softly, hugging me tighter.

"I love you too girl."

By the time I was dressed in the leggings and t-shirt, I was exhausted and starving. Walking out into the lobby I looked around, wondering if Nico was waiting for me or not, because apparently, I couldn't call him as I left my phone behind at his place that morning.

Nico was waiting in the lobby for me though, a pair of blue jeans on with a white t-shirt under his leather Devil's Psychos cut.

There was no missing him. His blond hair fell around shoulders and cocky as fuck smirk was plastered on his face as walked my way. "Hey, Little Dreamer. How was your day?"

I couldn't help myself; I smiled up at him. "It was pretty fantastic. Thank you."

"Anything for you, babe." He kissed my forehead and wrapped an arm around my waist, holding me gently. "Come on, let's get out of here." With his arm wrapped around my waist, he led me out of the spa.

I smiled as we left the air-conditioned building and headed out into the hot and humid late July evening. My leggings were already making me sweat and I wondered where he planned on taking me dressed in basically pajamas. "Nico, where are we going?"

Nico stopped walking in the middle of the parking lot. He turned and stood in front of me. Both of his hands came up to cradle the sides of my face, "Little Dreamer, I'm gonna need you to trust me tonight. Can you do that?" He was so serious. His blue eyes were so intense as he stared down at me.

My heart shuddered in my chest and my breath hitched in my throat. He was a stunning specimen of human male. God damn, he was gorgeous. But the intensity of his stare, and the question he asked after a day of pampering and relaxation, caught me off guard; I was incredibly vulnerable. "I—"

"Maya, please baby. Let me take care of you tonight."

"Nic." I bit my lip as my hands came up to hold both side of his leather cut. I needed something to ground me. I was losing myself in his gaze.

His thumb brushed over my lower lip, pulling it gently from my teeth. "You're so strong all the time. You carry the weight of the world on your shoulders. Let me take care of you tonight. Let me carry your burden."

My lips parted slightly as shock rolled over me. My heart hammered in my chest and butterflies exploded in my belly. This man would be the death of me. I licked my lips, trying to think of what to say, how to answer. I wasn't mentally ready for whatever he was planning. I needed space, needed time to build my walls back up.

I nodded my head anyways. Against my better judgement, I nodded my fucking head and agreed to go to with him. *Let's face it. There's nowhere on this earth where I wouldn't follow this man.*

Nico gave me a soft smile, his cocky smirk nowhere to be found. He leaned down and placed a gentle kiss on my forehead that had me eyes closing as I almost fucking swooned. He was stealing my heart all over again and if I wasn't careful, I would let him.

Maya

Hours later, I found myself back at Nico's townhouse lying on the couch. Tucked into his side, with my head on his shoulder, I zoned out on the movie he had playing. The lights were dim, remnants of our takeout food were strewn about the coffee table, and I was tucked under his arm, squeezed between his body and the back of the couch.

It was bliss.

After the relaxing day I'd had, I was barely holding on and about to doze off any minute. A contentment I hadn't felt in years settled over me. Nico's hand absently slid through my hair and his other hand was laced with my fingers on his chest, his thumb stroking idlily.

It was almost the most perfect night; it was just missing a few more people.

Maya

I woke to darkness. No longer on the couch, I was wrapped up in Nico's bed, his limbs entangled with mine. His soft breaths tickled the back of my neck. I blinked at the clock, noting it was four a.m. Feeling wide awake, anxiety gripped at me, I really didn't want to lay there for hours waiting for an awkward good-bye come morning.

I dreaded having another conversation with questions I couldn't answer, that would lead to yet another fight. Not after we had spent the most relaxing night together. It had been a soothing balm for my tired soul, and I didn't want to ruin that. If anything, I wanted that calm connection between us to last, the reminder of how it used to be between us, before life went to hell.

The weight of my responsibility settled on me, trepidation pooling within. I needed to leave, now. But how? Nico had purposely picked me up Friday night, making me reliant on him for a ride—just as he planned. Rideshares were out of the question, ever since that night ten years ago, I hadn't ever taken another ride share alone—not that I needed to, I rarely drank anymore. My punishment that night had made a lasting impression on me, leaving me with more baggage than I knew what to do with.

Just another reason I saw my therapist.

No, I would have to take his car. He could pick it up whenever he needed it, but for now, the sports car would be my getaway. I just had to sneak out of bed without waking him while he was wrapped around me like a damn octopus.

It took me close to twenty minutes to disengage, slowly sliding his leg and arm off me. Once I was out from under him, I headed downstairs, not bothering to look for the bag with my dress in it.

I'd get it back whenever. I found the keys to his car in the kitchen on the counter, next to a notepad.

Before I could leave, my conscious got the better of me and I left him a quick note.

Thank you so much for the
weekend. It was magical.
♥always
XOXO

I grabbed my own keys and purse from the counter, then I was down the stairs and into the garage a moment later. I wasted little time opening the garage door and starting the very loud engine. As I backed down the driveway, I adjusted the driver's seat forward with the electric button. My heart was racing, I was afraid that the noise from the engine would wake Nico and I really didn't want to still be here when he walked outside.

The drive home from Nico's only took ten minutes and I parked his car on the street in front of my parents' house, as to not draw attention to it. It was going on five in the morning when I let myself quietly into the house. Thankfully the house seemed quiet, so I headed down the hall to my bedroom and closed the door.

I wouldn't be able to get any more sleep, I knew, but at least I wouldn't draw attention to the fact that I was sneaking back in the house after a weekend away. Not that it mattered, I had spoken to my mother on Saturday morning before the spa, making sure everything with my father was good and to see if my mother needed anything.

Elaine, as usual, was fine. A little short and brisk on the phone, but when wasn't she? I still didn't want to draw attention to the fact that I came home at five a.m. and not after breakfast time. It made it look suspicious and I really didn't want to hear my mother's opinion on the matter.

I was tired of everyone's damn opinions.

It was my damn life, my fucking son's life, I could and would decide what was best of the two of us.

Or so I told myself as I sat in bed and brooded over my current state of affairs.

Chapter Twenty-Six

Jason

I LOOKED OVER AT a sleeping Luke and smiled wide. The kid had fallen asleep at the dinner table, his head resting on the table with his fork halfway to his mouth. We had spent the day fishing for salmon on a rental boat out on Lake White Buffalo. The weather had been fantastic, Luke had listened to everything Marcos and I had taught him, and our guide had been right on the fish all day.

We each had caught several keepers and after wrestling with the massive fish we caught, the three of us were exhausted. Marcos hadn't stopped smiling all day though. And every time Luke laughed or yelled with excitement, I laughed and smiled. It made me wish that Nico had been with us.

I had almost missed Maya at one point, too. Almost.

It had felt almost wrong to be enjoying such a beautiful and memorable day without her there. Especially when Luke started asking Marcos to take pictures to send to his mom. Or how Luke mentioned how much Maya loved to eat Salmon, something I hadn't known about her. It was a slap in the face of how much time had passed and how little I knew her anymore.

My heart hurt thinking about her and what could have been.

God, I hoped Nico was finding out the truth from her this weekend. We desperately needed answers, and I hoped Nico could get them through his own gentle ways versus anything Marcos or I would come up.

I could finally admit that there was something more to the story when it came to Maya. Things didn't add up. The Maya we knew back then was very head over heels in love with us and I didn't believe that night was the catalyst for her leaving. It may have played into her emotions, but there was some deeper reasoning behind her taking off the way she did.

If she wasn't being threatened and she felt the scene had gone too far, she would have kicked our asses to high heaven in the days that followed. She wasn't one to not speak her mind, despite having issues opening up. She would very much tell us off if she felt she was wronged.

It's why none of it made any sense. For as much as she had problems opening up about things, she also didn't have that problem with the three of us. She told us how she felt about anything and everything. They often spoke at length about scenes they were interested in, then planned them out, discussing at length—sometimes for hours—about safety or emotional issues that might arise.

Maya was not a meek or silent partner in our relationship. She had been the driving force of our relationship and her submission had been hard earned. Earned, not freely given. Maya had made us work for her submission every damn day and it had been glorious.

The more I thought about the past and how things ended, the less sense it made. Nico's reasoning that Maya being threatened back then was looking more and more plausible. Luke practically confirmed it when he mentioned someone was leaving her flowers that would make her upset.

Jason

"This weekend was so much fun guy! Thank you so much!" Luke grinned brightly from the back seat as Marcos pulled the truck into the driveway at Maya's parent's place.

My instincts kicked up at the sight of an unusual blacked-out dodge charger at the end of the driveway. I frowned, while staring at the vehicle, it was looked oddly familiar—eerily so—and not very street legal. It had to be a gang-banger's car.

Unease settled within me as I glanced at Marcos to see him point subtly to under his seat—where we had both stored our guns. Not wanting Luke to know that we were carrying—because we were always carrying—we had hid our weapons under the seats.

"You're welcome, buddy," Marcos answered Luke. "I had fun too!" His voice was even as he smiled into the rearview mirror.

"Do you think mom could come next time? She'd love that boat!"

My heart clenched with Luke's plea. He just wanted to have a normal childhood with both parents involved on a family vacation. The way things should have been if we had been in his life since the beginning—if Maya hadn't left.

"Yeah maybe," Marcos said distractedly, as he put the truck in park. "Listen, Luke, buddy."

"Yeah, dad?"

"I need you to listen to me carefully, ok?"

"Yeah." Worry edged into Luke's voice.

"There's a stranger in the house and it's not safe for you right now. I need you to stay here and lock the doors. I'll come get you when it's safe to come inside, ok?"

"Is mom safe?"

"I'm not sure, but we're going to check on her."

I kept my eyes on the house, watching intently while Marcos gave Luke instructions. There was no movement from the house. Unease rankled me.

Marcos nodded to me and we both got out of the truck and reached under the seat to pull out our weapons. We closed the truck door behind us and waited for Luke to hit the lock button. Holding our Glocks down by our thighs, we moved quickly toward the house when it was clear that Luke was locked in tight.

I followed Marcos up the driveway and onto the front porch. Glancing in the window, I saw two bodies pressed against the wall by the hallway leading to Maya and Luke's bedroom. It appeared to be a man pressed against a woman.

Marcos paused to take in the scene before he threw open the front door. I followed behind him, taking in the scene in front of me. Dax Hillcrest had Maya pressed against the wall, in what looked to be an intimate encounter.

"What the fuck is this?" Marcos's voice boomed in the small living room.

Maya jerked in Hillcrest's hold, looking over his shoulder to see both Marcos and I standing in the doorway, our Glocks raised and pointed at the two of them. Maya gasped.

Hillcrest murmured something softly into Maya's ear, and I watched as her eyes fluttered closed in response. As he slid his hand from around her throat to cup her face, Dax had the audacity to glance over his shoulder to smirk at Marcos and me before he turned back around and slammed his lips against Maya's and kissed her roughly, like he was claiming her. He lifted her chin and angled her head so he could deepen the kiss.

Maya wrapped her arms around Hillcrest, digging her fingers into his back. She kissed him just as passionately, holding him close as she moaned into the kiss.

"What the fuck is this?" I growled, shifting my weight on my feet, in an attempt to not storm across the room and rip them apart. Anger roiled through me, and I was a hair-trigger away from popping the safety off my Glock and firing my entire clip into Hillcrest's back.

Maya broke off the kiss. "What do you think it looks like Jason?" she asked rolling her eyes. Her fucking attitude pissed me off.

"It looks like you're fucking the enemy," Marcos growled, shifting beside me.

Maya laughed, "Guess, I am. But he's not *my* enemy." She smirked at Marcos and me, and licked her fucking lips before she tilted her head back against the wall and pressed her tits against Hillcrest's chest.

I saw red.

Hillcrest laughed deeply, his nasally voice sounded more like a wheeze than a laugh.

I was going to kill him. Kill her. The betrayal of all betrayals. Of anyone she could have fucking been with, she had to choose our fucking enemy. She was dead to me.

"You lost your chance with her," Dax goaded. "She's mine now."

"They just can't seem to get over the fact that I left them years ago," Maya drawled, rubbing her hands over Dax's back. "They're still holding a flame for me."

"Trust me, we're not," I growled. Not anymore.

"You're not bringing this piece of shit around my son," Marcos snapped.

She eyed us both warily, at least she still had some smarts about her. And she wouldn't be getting her son back, not if I had anything to do with it.

Marcos and I still had our guns held out in front of us, neither one of us were interested in putting down the weapon, not while our enemy was in sight.

Dax's hand left Maya's jaw and slid down her chest to grope her breast, while the other pulled her hair, yanking her head back farther. She moaned loudly.

"For fucks sake," I snapped, fed up with the bullshit. I wasn't going to stand here and watch this shit. "Come on, Killer. Leave the whore, we don't need her."

I walked out the front door, leaving Marcos inside. Marcos followed me out a moment later and we both booked it for the truck. I heard the lock click before I opened the door and climbed in.

"What happened?" Luke asked, as Marcos climbed in and slammed his door. He started the truck a moment later and was backing down the driveway before he answered Luke.

"Your mom had a friend over, someone not safe for you to be around. So you're gonna come back to my place for the night."

"What?" Luke asked, clearly confused.

I took a deep breath before I turned around in my seat to face Luke. "Hey, it's ok. Your mom is safe; she just has a man over that we don't really want you around."

"If he's not safe for me, then why is my mom hanging around him?" Luke asked.

Marcos pulled out of the driveway and threw the transmission into drive, speeding off down the street. "I don't know, buddy. Has your mom ever brought a man around the house before? Have you ever gone to dinner with her and another man?"

"Like a boyfriend? No. My mom doesn't have time for dating. She goes to work or my practices and then takes care of my grandparents."

I frowned and looked over at Marcos, he too looked just as confused as I felt.

"Alright, well for tonight you're gonna spend the night at my apartment. I'll bring you to summer camp in the morning, alright? What time is drop off?"

"Six-thirty," Luke answered. "Guess it's a good thing mom over packed my bag."

I forced a laugh. "Yeah, that's helpful."

Maya

TWENTY MINUTES BEFORE.

I was reading a book and dozing on and off on the couch Sunday afternoon while I waited for Luke to get home from his guys' trip with Marcos and Jason. I had enjoyed the weekend with Nico and had been surprised when my mother didn't give me much flack about being gone two weekends in a row.

There was a quiet knock on the front door before it opened. My head whipped over in surprise and then relaxed a bit when I saw Nico walking in the house. "Hey, Little Dreamer," he greeted me with a smile.

"Hey."

Nico doesn't say anything until he's standing before me, then he crouches down before the couch. "Why'd you take off this morning?" He's direct, as usual, and it makes my heart skip a beat.

"I got scared," I answered honestly.

Nico's mouth opened then closed quickly, as if he wasn't expecting my honest answer. "Scared," he repeated.

I sat up, turning to face him head on, my legs slotting between his squatted thighs. "Yes." I nodded. "I woke up at four this morning and got so overwhelmed. I needed to get away."

"From me."

I sucked in a breath and released it slowly. "From myself, my emotions at that moment."

"Why didn't you just wake me? We could have talked them out."

"I can't talk about it Nico. I've told you that."

"So is this about what's going on that has you too scared to talk to me or Marc or Jase."

I sighed and looked down at my hands, my fingers were twisting around a piece of the fringe on the throw pillow. God, I wanted nothing more than to reach out and pull his face closer to mine, to kiss him passionately. I couldn't do that, though. No matter how much I wanted to, I needed to put a distance between us again.

"Do you regret sleeping with me?" Nico asked, jolting me out of my head.

"I could never regret that, Nic," I admitted before I thought better of it.

"I love you, Maya. I hope you know I'd do anything to protect you." He reached out and tucked a stray hair behind my ear.

Tears welled in my eyes and I swallowed thickly. "I love you too," I murmured. "But we can't be together."

Nic ground his molars, the vein in his jaw popping, reminding me of Jason or Marcos's mannerisms. Nic was the happy one, not the angry one—I was clearly upsetting him. I couldn't blame him though, I knew how utterly ridiculous I was being. It was time to put up the wall between us again, force him to hate me. It was the only way to keep everyone safe.

"You should go."

"Maya."

"Don't Nic," I shook my head.

Clearly annoyed, he stood up abruptly and backed away. I stood up too, hoping to gain some even footing with him. "I don't understand," he said, his voice soft. "You know we can help you; you just need to tell me who it is."

I shook my head. "I don't need your help."

"Don't need, or don't want?"

"Both." I shot back, annoyed. I glared at him. "Just go already, stop pushing for something you're not going to get."

"Right," Nico said, sardonically. "You love me, but not enough to fight for me—for us."

I shrugged a shoulder and crossed my arms over my chest. "Stop being so fucking dramatic. Not everything revolves around you,

Nico. I'm only here for my parents and because Luke asked about Marcos."

He laughed incredulously. Shaking his head, Nico turned away from me. "Alright, Maya. Tell yourself that if you have too, but I'm not going anywhere." He walked out the door a moment later, leaving me standing in the middle of the living room feeling anxious. He wouldn't stop, I knew he wouldn't, and now I was worried Nico was going to tell Jason and Marcos, and all of three of them would be up my ass looking for the truth—more so than they already were.

I turned away from the door and just sat back down on the couch. I heard Nico's car drive away when I finally picked up my book again. Just as I was settling into my book again, the front door opened again. "Nico, I said—"

"Not Gage," a deep nasally voice said as he walked toward me.

Whipping my head to the door, I let out a quiet shriek of surprise. Jumping up, I tried to back away from the intruder, but he was on me too quickly. "Keep your voice down now," Dax Hillcrest growled, wrapping his hand around my throat. "Wouldn't want to alert your parents down the hall now, would we?"

I gulped as he shoved me back against the wall of the living room. "Please," I begged quietly. "Please, I haven't said anything to anyone."

"Trust me, bitch, if I thought you had talked, you'd be dead already." He squeezed my neck tighter. "But you're getting awfully chummy with Gage, Langford and Candella. Can't have you getting any ideas now."

"I haven't said anything, I won't." I tried to explain, but he only shook his head.

"You don't get it, whore. I will kill each and every single person you care about, starting with your little bastard chil—"

"Please don't!" I begged. "Please. I haven't said anything. I won't tell them anything. I'll keep my distance. Please don't hurt my baby."

"I don't thin—"

"What the fuck is this?" Marcos's voice boomed in the small living room.

I jerked in Hillcrest's hold, looking over his shoulder I found both Marcos and Jason standing in the door way, Glocks raised and pointed at us. I gasped.

"Don't you dare tell them," Hillcrest muttered in my ear.

"Dax, please?" I begged quietly.

"Better sell it." He slid his hand from around my throat to cup my face. Dax glanced over his shoulder to smirk at Marcos and Jason before he slammed his lips against mine and kissed me. His hand lifted my chin and angled my head so he could deepen the kiss, while the other wrapped around my hair, fisting it tightly, all while his fingers dug in painfully to my jaw, reminding me of my place.

Sell it, I told myself and wrapped my arms around his back, digging my fingers into his back, trying to stab him with my nails. Forcing myself to kiss the disgusting monster was something else though. I had to breathe through my nose and try not to gag. He tasted of stale cigarettes and whisky.

"What the fuck is this?" Jason growled.

I used his question to break off the kiss with Hillcrest. "What do you think it looks like Jason?" I asked, rolling my eyes.

"It looks like you're fucking the enemy," Marcos growled.

I laughed, "Guess, I am. But he's not my enemy." The words felt like ash in my mouth. I forced myself to smirk over at Marcos and Jason, forced myself to lick my lips and tilt my head back against the wall, and press my tits against Hillcrest's chest.

Hillcrest laughed deeply, his nasally voice sounded more like a wheeze than a laugh.

It took everything in me not to cringe or wince under his hand. He was a disgusting man, and having him so close to me was making me sick.

Marcos and Jason looked devastated—utterly betrayed. I needed to brandish that betrayal like a weapon and use it, hone it. Drive home the lie and push them away. It was the only fucking way.

"You lost your chance with her," Dax goaded. "She's mine now."

"They just can't seem to get over the fact that I left years ago," I drawled, rubbing my hands over Dax's back. "They're still holding a flame for me."

"Trust me, we're not," Jason growled.

"You're not bringing this piece of shit around my son," Marcos growled.

I eyed them both warily. Marcos and Jason still had their guns held out in front of them, neither one of them looked interested in putting down the weapons.

Dax's hand left my jaw and slid down my chest to grope my breast painfully, while the other pulled my hair, yanking my head back farther. I forced myself to moan instead of cry out as I wanted to. He was practically sexually assaulting me right in front of them and there was nothing I could say or do to stop it.

I needed Marcos and Jason to leave.

"For fucks sake," Jason snapped. "Come on, Killer. Leave the whore, we don't need her."

Jason walked out the front door, leaving Marcos inside. "I should just kill you now and save everyone the hassle," Marcos said.

My heart skipped a beat. Fuck, I wished he would. Killing Dax would solve most of my problems.

Dax laughed and pressed harder against me while looking back over his shoulder at Marcos. "Go head." Dax said it so nonchalantly, even I was dumbfounded. When he captured my mouth in another kiss, it took everything in me to not gag and push him away.

Finally, I heard the door slam shut and I pulled away from Dax. Looking over Dax's shoulder, I watched Marcos walk down the driveway toward the truck. I roughly pushed Dax away from me. "Get off me," I growled.

I was shaking with rage that I had been put in this situation.

"Remember, Maya, don't say a word, or all of your boys and your son are dead." Dax threatened me for the hundredth time. "I'm losing my patience. I will kill every single person you care about."

I watched out the front window as Marcos and Jason got back in the truck. Marcos started the engine and backed out the driveway immediately, taking Luke with him. My heart raced as it sunk into my belly. He was supposed to drop off Luke... where were they going?

"I get it! I won't say anything!" I pleaded.

Dax took his fucking time stepping away from me and leaving my house. Only when he was out the door and down the driveway, did I slide down the wall and crumple onto the floor in a sobbing heap.

My mother chose that moment to leave her bedroom and come out into the living room. Elaine's disappointment was evident on her face as she tsked softly and shook her head. "You should have come clean. That was the moment. Those boys would have saved you."

I sobbed harder, knowing in my heart that my mother was right.

Jason

AFTER LUKE WAS SOUNDLY sleeping in Marcos's bedroom, Nico and I pace around Marcos's small living room while the guy sits, staring at the blank wall, lost in thought. "You can't give him back to her," I pressured. "If she's dating Hillcrest, it's not safe."

"This isn't what it looks like." Nico shook his head and ran his hand through his shoulder length blond hair. "I was with her all weekend. She admitted she still loves me."

"She a master manipulator," I shot back, over Nico's fucking naivety.

"I straight out asked her if Dax Hillcrest was threatening her and she clammed up and wouldn't answer me. She got fucking scared. I guarantee what you saw, wasn't what truly happened." Nico spoke so adamantly, I wanted to believe him.

"You weren't there, man. She was into the kiss, she pressed against him and moaned and she wasn't fucking playing around," I said.

"She was fucking terrified when I brought up Trish and Hillcrest. I straight out asked her if he was threatening her and she immediately started hyperventilating and crying. I'm telling you, she's not willingly with him!" Nico yelled.

Marcos blinked out of his daze and looked at Nico. "You think he's threatening her?"

"Yes, and I think he has something over her. And whatever it is, it's enough for her to think she can't come to us." Nico took a deep breath. "You didn't see her man. She was almost inconsolable; she couldn't calm down. I've never seen her so upset. The way her eyes widened when I said Trish and Hillcrest's names—I'm telling you man, Hillcrest is up to something."

I ground my molars as I watched Marcos listen to Nico, looking for all the world like he believed what he was hearing. I didn't think Nico was lying...I just thought that Maya was a lying whore, and there was no telling what the truth really was.

Marcos sighed and hung his head. "Fuck," he groaned. "I'm gonna call Kara." He slowly got to his feet and patted the inside of his cut. He pulled out a joint and his lighter and headed for the front door of the small apartment. "Stay with Luke."

I ran a hand over my short hair and let out a deep breath as Marcos closed the door behind him.

"You don't believe me," Nico immediately turned on me.

I shook my head. "I believe you. I don't believe her. I think she's twisting your feelings for her."

Nico rolled his eyes. "You weren't there. You didn't see her, hear her. She's fucking terrified of someone. Luke even confirmed that with the damn flowers. Why is it so hard for you to believe that maybe Hillcrest fucking threatened her right before you walked in that house, and maybe she was just trying to save herself or her son? Hillcrest could be holding Luke against her, threatening to kill him if she doesn't cooperate. Don't you think that Maya would do anything she could to protect her son?"

Nico was making too much sense, and I didn't like it.

"She admitted she still loves us, man. She said leaving back then wasn't her choice—she didn't want to leave us, but she had to. That's how she worded it."

I took a seat on Marcos's couch and sighed heavily. Resting my elbows on my knees, I cradled my head in my hands and thought about what Nico was saying. It made sense...or we were stretching for the truth. "Luke said that Maya never brought a guy around, that she didn't have time between work, football practice and taking care of her parents." I admitted.

Nico nodded slowly, "We're with her at most of those football practices. Three nights a week, she comes straight from work to football. You've seen her calendar, how packed it is with doctor appointments and things for her parents."

"Yeah."

"Just think about it man. I don't think this is what it looked like."

"Did you sleep with her?" I asked, dropping my arms. I raised my head to meet my brother's gaze.

Nico's bright blue eyes were dark with worry. He blew out a breath and ran his hand through his messy blond hair. "Yeah."

I huffed out a laugh and shook my head in disbelief.

"Maya's not a cheater. She never would have slept with me if she was with someone else." Nico spoke softly, almost as if he was trying to convince himself as well as me.

"We don't know her anymore." I spoke just as softly, not wanting to fight anymore. "It's been ten years. We never thought she would have left us back then either, but she did. It's been ten years. People change."

"Not like that," Nico said. "She still loves us."

"She tell you that while you were fucking her?"

"Fuck you, man." Nico walked toward the apartment door. "Believe what you want, but I'm fucking telling you, she was terrified when I mentioned Hillcrest and Trish. He's threatening her. I guarantee it."

The door closed softly behind Nico, leaving me in the small quiet apartment, alone with my thoughts while Luke slept in the other room.

Marcos

I slowly smoked my joint while I dialed my sister's phone number and pressed the phone to my ear.

"Hey, Marquitos," Kara answered the phone.

"Hola, Manita." I smiled immediately upon hearing my little sister's voice.

"Uh oh, I know that tone. What's going on?" Kara asked, getting right to business.

"Have you talked to Maya at all lately?"

"No, I'm sorry. I've been so busy with the baby and the case with my dad, I haven't reached out. Is she ok?"

I sighed and ran a hand over my buzzed head. The fucking case with Vincent Carmichael was still on going—directly impacted by the fucking Las Serpientes—another thing weighing on my mind. "I don't know. I think she's in trouble," I admitted.

"What do you mean?"

"I walked in her house tonight and Dax fucking Hillcrest of Las Serpientes had her pressed against the wall, fucking making out and shit."

"Whaa?" Kara's shocked tone had me wondering if Nico was right. The more people thought Maya's behavior was unusual, the more confident I grew in agreeing with Nic.

"Yeah, it was strange. And like Luke mentioned last weekend that someone was leaving Maya flowers and whenever she found them, she became super upset. He said she was seeing a therapist for it."

"Damn. You think it's Hillcrest?"

"I don't know what to think," I admitted. "Nico confronted her this weekend while Stone and I were away with Luke, and he said that she immediately began freaking out when he asked her outright about Hillcrest and Trish—his girlfriend from ten years ago that came into the clubhouse. Nic said Maya became inconsolable or some shit."

Kara gasped.

"Nico couldn't get a straight answer out of her, he said she refused to answer, but he seemed pretty convinced that Hillcrest has been threatening her all this time and that's the reason she left."

"Holy shit," Kara breathed the words softly.

"Has she said anything to you?" I needed answers.

"No," Kara sighed. "I haven't really been pressing to be friends with her again, though. It hurt me too, when she left you. Even though back then, me and her weren't really talking that often, because I wasn't really talking to you at the time so it put a strain on our relationship too."

"Yeah." I huffed out a breath. The past was fucking filled with drama.

"I can reach out to Slade, I know she still talks to Maya. I could ask her what she knows?" Kara offered.

"Nico already went to Slade. It's why he's so adamant. Slade knows something, said to look deeper with Maya, and said something along the lines of 'why would someone like Maya need to see a therapist if there wasn't something going on?' Then told him to look deeper."

Kara gasped again. "Yeah, that sounds like there's something going on."

"I took Luke home with me." I changed the subject. "I was supposed to drop him off after my weekend with him, but that fucking scum bag was there and I left with Luke still in the truck."

"Fuck, Marcos." Kara sighed. "You can't keep him, not permanently."

"Why? He's my fucking son," I snapped. I hung my head and puffed on my forgotten joint. It had already burned down halfway. I took a long drag and held in the smoke while I listened to Kara hand me my ass.

"Because you said your name isn't on his birth certificate. Because you don't have parental rights established. She could call the police and have you arrested for kidnapping her child! Marcos, you need to bring him home."

Slowly blowing out the smoke I thought about what she said, knowing she was right. "What are my options for custody?"

"Fuck," Kara took a deep breath. "You need to establish paternity. You'd have to either get her to agree to a paternity test, or subpoena her for the test. That's basically suing her though, just so you're aware of the consequences that can of worms can open."

I nodded slowly to myself. "So I'd need a lawyer?"

"Yeah, Marquitos. I'll make a call; I have a friend in family law. I'll text you her info after I talk to her. If you want to go down that route, you have to know it's a slippery slope, and with your record—"

"I could lose Luke."

"Yeah, brother," Kara said softly.

"So, I sue for paternity and then have to wait for the results? We know that he's mine, he looks just fucking like me."

"Yeah, but you have to follow the law and that's sticking to due process. Establish paternity, then fight for custody. Not going to lie, brother, single fathers have a hard time getting full custody. It would have been different if you and Maya had been married. Unless you can get the court to rule that she's unfit to parent, you're only looking at every other weekend, or joint custody at best."

"Right."

"You need to talk to Maya, Marcos. Find out what's really going on."

"I know."

"If Nico's right, and she's been threatened this whole time, if that's why she left in the first place...that changes things, doesn't it?"

I couldn't answer her. That was the million-dollar question, wasn't it? If she's been threatened this whole time, what would that mean for us?

Why didn't she come to us?

There was only one person who could tell me the truth...only I didn't think she would.

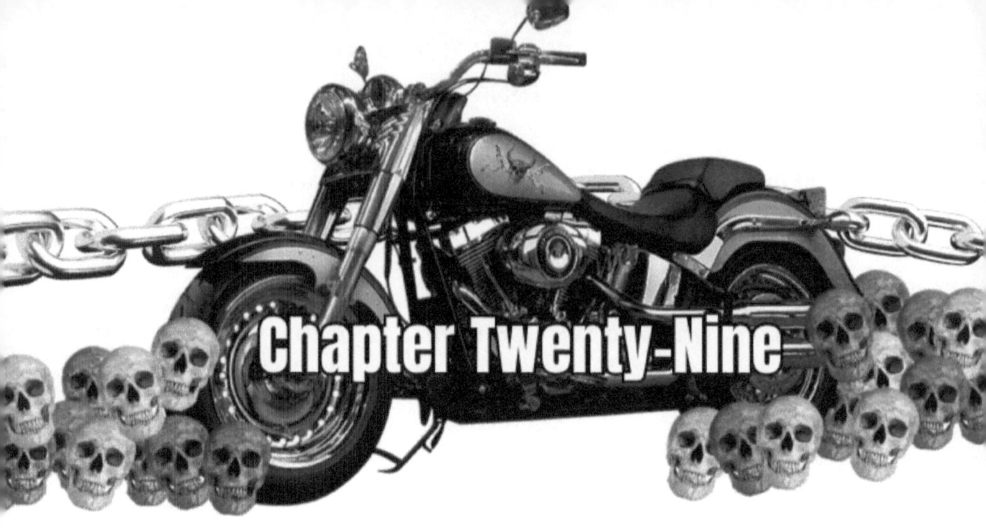

Maya

I PACED OUTSIDE THE school summer camp pick up area, waiting for Luke to come out. I had gotten off work early and called the camp stating I'd pick up Luke instead of sending him on the bus. When Marcos's hadn't brought him back home last night, I was terrified that Marcos was going to try to keep Luke away from me.

When I had texted him last night, Marcos's reply had been short.

Marcos:

I'll drop him at camp tomorrow

It was enough, I supposed. I had been so terrified though; my boss had let me leave an hour early to pick up Luke before camp ended. I needed to see my son.

A moment later Luke came walking out with his black hair mused and in need of a haircut and his dark brown eyes soulful and worried. "Mom?" he asked as he walked over to me.

I wrapped him up in a hug, lifting him off the ground. "Oh, my boy!" I cried. "I missed you so much!" I tried to play it off as missing him his weekend away, but knew I was worrying him.

"I missed you too. Mom, are you ok?" Luke asked, pulling away slightly to look at me.

I quickly set him back down and wiped away my tears. "Yes. I just missed you so much."

"Dad said you had someone at the house that wasn't safe." Luke's hands were still on my shoulders and he met my gaze with a stare that was older than his nine years of age.

I frowned slightly. "Yes. There was someone there that wasn't safe. It was a good thing your dad took you back to his place. But don't worry, he won't be coming back. The house is safe now."

Luke was watching me warily. "Dad asked if you were dating someone."

I sighed and shook my head. "No. I'm not dating anyone; it was just an old friend that came by who shouldn't have. He left right after your dad."

Luke finally nodded, accepting my explanation. "Alright. Why did you pick me up early?"

"I missed you! I thought I'd get off work early and we could go get ice cream and hang out since you don't have practice tonight."

Luke's whole face lit up as he smiled. "Yes! Awesome! Can we go that place on the river and watch the boats go by?"

"Skully's? Sure can!" I grinned and high-fived my son.

Maya

Luke and I had a wonderful evening, eating ice cream for dinner and watching the barges and speed boats on the Nevermore River. Skully's Ice Cream and Grill was an historical establishment right where the Nevermore River met the Illinois River, about thirty minutes south of Creekton. The restaurant overlooked the locks, where the water levels were changed so boat could travel from the higher Nevermore River to the lower Illinois River.

The hiking in the area was fantastic as well, and it had been my favorite place to go for day trips since I was old enough to remember. Luke loving the area just made it all the more special.

Now that Luke was in bed, I felt like I could finally relax. Yesterday had fucked me up mentally and emotionally. Not only had I had to deal with being sexually assaulted in my own home by Dax fucking Hillcrest, I had to lie to Jason and Marcos about it. On top of that, I went to bed knowing my son wasn't in the house, despite almost being dropped off.

My emotions were fucked up and I was exhausted. It was all beginning to pile up on me. It was fucking draining and I just wished I could come clean. But after what Hillcrest put me through yesterday, I knew my guys were lost to me, if I'd ever had a shot with them after all this time.

There was too much hurt there. Too many lies.

I heard a motorcycle coming down the road and looked up. It was dark outside and I couldn't see, so I grabbed a sweater and walked out the front door, hoping whoever it was knew to park at the end of the driveway as to not wake my parents with the Harley engine.

I had just slipped outside when the bike parked at the end of the driveway and the engine cut off. I wrapped the sweater around me, despite the seventy-degree weather, it was a little cool without the sun out. Walking down the driveway, I wondered which one of them had come for a late-night visit.

I half expected it to be Nico, coming to question me. I was sure the other two had filled him in on what happened after he left yesterday. It was a little surprising actually, that he hadn't been by yet. Maybe he was waiting until football practice tomorrow evening, where he could corner me without Luke hearing?

I reached the bottom of the driveway as the rider took off his helmet, but didn't dismount the bike. Marcos set his helmet on the handle bar, before he leaned back and crossed his beefy arms over his chest. He watched me as I moved toward him, not saying a word.

I wasn't ready for this; I was still too raw. My walls weren't built back up yet. I wanted more time before I faced Marcos again. I waited for Marcos to speak first.

"I talked to Nico," he said softly.

I swallowed thickly.

"He told me how you reacted when he confronted you about Hillcrest." That was the last thing I expected him to start with. I was sure he was going to ask about us sleeping together.

I crossed my own arms over my chest. I needed to push him away, not have him worm his way under my skin again. Not have him ride in and try to save me. "Nico heard what he needed to." I shrugged.

Marcos glared at me in the dark. I could feel the weight of his scrutiny despite the dim light. "So you could fuck him? That right?"

Again, I shrugged. "Thought I'd hit that for nostalgia sake."

Marcos let out a sardonic laugh and shook his head. "Jason said you were full of shit."

Hurt rankled me, but I tried not to show it, grateful for the cover of darkness. "Of course he did."

"You're fucking Hillcrest too? Nico gonna have to go get tested because you're whoring around?"

"Not like he's a saint either, all the whores the three of you fuck at the clubhouse."

Marcos chuckled softly. "I thought he was on to something," Marcos admitted, shaking his head. He ran a hand over his buzzed hair and sighed. "He was so damn adamant that you were being threatened by Hillcrest, that everything you've done for the last ten years—leaving us—was justified, was fucking worth it." Again, he laughed. "Guess the jokes on him, huh? On us again?"

I needed to drive the point home so they'd stop fucking questioning me about this. "Sure is. I left because I didn't want you anymore. I found out I was pregnant and didn't want to raise him around you or the club, so I fucking left. I only came back because of my parents' accident."

Marcos hand shot out and wrapped around the front of my sweater. He yanked me roughly against his chest, so I could see his face clearly. "Maya, I swear to fucking god, if you're lying and it turns out Nico's right—Mi Vida." He choked out the word as emotion clogged his voice. "Tell me please. Is Hillcrest threatening you?"

I bit the inside of my cheek to keep my emotions in check. I wasn't strong enough for this. "Marc—"

He cradled my face with both hands and kissed me, claiming my mouth and owning me as he kissed me passionately.

My hands gripped his forearms, holding on as he held my face. I kissed him back, holding his arms tight and moaning softly. Abruptly, I pulled away from him breathless, as I put space between us. "Don't."

"I know you still fucking feel that," Marcos growled, stepping toward me. "Don't fucking lie to me."

"Stop looking for something that's not there anymore. I left you. I'm with Dax now, stop pushing."

"But you still slept with Nic on Saturday. Classy, Henderson." He glared down at me.

I rolled my eyes. "You should go." I was already backing away from him though, before he could answer. I turned my back on him and headed for the house, ending the conversation.

"This isn't over," Marcos called to me as I reached the house.

I ignored him and slipped back inside, closing and locking the door behind me.

Marcos

I drove a couple blocks over to where Kara's house was. Funny, that Maya and Kara only lived a couple blocks from each other and never saw or spoke to each other anymore. *How did people that used to be best friends, grow so far apart,* I wondered. Probably the same way Maya grew so far apart from me and the guys. She changed and left us all behind.

I drove up the long driveway at Kara's place—Johnny's place—and parked my bike in front of the garage. It was late on a Monday night, but I saw the lights on inside, and knew it was still an hour or two before my sister would be going to sleep.

I knocked softly on the back door as I let myself in the house through the mudroom attached to the kitchen. Kevin was in the kitchen, washing bottles from the looks of things as I walked in. "Hey man," Kevin said, glancing at me over his shoulder. "You good?"

I immediately shook my head. I kicked off my shoes in the mud room, lining them up on a rubber mat, along the wall with the other boots. I walked into the kitchen and over to Kara's liquor cabinet. I helped myself to her bottle of Macallan, grabbing a glass out of a cabinet next to where Kevin was washing dishes. Pouring myself two fingers of whisky, I quickly tossed it back.

"That bad?" Kevin asked, raising an eyebrow.

Sighing heavily, I poured himself another two fingers of whisky, before I put the top back on the bottle and walked over to the island. I sat down with my whisky and shook my head.

"Marcos?" Kara's voice came from behind him, and I glanced over my shoulder to see her walking down the stairs with Johnny and Derrick behind her.

"Hey, Lil Manita," I greeted her, raising my glass.

"Fuck," she swore softly as she walked over.

I didn't see Lilah anywhere and glanced around the living room, realizing the baby wasn't in the room.

"We just put her down," Johnny said. "You good, man?"

"Not really," I grumbled.

"Oh no," Kara sighed. She walked over to the counter and grabbed her own glass and poured herself two fingers of Macallan.

"I confronted Maya. I asked her straight out if she was being threatened by Hillcrest. She denied everything. So either she's lying straight to my face and Nic got it wrong, or she's fucking Dax Hillcrest."

"Jesus Christ," Johnny growled.

Kara frowned, her blond hair framing her face. Her blue eyes darkened as she sipped her whisky slowly.

"Dude," Derrick grunted.

"Did you see her face to face?" Kara asked.

"I just came from her parents' place. I mean it was dark and we talked outside, but yeah, I saw her face. I don't know anymore, Kara. I don't know her like I used to, to know if she's lying or not. Nic seems to think she's being threatened; he questioned her Saturday night and she freaked out the minute he mentioned Hillcrest's name. Tonight, she said the opposite and told me she was fucking him." My voice choked up with emotion and I quickly sipped my whisky.

Kara reached across the island and grabbed my hand, squeezing it.

"I don't know her, man. But no one would willingly fuck Hillcrest," Derrick said.

I could only shrug.

"I called Slade," Kara said. "She was reluctant to talk about Maya with me, because I haven't really been friends with Maya in the last decade, but she did say she was, and I quote, 'scared for Maya and really worried about her'. We all know Slade doesn't scare easily, and it takes a lot of make her worry."

Johnny hummed low in his throat. "That's telling in itself. But if Maya's refusing to tell you anything, there's not much you can do."

"Short of killing Hillcrest," I mumbled darkly.

Kara sighed and squeezed my hand. "Not yet. Soon, I promise."

"Kara," I breathed heavily. "How much longer? Las Serpientes fucking kidnapped you, they played the Psychos like a fool, my club is gunning for retribution. I don't know how much longer I can hold them back. Couple of my guys have personal beef with the snakes too. They want to wipe them out."

"We're down for that," Johnny growled. "Trust me, the Knights are itching for this too."

"My father's trial starts the week after next. Depending on how it goes, will determine the date for sentencing. It would be faster if he took a plea deal though. If he admitted he was guilty and took the deal, it would give me what I need with the board and ensure the smooth transfer of the firm to me." Kara took a pull from her whisky.

"He hasn't agreed to a plea yet?" I asked, confused.

Johnny shook his head and paced away, rubbing his hands over his buzzed hair. Clearly, there was some contention on the subject.

"I've been worried that if he took a plea, the board wouldn't agree to transfer the firm into my name, but I just threw the bylaws at them *today*, and they've agreed that if my father enters a plea deal and pleads guilty, they will transfer everything to me. So if you can somehow convince my father to enter a plea deal..."

I sipped my whisky thinking. "What would that do to the timeline?"

"If he signs the plea deal, the D.A. is confident that we could get him before a judge by end of next week. Sentencing would likely be same day, but could take a couple days depending on the judge and the deal," Kara explained.

"So no trial?"

"If we can convince my father to a plea deal, no trial," Kara huffed.

"That going to be hard?"

"He's apparently had a change of heart since admitting to the crimes at the police station. He wants to go to trial," Kara grumbled.

"The fuck?" I turned to Johnny. "I thought you guys had the Bratva assisting inside?"

Johnny shook his head. "We're still rocky with Tarazov since shit went down with the Seratelli's. Until we get that smoothed over, Tarazov has us on ice."

"So a sit down with the Seratelli's is needed." I concluded.

"It would help." Kevin nodded.

"I'll talk to Nic, see if he can talk to his cousin again." I finished up the last of my whisky and glance around for the bottle. Kevin set it on the island in front of me. Pouring another two fingers of whisky into my glass, I continued, "Maybe we can knock out two birds with one stone, see if the Seratelli's have anyone inside that will convince Vince and get you that sit down you need." I ran a hand over my hair, thinking.

"I'd appreciate that, brother." Johnny nodded solemnly, always serious.

"It's going to take some time though. Nico and Leonardo had a falling out a couple years ago. He's tried reaching out recently and it didn't go well. He's talked to his mom about it, so we're in a waiting game until Nic hears back from his mom, or Seratelli."

Johnny let out a long breath, clearly not happy with the news.

"I know man," I said. "It's been one thing after another."

"Yeah," Johnny agreed.

I turned to my sister again. "Did you reach out to your friend? The one who does family law?"

"Yeah," Kara dropped my hand and walked over to the counter closest to the mudroom, where her purse was sitting next to her keys. She dug in her purse for a moment before she pulled out a white business card. Walking back over to the island, she handed me the card. "Michelle Lakeson. I had lunch with her today. She agreed to help. Give her a call in the morning."

"Shit man, you gonna sue for custody?" Derrick asked.

I shook my head. "I need to establish paternity first. I'm not even on his birth certificate."

"Shit." Kevin sighed.

"Yeah."

"You staying here tonight?" Kara asked softly.

I nodded. "Yeah."

"I'll make up the guest room," she murmured and walked away.

"You make this happen, we'll be in the clear," Johnny said. "One step closer to Dax Hillcrest being dead."

I could only nod as I nursed my whisky, feeling the weight of the world settling on my shoulders.

Marcos

"I SPENT THE NIGHT at Kara's," I told Jason and Nico the following morning when I saw them at the clubhouse. They both looked up from the car they were working on in the clubhouse's attached automotive shop. It was a new business endeavor that the Devil's Psycho's were starting, as the club needed to make more money—legal money—that we couldn't get from our different dealings with running drugs, guns, or other illegal activities.

"I went to see Maya last night," I continued when I had both their attention.

Nico looked relieved while Jason schooled his face into his usual stone-cold mask.

"I had to know for sure, one way or another. She denied Hillcrest threatening her and said she was fucking him."

Nico's head tilted back in disbelief, while Stone rolled his eyes. "I'm not surprised."

"She was clearly trying to cover up. If he went to her parent's house Sunday, then he's growing suspicious of our involvement. He probably scared her to make sure she wouldn't say anything." Nico's defense of her was admirable, but I didn't know what to think anymore.

"Or she's a lying whore," Jason deadpanned.

"It was dark, so I couldn't see her face clearly, but I kissed her and practically begged her to tell me the truth. I told her we would protect her and Luke if she was in danger and she just got angry. She denied any danger and said she was gladly fucking him." [update previous scene].

Nico sighed and threw down his wrench. "I don't fucking get what her deal is. Why won't she just trust us?"

"Because she lied to you Nic," Jason said softly, gently. "She was worked up, and in the moment, so she said what you wanted to hear. You want her to be lying so badly, that even when she keeps repeating the same thing over and over, you're looking for looking for something that isn't there."

Nic shook his head vehemently. "No. I don't believe that. You weren't there; you didn't see her. I'm telling you man. She was terrified."

I sighed softly. "Either way. We don't know. What I do know, is that I'm not on Luke's birth certificate as his father. If anything were to happen to Maya, I would not get custody of my son—not easily at least. That's not acceptable to me. So I talked to my sister about it and she hooked me up with one of her lawyer friends that practice family law—"

"Marcos, no," Nico snapped, shaking his head.

"I have to Nic!" My voice rose. "The lawyer is going to file a Petition to Establish Paternity. Maya can either voluntarily agree to a paternity test, or the court will order her to appear for testing. I need to make it legal that Luke is my son."

Jason hummed in agreement.

Nico stared at me with a loss for words. "You're not going for custody?"

"I need to establish paternity first. Custody maybe after, if Maya keeps up this bullshit charade with Hillcrest." I ran a hand over my buzzed head.

"Fucking hell, Marcos," Nic shook his head and paced away from the car. "You're gonna rip out her fucking heart."

"Like she did to us?" Stone shot back. "Like she keeps doing? You didn't see her Sunday! How she pressed against him—"

"No! I was with her Saturday night when she sobbed in my arms when I questioned her about Hillcrest! I saw the fear in her eyes! You weren't there when she confessed her love for us, before she clamped down on my cock!"

I let out a heavy breath.

"Point made. Heat of the moment," Stone said.

"Motherfucker" Nico shoved at Stone.

"Hey, hey, hey!" I shouted, pushing between Jason and Nico. "Come on! This isn't us! We don't fight over pussy!"

"Maya isn't just pussy, and you fucking know it!" Nico growled, pushing at me.

I allowed it, my back pressed against Jason's chest, until Jason backed off and walked a few steps away.

"Marcos, I'm telling you man, Maya is being threatened! I believe that with everything I have."

Taking a deep breath, I nodded slowly. "I hear you, Nic. I do. But there's nothing I can do about that—"

"So we kill Hillcrest!" Nico shot back. "Something we should have months ago! When Las Serpientes kidnapped your god damned sister! When they killed our fucking President! We've let them get away with everything for too damn long!"

I nodded, feeling every bit of Nico's rage. "I know, Nic, I know! I talked to Kara about that too. I told her the club is getting restless and seeking retribution. She said that she needs her father to accept a guilty plea deal. The board for the firm—"

"Fuck the board!" Nico shouted. "Since when do we give a shit about a bunch of corporate monkeys?!"

"Since my baby sister—the one YOU vowed to protect—asked us to!" I yelled, getting into Nico's face. He wasn't listening anymore and I needed him to.

Nic stepped away, breathing hard.

"Kara needs a guilty plea agreement signed, so the board will transfer the firm to her. Without the plea agreement, it goes to trial, which could take months if not years. With the plea agreement we can finish this maybe next week!" Marcos yelled.

"And he won't sign?" Stone asked, his voice calm.

"No. And Johnny said they can't ask the Bratva, because there's friction there after Mac reached out to the Seratelli's. The Knights need things smoothed over with the mafia and to back out of that agreement before things can be smoothed over with the Bratva."

"So we need a sit down with the Seratelli's," Stone deadpanned.

"Yep."

"FUCK!" Nico yelled. He turned to the work bench full of tools and shoved everything off of it in a fit of rage.

I gave him a minute to rage. Nico already knew what was expected of him; how much now rode on his back.

When he caught his breath, his back tense, he hung his head as he clung to the side of the tool bench.

"I'll call my mom. She never got back to me after I went to see her. Leo was not open to talking the last time I saw him. She said she would try, for Maya, but the family was upset with me. She's been asking him for the last three weeks to talk to me and he's refused every time."

I nodded, knowing this already. "We need you to try again."

Nico

I didn't end up calling my mother, instead I called my cousin directly. I half expected to be sent to voicemail, so I'm caught off guard when Leo's gruff voice answered the phone. "Hello?"

"Leo, can we talk please?"

Leo's heavy sigh is audible through the phone. "I answered, didn't I?"

I rolled my eyes and gritted my teeth; my cousin could be a real asshole sometimes. "Can we please talk in person?"

"The restaurant, Thursday night, 8 pm. Come alone."

"I was hoping we could set up a meeting with the club."

"No. You will come alone. You will answer to the family first, before I will agree to any sit down with your little bike club."

"I appreciate i—"

Leonardo hung up the phone before I could finish speaking. Shaking my head, I grabbed a pre-rolled joint and walked out into the clubhouse. I found Marcos and Jason in the president's office, both men kicked back on opposite couches, each smoking their own joints.

I sighed heavily and lit up my own as I took the chair in front of the desk and turned it toward the couches. I sucked back hard on the joint as I sat down and kicked my feet up. "He answered. He agreed to a meeting Thursday night at 8. I'm to come alone."

"Fuck," Stone grunted.

"Yep," I said and blew out the smoke from my joint. "He said I had to answer to the family first, before he would agree to any sit down with the MC."

Marcos nodded slowly. "And you think he's going to demand retribution Thursday night?"

"Definitely. You guys should probably be on stand-by across the street. I don't think I'll be walking out of there." I puffed on my joint.

Marcos grunted and rubbed a hand over his head.

It was fucked up. I prayed to God that I lived through it. We needed the Family's support when it came to both Vince Carmichael and Dax Hillcrest.

Chapter Thirty-One

Nico

Thursday night, I walked into Sera's and gave my name to the hostess. I was immediately led toward the back and down the hallway to Leo's office. This time, the hostess knocked and waited until it was opened by none other than Giovanni Seratelli, Leo's younger brother and Underboss.

I paused in the doorway, meeting my cousin's gaze. "Hey Nic," Giovanni smiled tightly.

"Hey." I nodded my head. The hostess left us and Gio opened the door further, showing the full scope of the packed office. All five of the Seratelli brothers were inside, along with another five men that I didn't know. Or maybe I did, because Fredrico Accardi, Leonardo's best friend, was standing against the wall.

"Come on in," Gio said. He stepped out of the way.

I squared my shoulders and steeled my spine as I walked into the Lion's den. I met the eye of every man in the room, stopping when I reached the center in front of Leo's desk.

Leo sat like a king on his throne, holding court before his Family. I thought that was an apt description, considering who Leo was to these men.

I met his gaze, as Leo watched my every move, looking for weakness. "Why are you here, Nicolai?" Leo asked, his voice deep and commanding.

Guess they were starting right away, huh? I cleared my throat and spoke clearly. "To apologize and ask for forgiveness from the family."

Leo's lips twitched slightly in the corners. Had I not been watching, I would have missed it. "Why are you here, Nicolai?" Leo repeated the question.

"To apologize and ask forgiveness from the family," I repeated.

Leo nodded, seemingly accepting my response. "Nicolai Gage, you have been disowned by your Don ten years ago. You turned your back on your family and chose to align yourself with another organization. By all rights, you should be dead."

A muttering of both approval and disapproval went around the room. I took the moment to eye the men that thought I should be dead—thankfully they weren't family—though Fredrico was one of the few that thought I should be dead. *Interesting.*

"For the debt you owe the family, your punishment is a stomping, to be carried out tonight, by the men present in this room. You will also give a formal apology at Sunday's family dinner, and you will work for the Family again."

"But—"

"You can keep your little biker club," Leo glared, speaking right over me. "But you will also work for the family. You'll be given a list of names we need eliminated, and you will do so, without question."

I swallowed and nodded my head once. It was the last thing I wanted to do. Contract killing was the main reason I wanted nothing to do with the family in the first place. I could kill if I needed to, but I wasn't a stone-cold killer like some guys—that shit ate me up.

I would do anything I had to at this point. Anything for Maya. Even if it meant selling my soul to the Devil. "My girl—"

"We'll talk about anything further *after*—or rather *if* you survive the beating." Leo stood up and the men along the walls straightened.

"Come." Leo stepped passed me, gripping my shoulder briefly as he passed by. He led the way out of his office and I had no choice but to follow.

With a wall of muscle behind me, and Maya and Luke's future in front of me, I followed Leonardo and Giovanni out of the office, across the hall, through another door and down a set of concrete stairs that went deep under the restaurant—like two floors underground.

The large concrete basement was much larger than the restaurant above it, like Leo owned the entire city block beneath the buildings. I swallowed; this was shaping up to be the worst-case scenario. I hoped that Marcos and Jason would be able to get me out of this at the end.

When we reached the center of the open basement, Leo turned around. "Search him."

Giovanni walked over and took my cut from me, while Augustino Jr. "Tino" gave me a tight smile as he started patting me down. "Sorry about this," Tino said softly.

I grunted in return, holding out my arms so Tino could finish quickly, while watching as Giovanni folded my Cut with care and set it gently on floor against the wall, out of the way. I had been hoping for the leather of the cut to protect me from most of the damage they planned to inflict, but they had thought about that as well. I appreciated my cousin's care and respect for the cut though, that meant a lot to me.

I waited in the middle of circle as my family and their guys circled around me. Leo made a show of taking off his suit coat and slowly undoing his cuff links before he rolled up his sleeves. I would have laughed and egged him on if it were just the two of us, if we were still as close as we had been as kids. But I couldn't, we weren't that close anymore.

I had burned that bridge when I left.

Kinda like Maya had, when she left.

I hadn't thought about how my situation could be compared to Maya's. We both walked away from family. We both came back looking for forgiveness. Or rather, asking for it because we needed *help*, though Maya didn't exactly ask for he—

I was yanked out of my musings by Leo's fist cracking against my cheek bone. I backed up a step, stunned and my ears ringing. The second fist landed on my jaw, before I even thought to bring my arms up to block my face.

It didn't matter though, because those two headshots delivered by Leo were the only ones anyone even tried to land. They must have gotten an order not to hit me in the head, because as one, they rained down punches on my torso. Someone got in a kick to my ribs that had me doubling over and that was all it took for them to get me on the ground and begin stomping on me and kicking me with their steel-toe boots.

I curled up into a ball to protect myself as best as I could with my arms up and protecting my head, but it didn't do much to protect me from ten guys stomping my ass. I would be lucky if I survived this beat down.

Jason

Marcos and I were led through the back door of the restaurant and down a set of concrete steps to an open basement that was massive. I did a quick sweep of the area, but it was mostly empty aside of Nico curled up in the center and the Seratelli brothers standing around him, smoking cigars.

I gritted my teeth as I took in the slightly ruffled Italians. There had never been any deep-seated friendship between the two crews. Though the Psychos used to run coke for the Mafia, it was only as a way to earn money. It was something the Seratelli's had come to us about, not the other way around. It had happened after Nico left the family.

It had been a mutually beneficial agreement, until it wasn't.

Mac Taylor going to the Italians to cut out the Bratva had been a huge upset to not only the amount of money the Psycho's were earning monthly, but also to the drug scene as a whole. It had started a whole cluster fuck of dominoes falling across the fucking board and he wasn't even alive to deal with the aftermath.

I was still pissed at the man over it. And fucking Buckley for teaming up with the fucking snakes to take on Taylor. It was all bullshit I didn't want to deal with.

Now, here we were, trying to pick up the pieces of that aftermath, and prayed to God that Nico was still breathing and this whole fucking beat down had been worth it. If his fucking cousins didn't accept his apology, then this was pointless.

They needed the Seratelli's help. Desperately.

"Leonardo," Marcos nodded at the Don as he shook his hand.

Leonardo Seratelli for the most part looked unruffled, though his suit coat was missing and his shirt sleeves were rolled up, but the overly handsome bastard was stone faced as he puffed on his cigar and watched them walk toward Nico's prone body.

"Jesus." I breathed the word. "You dead, man?"

"He's alive," Leonardo declared.

I still crouched down beside my buddy and pressed my fingers to his neck to check his pulse, not believing the Italian. Only when I felt it for myself, did I stand back up and meet the gazes of all five Seratelli brothers. "You guys get enough?" I goaded.

Leo had both hands shoved into his pants pockets and the cigar tucked between his teeth. He leaned back on his heels and raised an eyebrow at me.

"Stop." Marcos immediately held up a hand, motioning at me.

I ground my teeth as I shut my mouth.

A frown pulled at Leonardo's lips as he slowly pulled the cigar from his mouth. "We went easy on him. Remember that."

Marco helped me haul Nico up between the two of us. It was a struggle getting him up the stairs, but we managed. It was a good thing Nic was out cold, because this would hurt like a motherfuck-er.

Chapter Thirty-Two

Maya

FRIDAY AFTERNOON I WAS just finishing up with a patient when I walked out of the exam room. Jayla walked over to me looking concerned. "Hey Maya, there's a man at the front desk looking to speak to you."

Frowning, I nodded and followed her up front and through the door separating the clinic from the front desk. On the other side of the counter was a young man, mid-twenties maybe, dressed in a t-shirt and jeans. "Can I help you?" I asked.

"Sure can." He smiled warmly and handed over a flat brown envelope. I had just grabbed the envelope when the man said, "Maya Henderson, you have been served."

My heart dropped immediately. "Excuse me? What is this?"

The man shrugged. "Legal papers. My job was to serve them, that's all I know." He turned away and walked out of the office, leaving me behind, dumbfounded.

Jayla placed a hand on my shoulder. "Maya, are you alright?"

Shaking like a leaf, I nodded and shook my head and slowly opened the envelope. Inside I found a single piece of paper with the words Petition to Establish Parentage at the top of the form. My breath caught in my throat as I read over the document.

Marcos had filed for a paternity test through the local county courthouse. According to the legal document in my hand, I was to either agree to a Voluntary Acknowledgement of Parentage or appear in the court at the date listed in the document, and allow the court to administer the paternity test.

"What the fuck," I murmured softly, my hands shaking as I reread the paper.

I knew it was only a matter of time with Marcos. After last weekend with Hillcrest in my home, and our disagreement in the driveway the next day, I knew Marcos was upset. Lashing out for paternity rights was just the beginning, I knew. Once paternity was established, he would fight for legal custody.

I couldn't allow that to happen. I would be damned if I allowed Marcos to take my son from me. Regardless of how things looked, I knew the truth. I needed to protect Luke at all costs.

Looking at the court order, I double checked the date on the form. I had three weeks before I had to appear in court. It would have to do.

Marcos

The office at the clubhouse only halfway muted the sounds of the Friday night party raging behind the closed doors. I sat at my desk while Jason and Nico lounged around the room either at chairs in front of the desk or the couch off to the side. I was waiting on a phone call that would set everything in motion—change everything.

It felt like all I was doing lately was waiting—for the lawyer, for the realtor, for a house. I was in a waiting purgatory that was killing me slowly. I needed good news.

"The realtor scheduled the closing date." Jason announced, as if sensing his darkening mood. "It's next Thursday the 12th. I've been talking with the loan officer and submitted all our documents, so we're good to go for closing," Jason said. "The inspection came back pretty decent. It was mostly cosmetic issues and a couple issues with the GCFI outlets in the kitchen. Nothing we can't fix ourselves."

I smiled, feeling the weight lift off my chest. "Good."

We were one step closer to the end goal. I would have a house for my son to come home to when I initiated the next steps with my lawyer: custody arrangement. If Maya wanted to claim she was fucking Dax Hillcrest, then I was playing hard ball, no more kid gloves with her. There was no way I was allowing my son to be around the fucking prick that was Hillcrest.

My cell phone rang in my pocket and I quickly pulled it out. Seeing my new lawyer's phone number, I answered. "Hello?"

Jason and Nico both watched me silently.

"Hello, Mr. Candella. I'm just calling to inform you that the Petition has been served successfully," Michelle Lakeson cut right to the chase.

"Ok," I said, feeling both relieved and anxious at the same time. My mind kept playing different scenarios of how Maya might have reacted, like how heartbroken she might feel. I had almost called the whole thing off several times in the last week, but in the end, I knew it was what I needed to do. Without my name on Luke's birth certificate, I didn't have any paternity rights. And if Maya did something stupid like take off again with my son, I wouldn't be unable to fight for him.

"So now all we can do is wait, unless you speak to her before then and can get her to agree to do so voluntarily."

I nodded slowly. "I understand, thank you so much for the update."

"You're welcome. Have a good night."

"You too." I hung up the phone and set it on the desk in front of me.

"She's been served?" Jason asked.

"Yeah." I grunted. I thought I'd feel better about it—about being one step closer to our goal, but the guilt ate at me.

Nico sighed deeply and tilted his head back against the wall behind the couch he was sprawled out on. He should be at home in bed after the beating he endured from the Seratelli Crime Family the night before, not sprawled out haphazardly on the raggedy couch in the president's office.

I had tried to get him to stay home tonight, to miss the party, but Nico had said things needed to progress as business as usual—despite the fact that he was pissing blood from his bruised to shit kidneys. He didn't want anyone watching him to think he couldn't handle himself.

It was clear he was hurting, both physically and emotionally. He didn't agree with our plan; in fact, he had said he wanted nothing to do with taking Luke away from Maya—not that I was planning that yet. I wasn't sure I wanted to do that to Luke.

I was really curious as to Maya's reaction and almost wanted to call her, but knew it was unwise. I'd see her in the morning, though, bright and early for Luke's first game of the season. It would be soon enough.

I wondered if she would tell Luke. She'd been pretty open with him about everything else...so maybe. The last thing I wanted was for Luke to hate me. I needed to make it clear that I was looking out for his best interest.

"Have you talked to Maya this week?" Nico asked, his voice low.

"No," I admitted. "Not since Monday night. She hasn't been coming to practice early this week. She just pulls up as practice is ending and then waits for Luke to come out, then she pulls up and he gets in and they leave."

Nico huffed a laugh that ended into a coughing fit.

"That's it," Jason snapped, standing up. "I'm taking you to the ER."

Nico didn't move, not even to crack an eye open. "Fuck off." He grumbled.

Jason shook his head and ran his fingers through his spikey blond hair, making the bedhead style even more messy. It was an usual move for the usual stone-faced man. "We need to get a doctor on payroll."

"Too bad we couldn't go to our nurse," Nico shot back.

I shook my head. We probably could have called Maya to look over Nico tonight, if I wasn't worried that I already burned that bridge with her.

"I'm fine. Leo sent over a doctor before you guys picked me up. He said I'm just heavily bruised, but I'll live." Nico said.

That was news to me. "Just failed to mention that tidbit when we carried your ass in here?" I asked.

"No need. You were already brooding over your own bullshit. Mine's being taken care of. I'll go to the family dinner Sunday night and apologize in front of everyone. Leo will sit down with me after."

"You *hope* he will sit down with you after, asshole!" Jason snapped, leaning down into Nico's face. "You don't know for sure that he'll help at all. For all you know he'll make your ass wait fucking *years* for anything more."

Nico shook his head. "I made it clea—"

"You didn't even get to negotiate terms. He demanded what he expected from you to rejoin the family and that was it. Stop fucking lying to yourself that you got anything out of this deal."

I shook my head. The last twenty-four hours had been the same between the two of them. Ever since Nico woke up in the backseat of my pick-up truck and rambled on about Leo's demands, Jason had been ready to fucking fight.

It was a losing battle, but Nico was in no shape to fight back. I would have to find a task for Jason to keep him occupied or he was going to drive us all insane.

Maya

LUKE'S FIRST FOOTBALL GAME of the season dawned bright and early Saturday morning. An eight-a.m. football game on a Saturday morning should be illegal. I was still reeling from being served the legal papers the day before and didn't sleep much. I wondered if Marcos would be at the game that morning and anxiety gripped me. It was getting harder and harder to see my guys and not confess, to not break down and cry and beg them for forgiveness.

Life was just getting harder and harder to navigate.

After dropping Luke off at the school entrance, I drove over to the parking lot and took my time in the vehicle. The game didn't start for another twenty minutes, and I wasn't too worried about finding a seat in the stands; it's not like I couldn't just squeeze in anywhere being there by myself. I really didn't want to be there too early and then get trapped by one of the guys—Marcos or Nico especially.

Sitting in my car, listening the music softly, I looked around the parking lot of all the happy families laughing and joking as they headed toward the football field. Tears lined my eyes of how much I missed out on—how much I denied my son—by leaving. When we were in Chicago, we'd had that with Jenna and Brad—family outings and happy mornings—but those were hard too with how expensive everything was in the city and I was a single mother, not making anywhere close to what Jenna and Brad were making.

And there were only so many times I could handle my sister offering to pay. It just sucked.

I was ruminating over my life when my passenger door opened unexpectedly and I startled. "Probably should start locking your doors, Maya." Hillcrest's nasally voice grated on her nerves.

Turning to face him, I finally snapped. "Fuck off, already. I'm tired of playing you—"

Hillcrest's hand wrapped around my neck and he slammed my head backwards into the glass of the driver's door behind me. Choking me, he leaned into my space, despite the center console between us. "Ah, ah, ah," he tsked, squeezing my neck tighter. "You've been a bad, bad girl."

I gulped—or tried too—as I stared at him in fright.

"I think you've forgotten what's at stake here," he continued.

I tried to shake my head vehemently. "I haven't! I haven't said any—"

"Stop lying!" he shouted in my face. "I saw you Monday night, making out with Candella at the end of your driveway. And you spent the night at Gage's on Saturday. I'm done playing around, Maya. Now you get to deal with the consequences of your actions." The let go of my throat abruptly and pulled away.

I'm left gasping against the door as Hillcrest climbed out of my car. Fear gripping my heart as the reality of what just happened settled on me. *I'm done playing around, Maya. Now you get to deal with the consequences of your actions.*

Fuck.

My heart pounded in my chest. My ears rang and my breathing started coming out in short, fast puffs. Oh fuck.

A knock on the window behind me had me whipping around in fright, yelling out. Slade's bright smiled dimmed as she saw the utter terror in my eyes. "Maya?" she called through the closed car door. Slade opened the door and crouched down beside me, her hands cupping my face gently. "Maya, what's going on?"

I gasped for breath, clinging to Slade's wrists. "I fucked up. Dax saw me kiss Marcos Monday night. He was just here, in the car. He said he was done playing around and I would have to deal with the consequences."

"Fuck. Maya you have to tell them. Right now."

"I can't, I can't," I shook my head vehemently.

"If you don't, I will!"

"No, no, no! Please, Slade. Please don't," I begged her frantically. I held Slade's wrists tighter; I needed her to listen. Slade couldn't say anything.

"Ok, ok," Slade agreed, soothing me. "Shh, it's ok. I won't say anything."

"Promise me!" I said, my eyes flaring wide as I stared at Slade. "Promise me!"

"I promise, I promise," Slade said, nodding. "Maya, I promise you."

I looked around the parking lot frantically. "He has people watching me always. He always knows what I'm doing, who I'm with. He will know if you say something."

Slade stiffened, but nodded. "Ok. I promise. I won't tell anyone."

I took a deep breath and slowly let go of Slade's wrists. "What are you doing here?" I asked, after moment.

Slade chuckled softly and shook her head. "I thought I'd come see Luke's first game. Come support you, too. I didn't want you sitting alone for his game—in case things were weird with the guys."

I laughed and then continued to laugh hysterically, until I was almost sobbing in front of Slade.

"Fuck, Maya." Slade sighed.

"I know, I know. I'm a fucking mess." I shook my head. Hastily wiping my eyes, I tried to calm my breathing. "Fucking hell." I let out a deep breath. "Girl, I have so much to tell you."

Slade chuckled lightly. "I bet." Standing up, Slade stepped away from the car, giving me the space to get out of the vehicle.

I composed myself, checking my make up in the rearview mirror and cleaning up my eyeliner. Slapping my sunglasses over my puffy eyes, I grabbed my ice coffee and keys, before I climbed out of the car and closed the door. "Fucking hell," I said, glancing around the busy parking.

"Yeah, game's in five minutes. We gotta roll," Slade said, glancing at the time on her phone.

"Shit. Let's go."

Maya

The game turned out to be not that bad. Slade and I found a spot on the opposite end of the bleachers than where Marcos, Jason, and Nico were sitting. I managed to ignore them for most of the game, cheering on Luke with all my might. I tried not to show that anything was amiss with me, which should have been easy after all the practice I'd had lately, but it was still torture.

Slade was fantastic though. After telling her all about the paternity test subpoena I had been served the day before, Slade glared over at Marcos as much as possible throughout the game. She had kept up a constant stream of chatter too, keeping my brain off of everything going on. She even managed to make me laugh a couple times and cheered like a crazy person when Luke scored a touchdown.

She had been a complete life saver.

A couple of the moms had walked over to me after the game, introducing themselves as mothers of other players—names of boys I recognized because Luke talked about them. It was nice to meet other moms, especially in the area.

After we exchanged phone numbers, the women left, leaving Slade and I alone to wait for Luke. He was still on the field with his team, huddled around the coach. While the kids all listened and ate a snack, I thanked Slade for coming. "Seriously girl, I don't know if I could have made it through this without you."

Slade wrapped an arm around me and hugged me close. "After what you said about everything lately, I don't know how you're still standing."

I wrapped an arm around Slade's waist and sighed. "I just have to keep moving forward."

The huddle on the field broke apart and Luke came running off the field. He stopped halfway to the stands, looking back and forth between Marcos and I at either end of the bleachers, wondering who he should go to first.

I smiled sadly and waved him toward his dad. "Go on!" I plastered a smile on my face, so he'd know I didn't mind—even if my heart was breaking.

I wished so badly that things were different, that Luke didn't have to choose.

Even though I told him it was ok, he still bounded over to me and Slade. "Slade!" he shouted, wrapped himself around her in a giant hug.

Slade laughed and hugged him back. "Hey Luke, buddy! Great game!"

"Thanks, Slade!"

"Nice touchdown, honey! That was awesome!" I said when Luke finally threw himself into my arms.

"Thanks Mom." Luke grinned brightly and hugged me tighter before he let me go. "I'm gonna go say hi to dad and the guys."

"Go head! I'll be here."

"He's so grown up, it's amazing to me," Slade said, sitting back down on the bench while Luke walked over to Marcos and the guys.

I sat down as well. "Yeah," she said softly.

"How does he feel about all of this?" Slade asked, looking over at me.

"He wishes things were different. He hasn't asked me out right why I'm not with Marcos, not anything more than when he first asked last year and I told him that we just didn't work out, but I know it's coming. I can feel him needing to know more."

"Yeah, it's only a matter of time, especially when he has to submit to a cheek swab." Slade sighed.

"Thank you for today," I murmured, looking down at my hands. I twisted my fingers around a frayed edge of my cutoff jeans.

"No worries. I had fun. Want me to kick Marcos's ass for you?"

I chuckled softly. "Nah... maybe Jason's though."

"Consider it done."

My phone rang and I picked it up from the bench beside me and sighed when I saw my mother's phone number. "Hey mom," I answered the phone.

"Maya!" My mother screamed on the phone, frantic. "Maya, your father! He's gone!"

I gasped loudly; fear immediately griped my heart as it sunk into my stomach. "What?" I asked in disbelief.

"You need to come home! Please!"

"Yeah, mom. I'm on my way." I hung up the phone and snapped into action. "My dad's gone."

"Shit," Slade swore.

"Yeah. I gotta go." My eyes snapped over to where Luke was laughing with his dad and Jason and Nico. Nico's eyes were on me, watching intently as I slowly stood up.

I steeled my spine as I descended the bleachers and walked over to Luke. Marcos looked up as I walked over and I watched the smile slide right off his face as he met my gaze. "Can I talk to you a minute?" I asked.

He nodded once.

I walked a few steps away from everyone and turned to Marcos. "Can you watch him today? Something just came up."

Marcos's eyes narrowed on me. "It's not my weekend."

Disbelief and astonishment flashed across my face before I schooled myself. "Never mind." I shook my head and turned away.

"Wait," Marcos said. "He can hang with me today."

I walked over to Luke like I didn't hear Marcos, shutting him out. "Luke, buddy," I said, getting his attention. "I've gotta go, your grandma needs me. Your dad said you can hang with him today. There are extra clothes in your bag, and your phone. I will call you later on, ok?"

Luke grinned brightly and nodded. "Of course! Thanks mom!" He wrapped me in a bear hug.

I hugged him back and pressed a kiss to his forehead before I turned and walked away, not looking at either of the men standing with my son.

Slade caught up to me quickly. "Come on, I'll drive you."

I shook my head. "I need my car. I'm ok to drive. Just follow me." I glanced at her.

"Of course."

Maya

My parents' house was already crawling with emergency responders when I drove up. I wasn't able to pull in the driveway due to all the vehicles, so I parked as close as I could and ran the rest of the way to the house.

"Mom?" I called out, as I ripped open the front door.

My mother was standing in the living room, talking to uniformed officer, with the hospice nurse, Clarice, was standing beside her. "What happened?" I asked, interrupting the conversation.

Elaine turned to me, teary eyed, and reached for me. "He just stopped breathing. I went to start breakfast and was gone maybe ten minutes. No longer than we'd usually leave him and he stopped breathing in that time."

I hugged my mother tightly. "It's ok, it's ok." I murmured soothingly to her, rubbing her back as tears fell down her face.

Clarice met my eye over my mother's shoulder. "This was always going to happen. We can't predict these things." She spoke calmly and soothingly.

I nodded and closed my eyes, hugging my mother as the tears poured down my own face. I knew that, had known that, but still it felt too soon. I looked over at the police officer who was pocketing his notepad. "Everything ok?" I asked.

He nodded, "Yes, it's routine that we come when there's a death involved, even with hospice. After the speaking with the nurse, I've got everything I need. I am very sorry for your loss." The officer headed toward the door and walked out of the house.

I nodded once. "Thank you." I turned to look down the hall toward her parents' bedroom as I pulled away from my mother. Slade shifted in the living room and I sought her out. "Slade, shit." I sighed. "You don't have to stay. Thank you for following me. I appreciate it."

"No, no." Slade shook her head. "You do whatever you need to. I'll be here if you need anything." She picked up my book from the couch and held it up. "I'll be good."

I nodded absently and turned back to the hallway, mustering up the courage to walk that way.

"His body is still there. You can say good-bye if you'd like. It'll be a while yet before the coroner will be here to pick up his body," Clarice said gently.

I walked slowly toward my parents' bedroom, wondering what I might find. The first thing I noticed was the window was open. *Why was the window open?*

My father looked peaceful though, so I supposed that was a plus. His once handsome face was lined with wrinkles and gray in pallor. Other than that, he looked peaceful, like he had just fallen asleep. I took the chair next to his bed and slid my hand into his. His skin was cool and his fingers stiff as rigor mortis was setting in already.

I bowed my head over his hand and let the sobs take me. I knew this moment was coming, but it still wasn't easy.

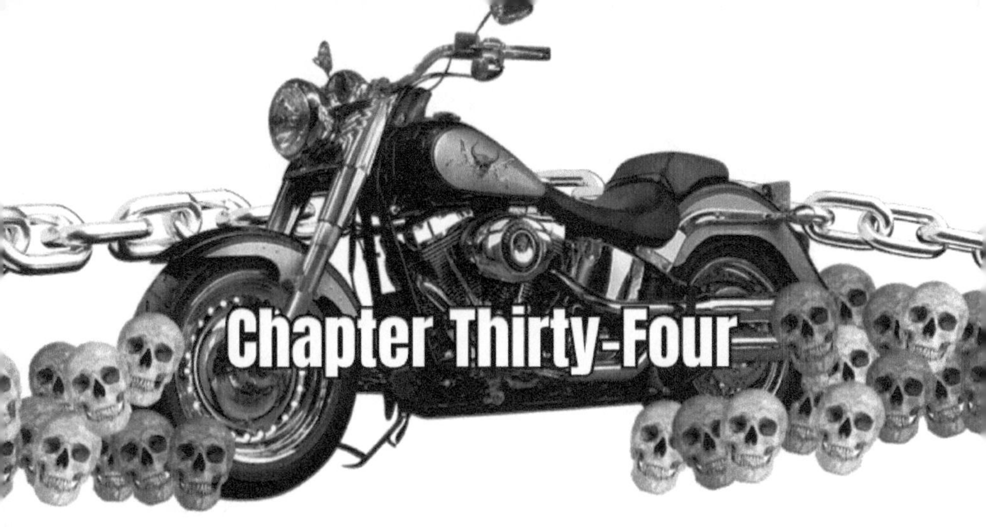

Chapter Thirty-Four

Marcos

I FROWNED AS I read Maya's text.

Hey, sorry to run after the game. My mom had called. My dad passed away.

"Is that Maya?" Nico asked.

The three of us had headed back to my small apartment with Luke after the game. We had stopped at the store to pick him up some clothes to keep at my place, and then Luke hit the shower right when we got back.

"Yeah," I said, absently. I looked up to see where Luke was, but him and Jason were in the kitchen cooking lunch. I handed Nico my phone, so I didn't have to speak the words.

"Shit," Nico said, reading her text.

"Yeah."

Maya sent another text a moment later.

Maya:

Can you bring Luke home after dinner?

I had half a mind to keep Luke for the weekend, despite it not being my weekend. We hadn't established any kind of custody schedule—Maya had been letting me hang out with Luke whenever I wanted—I didn't feel right about it.

Maya was specifically asking for Luke. If she needed space, she would say that, right?

I didn't know what to think anymore. I almost regretted the court order paternity test; it was making me question things.

"Fuck, dude." Nico sighed and gingerly sat back on the couch, his body still healing from his beat down Thursday. "You should do as she asks. Give her whatever she wants, bro. Her dad just died. Don't be a dick to her."

I nodded absentmindedly. "Yeah."

Maya

Later that night, once Luke was home and tucked into bed, I sat in the living room with my mother. The TV was on with the volume down low, but neither one of us paid much attention to it—both seemingly lost in our own thoughts.

"Your father was murdered," Elaine said softly.

My head shot up and whipped over to look at her. "What?"

Elaine nodded. "It was Hillcrest. I saw him jump out the window when I came back to the room with lunch. He turned and looked right at me. He told me to keep my damn mouth shut or he would shut it."

My mouth dropped open in shock. My heart lurched in my throat. "Mom!"

"I didn't tell the police. I know what it means, Maya." Elaine spoke so calmly while I was struggling to comprehend the situation. "You need to tell those boys, so they can deal with him."

Again, my mouth dropped open. That was the last thing I expected out of my mother's mouth. My mother had always hated Marcos, Jason, and Nico, and everything they represented with the club. "Why are you so calm about this?" I finally asked.

Elaine looked down and toyed with the nail polish on her fingers, chipping at it. It was the only sign of distress she allowed. Sighing heavily, she looked up at met my gaze. "We both know your father wasn't well. We've been slowly watching him die this whole time and he was barely holding on. Hillcrest suffocated him with a pillow. He made it quick. It was for the best."

"What?"

Elaine nodded. "The pillow was still over your father's face when I walked in there. Harry must have struggled a bit, because blankets were strewn on the floor too, like he flailed around. I set everything to rights again before I called hospice and the coroner."

I sat there dumbfounded as I listened to my mother calmly explain how she covered up a murder. For Dax fucking Hillcrest.

"It's almost a blessing. Harry was miserable. This way he went quickly."

I shook my head as a hysterical laugh bubbled out of me and quickly turned into sobs. Fucking hell. My life was a mess.

The sobs wracked my body for several minutes. My mother got up and sat down next to me on the couch, her own tears sliding down her face as she held my hand tightly. I wished like hell Jenna was there, she'd know what to do or say, but she couldn't get off work until tomorrow. Thankfully she'd have the week off to come down and help plan our father's funeral.

Instead, I sobbed, letting out all of my pent-up emotions and stress and heartbreak from the last six months and clung to my mother's hand. When I finally started to calm down, my mother handed me a tissue to blow my nose, and stood up and walked back over to the recliner. I wasn't even surprised. "What are we supposed to do now?" I asked, half in a daze.

"You need to tell your boys." My mother said it so mat-ter-of-factly that all I could do was nod my head.

Yeah, I need to tell them, I agreed mentally.

Chapter Thirty-Five

Nico

I STOOD OUTSIDE LEONARDO'S mother's home—his family home—dressed in a suit and tie that I tugged at awkwardly. The suit was new, something I had gone into Mourningside for that morning to pick up. It had been years since I had to wear the get up and I had bulked up since then. Nothing in my closet at my mother's had still fit from when I was a scrawny little teen.

I had made a point to go to Ralph Lauren for something off the rack. I didn't have time for some tailored bullshit like the Seratelli's always wore. Leo wouldn't be caught dead in anything off the rack. He was highly ostentatious.

Struggling with feelings of inadequacies, I stared up at the imposing marble staircase outside the ridiculous mansion that boasted a cliché circular drive with a fountain in the middle of it. The whole place was so ridiculous, as were half the people inside.

The dining room was sure to be packed with fake women, dressed to the nine's in layers of silk or tulle or some other bullshit fabric I couldn't give two shits about. They would laugh their fake airy laughs and throw their heads back and noses up in the air like it was the most hilarious thing in the world...and I would have to sit through it all, with a smile on my face and bear through it.

The thought alone made me miserable.

A car pulled up behind me and I glanced over my shoulder to see Leo climbing out of the back of a blacked-out Escalade. Talk about your cliches. "Nice shiner," Leo commented.

I smirked back. "Can't all look this beautiful."

Leo rolled his eyes. When he stepped closer, I waited warily. "I'm glad you're doing this." He rested a hand gently on my shoulder. "I've missed you."

I was slightly dumbfounded as I stared at my cousin. "Uh—"

"Apologize to the family at dinner, then after, we'll talk about your girl." Leo squeezed my shoulder before he dropped his hand and walked up the marble stairs. "Come on, no one makes my mother wait." Leo called over his shoulder, shooting me a smirk.

That got my ass in gear. I bounded up the steps after Leo, knowing just how hot-headed Lita Seratelli could be if anyone missed her cooking—not that she didn't have a team of chefs in the kitchen helping her, but no one would dare to tell her otherwise.

Inside the house was just as ostentatious as the outside, or even more so, given all the intricate woodworking details and gaudy gold accents covering everything. I could admit the wood was cool, the gold everything on the other hand was overly flashy for no reason. In short, it was stupid.

I followed Leo into the parlor where guests—family members—mingled. Leo was stopped almost immediately by a group of ladies, but I carried on to the full bar in the corner of the room where a bartender was serving drinks. I ordered a whisky neat, going for Kara's favorite Macallan, not feeling a damn bit wrong for drinking Leo's top shelf liquor.

While I waited for my drink, I scanned the parlor area, searching for my mother, even though I knew she'd either be in the kitchen helping Lita, or in the living room chatting with one of the girls. She didn't like that Leo allowed the gentlemen to smoke in the parlor. She said it was bad for her skin and lungs, despite Augustino Sr. shelling out big money to install exhaust fans and ozone filters.

I knew I should find her before dinner so we could sit near each other at the ridiculously long table, but I was in no rush to hear her fuss over my very black eye. Leo had been precise in his two hits to my face—aiming for my eye and jaw—to leave a very dark bruise.

I thanked the bartender as he set my drink on a napkin before me. Turning to survey the room, I sipped on my whisky and nodded occasionally at people as they met my gaze. No one had dared to come over to me and I knew they wouldn't until Leonardo gave the ok that I was welcomed back into the family.

When it was finally time to be seated, a staff member announced dinner and the guests all made their way into the dining room. I met my mother at the door from the living room and gave her my elbow as I led her over to the table—or rather she led me to where she'd like to sit—in the middle, closer toward the head of the table where Leonardo stood, facing us all.

I ended up seated right next to my cousin Tino. The five Seratelli brothers were seated closest to Leonardo, with Fredrico Accardi seated across from me. Freddy glared at me, but I ignore him, taking in all the faces along the very long table.

Everyone waited for Leonardo to motion to us to sit, before we actually took our chairs. Then it was a flurry of activity as everyone sat down and kitchen staff began bringing out plates. Everyone was served a plate full of food by the staff, while platters were set in the center of the table for people to serve themselves seconds as we finished our plates.

Nothing had changed. Not one damn thing.

I didn't know whether or not to laugh or cry at how familiar it all was. I didn't know why I expected change. Just because my Uncle Augustino was gone, didn't mean the family would change how things have been for decades. Leonardo was more like his father than he realized.

Conversations around the table ranged from different movies to plays that people had seen that week, to different remodeling project updates people were going through. One of my aunts was having a knee replacement the following week, so a couple of the women were fussing over her.

One thing that I noticed about the Seratelli men was that none of the younger generation—my generation—had women. They were all single.

I didn't know why it stood out, but it had. Leo was my age, just having turned forty, so it was a little unusual for someone in his position to not have an heir yet. He'd been head of the family for ten years now. I would have thought that securing an heir would have been a priority for him.

I glanced around the table looking for Alessia—Leo's youngest sister—but couldn't find her. "Where's Alessia?" I asked my mother, keeping my voice low.

"She's away at college," Leo replied, having heard me.

I turned to my cousin, wondering if I was permitted to ask more. It had been so long since I was in a social setting regarding the family, I didn't know how Leo acted during dinner, or where I even stood with the man. He'd been agreeable before dinner when we'd been one on one, but surrounded by the entire family, Leo might act different.

"She's studying to become a nurse practitioner. She's up north at the University of Chicago, downtown," Leo elaborated.

My eyebrows rose as I nodded. "Good for her."

Leo smiled wryly. "As she keeps telling me."

His brothers laughed around us and I felt like I was missing the joke.

"Alessia is...strong-willed, you could say," Leo said, choosing his words wisely. His eyes crinkled in the corners as he smiled. His sister was twenty years younger than us and sounded like she was coming into her own.

I chuckled. "Well, good for her."

Leo nodded and looked around the table at all the people gathered. "Ready?" Leo asked me.

I shook my head *no*, but wiped my mouth anyways.

Leo stood up, making a formidable sight at the head of the table, and everyone fell silent as conversations tapered off. "Thank you everyone for coming. Sunday family dinners have always been important to our family, and I love that all of you make it a priority as well. Though we've all had our differences over the years, we've always tried to come together and put family first. While individual needs can at times feel more important, family should always be included in our priorities. That being said, I want to welcome Nicolia back to the family." Leo motioned toward me.

As one, everyone at the table turned to me. I swallowed and slowly stood. Not one to be nervous, I still felt on edge. My mother was here. I didn't want to disappoint her further than I already had in the last ten years.

"Hey everyone," I greeted, looking around the table as Leo sat down. "I know I've been gone for some time now, and I only have myself to blame for that. While I might have always marched to the beat of my own drum, and maybe I didn't always prioritize this family, I always loved this family. Ten years ago, I was in a bad place and I found myself in some trouble. Uncle Augustino and I may have never seen eye to eye, but I always respected him. When he told me he couldn't help me, I was hurt. I had just lost the love of my life, and in my pain, I lashed out at Uncle Augustino." I paused, looking down at the table, gathering my words. "It wasn't my finest moment." I paused again and took a sip of my whisky. "I've recently come to learn just how severely my actions back then had truly impacted those in my life, my family included.

"I've come to dinner tonight to apologize to our family and to beg your forgiveness," I glanced at Leonardo as I spoke this part. "I am deeply sorry for the hurt and disrespect that I have caused you, your brothers," I glanced to my other cousin's, "your mother, and to the rest of this family, by not going to Uncle Augustino's funeral. I apologize for not being someone this family can count on. If you'll agree to me returning, I'd like to prove that I can be relied upon by this family."

The room was silent as I finished, all eyes on Leonardo as he stood again. Leo smiled broadly and rounded the table. "Apology accepted. Glad to have you back, cousin," Leo said formally.

Relief swept through me so hard that my damn knees felt weak. Cheers and clapping erupted around the table as Leo clapped me on the shoulder and pulled me into a full hug, no bro slapping half hugs that I did with my brothers. Leonardo hugged me tightly and I had to hide my wince as Leo purposely crushed my ribs. "Welcome back."

I covered my wince with a cough and forced a smile on my lips. "Thanks, cousin." Purposely using the term that Leo had agreed upon, after rebuking me not that along ago.

"We'll talk after dinner." Leo nodded his head as he patted my shoulder one more time, before stepping away to leave room for his brothers to embrace me, much the same way Leonardo had, hard squeeze and all.

Nico

By the time dinner was finished, I was aching and exhausted. I wanted nothing more than to go home and lay down, but I needed to get through the after-dinner drinks in Leonardo's study to discuss the family helping Kara and then Maya. We needed to take care of Vince Carmichael in prison to get him to agree to the plea deal for Kara. Kara could finally inherit her father's law firm, and we could finally kill Dax fucking Hillcrest for being a douche. Hopefully then Maya would admit that he'd been harassing her all this time.

I didn't know for sure, but I had a hunch that was why Maya was so adamant to stay away from us. If Luke's explanation of her being terrified of flowers was anything to go by. I would do whatever I had to for the family—and I'd already done two of Leonardo's three requests—to ensure Maya would be safe.

Once the plates were cleared, Leo rose and so did his brothers. I followed them through the house to Leonardo's—Uncle Augustino's—study in the back of the house. The old school mahogany paneled office dripped of old money. Italian leather couches sat in front of a massive fireplace, bookcases lined the walls full of likely first editions of the classic literature, most of which was probably never read by one in this house.

It was a very showy and opulent room, made to intimidate those who visited it. I had spent several nights in this office, biting my tongue as my uncle raged at me over my short comings to the family. Choosing to 'hang out with delinquents in the ghetto of Creekton when he was raised in Crestwood was a dishonor to the family'. Then later when I joined the Devil's Psychos, I had 'brought dishonor to my mother for not following the family business'.

To say I did not have found memories of this study was an understatement. I could only hope that Leonardo wouldn't force me to come back here too often.

Taking a seat at a couch by the fireplace, I took the offered cigar from my cousin Tino and nodded in thanks.

"Alright cousin," Leo started, sitting at an armchair facing the couches and fire, like he was holding court. "Tell us about your problem."

I took a deep breath and began. I explained how Kara's father had embezzled money from his own firm and pinned the crime on Mac Taylor, president of the Ravager Knights MC. I explained how through Kara's involvement, she had her father arrested and currently awaiting trial. "Marcos Candella's sister Kara, needs help convincing her father to accept a plea deal. In order to inherent the firm, she needs him to either plead guilty, or be found guilty in trial."

"So why not just wait for the guilty verdict? It sounds like she has a solid case," Leo asked.

I sighed. "We can't wait that long. The trial and sentencing could take months. We need this to happen ASAP. Kara is under the impression that if she can get her father to change his mind, then she can get him sentenced by end of this week."

Leo frowned and sucked on his cigar; his eyebrows furrowed together as he thought. "How does this effect you?"

I took a deep breath and continued, feeling the weighing gaze of all my cousins in the room. "Kara was kidnapped by Las Serpientes last year."

The room erupted into growled curses and raised voices.

Leo glared hard and raised a hand silencing everyone. "The snakes?"

I nodded. "Yeah. Because of their involvement with my president Buckley, Mac Taylor was killed, and Kara was kidnapped while she was pregnant."

Again, the room erupted into angry voices. This time, Leo let them spit their angry vitriol. There was one thing the Seratelli men all hated more than anything and that was abuse against women. The second thing they hated more than anything? That would be Las Serpientes.

I took a sip of my whisky as the room slowly quieted. "Kara has refused to let anyone kill Dax Hillcrest. She believes—and we agree—that if we kill him now, his guys in prison will retaliate against her father in prison before he can be sentenced. She needs control of the firm, before that happens, or everything she's worked for all these years goes down the drain."

Leo frowns. He takes a sip of his own whisky and stares contemplatively into the fire. "And the Knights can't help with that?"

The moment I've been waiting for, "No. Apparently there's tensions with the Bratva, because of the coke deal."

A hiss sounded from someone in the room, and I braced myself for Leo's impending wrath.

Leo shook his head slowly. "I should have known there would be more."

"Johnny Taylor said you refused a sit down, so his hands are tied with the Bratva. He can't get anyone inside to sway Carmichael, so Kara can't get the verdict she needs. Without that verdict, I can't kill Hillcrest." I pressed on quickly before Leo could stop me. "My girl, Maya. She came back. She's being threatened by Hillcrest. He's stalking her."

"So fucking kill him," Leo snapped, glaring at me.

"I would, if I could. Kara's like a little sister to me. She made me vow—all of us vow—that we wouldn't kill him until the shit with her dad was finished. As she was the one that had been kidnapped by the piece of shit, we told her yes. That was *before* I found out the love of my life was being threatened by him. It's why Maya left me in the first place ten years ago."

I wasn't sure if it was true or not, but all evidence that I had pointed that way. Leo didn't need to know that Maya hadn't confirmed any of it yet. We needed Leo to agree to have someone inside put pressure on Vince to accept the plea deal.

Leo stared at me, assessing me, as if seeing me clearly for the first time.

I could see his wheels turning, knowing Leo was wondering where my true loyalties lied. That was the thing, Leo would always put *his* family first.

"Alright," he agreed.

There was a shifting around the room as Leo's brothers either disagreed or agreed, they kept their mouths shut at least. I was grateful for that. "Thank you."

Leo shook his head slowly. "I will have someone reach out to our guys in the prison, but you have a list to work through. Twenty kills, Nicolai." Leo's voice was deep and authoritative; it held no room for disagreement. "I don't care if you enlist help from your biker buddies, but each name on the list must be killed. I want proof."

I swallowed thickly. I nodded slowly. "Do they have to be killed before you'll reach out to your guys?"

Leo's eyes narrowed. "Better act quickly."

Chapter Thirty-Six

Marcos

I WALKED AROUND THE empty house in bit of a haze of disbelief. Everything was almost exactly the same as it had been when we moved out ten years ago, minus some odd color choices, but still almost the same.

I couldn't believe we were able to get this house.

I couldn't believe I owned a house.

The three of us had bought a home together.

Our home.

The last place we had all been together and truly happy.

I had been the first to leave—after Maya. I couldn't bear the idea of being in the house without her here. Nico had been the last of the three of us to leave, holding on hope that she would return.

Now here we all were, moving back in, without Maya. Only this time, even I was slightly hopeful that Maya might return, though I'd never admit that out loud. I didn't want to get my hopes up. I had only agreed to buying a house because I needed to for Luke, because if things went sideways, I would need a home for him.

Thankfully, Jason had handled everything we needed regarding the lawyer, the realtor, and the loan officer, because I hadn't had a clue. Jason had scheduled everything and moved money around to make all of this work. All I had to do was show up to closing and sign my name.

Walking around the house now that it was officially ours felt completely surreal.

"Do you have specific paint colors you want?" Jason asked as I walked into the kitchen. He was standing at the counter with a legal pad in front of him, a list already in process.

"Nah." I shook my head. "Neutral colors, earth tones maybe? I don't fucking know, just get rid of this shit." I twirled my finger around, pointing to the room at large.

Jason snorted a laugh and nodded. "Yep. I'm gonna hire someone to paint the whole house in one go, the kitchen cabinets included. I figure the cabinets are in good shape, we can upgrade the counters to granite."

"Sounds good," I agreed.

Nico came in from the back door, a smile on his face. "Garage looks the same."

"What else do we want to be done before move in?" Jason asked. "I'm assuming we want in as soon as possible?"

"Yeah," I said. "Throw the bathroom cabinets in for the painter and counters. The bathrooms are relatively decent; paint and new counters will help a lot."

Jason made a note on his list. "Which room are you giving Luke?"

"I'm not sure."

"Can we leave the master bedroom open?" Nico asked.

Jason tensed immediately and I paused. "Why?"

"Please. Just for a while. Can we just move back in like how it was before? We all had our own rooms upstairs and Maya's was the master. Can we just leave it empty for now?" Nico said tentatively.

I sighed and rubbed a hand over my head. "Bro."

"Please, just for a while," Nico pleaded. He looked so damn earnest, that I immediately wanted to cave.

I turned to Jason who was still tense. "I don't see the harm."

Jason shook his head. "I don't see the point."

"Please?"

"Where would Luke sleep?" Jason asked.

"He can have my old room. I'll take the bedroom down here that used to be Kara's," Nico said.

I nodded thoughtfully. Nico was thinking that Maya would move back in. I could see the hope in Nico's eyes. I didn't want to be the one to crush that. "I'm fine with it."

"Fine," Jason said. He shook his head slightly. "What color do you want his room?"

"I'll ask him when I tell him about the house. I want him to have a say," Marcos explained.

"And when do you plan on telling him?" Jason asked.

"Tomorrow at the funeral."

The three of us grew silent while we thought about tomorrow's plans. Maya had never said anything regarding being served the papers for paternity. Granted, she had a lot going on right now, but it would be the first time we've seen her since Saturday—at least closer than we had when she picked up Luke from football practice without getting out of the car.

Her father's funeral was going to be hard on her. I had thought about reaching out to her several times regarding everything, but it hadn't felt right. I'd seen her when I brought Luke home, but we hadn't really spoken much. I did give her my condolences about her father, but that had been about it.

Maya had kept up a stone-cold wall that even Jason couldn't beat.

"Do we say anything tomorrow to Maya?" Nico asked.

I shook my head. "Nah, she'll probably be busy. We'll talk to Luke about it. I'm sure he'll tell his mom at some point. Otherwise, I'll tell her when I have him for the weekend again."

Jason hummed noncommittedly while Nico nodded absently.

I sighed. We finally had the house of our dreams, but it was obvious it would be missing the key person that would make it a home.

Chapter Thirty-Seven

Maya

T HE FUNERAL FOR MY father took place on Friday. A single-day Celebration of Life, that included a viewing at the church, followed by Mass, then a progression to the burial site. From there we headed back to my parents' house for a potluck repast that everyone was invited to.

It was a lot. I was both emotionally and physically drained. Jenna had been a godsend, organizing everything and running around like a headless chicken. It helped that she was a little more detached from the situation, a little more pragmatic about it. She was still sad, but as a doctor, she understood that her father had only been living on borrowed time since his accident.

While I had known that as well, it was harder for me after being here taking care of him this whole time, and knowing in the end, my father had been murdered. I didn't have the heart to tell her about Hillcrest. Jenna already knew that he'd been harassing me; it would only add fuel to the fire and Jenna would demand I tell the guys. Or she would tell them herself, like my mother was promising to do.

My nerves were shot, having to play hostess and conversate with a million people I hadn't seen in years was tiresome. Though I had about died when Karma and Arturo Ventura showed up, along with Stephanie Stonewall, and Hunter Maxwell—my ex from college—and his roommate Travis Miles. It had been a blast from the past that had immediately reduced me to tears over the friendships and life that I had lost when I had to move away.

No one had understood why I had left Marcos, Jason, and Nico. I hadn't been able to tell any of them anything. And then my abrupt move to Chicago had put a strain on my friendships that were already drifting apart after college. Only Slade had stuck around, mostly because Slade had gotten the truth out of me one night in Chicago after a long grueling tattoo session—where I had broken down in tears and confessed everything.

Seeing everyone again today was heartbreaking—the whole damn day was heartbreaking. Even Marcos, Nico, and Jason showed up, which I really hadn't expected. But I was glad, because they had kept Luke company.

The repast at the house was finally winding down, and my mother and I were in the kitchen cleaning things up, but it was clear my mother was in a tizzy about something. "What's going on?" I narrowed my eyes on her, trying to keep my voice down from anyone in earshot.

"I'll talk to you in the garage." Elaine walked away before I could respond.

I bit back a snarky comment as I followed her into the garage. The entrance was off the hallway that led to my parents' bedroom. I closed the door behind me as I walked outside. The overhead garage door was wide open on the beautiful summer afternoon, and I was immediately sweating as I stood before my mother, wondering what the hell was on her mind that couldn't wait until everyone was gone.

"You need to tell them," Elaine started immediately, turning to look at me with anger in her gaze.

I sighed deeply. "No, I don't. It's fine, everything is fine."

"No, it's not *fine*," Elaine snapped. "Your father is dead because it is not *fine*! You need to tell Marcos and those boys!"

"I can't tell them! Hillcrest already killed dad!" I yelled at my mother, losing my cool. Emotions warred inside me; anger, fear, anxiety and grief all swirled within me, threatening to pour out. This was not the time for this conversation, not when we had a house full of guests. "He's already threatened Luke's life if I say anything! He already thinks I'm too close to them! He said he would kill them next." A sob tore out of me. My shoulders hunching in as I sobbed.

"You tell those boys, tell Marcos, or I will," Elaine said. She spoke so calmly, her eyes drifting over my face and then past me to the inside garage door behind me.

"Tell us what?" Marcos's deep voice rang out from behind me, sending a shiver down my spine.

A startled 'eep' escaped me as I glanced over my shoulder to face not only Marcos, Nico, and Jason, but also Kara. The guys looked pissed off and had clearly heard everything, while Kara looked at me concerned.

Kara pushed past the boys and walked over to me, immediately wrapping her arms around me. "Did we hear you right? Dax Hillcrest killed your father?" Kara's voice was gentle and soothing as she pulled me into her.

"Yes," Elaine spoke up. "I walked in on him leaving, the pillow was still over Harry's face and Dax was climbing out the window. He looked back and I saw his face clear as day. He said if I said anything to the three of you, I'd be next."

"Motherfucker," Marcos swore, stalking toward me. "Why the fuck haven't you come to me before?" he growled.

I flinched away from him.

"Back off, Marcos!" Kara snapped, holding me tighter.

Marcos didn't budge; he still loomed over me.

I lifted my chin and channeled my rage. "He threatened Luke!" I shouted at him. "He said if I told you guys, he would kill Luke!"

"And why the fuck would he even care about Luke? What's he got over you? Why does he even care about you?" Jason's deep voice cut me to the bone.

"I saw something I shouldn't have. Back then," I admitted, my breathing labored.

Nico

Finally, we were getting somewhere! I thought as Maya gasped for breath. I pushed away from the doorway and walked over to her and Kara. Marcos hovered over them, but I didn't care, I pulled Maya and Kara into my arms, holding them both against my chest as a way to gather Maya to me, without ticking off Kara. "Little Dreamer, what did you see?" I asked softly.

Maya buried her face in my chest as one of her arms wrapped around me tightly. "I saw him kill someone. Ten years ago, I was at the gas station one night after working late. I was getting gas when Hillcrest came flying in, following this BMW. They both got out of the car, Hillcrest and this older white man—I later found out he was the mayor—but Dax fired several rounds into his chest, killing him. Dax saw me watching them and got in my face, he grabbed my work badge and said he now knew who I was and where I worked, and if I said anything, he would kill me too." Maya took a shuddering breath against my chest and clung to me tighter.

"Motherfucker," Marcos swore again.

I met his gaze over the girls' heads and shook my head, trying to get Marcos to back off. "Then what happened, Little Dreamer?" I asked softly, rubbing her back. I needed to know every single detail. All of it.

"Then he figured out who you guys were, that's when the flowers started showing up—at work or in my car, taunting me. He started leaving notes that said he would kill the three of you next. Then one day it was like he got bored with it, or something happened with the club, I don't remember, but he cornered me at the grocery store and told me to leave town or he was going to kill you guys, and give me to his crew to play with."

Jason hissed over by the door, and I looked over at him to see him leaning against the wall, with his arms crossed over his chest.

Ignoring him, I pushed Maya further. "Then what happened?"

"Then I told him to f-off. I wasn't going to leave! I swear, I didn't want to! I promise you I didn't want to!" She sobbed harder against my chest.

"Shh, it's ok, it's ok," I murmured. "I know, baby girl. I know."

"But he had already shot Marcos and Jason the week before." Maya's voice caught in her throat again.

I made eye contact with Jason as he watched on quietly, while I slowly coaxed the truth from her. "Yeah, I remember how rattled you were then," I muttered.

"I was so fucking scared!" Her voice broke as another sob tore through her. "Then, the party at the clubhouse. I wasn't feeling well from when we played in the woods. I couldn't get ahold of you guys. I tried calling, but no one would pick up! I was going to stay home."

"I know, baby," I soothed. "We saw the missed calls and heard the voicemails."

"My head wasn't right after how we left things during the scene—when Marcos brought up renegotiating in the middle of the scene—it fucked with my head, I didn't know what to think. Then I woke up alone that morning, and I was still experiencing sub-drop and some after effects from the hypothermia—I wasn't in a good place."

"We never should have left you alone," I said.

"I knew I had to see you, if you weren't answering the phone. I was going to ask you take me to the hospital—I knew something was wrong."

I sucked in a breath, my eyes darting to Marcos and Jason.

Marcos face had fallen, his tan skin looking almost pale, while Jason's mouth opened, like he was going to say something, but quickly closed it.

"But then at the clubhouse... I saw Marcos smiling at her—at Trish—and I just lost it. During our fight Trish told me who she was to Dax, and passed along a message from him, the same message he delivered when he cornered me in the grocery store: leave town or he'd kill you guys and my parents."

Maya shook her head and tried to pull away from me, but I held her and Kara tightly still. "I don't know, it hit different coming from her, seeing her in the clubhouse, like nothing was safe anymore. Then you got arrested that night, Nico, and Marcos texted that Hillcrest had you framed for false charges..." She broke off shaking her head. "In my mind, I had to go. It wasn't safe anymore. Hillcrest could get to you guys at any time and he had the power to have you arrested. I couldn't be the reason you guys were killed...so I left."

"Jesus fucking hell." I let out a deep breath.

"And Luke?" Marcos's voice was gruff, but soft.

Maya pushed away from me, and I finally let her so she could turn to face Marcos directly. "I didn't know I was pregnant until I was in Chicago for a week. I swear, I didn't leave here knowing I was pregnant."

Marcos looked absolutely gutted. The emotion in his dark eyes was heart breaking. I felt it too, but right now wasn't the time to fall apart in front of Maya. We needed to be strong for her, we could fall apart later.

Maya's face was wet and blotchy, her makeup was mostly rubbed against my dress shirt, but I didn't care, she was still the most beautiful woman I'd ever seen.

"Why didn't you come back?" Jason asked, his voice so hoarse and soft I almost didn't hear him.

Maya wiped at her eyes as she started crying again. "I wanted to. I was going to, but then I heard you and Marcos were arrested and sent to State—"

"Fuck," Marcos swore.

"Everything I heard from Creekton wasn't good." Maya shrugged a shoulder. "All I knew was that Creekton or even Mourningside wasn't safe, and I had my baby to protect, so I stayed away."

Jason nodded his head once, as if the answer was enough for him.

"Maya," Kara spoke softly. "I'm so sorry. I wasn—"

"Don't." Maya shook her head as more tears fell. "You had your own shit going on. Don't do that. I can't hand—" A sob broke out of her again and I pulled her back into my arms, tucking her head under my chin.

"Thank you for telling us the truth, Maya." I pressed a kiss to the crown of her head.

"I'm sorry," Maya cried, as sobs wracked her body. "I'm so sorry!"

There was nothing we could do to change the past, but hopefully with time, we could move forward.

Chapter Thirty-Eight

Maya

I T FELT LIKE A weight had been lifted off my shoulders since I admitted the truth to Marcos, Jason, and Nico. The pressure was gone and in its place was a bit of hope. I was still scared, nothing had been resolved with Hillcrest, but now my guys knew everything and would protect me.

Marcos had already stationed guys outside of my mom's house and told me I wasn't to deviate from my regular schedule until things with Hillcrest were taken care of. Which was fine by me, because I had become a creature of habit and rarely deviated from my schedule during the week.

Things with my guys were still unresolved. I hadn't seen them since Friday when the truth came out in the garage. Since then, I spent a quiet weekend at home relaxing, while Luke played video games with friends—we had even skipped his game on Saturday morning to sleep in. I wasn't letting Luke leave the house and roam the neighborhood like I sometimes did, but he could at least hang out at home with friends while things got figured out.

Monday, I called into work, or rather I texted my boss and went back to sleep. I needed another day before I had to be an adult again. Luke would sleep in unless I woke him, so I wasn't worried about him as I drifted off to sleep.

I woke to the bed dipping as someone slid into bed beside me. "Luke?" I asked groggily.

"Nuh uh, Little Dreamer." Nico's voice was smooth in my ear as he slid one arm under my pillow and the other arm draped over my waist and pulled me into him.

I mumbled sleepily and rolled into his very naked chest. He was so warm and his skin was so smooth as I ran my hand over his ribs. "What are you doing here?"

"Saw you didn't go to work; thought I'd check on you." He pulled my leg over his and wedge his thigh between mine.

"Luke's here," I mumbled, my brain trying to catch up.

"Nah, I dropped him at camp. He was only a little bit late. Thought you would enjoy the day without responsibility. Don't worry, we've got guys at the school."

My heart fluttered in my chest. He was so thoughtful all the time. "Thank you." I nuzzled into his neck.

He held me tighter, one hand splayed across my back, while the other was tucked under my pillow. I was dressed in my usual PJs that consisted of a t-shirt and undies. My pants were on the floor where I took them off before bed, and within easy reach to grab in the morning to put back on before I left the room.

"I missed this so much," he murmured. Kissing my forehead, he let out a heavy sigh and seemed to melt into the mattress.

I murmured in agreement, my hand absently rubbing over his smooth back. He had stripped down to his boxers and his skin was so soft.

"I realized this morning that we didn't have to hide anymore."

I stiffened and my eyes opened, as if realizing the same thing. "What do you mean?"

"I mean, you are mine, Maya Henderson. You never stopped being mine, and I am claiming you again." His voice was deep growl in my ear that sent shivers down my spine.

A whimpered moan escaped my lips.

Abruptly, he flipped me and pressed my body into the mattress. "You like that idea, don't you, Little Dreamer?"

"I want that more than anything, Nico. I'm so sorr—"

He cut off my apology with a fierce kiss that stole my breath from my lungs. "No more apologies, not to me." He shook his head, his blond hair framing his face as he stared down at me with those sparkling blue eyes.

I was panting and breathless. "But we can't just go back to the way we were."

"I'm not saying that, Maya. I'm saying, I understand why you did what you did, and you don't have to apologize to me for that anymore. As for anything else, I'm— Fuck, I guess I'm asking for permission to be able to hold you and kiss you again anytime I want, to be able to fuck you again. I don't want walls between us anymore."

He looked so vulnerable as he hovered over me, his dark blue eyes darting between mine, waiting patiently.

I smiled softly and reached up and cupped the side of his face, caressing his cheek with my thumb. "I'd like that, but we need some boundaries. I can't go back to what we were, the twenty-four-seven dynamic. There's too much there that we need to discuss and unpack, and with Luke around—I just can't."

"I get it, Maya. I do. We have a lot to discuss and work out. But I missed you for so damn long, all I want is to be able to hold you and love you again."

I smiled easily and pulled him down to kiss his lips softly. "I want that too. Let's take things slow, though, keep things relatively *vanilla*." I smirked at him. "But I'm not opposed to touching and showing affection, and I'm ok with more behind closed doors."

A wide grin split his face, and he leaned down and captured my lips in a passionate kiss.

He moved languidly, despite the passionate kiss. He slowly slid my panties down my legs and then pulled off his own boxers. Hovering over me, he guided the broad head of his thick cock through my slick folds, before he notched himself at my entrance. "So beautiful," he murmured against my lips.

I gasped as he slowly slid inside me, lowering his body to fully press against every inch of mine while he slid home till the hilt. I wrapped my arms around his back and held him reverently as he as leisurely thrusted in and out of me, taking his time.

Moaning, I arched my back and clung to him. He kissed his way down my jaw to my neck, where he gently sucked and nipped at my skin. "Nico." My voice was raspy as I panted.

He grabbed my hips and angled them so he could drive in deeper. "So fucking good for me, Little Dreamer. This pussy is mine. I'm never letting you go."

"Please," I begged. My pussy fluttered around his cock, teetering on the precipice, but refusing to fall over.

"Shh, baby," Nico crooned. "Let me take care of you."

I clung to him tighter, my fingers digging into his back.

"Please, please, please," I babbled endlessly.

He captured my lips and nibbled on my bottom lip, cutting off my nonsense.

"Ahh," I groaned.

"I will take my fucking time with you," Nico growled, slowly his pace. "And you will let me."

"Nico," I gasped. I enjoyed every damn bit of his dominance. Despite my speech about keeping things *vanilla*, I knew that was next to impossible for the both of us. Nico was a pleasure dom through and through, and I was a bratty submissive to my core, there was no way we'd ever have completely vanilla sex even if we were making love.

"You'll come when I say you can, Little Dreamer." Nico snapped his hips harder, jolting me forward.

"Oh," I gasped.

He swiveled his hips and reached between us to circle his thumb over my clit.

"Please, Nico. Please."

"Come for me, Little Dreamer," Nico finally said.

I buried my face into the crook of his neck and bit down, sucking a mark into his neck as I muffled my moaning. My body shuddered against his and he picked up his pace, fucking me harder.

Nico groaned as he picked up his pace. Grabbing both of my hips, he slammed into me until he was groaning deep in his throat. His hips stuttered as he stopped thrusting, his whole-body stiffening as he came with a low groan, before he collapsed onto his elbows, keeping most of his weight off me. "So good for me, Little Dreamer." He kissed my cheek gently.

I smiled faintly, patting his back.

"Maya," Nico murmured. "I love you so much." His voice was thick with emotions. "I don't want to ever lose you again."

My heart pounded in my chest at his emotional confession. Tears gathered in my eyes as I met his passionate gaze. The love I saw in his beautiful blue eyes only made me fall for him harder.

"I love you too, Nico. I never stopped."

"Good." He kissed me slow and sensually, making my toes curl with delight.

I giggled softly and held him, reveling in the moment. "What's your plan for today?" I asked, when it was clear he wasn't moving off me any time soon.

"Maybe some breakfast, but then we're getting back in this bed for round two."

"My mom—"

"Has been made aware that you need some adult time."

"Nico! You didn't!"

Nico laughed diabolically. "I sure the hell did! Relax woman, she didn't seem upset."

I shoved at him, but he barely budged. "Of course she wasn't upset to you! I'll have to hear all about it later when she tells me how I'm being a bad daughter or a bad mother."

Nico frowned slightly. "She still does shit like that?"

I sighed. "Not as bad as before, but it's like she can't help herself. She'll make a back handed comment about something and it just hits to the bone, you know?"

Nico nodded slowly. "I'm sorry you have to deal with that still."

I shrugged. "Now that my dad is gone—" I paused to swallow my tears. "She should have more time for her own health. She needs to get back to physical therapy. I need to look into senior ride services to get her out of the house during the day. She can still do things for herself, but she can no longer drive."

"Let me know what you find out, otherwise we can make the Prospects drive her."

I barked out a laugh. "Fuck, I'd pay to see that happen!"

"Little Dreamer, you don't have to pay for shit! I'll make it happen today, if you want!" Nico grinned.

I just grinned up at him, feeling happier than I had in a long time.

Nico

Later that night, I drove Maya to pick up Luke from day camp. "Hey mom, did you know school starts Wednesday?" Luke asked as he climbed into the back seat of the Civic.

Maya turned fully in her seat to look at him as I pulled away from the pick-up lane. "Fuck," Maya swore.

I glanced over at her surprised; she usually tried to censor herself in front of Luke.

"I completely forgot! With everything going on, I forgot school was this week! I'm so sorry, honey! We need to get you supplies still!"

"Can we afford that?" Luke asked, his voice lowering as if ashamed about it.

Maya's face fell and I looked over to see tears welling in her eyes.

"Don't worry about that," I said. I smiled broadly and looked up into the rear-view mirror at Luke. "I'll get the supplies, my treat."

Luke's immediate grin had my heart clenching. God, that kid made me happy.

Nico

Later that night, after Luke was tucked in, I held Maya tightly.

"How long have you been having money issues?" I asked. After her near panic attack in the car after we picked up Luke from camp, I had quickly calmed her down, but when she started to cry because Luke had asked if they could afford school supplies, I had to step in.

Luke had quickly perked up when I offered to buy, and Maya, though resigned, seemed grateful. I had even taken them out to dinner—well, breakfast for dinner at Luke's insistence. Gramma's

Table was a quaint family restaurant near the house and Maya had admitted to wanting to try it since they'd moved in.

Luke had wolfed down a stack of pancakes and sausage links and I had ordered him an omelet afterwards to make sure he wasn't still hungry. Dude was a growing boy; he needed the calories.

Maya had a smile on her face while she drowned her entire plate, not just her pancakes, in syrup. She even laughed when I called her out.

It had been good a night out and had felt like something a family would do.

I had desperately wanted that. Craved that.

"Since we've moved back." Maya sighed. "I took a huge pay cut to come here. And the small doctor's office has been great as far as having normal hours and being flexible when I need to leave for Luke or my parents, but they don't pay anywhere near what I was making at the hospital. And I've been helping my parents with their medical bills. My dad's care was expensive."

I sighed heavily and hugged her closer. "I wish so much was different, Little Dreamer."

Maya sighed as well. "Me too, Nic. Me too." She turned her head into the crook of my neck and drifted off, leaving me wide awake, thinking of all the things that should have been.

Chapter Thirty-Nine

Jason

I COULDN'T SETTLE. I was too keyed up. For days since Maya finally told us the truth, and I'd been on edge, waiting for something, anything to happen. I didn't know what I expected. Marcos had taken control of everything, and Maya hadn't uttered one complaint—not that I'd heard.

Nico had spent the day with her Monday, taking Luke to camp so he had some alone time with her. I wasn't sure if I was jealous or not. I was still so angry with her.

Ten years down the drain. All because she chose to listen to threats of some low-life piece of shit, and not come to us in the first place.

Seeing the fear on her face and listening to her sobs had gutted me—ripped my fucking heart out. Her story and the way it lined up with all the facts I knew firsthand… it was obvious that she had finally told us the truth.

The way Maya's mask had been completely stripped away—I had finally caught a glimpse of the woman I had been in love with—and she was broken. It made my heart hurt.

She hadn't trusted me enough to come to me to protect her.

I felt like I was drifting aimlessly through time, without a plan or a goal to move forward. How did we ever reconcile things? Did I even want to?

Nico spending the day with her, even going so far as to stay the night, had apparently bothered me more than I thought. I couldn't go see her, not after what I'd done to her. She already didn't want to be alone with me. She barely even acknowledged my presence at football practice—not that I blamed her.

That was a different problem for different day.

Today, I needed to do something. I couldn't sit around anymore and wait. That's all we'd been fucking doing.

Nico had messaged us Sunday night after his family dinner at the Seratelli home, and gave us the list he'd been given, and told us Leonardo wouldn't help until the list was finished.

A week had gone by since then, and all of the list was completed—except for the three fucking names that we were all pussy-footing over. Kara was getting antsy, as her father's trial neared, and what does Nico do? He spends all day at fucking

Maya's house and even spends the night, leaving Marcos and I, and our club to do the dirty work.

Dirty work that involved killing three of Hillcrest's crew.

How the fuck were we supposed to stay under the radar with Hillcrest, and not draw attention to our plans, if we had to kill three of his men? Thankfully, Sunday night after Nico returned home, Marcos had the sense to call an emergency church session at the clubhouse. Nico had shared what happened with his family and had handed over the list, saying that the club was allowed to help. But the Seratelli's wouldn't agree to either a sit-down, or convincing Vince inside, until the list was complete.

Most of our crew had jumped all over the list, fighting over which names to take. Most of the names were known low-lives that had wronged the club at some point or another, so it was no skin off our back to help the Italians.

Except for the three fucking snakes on the list that were a little too fucking close to Hillcrest. Not quite his lieutenants, but the men held long standing positions of power within Hillcrest's little street gang.

I had to do something.

I left my dorm room at the clubhouse and headed down the hall to the main barroom. I paused in the doorway, looking around. It was a Tuesday night, so it wasn't all that busy, but I found exactly who I was looking for sitting at a table in the corner: Axel, Phoenix, and Blaze. The three patched members were a tight unit, but didn't interact too much with Marcos, Nico and I.

They were good guys and had always come in clutch when needed. And they were exactly who I needed right this moment: Axel Jones, Blaze Thomas, and Phoenix Kendrick. The three men were huddled around a table in the corner of the clubhouse, playing cards and smoking cigarettes.

I knew that Axel's little brother had been killed by Las Serpientes when he was in high school, so the three men had joined the Psychos together around that time. They were out for blood when it came to the snakes, and I would play into that by inviting them along.

I walked over to their table, watching the cards on the table, vaguely wondering game they were playing but also not giving a fuck. "How you guys doing tonight?" I asked.

"Fine," Axel said, glancing up at me, a bored expression on his face. "What's up?"

I chuckled softly. Axel was a man of few words, a lone wolf most of the time despite the two guys attached to him. They were a solid unit, rarely seen without the other two. "Need to get out of here, going stir crazy." I stated. "Was going to go look for trouble on the southside."

Axel raised an eyebrow at me. He was a bald man with a thick dark beard and heavy brows. He was serious all of the time, and I wasn't sure if I've ever seen the dude smile. His eyes were dark as night and looked like they were staring through you most of the time. With his thick chest and heavily muscled arms, he was a scary motherfucker that even I didn't want to cross.

"You guys in?" I asked.

Blaze chuckled darkly. His white teeth flashed in the dim light, a perfect fucking smile to along with the model worthy mug shot. He had light brown hair that was slicked up in some faux hawk style shit that the ladies swarmed over. There was something sinister in his icy gray eyes that saw everything. He looked like he should be seated in a board room, not in a dingy corner of a biker clubhouse playing cards. "We're in." His voice was as smooth as his face, and I knew he could sweet talk just about anyone into doing what he needed them to.

My eyes jumped to Phoenix, taking in his long black hair and trimmed goatee. The beard was a couple inches long, that he would sometimes braid. His black hair was usually pulled back into a braid with some kind of rope or some shit in it. I thought the man might have been native American, but I didn't know for sure—he definitely had an olive skin tone. Phoenix was the most easy-going of the three of them. His green eyes usually were crinkled in the corner and his plump lips were pulled wide as he smiled up at me. "We going after—"

"Shh." I motioned down with my hand, indicating for the man to keep his damn voice down. "Yes."

"Why aren't we telling anyone?"

"Because the less that want in, the easier it should be. Hopefully we're in and out. I'll meet you out front. Grab your weapons." I turned and walked away, off to gather my own weapons and gear. I didn't want to draw attention to the fact that we were headed into enemy territory. We needed to finish this—tonight—so Kara could get what she needed, and then Maya could be safe.

Maybe once she was safe, I could figure out my shit regarding her.

Jason

"Fuuuuck," I groaned, cradling my shoulder. The gunshot wound was bleeding profusely and hurt like a motherfucking bitch. My whole arm hung limp, too painful to fucking move. The force of the bullet tearing through my upper arm had dropped my ass to the ground, and I was struggling to my knees while still aiming my gun at our enemies.

I fired another round down the alley way, at the group of three guys that we'd followed here tonight. The three fucking Las Serpientes we need to kill. It was fucking stupid that I got shot first.

"Jesus, Stone." Phoenix groaned and looped my arm over his shoulder and pulled me to my feet.

More gunfire erupted down the alley, aimed at us.

"Fuck!" I shouted as another bullet tore through my calf.

"Move!" Axel shouted.

We had just turned around when the burning in my neck hit. I hissed in pain and dropped my Glock.

"Oh fuck," Phoenix groaned. "Come on, man." Phoenix helped me limp to safety, taking cover behind a damn dumpster in the alley. Phoenix lowered me to the ground and I landed heavily on my ass. Phoenix immediately prodded at the wound in my neck and sighed heavily. "Just a graze, but its bleeding like a bitch." He pulled his bandana off his head and folded it up until it was an inch thick, then he wrapped it tightly around my neck and tied it off, holding pressure on the wound. "Can you breathe, ok?"

"Yeah, I'm good." I groaned; my voice raspy.

"Good. Stay here." Phoenix turned away then, and went back to helping his brothers, leaving me propped up against the dumpster.

Annoyed as shit and bleeding out, I reached into my leather jacket and pulled out my cell phone. There was no way I was going to be able to ride out of here, I'd need someone to come get me. *So much for being fucking discreet.*

I pressed dial on Marcos's number, listening to the gunshots continue down the alley. "Yo," Marcos answered on the third ring. "What the fuck?" he demanded, clearly hearing the gunfire.

"Hey, I need a pickup. Probably back up too. I'm hit. Axel, Phoenix, and Blaze are under heavy fire."

"Where?" Marcos demanded.

I rattled off my last known cross streets then said I'd drop a pin for Marcos to find me. I hung up the phone and immediately dropped the pin in the group chat with Marcos and Nico, knowing both men would come immediately.

My vision swam in an out, probably indicating I was losing too much blood. Things grew quiet in the alley—or I dozed off, I didn't know which. But the next thing I knew I was being jostled as Marcos and Nico hefted me off the pavement. "You dead, man?" Nico asked.

I rolled my eyes. "Didn't I just ask you the same question last week?"

"He good?" Axel's voice broke through the haze that I had fallen into.

"Right as rain," I said. "You get them?"

"Yeah. Snapped a picture and sent it to Nico to send to his cousin," Blaze said.

"Awesome. Good work." I huffed out a breath as Nico and Marcos dragged my sorry ass over to the back of Marcos's pick-up truck.

"I'll ride his bike out of here," Nico said. "Where you taking him?"

"Can't go to the hospital. And he'll need round the clock care." Marcos sighed.

He must have said something else that I missed as they transferred me into the backseat of the truck, because Nico said. "Yeah, I'll meet you there."

Chapter Forty

Maya

I WAS ROUSED AWAKE to the overhead light in my bedroom turning on and heavy boots stomping on my floor. "What the fuck?" I snapped, sitting up.

Marcos and Nico were carrying a very limp Jason between them. He had bloody gauze wrapped around his shoulder, neck, and calf.

I jumped out of bed and ripped back the top sheet and blankets, tossing them out of the way. "Sorry about this," Nico said, as he and Marcos maneuvered Jason onto the bed.

"Doctor's on his way; we couldn't bring him to the hospital," Marcos said.

"Why here?"

"He's going to need round the clock medical care. We'd hoped you'd help." Nico shot me a tight smile.

I ignored him and dove for my closet. I pulled out the tackle box and duffle bag of medical supplies I kept on hand; things I'd grabbed from the hospital or the office over the years. It had been a habit that I still hadn't broken since the days I dated the guys. Thank God I kept up the habit too, because they were in serious need of supplies.

"He looks like he's lost a lot of blood," I said, slipping on gloves.

"Doctor's on his way with blood. He'll help you," Marcos replied, stepping out of my way.

"The neck wound, how bad?" I asked.

"They said it was graze, but deep," Nico answered.

I nodded and grabbed scissors, going to work on cutting off Jason's shirt. Someone had already field dressed his wounds, so he was no longer dripping blood everywhere, but he was still heavily bleeding.

"Nic, in the hallway linen closet on the floor is a pile of junk towels. Grab them," I delegated.

A phone rang as I was cutting the gauze wrapped around Jason's upper shoulder, where the bullet had penetrated his deltoid muscle. It didn't look deep, but I didn't have any local anesthetic on hand anymore, so it was going to be painful once I started digging around.

Marcos answered the call and walked out of the room, just as Nico walked back in with the towels. "Here," Nico said.

"Fold one under his shoulder." The last thing I needed was my mattress getting ruined.

Nico did as he was told and I grabbed a pair of hemostats. I was gathering up the rest of the supplies I'd need to remove the bullet and pack the wound with gauze before I wrapped it up. It was shallow enough that it didn't look like it needed stitches.

"You realize I'm not a doctor," I said wryly.

"Good thing, I am." A male voice spoke from behind me.

I glanced up to see a familiar looking man carrying a cooler and a duffle bag of his own. He was tall with a bald head and warm chocolate eyes. "Dr. Griffin?" I asked.

"Yeah, Katalina's friend, right?" Doctor Griffin asked.

"Maya."

"Alright Maya, what do we have?"

"Two GSW's, one to the deltoid muscle and the other to the upper gastrocnemius. I haven't looked at it yet. Deltoid looks superficial. Possible graze to the neck. He's lost a lot of blood." I rattled off his vitals, while Griffin unzipped his bag and pulled on his own set of gloves.

For the next half hour, the two of us worked as a team to tend to our patient. Occasionally, I delegated tasks to Marcos and Nico, like grabbing a hanger from the closet to hang from the curtain rod to set up a makeshift IV pole.

Griffin had a bag of saline, antibiotics and universal donor blood on hand. I had quickly started a line for the blood transfusion and a saline bag in his elbow. "We'll hold off on antibiotics for now," he said. "He should still be ok. I'll leave pills behind in case he needs them."

I nodded and pulled out a blood pressure cuff. I checked his vitals again, repeating them to Griffin.

"Good." Griffin finished up with the dressing on Jason's calf. Neither gunshot wound would be stitched up, rather we packed the wound with gauze before we wrapped it tight with a self-adhesive bandage.

The bullet that had grazed Jason's neck had left a two-inch-long gash that thankfully had not hit anything vital. The wound had required stiches though, and Griffin had used a local pain anesthetic to relieve any pain Jason might feel, in case he woke up.

Jason, thankfully, had stayed unconscious the whole time we worked on him. Griffin had brought several vials of anesthetic and syringes with him, but we hadn't needed it. "I'll leave this stuff with you. I can get more," Griffin had muttered off handedly while we worked.

I had thanked him profusely. I no longer had access to those kinds of things working at the family clinic.

"Aright, I think that's about it for me," Griffin said when we finished up. He started packing up his things, while he pulled out other supplies and stacked things on my dresser. "You can have all this. I'll grab more from the hospital."

My eyes widened at the bags of saline and antibiotics, and other medical supplies. "Thank you, Griffin. I really appreciate it."

"Yeah, no worries. Call me if anything changes. After the blood bag and saline are finished, you could remove the IV."

"Yep," I nodded.

"I'm sorry about your guy here."

"Thanks," Marcos spoke up from the doorway of the room, where he'd stationed himself, watching on while we worked. "I appreciate this doc."

Griffin smiled and nodded. "No worries." He shook hands with Nico and then me, "You did good." He nodded at me, then he grabbed his bag and cooler off the bed and headed toward the door where Marcos was standing.

Marcos pushed off the door and turned around, leading Griffin out of my room.

I took a deep breath in the quiet that descended over my small bedroom. My limbs began to slowly shake as tears welled in my eyes.

"Oh, sweetheart," Nico crooned, moving to me immediately. He wrapped his arms around me and held me tight. "You did so good, baby. I'm so proud of you."

I clung to him as I broke down in his arms, the overwhelming emotions pouring out of me now that the traumatic event was over.

When I heard footsteps behind me, I took a shaky breath and cleared my throat. I pulled away from Nico and wiped my eyes, putting on a brave face again, just as Marcos walked back in the room. Ignoring him, I turned back to Jason, who was still unconscious in my bed. The IV fluids were still flowing and Jason was still breathing, so there wasn't much for me to do.

"Thank you." Marcos spoke so softly, I almost didn't realize he was speaking to me.

"Yeah."

I busied myself by picking up the blankets from where I'd tossed them on the floor earlier. I started making the bed, when Marcos came up and gently pried the blankets from my hands. "Maya," he murmured my name softly, his hands so soft on mine.

A tortured sob ripped out of me.

Marcos sat on the edge of the bed and pulled me into his arms, settling me on his lap. "It's alright," he said, "let it all out."

I clung to him, burring my face into the crook of his neck, breathing in his familiar scent of leather and mint. He rocked me gently, careful not to jostle the bed too much as he rubbed my back and whispered softly in my ear. I ignored all the shit between us, and held on, savoring his warmth and his strength—I had needed it more than I thought.

A while later, I felt strong enough to pull away. A glance at the clock told me it was going on four in the morning and my alarm would be going off in two hours. I already knew I wouldn't be going to work, though. So I grabbed my phone and texted my boss that I'd had a rough night and needed the day.

My boss had been extremely understanding since my father's passing and had told me if I needed more time, that it was ok to take additional days. This wasn't exactly what my boss probably had in mind, but I didn't care. I needed the day.

It was also Luke's first day of school. The new school year had crept up on me and I didn't want him to miss anything. It felt like life was too unstable these days, too many unknowns kept popping up. We needed routine.

"You call in?" Nico asked as I set my phone back down on the nightstand.

"Yeah," I murmured, my voice raspy. I picked up the sheets and blankets again, and this time Marcos helped me remake the bed, covering Jason and tucking the sheet and blankets under the mattress. "I'm gonna try and get some more rest before I have to get up with Luke," I told them, looking between Nico and Marcos.

"I'm gonna drag the recliner in here," Marcos declared.

"I'll help you."

I let them do what they wanted and slid under the covers next to Jason in my queen-sized bed. At one point during our care for him, I had Nico grab the extra pillows out of the hallway linen closet to prop him up with, so I could use my own pillow to curl up next to him.

Marcos and Nico carried in my father's recliner from the living room, and the stack of cushions from the couch. They set up the recliner in the corner, and Nico threw the cushions on the floor at the end of the bed before he left the room again. He came back a moment later carrying two throw blankets and a throw pillow. He tossed one of the blankets at Marcos—who raised an eyebrow at him—and then made himself a bed on the couch cushions.

I chuckled softly and shook my head at Nico's antics. I fucking loved him, though, and I was so grateful that they both were camping out in my bedroom with me, while we waited for Jason to recover.

"Marcos, the lamp next you has a super dim nightlight feature. Turn it on, please?"

"'Fraid of the dark, Mi Vida?" Marcos voice rumbled through the darkness.

My gasp of surprise at the term of endearment, carried louder than I'd intended.

Both men ignored it, and Marcos turned on the nightlight.

I thought it would be impossible to sleep, but with all three of my men in the room, I drifted off to sleep almost immediately.

Marcos

Despite the late night, Maya's alarm woke us all up at six o'clock that morning. I stirred in the recliner, surprised that I actually fell asleep. I had planned on keeping watch over Stone, but once Maya cozied up to him in bed and said to turn on the night light, I hadn't stood a chance.

Despite my fear for my brother, I had felt more content than I had in a long time. Maya's gentle calm, despite her tears, was a balm to my weathered soul. I needed her calming presence around me always. After she let out her emotions and relaxed again, it was a like drug that permeated the air.

The second time Maya's alarm went off, she slowly sat up. I watched her grab Jason's wrist and push her fingers into his pulse point, while reading the analog watch on her wrist. She sighed when she dropped his wrist back to the mattress, before she turned to press the back her hand to his cheeks, checking his temperature.

Seemingly satisfied with what she felt, she pulled away from him and slowly got out of bed. The short tank top and booty short set she wore to bed flashed a lot of skin, and I felt my dick stirring in my jeans. She had always been gorgeous, ever since the day we met her. But in the last ten years, she'd only grown more beautiful.

Maya headed into the attached bathroom and shut the door behind her. Nico sat up from his makeshift bed on the floor and rubbed his face. The lack of sleep last night was hard on everyone, but our brother was still alive, and that was all that mattered. "How's he doing?" Nico asked, his voice thick with sleep.

"Maya checked his vitals when she woke up. She seemed content with whatever she found." My jaw cracked as I yawned deeply.

"That's good." Nico stood up and left the bedroom, probably in search of the main hallway bathroom.

I stood and stretched, before I left the room to go wake up Luke. I was honestly surprised that he never woke amidst all the commotion the night before, but I was grateful for it too. "Morning, Luke," I greeted as I flipped on Luke's overhead light and walked into his bedroom.

Luke groaned deeply and pulled the covers over his head. "Go away," he mumbled.

I chuckled softly and walked further into the room. "Time to get up," I said in a sing-song voice. "It's the first day of schoool."

Luke's groan was deeper this time, more annoyed.

I laughed and shook the mattress, jostling Luke around like an earthquake was happening.

Luke laughed faintly beneath the covers and I grinned proudly. I really was getting the hang of this whole dad-life thing. "Come on! Up you go!"

Luke sighed and slowly peaked his head out from under his covers. "What are you doing here?"

"It's your first day of school! I wouldn't miss it for the world!"

I could see Luke slowly processing that as he stared into space. It was a painful reminder of how much I had missed. Both Luke and I were still wrapping our heads around it, knowing the matter had been out of both our control.

Finally, Luke sat up and slid out of bed, just as Nico walked in the room with a bright grin on his face. "Morning, dude! Ready for your first day?"

"Ugh," Luke groaned, a faint smile on his face. "Why are you so chipper first thing?"

I laughed loudly. "You'll get used to him."

"The sun is shining! It's a glorious day!" Nico said, being extra exuberant.

Luke walked out of the bedroom in just his boxers, shaking his head. I heard the bathroom door close a moment later.

"What's the plan for today?" Nico asked.

"We should head to the clubhouse and see what's happening with Axel, Phoenix, and Blaze. Did you hear back from your cousin?" I asked.

Nico shook his head. "A simple text stating he received it would be nice. But it was the middle of the night, and it is still early."

I sighed and nodded. Leonardo Seratelli didn't strike me as the type of man to sleep in during the week, though.

In the next hour we made breakfast for Luke and got him dressed and his lunch packed. I helped Maya with it all, and then we did a mini photo shoot in front of the house. Maya busted out a mini blackboard that had things like grade and age and favorite subjects. Maya asked Luke his favorite things while she wrote on the blackboard with neon colored chalk markers.

Luke was a good sport, indicating that he had done all of this before. I watched on as Maya snapped picture after of picture of Luke holding the board and his backpack in front of the house. Then she made me get in the photos as well, and I couldn't keep the cheesy ass grin off my face when I wrapped my arm around my son.

"You get in there too!" Nico said, pushing Maya toward me and Luke.

Maya opened her mouth to protest, but Luke immediately agreed. "Yeah mom!"

And so we snapped a bunch of family photos for the first time ever.

I wasn't even upset about it. When I stepped away to give Maya and Luke a couple photos alone, I still had a broad grin plastered on my face. Despite the shitty early morning events, the day was shaping up to be better than I expected.

Marcos

My phone rang later that afternoon, just as I was pulling my truck into Maya's driveway. A quick glance at the truck screen showed it was my sister. My heart leapt into my throat as I quickly answered the phone while throwing the truck into park. "Hola, Manita."

"Hey, Marquitos." Kara's voice was upbeat and happy, that had to be good news right? "I just got off the phone with D.A. Lacey Winters. She just left the county jail. My father has signed the plea deal."

"Thank fuck," I said, leaning back in the driver's seat. I hadn't realized how tense I'd gotten.

"Yeah," Kara agreed. "Lacey thinks she can get this before a judge by the end of the week. It's Wednesday, so she's optimistic. Once my father is sentenced, the board will convene. Hopefully, you'll have an answer by this weekend regarding Hillcrest."

"Thanks, Kara." I sighed and rubbed a hand over my face.

"How are things, otherwise?"

"There's some stuff going down that I can't talk about over the phone. Jason was shot last night, though." At Kara's gasp, I pressed on talking faster. "He's doing ok, now. He's at Maya's. We called in the doc and he and Maya got him stable last night. He's going to be ok."

Kara let out a heavy breath. "Thank God."

Chapter Forty-Two

Nico

I FROWNED AS I watched Maya catch a midday nap in bed next to Jason. In the two days since Jason was shot and brought to Maya's house, she'd barely left his side. She had taken the rest of the week off of work, and had taken care of Luke and her mother, of course, but she'd barely left Jason's side if she didn't have to.

At night, I'd catch her sitting up, wide awake, keeping watch. She took his vitals several times a day and wrote the numbers down in a little notebook she kept on her nightstand. Dr. Griffin had returned on Wednesday with more supplies for Maya, including a catheter, since they wouldn't know how long Jason would be out for.

Griffin had been fantastic and had reached out a couple times since then to check on his patient, and Maya had given a detailed account of his well-being each time. If she wasn't sleeping in the bed beside Jason, she was curled up in the recliner in the corner. Marcos and I had carried her to the bed a couple times, just so we could use the chair ourselves.

The stress of the ordeal was weighing heavily on her. Elaine had told me that she was barely eating, despite Elaine cooking meals for us. I had stocked the fridge with groceries, knowing money was tight. The life-insurance policy had covered the funeral expenses, but there wasn't enough to cover other expenses, not until Elaine was able to sit down and finalize things with her lawyer to get access to Harry's 401k.

I understood it was a stressful time, and adding Jason's injury to the list wasn't helping. Helping out with groceries was the least I could do. Marcos was busy with running the club and taking care of Luke. With it being the kid's first week of school, he had homework on top of football practice, and he had another game tomorrow morning that Marcos was insisting Luke still attend.

Life was busy and still moved forward despite one of our brothers lying unconscious in bed for days. We still had jobs to do.

Marcos walked in the bedroom while I was lost in thought. "Kara just called; the D.A. got Carmichael before the judge this morning. He's been sentenced to the ten years for racketeering and fraud for the shit against the firm, then an additional twenty years for the murder of Mac Taylor. Kara's on her way to the board meeting to find out the status of the firm."

"So we should know soon?"

"Yes." Marcos nodded. "She said that it could take a couple hours, but she felt confident that by the end of the night she would be in possession of Carmichael & Associates.

"That's great news," I said.

Jason

I woke to the low rumble of male voices talking around me. My whole body was on fire, pain radiating out of certain places. My leg and shoulder were the worst. There was a dull aching in my neck that burned too.

I groaned and slowly opened my eyes.

"Hey man," Nico said, leaning over me. "How you feeling?"

"Like I've been run over." My voice was a rough gravel that hurt my throat. "Water."

"Yeah, hold on," Nico said. "I'll fill the bottle."

I watched him grab a hospital mug with a straw from the dresser and leave the room. I looked around the room and realized I didn't know where I was, but Maya was sleeping in the bed beside me. "What happened?" I asked Marcos, though my eyes stayed on the sleeping Maya. There were bags under her eyes and her hair was a mess. She looked thinner too. Like the stress of the last several weeks had caught up to her.

"You remember going out with Axel, Blaze, and Phoenix?" Marcos asked, walking closer to the bed.

"Shit," I swore. "Yeah, I got shot."

"Yeah. You got shot," Marcos deadpanned.

"How long have I been out?"

"Two days. It's Friday afternoon."

"Where are we?"

"Maya's house. This is her bedroom."

Nico walked back in the room with the hospital cup filled and ice sloshing inside. He held the straw to my lips and I tried to lean forward to take a sip, but groaned deeply when the stitches in my neck pulled.

Maya startled awake on the bed next to me, sitting up abruptly and looking around for trouble. She frowned when she saw Nico attempting to give me water. "Gimme that," she snapped and grabbed the cup from Nico and held it closer to my mouth, angling the straw down to make it easier for me. "Small sips." Her voice was groggy and thick from sleep, and her eyes lids were still heavy.

I watched her warily as I took a small sip of cold water. When I was done, I shook my head and she pulled the cup away. "How's the pain on a scale of one to ten?"

"Seven?" I answered.

Maya was already up and moving around the bed as I spoke. She came around my side of the mattress and set the cup down. "I'll get you something to eat so you can take some pain pills." She bustled out of the room before the three of us could say anything.

I frowned as I watched the door she disappeared through. "How's that been?" I asked, regarding the situation with Maya.

"Tense, weird," Marcos admitted. "We haven't talked about anything substantial."

"She hasn't left your side, man," Nico added. "She's been here day and night, called into work this week. She only left the room if she needed to for Luke or her Mom."

I frowned, my brain was struggling to keep up with what they were telling me. "She patched me up?"

"Yeah, her and Doc Griffin. But it's mostly been her taking care of you," Nico said.

A moment later Maya walked in carrying a plate of food. "I got toast and a PBJ. Try the toast first, and we'll see how your stomach handles it with the pills." She set everything on the nightstand. "Nic, grab those throw pillows. Marcos come help him sit up."

I watched as my brothers did what Maya told them, and a moment later I was propped up against the pillows, with two throw pillows under my left arm to support my injured shoulder. I scarfed down the toast and swallowed back the pills quickly before Maya shooed Marcos and Nico out of the room, so she could remove my catheter.

"Catheter? Seriously?" I glared at her.

"You were unconscious for over forty-eight hours; I wasn't having you piss in my bed. Never was one of my kinks." She slipped on gloves as she spoke, and I took the time to admire her form. She was utterly gorgeous despite the bags under her eyes and the messy hair. She was dressed in her usual tank top and booty shorts that show off her great ass and way too much skin.

I had no idea how I was going to handle her *handling* my dick, while she pulled out the catheter. "Maybe we should wait for the doc."

Maya chuckled softly. "Doc wouldn't know what to do. Catheters have always been the nurse's job." She gathered up a bed pan and smirked at me. "Don't worry Jason, it's not like I haven't see your dick before."

I rolled my eyes and stared at the ceiling as she gently pulled back the blankets and sheet to reveal my naked ass. Her hands were gentle as she worked the plastic tubing from my pierced cock and I groaned softly once it was fully removed. She disappeared into the attached bathroom carrying the tube and attached bag that was full of urine.

Sighing, I pulled the sheet back over myself, so I wasn't just sitting there naked while she emptied things and cleaned up in the bathroom. A couple minutes later she came back in without her gloves on and grabbed a duffle bag from the floor by the door and set it on the bed. She riffled through it before she pulled out a pair of basketball shorts—my basketball shorts.

"Nico went by your place," Maya said as she walked around the bed. She pulled back the sheet and quickly got to work slipping the shorts over my feet and tugging them up my legs. I helped her when she got to my ass by lifting my hips.

I grunted slightly in pain, but we managed to get me half-dressed without causing me too much discomfort. She covered me back up and then handed me the plate with the PBJ. "Think you can eat this?" She put the plate on my lap.

"Yeah." I grunted.

Maya went and opened her bedroom door, letting Marcos and Nico back into her room. Both men walked in after Maya walked out.

"So what'd I miss?" I asked.

"You guys got those three snakes we needed dead. Seratelli followed through on his end, Carmichael accepted the plea Wednesday. The D.A. got him before a judge and sentenced this morning, and Kara's meeting with the board right now as we speak. We're just waiting for a call from her, before we head to the clubhouse to call a vote on taking out Hillcrest."

"Good, let's go." I tried to sit up fully.

"Fuck no," Marcos snapped. "You're not going anywhere. You've been knocked from blood loss for the last two days! You had to get a damn blood transfusion. Your ass is sitting here till Maya says you can leave. And not a second before then!"

I grumbled, but leaned back against the pillows.

Marcos's phone rang and he quickly pulled it out of his jeans pocket. "Lil Manita," he answered the phone.

I waited, watching as my brother smiled broadly.

"Congratulations, Kara! I'm so proud of you!" Marcos beamed.

I sighed in relief. Kara had called with good news. That meant good news for the rest of us. We could kill Hillcrest.

"Alright, you have a good night! Go celebrate with your guys. Love you too." Marcos hung up his cell phone and slid it back in his pocket. "We're a go for Hillcrest."

"Hell yeah. I'll call church," Nico said, reaching for his own phone.

I sighed, knowing they were about to take off and leave me behind.

"By the way, I got your bike from where you left it Wednesday. It's back at your place."

"Thanks. Call me later for the vote." I sighed.

"Will do. Rest up brother." Marcos walked over to the bed and pounded his knuckles against mine.

I nodded and the same with Nico. "Go easy on Maya, yeah?" Nico said.

I huffed and shrugged my good shoulder. "We'll see."

Jason

I woke up the middle of the night, pain radiating from my body and my bladder screaming. I hissed when I tried to sit up.

"What's wrong?" Maya asked, jumping up from the recliner in the corner of the room.

I hadn't even noticed her over there before. "Bathroom," I grunted.

"Alright." Maya walked over and pulled back the blankets before she wrapped her hand around my right hand, looping our thumbs together. "I'm going to pull you forward and swing your legs out of bed. We're going to try and do this at the same time, ok?"

"Yeah."

Maya pulled, surprising me with her strength as she easily pulled me upright. I swung my legs out and over the edge of the mattress at the same time as I sat up. I let out a relieved breath when my body didn't scream in pain with the move. "Alright, step two. I'll help you to your feet, but only put weight on your left leg. You're going to use me as a crutch and we'll hobble to the bathroom."

I thought the idea was crazy, Maya was so small compared to me. But I nodded and did as she said, and I was standing on one leg feeling only slightly lightheaded.

"How you doing?" she asked.

"Kinda lightheaded."

"That's normal, you lost a lot of blood."

I grunted and stepped forward. Maya moved with me and once again I was surprised by how easily she handled me and moved me around. A moment later we were around the bed and at the attached bathroom. She flicked on the light and got me as far as the vanity, before she slipped out from under my arm. "Alright. I'll be right outside if you need anything."

She closed the door behind her, and then I was alone in the bathroom.

I leaned on the counter to limp my ass over to the toilet and quickly emptied my bladder. While I stood there, I thought about everything we'd learned about Maya in the garage, during the repast after her father's funeral.

Even with everything we learned and now knew, I still didn't have the answers for why. But I was going to get them.

I finished my business in the bathroom, washed my hands and limped my sorry ass out of the bathroom. Someone how I made it around the bed and managed to get myself tucked back under the sheets. Maya was nowhere in the room though.

I huffed a sigh and wondered where the hell she went. The recliner in the corner of her bedroom still had the footrest up and blanket pushed to one side, like she had been sleeping there and jumped up when I woke, not bothering to push the footrest down before she rushed to my side.

I didn't have to wait much longer though when she walked in the room carrying a plate of food and a glass of milk. "I heated up some leftovers. My mom made a pot roast for dinner."

My stomach let out a loud grumble that had me rolling my eyes. "Thanks," I muttered as she set the plate in my lap. There was a dim nightlight on the lamp on the dresser that gave off enough light in the room to see my food. I started eating as Maya grabbed a pill bottle on the dresser and popped the top off. She dumped a couple into the palm of her hand and put the cap back on.

Maya turned and walked over to me, handing me the pills and then held up the glass of milk. I quickly downed the pills with a gulp of milk before I went back to eating. The food was pretty good, even reheated. I was starving—because apparently, I hadn't eaten in two days.

I watched Maya return to the recliner, out of the corner of my eye. She curled up and wrapped the blanket tightly around her. I hated the fucking awkwardness that settled over the room while I ate in quiet. Maya might not even feel it, because of the looks of her, she had closed her eyes and was trying to doze back off, but I felt it sitting heavy in the room.

Awkwardness and unspoken words.

I fucking hated it.

"Why didn't you come to us? Back then, we would have protected you. Why didn't you come to us?" I finally demanded.

Maya startled in her chair, as if she really had dozed off again.

I almost felt bad, but I needed to know the truth. "Why didn't you trust us to protect you?" I hated that the pain in my voice was leaking out, but I was tired of hiding how she fucking ripped out my heart and stomped on it when she left us.

Maya gasped.

"No more lies, Maya. Why didn't you just tell us what you saw the next day, or that night when we got home? Why keep that from us? We would have protected you."

"I don't know," she said softly. "At first, I was so utterly terrified. I'd never been in that situation before. I thought if I just kept my mouth shut, it would go away."

"But it didn't."

"No." She shifted in her recliner, pulling the blanket tighter around her. "Then he started stalking me. He had figured out who you guys were, and he wanted to make sure I wouldn't tell you. He constantly terrorized me, followed me."

I hissed, letting the fork hit my plate as my head came up to look at her. Even in the dim light of the room, I could see the terror etched into her face. "Maya."

"I was scared, Jason. I was fucking terrified and I didn't know what to do. Yes, I should have fucking told you guys. I know that now. I fucked up and was I scared. I don't know what else to tell you, I thought I was protecting you buy not saying anything. The day I decided I was finally going to tell you guys, you and Marcos got shot by Hillcrest. I was pulling bullets out of both you in the kitchen and wondering if the next time you might not make it." Her voice broke on a sob and she covered her face.

I sighed and set the plate on the nightstand. "How long was he threatening you before you decided to leave?"

"About a week and half. It wasn't that long. Like I said, by the time I finally decided to tell you guys, you two were shot. Then the night Trish was at the clubhouse she said that Hillcrest wasn't going to miss next time. He said he'd kill the three of you and give me to his crew." She'd already told me all this, but hearing her say it again, seeing the truth on her face *finally*, after seven months of her showing zero emotion behind her stone-cold mask, it sunk in in a way that hadn't really before.

I was sure it would still take some time before I really wrapped my head around it. If I ever could.

"I thought if she could just walk into the clubhouse without anyone realizing who she was—being Dax's girlfriend—then any-one of his crew could just walk in and you guys wouldn't know. The danger became more real for me, and I freaked out. Those last two days before I left were a lot. I was not in a good place mentally and then the scene in the woods—"

"We went too far," I surmised. My head fell back against the wall behind the bed.

"I don't know, maybe." She shook her head. "I think everything had gotten to me those last couple days. I knew what I was doing when I went to Karma and Arturo's. We all played a role that night and I should have safe-worded." Again, she shook her head, as if lost in thought. "I don't know, we're not talking about that night." She paused to take a deep breath. "All I'm saying is that those last two days I was here—shit, even those last two weeks—I was not in a good place mentally and all of that played a part in my leaving."

I looked away from her, trying to process what she was saying. It was finally sinking in how difficult everything had been for her back then.

"I'm sorry for that."

"I can't—" It was my turn to shake my head, letting my sentence trail off.

"I don't expect you to," Maya whispered.

I swallowed thickly, feeling myself getting emotional. I didn't like that she was across the room. It was dim enough that depending on how she shifted, her face would move into the shadow and I couldn't get a read on her—not that the tears and choked voice and labored breath were enough. Maya usually wore her heart on her sleeve; her face was the window to her mind—or at least it used to be—and I hated that I couldn't read her.

Maya yawned deeply and I sighed. It was the middle of the night and she'd clearly been taking care of me nonstop, on top of the stress of losing her father recently.

"Come back to bed," I muttered.

Maya didn't move; I could see her blinking at me though.

"It's your bed. You were sleeping in it before I woke up. Come on."

Maya

I STARED ACROSS MY dimly lit bedroom at Jason wondering if he had lost his damn mind. Maybe the pain killers were getting to him. Was he high? Either way, I didn't move.

"Maya!" He barked, that dominate tone immediately sending shivers rushing down my spine.

I jumped, startled and quickly sat up. Kicking off my blanket, I stood from the recliner and walked around the end of the bed. I climbed into the space next to him on the queen-sized bed, on the other side of the throw pillows that he was resting his injured arm on.

It wasn't until I was climbing into bed that I realized how easily and how fucking quickly I'd followed his order.

He chuckled softly when he saw the surprise flash across my face. "I'd call you a good girl, but we both know you're not."

I flushed a bright red and turned away. I wasn't going to sit here and listen to his teasing. I went to walk away, but his hand shot out and grabbed my wrist.

He immediately groaned and let go. He grabbed the bullet wound with his good hand and slowly fell sideways in agony. "Fuuuck." He panted.

"Shit, Jase," I squeaked. I tucked his head against my chest and I held him loosely. That had to have hurt.

He straightened out his arm, still cradling his injury, but left his head resting against my chest. "I think you just wanted my face in your tits again." His voice was hoarse, a rough gravel that sent a shiver down my spine.

I missed his voice.

"I uh—"

He chuckled softly, his breath fanning against my cleavage.

I held him, in disbelief that it was happening after everything that had happened. That I allowed it and that he did as well. I believed it was the magic of the darkness; things happened under cover of darkness that wouldn't happen otherwise.

A moment later he groaned and pulled away, he leaned back against the wall, because there was no headboard on the bed, and tilted his back, sighing. His good hand came up to run over the bandage covering his stitches on his neck, and I bet they were being pulled while he was leaning forward.

Jason closed his eyes and took a couple deep breaths. "Why didn't you come back?"

The question hit out of the blue that I was stunned speechless. I licked my lip and ran a hand through my hair as I thought about the answer. "I thought about it a couple times. I thought about telling Marcos about Luke sooner. I came down here a couple times, but somehow Hillcrest always knew... and the updates I'd hear from Slade... they weren't good." I took a deep breath to gather my thoughts. "About two years after I left, I decided it was time, that I needed to tell you guys. I went as far as to come down here and look at apartments..." I trailed off as emotion choked my voice.

"What happened?" Jason asked, not opening his eyes. His voice was rough.

Tears flooded my vision and I curled up against the wall, hugging my pillow to my chest. "I was in town for two days. I looked at three apartments and was going to put a deposit down on one. I was at the bank when a courier brought me a bouquet of orange carnations—did you know there's a whole language to flowers?"

He raised an eyebrow, keeping his eyes closed.

"Yeah, I didn't either, but I've learned a lot about the language of flowers in the last ten years." I gave a shaky laugh before I continued. "There was a note in the bouquet. It said that what was about to happen, was my fault, and that I should have stayed away." I took a gasping breath as tears fell down my face. "I was in the bank across the street from the clubhouse. I stood there and watched the clubhouse get raided."

Jason's eyes shot open and looked to mine, searching my gaze. "You were there?"

I nodded, tears falling down my face. "I saw you and Marcos getting arrested in front of the clubhouse." I had to take a deep breath before I continued. "I stood in the entrance to the bank across the street, watching in horror as Marcos was slammed on the hood of the cop car and handcuffed. A moment later they led you out of the clubhouse, already in cuffs. You looked like you were cussing out the cop that was leading you."

Jason frowned, a line forming between his eyebrows.

"I was terrified. I had no idea how he'd known I was even in town or thinking of moving back. I looked through the flowers again and found a second note stuck deep in the bouquet. It said if I left town, he'd make sure the sentences were low, but if I stayed, he would make sure you received ten years."

"What the fuck?" Jason demanded.

I let out a soft sob as emotions rocked me. "I later heard from Slade that the two of you were sentenced to two years at Illinois State Prison. So I didn't bother coming back."

He sighed and looked away from me. Anger was radiating off him and I knew he wouldn't still be laying in this bed if he could get up and walk away. I needed to change the subject, but had questions of my own I needed to ask. And what better time than when he was laid up in my bed, unable to leave?

"Why didn't you guys come for me?" I turned the question around on him. "You had to have known I would have gone to my sister, knowing I wasn't on good terms with my parents. I know you have ways of finding people."

Jason nodded slowly. He rubbed a hand over his face, which was way out of character for *Stone*, but he was never that person when it came to me. Never used to be at least. I was getting a glimpse beneath the mask he'd been keeping up whenever I was around and it was nice. "I did come up there."

"What?" Shock and disbelief rocked through me.

"I came up about a year after you left. None of it felt right. I kept replaying everything in my head from both that night and the night in the woods. I knew we fucked up and took things too far, but after Trish... things didn't feel right. We never got a chance to fully question her. Buckley killed her before the three of us could get answers."

I frowned. "Why would he do that? Isn't he your president?"

"Was. Was our president. Buckley was in business with Hillcrest. They teamed up together against the Ravager Knights. They organized the hit on Mac Taylor, Johnny's dad. Before they killed him, they had him framed for a bunch of white-collar crimes that Vince Carmichael is currently awaiting trial on."

"Your president is in league with Hillcrest?" I asked incredulously, my voice rising.

"Was. He was our president. He's dead now." Jason said. He reached out with the hand of his injured arm and grabbed my hand.

My heart pounded. "You don't think he—"

"I don't know what to think, Maya." Jason squeezed my fingers.

"Jason, if your president and Buckley were involved back then, and he had a hand in driving me away, it changes—"

"It changes nothing," Jason said forcefully, his hand dropping mine.

"How can you say that?!"

"Because you still fucking left us! You didn't come to us! You didn't trust us to take care of you!" Jason's voice rose with each word. He barely managed to keep his voice down as to not yell in the middle of the night and wake Luke or my mom, but his anger was still epic.

"You're right," I choked out, stifling a sob.

"Maya." Jason sighed and tried to grab my hand again.

I evaded him and hugged my pillow. I buried my face into the cool fabric and let it soak up my tears. Life really wasn't fair sometimes.

"You said you came up to Chicago?" I asked, needing him to finish that explanation.

"Yeah," he huffed out. "About a year after you were gone. I went to the hospital you were working at. I saw you on the ICU floor. You were standing at the nursing station with two other women. You looked happy. You were laughing and you looked like you had a nice tan. It was summer."

I frowned and pulled my face out of the pillow. About a year after I left, I would have just been back to work. Luke would have been about three or four months old. I was probably fresh off maternity leave where I had spent as much time as I could in the sun, soaking up the vitamin D before I was due back to twelve-hour days under florescent lights. "Why didn't you say anything?"

Jason shrugged his good shoulder. "I ask myself that all the time."

An uneasy silence settled between the two of them and I shifted uncomfortably. A yawn burst out of me, cracking my jaw with its intensity. "Where do we go from here?" I asked, my voice soft.

He sighed deeply. His hand rubbed over his face tiredly and he shook his head. "I don't know."

I rested my head on the pillow looking at him, feeling lost. "We have to figure out a way to coexist."

Jason nodded slowly. "Yeah. Truce?" He looked over at me and raised an eyebrow.

"Truce." I agreed.

"Alright, get some sleep," he ordered. He shifted himself until he was laying down again and I had no choice but to also lay down.

I rolled onto my side, facing him, and slowly dozed off.

Chapter Forty-Four

Marcos

I WALKED INTO MAYA'S bedroom first thing Saturday morning, after letting myself into the house. I kept quiet, as not to disturb anyone as it was barely seven in the morning. I hadn't slept the night before and needed to reassure myself that Jason was ok. I had been spending the night at Maya's since Jason's attack, but I hadn't been sleeping all that great in the chair.

Now that Jason was conscious, I thought I'd go home and try to get some real sleep. It hadn't worked. I slipped into Maya's room silently and stopped dead at the end of the mattress. Maya was tucked into the bed beside Jason, her curvy body curled around Jason's arm that was propped up on the throw pillows between them. Her face was pressed against his arm, while both her arms were wrapped around his, holding him close.

It wasn't just the reverent way she grasped his arm, but the way Jason allowed it. He was currently awake, leaning back against the several pillowed piled up behind him, and scrolled lazily on his cell phone. Jason glanced up at me and raised an eyebrow, but didn't say anything.

"How long have you been up?" I asked quietly. I walked over to the recliner in the corner of the room and picked up Maya's blanket and tossed it over the back of the chair before I sat down.

"We woke up around two, had to pee. Then we started talking and I dunno, it was close to four when we dozed back off. I woke up about twenty minutes ago."

I nodded, watching Maya's face as she slept on peacefully. She was beautiful—as usual—but there was something serene about her. "You guys get everything figured out?"

Jason grunted softly. "Not really."

I rolled my eyes. "Why am I not surprised?"

Jason ignored me and kept scrolling on his phone.

"Nico said he's back together with her. Said he's all in."

Jason huffed a quiet laugh. "Why am *I*, not surprised?"

I smirked. "He's been waiting for this moment for a long time."

Jason let his phone fall against his chest, nodding absently. He glanced over at Maya, as if lost in thought. "Where do you stand in all of this?"

I ran both my hands over my face. "I don't know man. This is a lot."

"While we were talking last night, she told me that she came down here about two years after she left. She was going to move back, even went as far as looking at apartments. She was at the bank to pull out money for the deposit when Hillcrest basically sent her flowers and told her that what was about to happen was her fault, and that she should've stayed away. She watched us get arrested for those battery charges."

"What?" I snapped, my eyes narrowing.

Jason nodded solemnly, watching Maya. Her breathing was still even; she hadn't moved yet. She still looked like she was out cold, but I would have to keep my voice down otherwise we risked waking her.

"Yeah. He threatened her again and told her that if she didn't leave, we'd get ten years, and if she left, he would get the charges reduced."

I shook my head. I leaned forward in the chair and rested my elbows on my knees.

"She watched us get arrested, man. She stood across the street and watched it, and was told it was happening because she came back."

"I'm going to fucking murder him." I growled, deep in my chest.

"That exactly how I feel. And the more we talked about the past and I explained what's going on with Carmichael and Buckley and Hillcrest...it made me wonder how much did fucking Hillcrest play a part of our club life, and if he's been dealing with Buckley for years? Did Buckley help Hillcrest get us locked up? Did he play a part in pushing Maya away? I mean, Buckley killed Trish before the three of us could even question her directly."

Again, I growled deep in my chest. How the fuck did this go on for so long and we didn't know? Was Buckley that utterly corrupted? "We need to kill Hillcrest. Now."

"What'd the club decide? You guys didn't call last night."

"Never voted. Never got close. They immediately started arguing about *how,* and the far-reaching implications that we don't know yet. Basically, it's clear that he's well connected and protected. Half the club wants to do recon; the other half wants to go in guns blazing."

Jason shook his head. "I need to talk to my dad."

"Probably a good idea. I think we should bring this up to Bear too. He was there the night Trish died. We need to know more about what they heard."

"Exactly. What happened BEFORE Buckley pulled the trigger."

I stared at the floor in horror as the past became crystal clear in my mind. We had been played by our God damn club president. "We need to get the answers out of Hillcrest. We need him alive."

"Yep."

Maya shifted on the bed, letting out a little snore before falling silent again. Both of us eyed her warily, waiting. Not that we wouldn't speak about this in front of her, but more that we knew she needed sleep still.

"I think Nico might be on to the right idea here, brother," I finally admitted.

Jason nodded slowly, his eyes on Maya. "Yeah, I'm feeling that too."

"Yeah. We've lost too much already. Time to move on. Together."

Maya

I woke up to male voices rumbling in the room. I stretched, arching my back and the voices tapered off. Slowly I blinked open my eyes opened, and realized I was staring into the skin of Jason's arm, the arm I was currently wrapped around like a koala. I looked up to see Jason looking down at me. "Hi," I muttered.

His lips curved into half a smile and my heart pounded in my chest. I blinked up at him, not awake enough to comprehend what I was seeing. It was the first time in the seven months that I'd been back that I ever saw something more than a frown or a glare from him—or his stone-cold mask.

It was a little unnerving, but as I was still half asleep, I chose to ignore it.

Turning my head, I found Marcos sitting in the recliner in the corner and Nico standing propped against the dresser. How had I slept through all three of them talking? "What time is it?" My voice was scratchy and I groggily rubbed my face.

"Almost nine," Jason said.

I grumbled and closed my eyes. I could feel the weighted stares of all three of them watching me. It was unsettling. They had to have been talking about me if they were staring at me. "Luke's game is at eleven today," Marcos said.

"Mmmhmm," I murmured. "Coffee."

Nico chuckled softly. "I got you, Little Dreamer. I hit the coffee shop on the way here."

"Love you," I muttered, not even thinking about it.

I heard the intake of breath from Marcos before he quickly covered it with a cough. Maybe it was too soon? Nico and I had already admitted our feelings weeks ago though when I was still trying to hide the truth. Now that it was out in the open, and Nico felt the same way, I wasn't going to hide it anymore. Hopefully one day Marcos and Jason would come around, or maybe they wouldn't, but I was done hiding.

"Get up, go shower. I'll start breakfast," Nico said, his voice getting closer as he walked across the room. He pulled back the covers and smacked my ass hard. The loud slap echoed around the room. "Look at that ass jiggle." Nico smacked my ass again, before he palmed it roughly and shook one of my ass cheeks.

"Fuck off," I grumbled, rolling over onto my back so he couldn't get my ass.

His wide grin and bright blue eyes twinkled down at me as he leaned down. "Morning, beautiful."

"Hi." I felt a dopey smile settle on my face and didn't even care.

He wrapped his arms under my shoulders and my knees and lifted me effortlessly from the mattress. I curled into him, wrapping my arms around his neck as he smirked down at me. Nico carried me into the bathroom and kicked the door closed behind us.

I giggled softly. "You joining me for that shower?"

"Hell yes, I am." He set me on the counter and ripped my tank top over my head before he lowered his head to my pebbled nipples and sucked it into his hot wet mouth.

My head fell back as my mouth dropped open and a deep moan fell from my lips. "Nico." I moaned and slid my fingers through his hair.

He chuckled against my breast and roughly tugged my booty shorts off me. It was such a quick move; he managed to get the out from under me while I remained sitting on the counter.

"That was hot." I giggled.

He grinned wickedly, before he dropped to his knees before me and pulled my legs apart, spreading me open wide on the counter. Shouldering his way between my parted thighs, Nico used his thumbs to pull open my folds and then he descended. His tongue licked me from asshole to clit in one long swipe.

"Oh fuck, Nico." I panted, winding my fingers through his hair. I tried to keep my voice down, not wanting to wake up Luke and have to explain what had happened, but at the same time I didn't care. Marcos was there, he could deal with the fall out, I wanted to enjoy the moment.

Nico went to work on my clit, licking and sucking and flicking his tongue over it. Two fingers entered my cunt and slid in, in one slow thrust. I arched my back and pushed my hips, trying to grind on his face, but his other hand gripped one of my hips tightly and held me in place.

Curling his fingers in a come-hither motion, Nico pressed them forward against that spot inside me that made me gasp. It didn't take long for me to come undone, right on the counter. "Oh fuck, oh fuck, oh fuck," I chanted, panting hard. My body jerking as I folded over his head still lapping at my sensitive folds. "Nico," I muttered.

He chuckled softly against my skin before he slowly pulled off my clit with an audible pop. "So fucking good for me." He stood up and kissed me senseless. I opened for him, letting him slide his tongue against mine and taste myself in the passionate kiss.

Nico broke the kiss abruptly as he pulled away from me. He walked over to the shower and quickly got the water started. "You still take scalding showers?" he asked over his shoulder.

I smirked. "I take warm showers."

"Burn the skin off your body, it is then." He nodded once.

I laughed and slid off the bathroom counter. Sticking my hand into the water stream, I rolled my eyes and adjusted things warmer. Nico hissed dramatically as he watched me do so. Laughing, I shook my head. "You'll survive."

I stepped over the tub and into the shower, pulling the curtain closed behind me. I slipped into the hot water and tilted my head back to wet my hair. I closed my eyes and dropped my head forward, letting the water massage my shoulders.

A moment later, Nico was pulling the curtain back, and my eyes opened to take in the sight of his naked body. He stepped over the tub as he climbed in the shower and closed the curtain behind him. It was a standard tub and shower combo, nothing fancy, and not very roomy. Moving toward me, he pressed his body against mine and hissed when the hot water hit him. Nico reached around me and turned down the temperature slightly.

I kissed his chest and wrapped my arms around him as he pushed into my space. His hard dick bobbed between us. Once he had the water adjusted to a more suitable temperature, he stood up straight and pushed his erection into my belly. "We don't have much time." I smiled up at him and wrapped my fingers around his rock-hard cock.

"I don't need much time, Little Dreamer." He smirked and hauled me up into his arms.

I wrapped my legs and arms around him tightly and held on for dear life as he pressed my back against the cool vinyl surround. He slipped into my cunt a second later and I moaned low in my throat as he stretched me open deliciously.

Sinking on to his cock, I captured his mouth and kissed him thoroughly. Nico rocked his hips against mine, starting off slow. We made out beneath the warm water as he thrusted in slow and steady, keeping a gentle pace, fucking making love to me in the shower.

It wasn't long before I was falling over the edge, my body shuddering in his arms as my pussy clenched down on his cock. "That's it, baby." He groaned. "Milk my dick."

All I could do was pant and whimper as shockwaves from my orgasm radiated through me.

"So fucking perfect," Nico murmured.

I smiled and rested my forehead against his. "I love you."

"I love you too, Little Dreamer."

Maya

AFTER I FINISHED SHOWERING with Nico, where we actually washed up, we had gotten dressed and left my empty bedroom. Jason was missing from the bed and I found him and everyone else in the dining room eating breakfast. "Food's on the stove," Marcos said, glancing at us both as we walked in.

I blushed slightly, wondering if Luke had heard anything, but he was talking animatedly about the upcoming game to Jason. Jason was seated at the table with his bad shoulder propped awkwardly on the table and I immediately felt bad. "I'll be right back."

Rushing back into my room, I went over to the pile of medical supplies Griffin had left me and pulled out the sling. I grabbed it and headed back out into the dining room. Not giving Jason the option to object, I loosened the strap and slipped it over his head.

He jolted slightly in surprise, but didn't say anything when I held open the sling part and said, "Put your arm in here." Gingerly, he followed my direction, only hissing slightly as his shoulder shifted to move into the sling.

Once Jason's arm was situated comfortably, I tightened up the strap and nodded, mostly to myself, before I walked into the kitchen and started making myself a plate.

Breakfast was a comfortable affair, and I mostly talked with my mom and Nico, while Marcos and Jason talked football with Luke. I knew how much both men loved that Luke was playing their sport.

After breakfast was cleaned up, Luke changed his clothes and got ready for the game. We all headed over together—Jason too—despite my minor protests. We had to take two cars, but Nico drove mine so my mother could sit down easily in the lower riding car and I sat in the backseat so she didn't get carsick. Marcos drove his truck with Jason, and Luke over to the school.

I couldn't keep the smile off my face all throughout the game. We all sat together in the front row of the bleachers, with me between my mother and Nico. Marcos and Jason were on his other side, and we all talked easily enough about the game, cheering loudly for Luke.

I felt happy for the first time in a very long time.

Maya

After the game, we watched as the boys cleared the field and headed back into the locker rooms in the school. Luke gave us all a great big smile and wave as he walked by with his friends. I knew he was on cloud nine having us all here, acting like a real family.

The way things should have been all along.

The stands slowly began to clear out as families headed to the parking lot to go home or wait for their player to come out of the school. My family and I stood up and stretched, feeling the ache from trying to sit on the bleachers for two hours. "Let's go wait by the car," I suggested.

The guys nodded and my mother moaned about the uncomfortable bleachers, and the five of us ambled off toward the parking lot.

"How are you feeling?" I asked Jason as I fell into step beside him.

He glanced down at me and shrugged his good shoulder. "Tired. Sore. But not horrible, I guess."

My lips parted slightly in surprise. I was not expecting him to be so open about how he felt. He'd barely talked to me since he apologized for choking me that night weeks ago after Sunday dinner. "That's uh—good—not good, I mean. I mea—"

Jason chuckled softly at my stammering response and I felt myself blush. "It's not great, but I'm not dead. I'll take it, and a nap when we get back to the house."

"Yeah." I nodded, glancing away.

The guys talked about the game while we continued to wait. As the parking lot steadily emptied, a pit of worry began to gnaw at my mind. Something was wrong. It never took Luke this long after a game to change. Most of the time he didn't bother, he just threw his shoulder pads in his duffle bag and wore his cleats and lower body pads home.

"Something's wrong," I said, looking around. I immediately began walking toward the school, that pit growing larger inside me. Something was wrong. I knew it.

I took off running for the school doors without looking back to see if anyone was following me. I needed to find Luke now. I ripped open the school door and yelled down the hallway as I ran toward the locker room at the end. "LUCUS! LUKE!"

"LUKE!" Marcos shouted from behind me.

We burst into the locker room, looking around at all the bewildered faces. "Is Luke Candella here?" I asked.

Marcos's eyes snapped to me; the shock apparent on his face. Guess I never told him that I gave Luke his last name. Now was not the time to discuss it though. I stormed through the locker room to the door in the back.

We went through the door to come out into another hallway, this one dimmer, extra-long, and clearly used for storage, but there at the end was Luke. Someone was dragging him kicking and screaming away from me.

"Luke!" I shouted.

"Mom!" he yelled.

The man dragging him turned and looked our way, grinning wickedly. I would recognize that jagged scar and those dead eyes from anywhere, even from a hundred yards away.

Dax fucking Hillcrest.

"LUKE!" I shouted, sprinting after them.

There was too much shit in the way, and some if it had been turned over, like Hillcrest had knocked it down, knowing someone was likely to follow him.

"MOM! DAD!" Luke cried, tears pouring down his face.

"Watch out," Marcos said, pushing me gently out of the way. He took off, running faster, climbing and jumping over things, trying to get to Luke.

Hillcrest pulled Luke out of the door and into the bright light of the outside world beyond. "No!" I cried out, trying to keep up.

Marcos was on his ass, but they had a head start.

"Please no," I whimpered as I climbed over a turned over bookcase, then a desk. Garbage and debris littered the space. Dust was kicked up, coating my skin and lungs.

It felt like an eternity before Marcos stormed through the door. It took me even longer.

Finally, I ran outside to the gravel driveway behind the school. Only there was no one there. No Luke. No Marcos. No Dax fucking Hillcrest.

"Luke!" I screamed out in anguish. I dropped to my knees as broken heart-wrenching sobs tore out of me. My heart shattered in my chest when I realized that even Marcos was gone. Despair tore at me.

Footsteps pounded on the gravel behind me and I whipped my head around to see Jason and Nico running toward me. "What happened?" Jason demanded.

Nico dropped to his knees besides me. "Maya, what happened?"

"Hillcrest!" I sobbed. "Hillcrest took Luke. He took my baby."

Nico's face fell as disbelief as his arms came around me.

"Where's Marcos?" Jason demanded.

I couldn't breathe, my heart was pounding in my chest and my lungs were constricting with dust and exertion. I tried to calm my breathing so I could explain through my tears. "We followed Luke and Hillcrest out of the door. Marcos got here first. By the time I got out here they were all gone!"

"Motherfucker!" Jason swore, kicking at the gravel drive behind the school.

Nico pulled me up and pushed me at Jason, before he took off running down the gravel drive and around the building in the opposite direction as he'd come.

Jason's good arm immediately wrapped around my shoulders and pulled me into his chest as tightly as he could. "Jason." I gasped his name as I clung to him. "My baby. He has my baby."

"I know, Darlin', I know. We'll get him back. I promise you, Maya. We will tear the world apart to get him back to you." Jason's voice was gravelly and deep, rough around the edges.

I sobbed into his chest, holding him tightly. We stayed that way until footsteps sounded behind me and I pulled away to turn around.

Nico and Marcos were walking back our way, looking complete dejected.

"No," I cried again, seeing the look of utter despair on both of their faces.

"I got the plate number, but they got away." Marcos's voice was scratchy and hoarse, as if he'd been screaming. Marcos walked right to me and grabbed me by both shoulders to turn me to face him, before both of his large hands came up and cupped the sides of my face. "Mia Vida, I swear to you, on my fucking life. I *will* find him. I *will* bring home our son."

Tears poured down my face as I whimpered and clung to his leather cut. "Marcos."

He yanked me into his arms and pressed my face against his chest.

Maya

We eventually went back to the parking lot and found my mother still waiting by her car. Nico had to explain what happened to Elaine, as he got her settled into the passenger seat of my Civic. I couldn't be parted from Marcos. I clung to him, needing the father of my child close to me.

I rode back to my mother's house with my hand wrapped tightly around Marcos's while he drove. Jason had sprawled out in back, taking up the length of the back seat to put his injured leg up. He had stuck his arm through the opening between the front seats to rest his good hand on my shoulder.

As soon as we got home, Marcos started making phone calls while my mother and I settled onto the couch. Marcos called their entire club to my mother's house and I listened in as the club convened in the garage. Deep booming voices that shouted and yelled over one another, angling to be heard. I had watched as all of my men had argued with their own club members on how to best rescue my son.

When it became too overwhelming, I left the garage quietly—not that anyone had noticed I had been there to begin with—and went to my bedroom.

I pulled my phone out as I sat down and frowned when I saw a new text message notification sitting on my lock screen. Unlocking my phone, I opened the message and covered my mouth to stifle a cry.

There was a picture of my son, his face bruised and bleeding in the message. Below the picture was an address.

Unknown Number:

Come alone. I will let him go free if you turn yourself over.

My heart pounded so hard in my chest, even as it fucking dropped into my stomach. Fear gripped me in a chokehold.

Maya:

How do I know you're not lying?

Unknown Number:

Only one way to find out. You have until nightfall, then I'll kill him.

My hand flew to my mouth to stifle my cry dismay. He was going to kill my baby if I didn't turn myself over to them.

An even trade sounded good, but would he keep his word? I didn't fucking know, but I knew what was happening out in the garage was not helping get my son back.

I needed to act. Now.

I entered the address into the GPS app on my phone and saw the house was just outside my neighborhood, across the Evermore River and into Creekton. It was located in The Edges, what the locals called the land between Creekton and Mourningside that no one knew which town it actually belonged to. The land was mostly owned by the Seratelli family.

It was within walking distance, maybe half an hour away. I wouldn't be able to take my car, not with the million bikes parked at the end of the driveway, and there was no way my guys were going to let me carry out this plan of trading myself for Luke.

I would have to sneak out of the house and walk, or run, as fast as I could to get to Luke. It was the only way I could save him. I needed to save my baby.

Before I could change my mind, I slid open the window and popped the screen up, crawled over the dresser and snuck outside.

On the way over to the address I was given, I thought out my plan, praying to all that was holy that I was making the right decision.

When I was two blocks away, I called Marcos and he answered on the second ring. I could hear the guys yelling in the background. "Maya, I'm sorry about the yelling. We'll be done soon."

"Marcos," I breathed his name. "I'm sorry."

"What do you mean, Mia Vida? This wasn't your fault. Give me a minute to finish up with the guys and I'll come in there."

"I left, Marcos. I'm not there."

"What the fuck, you mean you left, Maya?" Marcos's voice shouted over the arguing voices, silencing them.

"I got a text from Hillcrest. He said if I turned myself over to him, he would release Luke. A simple trade," I explained.

"What the fuck, Maya! It's a god damn trap! Turn around now!" Marcos screamed through the phone.

I had already thought about that, but I didn't care. I would either be with Luke, or Hillcrest would keep his word and release my son. Either way, I would save my son. "I'll text you the address, but I'm already here."

"Maya—"

I hung up on Marcos before he could yell some more. I forwarded the text message from Dax so Marcos would have his phone number as well, but I knew full well that it was likely a burner cell and nothing traceable.

My phone rang immediately after, and I quickly silenced it. I didn't outright shut it off, but I turned off the ringer so I couldn't be distracted from my mission. Tucking the phone in my back pocket, I walked the final two blocks to the house and waited on the sidewalk in front of the run-down house that looked more like a shack than a home.

Huge sections of the roof were missing. Clearly it hadn't been lived in for quite some time. This was a clearly just a meeting place, and that was it. They probably wouldn't keep me here very long at all. I would likely be moved to a different location.

I would need to stop them from moving me. My life would depend on it. I had called Marcos though. They were maybe five minutes away by motorcycle, they would get to me before I got moved. I was sure of it.

Swallowing hard, I steeled my spine and then walked up to the front door. It opened just as I stopped on the front step. Dax Hillcrest stood with my son held in front of him and a gun trained on his head. "You come alone?" he demanded, his milky white eye catching the light and making him look more deranged.

"Yes," I muttered, my eyes on my son's bruised face.

Hillcrest motioned me closer with the gun, but I held my arms out for Luke. Hillcrest pushed my son into my arms and I held him tightly to me, bending down to whisper into his ear. "My phone is in my back pocket. Grab it and run as fast as you can. Call your dad."

"Mom," Luke cried.

"You do this, Lucus." I whispered fiercely into his ear. "Now." I snapped a little louder and shoved him to the side. I felt my phone get lifted out of my pocket and then heard the pounding of Luke's feet as he ran as fast as could.

Hillcrest aimed the gun on me and smiled wickedly. "You stupid bitch. You'll pay for that."

The gun fired.

And everything went black.

And my body fell to the ground.

To Be Continued...

Maya's story continues in the Devil's Psychos book 3: Brandishing Balance!

Coming October 3rd. Pre-order today!

Coming Soon...

Loved the Devil's Psychos?

Please take a moment leave a review on amazon here!

Sign up for my newsletter here, for the latest updates and sneak

peeks on what I'm working on.

Follow me on social media!

amazon.com/author/methornwood

facebook.com/methornwood

instagram.com/midnightdreamingwriting/

goodreads.com/author/show/45144764.M_E_Thornwood

M.E. THORNWOOD

tiktok.com/@me.thornwood.author

https://twitter.com/ME_Thornwood

Brandishing Balance

by M.E. Thornwood

Also By M.E. Thornwood

Missed out on the Ravager Knights MC?
Start with Courting the Consequences!

Check it out here!

Choices have consequences, and some consequences cannot be undone.

Fighting to survive is all Kara Carmichael knows. Whether it was surviving the streets as a poor kid on the southside of Mourningside, Illinois or fighting the legal injustices in the court room, Kara prides herself on her ability to fight and win.

She also knows that every choice you make, has an outcome or consequence.

As the managing partner of the most prestigious law firm in the city, Kara had fought her way into a good life. She had made all the right choices.

Or so she thought.

When the Ravager Knights MC rolls into her law firm and kicks up trouble, Kara has a choice to make.

Fight the soul burning attraction of three rough and tumble bikers? Or fight for the prestigious job and gilded lifestyle she worked her entire life building?

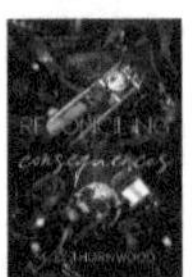

Check out Reconciling the Consequences here!
Make a choice. Consequences be damned.
Kara made her choice, and the consequences of her choices left her burned and beaten.

After her father's hitman failed to kill her and her ex-boyfriend carried her body from the burning house, Kara wakes up in hospital... alone.

Without a home to return to, and her father still out for blood, Kara has only one choice left... beg for forgiveness from the three men whose hearts she deliberately broke. Or die trying.

Will Johnny, Derrick, and Kevin accept her apology and move on? Or will Kara have to face the consequences for her choices and save herself from her father?

Check out Embracing the Consequences here!

Not all consequences are bad. Some consequences are meant to be embraced.

Kara Carmichael knows first-hand that not all consequences are bad. She never would have met her boyfriends had her father not framed Mac Taylor for embezzlement and the list of other alleged crimes.

With her father locked away, Kara and her guys are faced with a new reality and a new family dynamic.

But when new threats and old enemies rear their ugly heads, new challenges are once again thrown their way.

Can Kara embrace the consequences for her actions or will it all come crumbling down around her?

Check out Brandishing Beginnings here!

They say trouble comes in three... as in the form of three rough and tumble bikers.

They make my heart race and my skin sizzle. They push my boundaries like no one else, introducing me to the dangerous world of the *Devil's Psychos* motorcycle club. And they're completely wrong for me.

When my college friend invites me to her family's home for the holidays, I didn't expect to see her brother Marcos—a gorgeous man I haven't been able to stop thinking about since we met—and he didn't come alone. His two best friends are hot as hell and downright dangerous... and they all want me.

One night I give into temptation. They teach me to submit, and it's hotter than I ever could have imagined.

Afterwards, I try to dismiss our passion as a one-time thing. But I can't stop thinking about Marcos's demanding presence and chiseled jaw. And Jason and his sexy piercings and sultry voice. And I miss the way Nico seemed to balance the two and always make me laugh.

When I need a place to stay, they take me in, and things heat up quickly. It turns out the three of them really like being in charge... and I find that I like that, too.

But a dangerous encounter reminds me of the risky world they live in—a world that could make me a target. For these guys, I'll risk losing my heart, but could that mean putting my life on the line as well?

Acknowledgments

Thank you to my readers.

As always, thank you to my husband. You are my rock, without you, I wouldn't be able to do this.

To Jessica Baker! Thank you for always listening to me rant and ramble!

To my girl Megan at Cantina Book Club! Thank you for being my friend for the last 20 years!

To CNRW! You are all such amazing writers and I'm excited to be apart of it.

Once again you readers, thank you so much for reading my books! I appreciate each and every one of you!

M.E. Thornwood is a contemporary Why Choose romance author that enjoys writing about dark themes, thrilling suspense, and hot hot spice. She loves her alpha males and the women who don't put up with them. Writing has been her passion since she was a little girl.

She lives in the Midwest with her husband and two children. When she's not writing, she's enjoying camping with family and friends, hiking with her kids, and reading books with her loveable fat cat Midnight.